After a successful career as a television writer and producer on series such as *A Touch of Frost*, *Midsomer Murders* and *Between the Lines*, **Michael Russell** decided to write what he always intended: books.

The City in Year Zero is the tenth of his Stefan Gillespie stories of historical crime fiction, taking a sideways look at the Second World War through Irish eyes, and exploring unexpected corners of the conflict, such as pre-war Danzig, New York, Franco's Spain, Malta, the Vatican and, in *The City in Year Zero*, life in Germany after the final collapse of the Third Reich. Four of these novels – *The City of Shadows*, *The City of Strangers*, *The City in Darkness* and *The City Under Siege* – have been shortlisted for Crime Writers' Association awards.

Michael lives with his family in rural Ireland, not a million miles from the mountains that surround Garda Inspector Gillespie's own home.

Also by Michael Russell

The City of Shadows
The City of Strangers
The City in Darkness
The City of Lies
The City in Flames
The City Under Siege
The City Underground
The City of God
The Dead City

The CITY in YEAR ZERO

MICHAEL RUSSELL

CONSTABLE

First published in Great Britain in 2026 by Constable

Copyright © Michael Russell, 2026

1 3 5 7 9 10 8 6 4 2

The moral right of the author has been asserted.

All rights reserved.
No part of this publication may be reproduced, stored in a retrieval system, or transmitted, in any form, or by any means, without the prior permission in writing of the publisher, nor be otherwise circulated in any form of binding or cover other than that in which it is published and without a similar condition including this condition being imposed on the subsequent purchaser.

A CIP catalogue record for this book
is available from the British Library.

ISBN: 978-1-40872-006-6

Typeset in Dante MT Std by SX Composing DTP, Rayleigh, Essex
Printed and bound in Great Britain by Clays Ltd, Elcograf S.p.A.

Papers used by Constable are from well-managed forests and other responsible sources.

Constable
An imprint of
Little, Brown Book Group
Carmelite House
50 Victoria Embankment
London EC4Y 0DZ

The authorised representative
in the EEA is
Hachette Ireland
8 Castlecourt Centre
Dublin 15, D15 XTP3, Ireland
(email: info@hbgi.ie)

An Hachette UK Company
www.hachette.co.uk

www.littlebrown.co.uk

For
Krystyna Green
who gave Stefan Gillespie a road
and
Martin Fletcher
who kept him on track

Vorbei sind die Kinderspiele,
Und alles rollt vorbei,
Das Geld und die Welt und die Zeiten,
Und Glauben und Lieb' und Treu.

Gone are the games of our childhood,
And all things pass, as they must,
Wealth and the world and the ages,
And faith and love and trust.

Kinderspiele
Heinrich Heine

PART ONE

IM DIENST

THE LINE OF DUTY

Glad to know you have arrived in Switzerland. Assume you did not leave any secret records in Babenhausen. Please confirm ... I should like to let you know how very much the minister and all of us here appreciate your excellent work in Germany. We appreciate very fully the trials and difficulties which you and your wife had to overcome and we are profoundly grateful that both of you took the whole experience as a great adventure.

Joseph Walshe, Department of External Affairs,
to Con Cremin, June 1945

The British Union of Fascists ... has instructed me to write to your Excellency to express its deep appreciation that the secretary to the president of Eire called on the German minister in Dublin to express condolences on behalf of the president on the death of Adolf Hitler ... and to convey its gratitude to the government of Eire for thus honouring the memory of the greatest German in history.

Letter to the Irish Minister in London, May 1945

1

DIE WEISSEN FAHNEN
WHITE FLAGS

Germany, Saxony-Anhalt, Ilsenburg, April 1945

On the steep hill overlooking Ilsenburg, above the River Ilse, lay the castle and the abbey, a crumbling mansion and what was left of the Benedictine monastery, just the church and the pillared refectory and the shape of what were once cloisters. They were crumbling too. Extending back into the thick woodland that marked the first slopes of the Harz Mountains, some straggling outcrops of grass-covered stone mapped what had collapsed entirely centuries earlier. Not so long ago, the thin, sour soil that lay between these remnants of the abbey's walls was left to itself and the scrubby growth that crept out from the encroaching trees. Now, among the stones, patches of earth had been dug and raked and planted. Nothing thrived here, but something grew. That was enough. There were the black-green leaves of potatoes, and cabbages and kale. There were heaps of manure at intervals, to feed the unresponsive soil, and on this warm April day, flies hovered over them. A group of men spread out among the vegetables, digging in the dung and earthing up potatoes. They were noticeably thin. They were unwashed. Their clothes were filthy, ragged, torn. Some wore grey trousers or khaki tunics, but part of every man's outfit carried the stripes that marked them out as forced labourers.

The girl walked past the prisoners without seeing them. There was, after all, nothing to see. In any case, she had more important things on her mind. She moved quickly, with a determination that wasn't just about purpose, but anger. She carried on past the abbey buildings and out through the arch to the path that led down to the town. She heard voices. They were young voices, shouting and laughing. She didn't register them either. But as she walked towards the Marienkirche there was a louder, sharper sound. A gun shot. She stopped. There was another shot. Then an indignant voice. The voice came from somewhere above her. And she looked up.

'What the fuck are you doing, you arseholes!'

In the arched window of the squat tower below the church's spire was a face she knew. Erich Schröder, in the black and tan of his Hitler Youth uniform, was halfway out of the arch on to the narrow ledge that would let him climb up higher.

'You won't shoot it down!'

Above the yellow brick, where the dark slates of the spire began, she saw the white flag on a pole, no more than a piece of torn sheet nailed to a broomstick. But she knew what it meant. And the anger she already felt grew. The laughter that answered Erich came from below. She looked down again to see three more boys. And they were all boys, thirteen and fourteen, dressed in the mix of uniforms that made them members of the Volkssturm, the army of children and old men that was going to halt the advance of Germany's enemies when Germany's army had finally failed to do it. There were Hitler Youth shirts, naturally, along with Luftwaffe jackets and army forage caps. And there was the rifle, the one rifle they had, that Klaus Voss had been firing up at the humiliating flag of surrender someone had fixed to the Marienkirche steeple.

'It's all right, Erich, we're aiming at the flag, not you!'

'That's what I'm afraid of Klaus! You never hit what you aim at.'

There was more laughter.

'I'll get it! Save the ammo for the Yanks!'

'OK. Don't fall off!'

Only now did Erich see the girl looking up.

'I've done this before, haven't I Krista?'

'You were ten then,' she called, laughing. 'And not so fat!'

The boy grinned and pulled himself out and up towards the flag.

'Who did it?' asked the girl, moving closer.

The other boys shrugged.

'Could have been anyone,' said Klaus.

It was a reply that instantly turned the girl's attention back to what she was doing. What she had to do. No, not anyone. There couldn't be so many traitors in Ilsenburg that it could be just anyone. She turned away abruptly, and walked on, faster and more determined than before. As she reached the steps down to Schloßstraße, her head was too full again, too angry again, to hear the cheer behind her as Erich Schröder threw the white flag down from the church tower.

In her bedroom in the Yellow House, in Mühlenstrasse, the girl was looking at herself in the mirror. She had changed her clothes. She had on the uniform of the Bund Deutscher Mädel, the League of German Girls. She was thirteen now, not as close to fourteen as she wanted to be, but old enough to move up from the Jungmädelbund and wear the long blue skirt she had made herself from precious, hoarded material, the white blouse with its patch pockets that somehow her mother had found for her, and the black neckerchief held in place by the knot of woven leather. It was right that she was wearing her uniform. She had no doubts about what she had to do, but it still made her feel stronger. She turned away to the door. As she did, she looked out through the window to the street. The river was there and above the river the hill. And on the hill the Schloss and the abbey behind it. She had seen him go into the abbey earlier. She had followed him after she spotted him by the telegraph wires. He could still be there. He was often in the chapel for hours, playing the organ. She didn't know why that thought came into her head, except that they might find him there, if he hadn't gone home. It didn't matter.

The girl came downstairs. The noise her marching shoes made on the wooden steps startled her mother, coming into the kitchen through the back door.

'What's all that clatter for?' she said, grinning.

And then she stopped grinning. This wasn't a time to put on that new uniform and walk out in it. She had already decided it was time to get rid of her own uniform. The time for uniforms was over. If there were people who couldn't see that, good luck to them. She knew better. Everyone knew the Americans were coming, even those who wanted to pretend they could be stopped. And if no one would quite say it out loud, everyone knew too that they were coming in days, not weeks. The rolling thunder of heavy guns had been a part of their lives for a long time. Distant and then less distant, constant and then intermittent, and now, barely heard. You didn't need to ask what that silence meant. There was no one to fire the guns. In Ilsenburg, the Luftwaffe camp outside the town had been empty for a week. The soldiers had gone. The SS men had gone. The forced labourers who marched out every day to work at the camp were digging up roads, supposedly to stop tanks, or just planting more vegetables in the abbey grounds.

But it wasn't the unexpected sight of her daughter in her BDM uniform on its own that surprised her mother. It was the expression that went with it. Hard and purposeful in a way that didn't go with her thirteen years. Something was wrong.

'What are you doing?'

'I'm doing my duty, Mother.'

The girl turned and walked away. She went to the hall and out through the front door of the Yellow House. For a moment there was the stiff clip-clop of the black boots on the stone path to the gate. There had been something like contempt in the words the girl had thrown out. Her mother had heard that contempt before. And she had heard that word: duty. It echoed in her head, and what had gone with it. Her daughter had been eleven then. She had learned to be afraid of her.

*

Anselm Ebbers sat at the keyboard of the great organ that seemed somehow out of place in the bare space that made up most of the chapel. But it wasn't all that was out of place. Cold, empty stone made up the narrow, truncated Romanesque building that was the church of St Peter and St Paul. The stone almost smelt of its Benedictine antiquity. But around the altar there was an elaborate, Baroque surround of richly carved wood that stretched from wall to wall and floor to arched roof with scenes from the crucifixion at its centre. And above it, in peeling, fading paint, the blue and white clouds of heaven sailed across the plasterwork. The organ, like the altarpiece, was somehow bigger than its building. So was its sound.

However, what the young organist was playing was quiet and mediative. He didn't excel at the organ. He was competent rather than good. He played often now because no one else did. The chapel was hardly used. It was part of life in

Ilsenburg that had ended even before the war came to put an end to many things, slowly at first and then faster. The abbey had been a home for those parts of the Protestant Church that had resisted, in whatever way they could, the new Germany that National Socialism had brought into being. As resistance went, it probably didn't amount to much, except to try to maintain at least some distance between God and the great maw of the state that would consume all things. But if it wasn't much, it was still too much, and in 1936 the little evangelical college at the abbey, that trained missionaries for the wrong kind of mission, had been shut down. The chapel was surplus to requirements, the organ almost never played. Anselm Ebbers, a theology student whose studies had come to an unsurprising halt in the middle of a war that had no place for theology, made a point of playing it, perhaps as a kind of prayer.

He played the last chords of Buxtehude's chorale, 'Saviour of the Nations, Come', slowly and quietly, letting the resonance fade into the air around him before he lifted his hands gently from the keyboard. Luther's words were in his head as he sat back in the silence that followed. 'Praise to God the father sing, Praise to God the son, our King, Praise to God the spirit be, Ever and eternally.' It was only as he got up that he turned and saw the policeman and two boys who stood beside him. Wachtmeister Vennemann, Erich Schröder, Klaus Voss. He smiled for only the few seconds it took him to realise they had come for him. The combination of awkwardness and disdain in their faces told him that. He understood even before he registered the rifle Klaus carried. It hadn't occurred to him, when he saw Krista Friesack earlier, on the road behind the abbey, that it meant anything. He had only seen her walk away. But he knew now that she must have been watching him. His first reaction was simply surprise. He thought of her as a child. What had she said?

'You'll come with us, Anselm,' said the policeman.

Anselm Ebbers nodded. He bent down beside the organ stool.

'What are you doing? Keep your hands in sight!'

The rifle was pointing at Anselm as he stood up, holding the leg iron of leather and steel he wore on his left leg, a permanent souvenir of childhood polio.

'I need this on, Herr Vennemann. I take it off for the foot pedals.'

He sat back down on the stool and tightened the straps of the leg iron.

In the dark, wood-panelled room at the front of the townhall, three men sat a table. On one side, Wachtmeister Jürgen Vennemann, sixty, gaunt, a little deaf. All that was left of Ilsenburg's police force. In the middle the mayor and Nazi party leader, Oskar Mommsen, fifty-five, lazy, officious and today clearly uneasy. He didn't like this. He had no choice about what had to happen, but he wished the damned girl hadn't seen anything. Couldn't she just have ignored it? Did it matter now, any of it? His thoughts were on a future that was very close and as a man who had always sweated, he sweated more now, more than ever. He was afraid. As for this, he wanted it over and done with. On the other side of the mayor, the town's military commander, Hauptmann Rainer Becker. He had lost an eye fighting in Poland at the start of the war. He wore an eyepatch, and he was in the habit of rubbing it continually as he spoke. It could be said that he wore the patch with a sense of gratitude. It had kept him alive, unlike most of the men he served with, whose bodies were scattered across thousands of kilometres of Russia between Leningrad and Stalingrad. Now, with the departure of the troops at the Luftwaffe camp and the SS men who did whatever it was they did there, which never seemed to be very much, preparations for the defence of the town had fallen on him. There were no soldiers left, only the old men and boys who made up the Volkssturm. They would make a good show of it. The enemy would pay dearly for every metre of German soil. That's what he told them. There could be no question of defeat. This man Ebbers, this traitor to the Fatherland, would make that point.

Anselm Ebbers stood to one side of the table, flanked by the Hitler Youth uniforms of Klaus and Erich. A group of townspeople sat on benches or stood at the back of the room. Mostly they were the party faithful, gathered together by the mayor. He had wanted a bigger crowd. It wasn't long ago that he would have got one. But as the news of what had happened spread through Ilsenburg, most people closed their doors and stayed where they were. But there were enough people there, enough at least to give Mommsen the sense of legitimacy he needed to feel.

The only witness was Krista Friesack. She stood in front of the table.

'I saw Anselm – Herr Ebbers – when I was walking behind the abbey.'

'Where was he?'

'I saw him on the wall by the stable yard, at the back of the Schloss.'

'And what was he doing?'

'He got up onto the roof and crawled along to the corner of the building, there's a telegraph pole, and the wires come down, across the yard, into the back of the Schloss. He could reach the wires from where he was standing. He cut them.'

The police sergeant held up a pair of long-handled shears.

'These were found at the house of the accused.'

'What happened then, Krista?' asked the mayor.

'He got back onto the wall and then climbed down to the road.'

'Did he see you?'

'I know he saw me when he was walking back towards the town. That's all. I don't think he knew I'd seen him up on the roof. He didn't know I was watching.'

'And you came straight to tell me what had happened.'

'I knew my duty, sir.'

The three-man tribunal nodded in unison.

'You can go, Krista,' said Mommsen. 'You should go home now.'

The girl hesitated. For the first time she looked at the man standing only a little way from her. He shrugged and there was almost a smile. For the first time, there was a question in Krista Friesack's head. She didn't even know what it was, except that she didn't like it much. Everything had stopped. What happened now?

'Your acts will be recorded,' continued the mayor. 'But we're done.'

As Krista turned to leave, there was a murmur of approbation running through the onlookers. Someone started clapping. Then they all clapped, including the judges. She put her head down. She knew she was blushing. She walked out.

There was silence. The three men stared intently at Anselm.

'You obviously know, Ebbers, that my office is in the Schloss.' It was Hauptmann Becker who spoke. 'The telephone wires you cut connect that office to other military commanders and bases. Your purpose was to sabotage the defence of the town and deliver it up to the enemy. It's very simple, very clear. Treason.'

There was nothing for Anselm to argue about, except his reasons.

'Everyone knows how close the Americans are. I've seen towns flattened by the bombing. I've seen the bodies in the streets. There aren't even any soldiers here now. They've gone. You know they've gone, Hauptmann. All I wanted to do was to stop the town's destruction, to stop us all from being killed for no reason at all.'

There was a hiss of anger in the room. Becker got to his feet.

'Surrender? Is that how you keep your oath to the Führer? You piece of shit. And you're not alone. There's evidence. You're one traitor. Who are the others?'

The mayor and the police sergeant felt obliged to stand now. The room had erupted. Indignant abuse was being hurled at the young student from everywhere.

'Look at these!' shouted the military commander, holding up some pieces of paper. 'These call for surrender. Found in your house. But who printed them? Where do they come from? And this.' He held up the white flag that had fluttered over the Marienkirche that morning. 'You didn't climb up there, you crippled bastard. You might manage a wall, but not a church steeple. So, who put this up?'

Mommsen picked up a wooden gavel and banged the table.

'Order! Let's have order. I understand how you feel. We all feel the same.'

The noise subsided into a low rumble of continuing outrage.

'Who else is involved in this?' The mayor, still standing, was looking at Anslem again. 'Where do these leaflets come from? Who put up the white flag?'

'No one else is involved.'

'Names. Give us names. Give us names and you might save your life.'

Mommsen looked at the other two judges. Jürgen Vennemann nodded. Rainer Becker shook his head decisively. The room was suddenly very quiet. The words had been spoken. Death was coming. No one was surprised, and by now that included Anselm Ebbers himself, but saying it aloud for the first time hit home.

'There are no names. The leaflets are mine. All they say is that when there's nothing left to fight for, then there's no reason to die. As for your white flag, I've never seen it. But am I alone in knowing it's finished? I don't think so. Am I?'

The last question was addressed to the room. There were a few people who looked down at the floor, but for the rest, it was enough to restart the rage. Whether that came from belief or desperation, it came, loud and strong. The death sentence was given in seconds, called out by Oskar Mommsen over the competing voices.

There would be no reflection. There would be no last moments for the condemned man. The sentence would be carried out immediately. The urgency of the drumhead had taken over. It needed doing. It needed doing quickly. This was the example Hauptmann Becker wanted. Everyone wanted it.

Anselm was already being dragged out of the room. Men and boys of the Volkssturm surrounded him, among them Klaus and Erich. As he was pulled through the crowd there were punches and kicks, and spit covered his face. They poured out into the marketplace. Anselm was struggling, but he was held too tight to move. He was pulled and pushed across the cobbles towards the little lake at the edge of the town. There was a stone arch that led to the waterside. The sun shone on the water. It was sparkling and bright. On the other side of the lake, the tree-covered hills rose towards the Harz Mountains. But no one saw any of that. No one in the marketplace saw beyond the scrum of angry, jostling, shouting men and women they were part of, pushing the terrified man towards the arch and the lake.

A noose hung from the arch. It had been thrown up there even as Anselm Ebbers walked into the room for what the mayor of Ilsenburg had recorded as a trial. He had added the words *in extremis*. That, he felt, covered all eventualities. There had never been any doubt what would happen. Everyone knew it. For now, Mommsen stood at the back of the crowd, on the townhall steps. He lit a cigarette. He was drenched in sweat. Somewhere in the throng were Hauptmann Becker and Wachtmeister Vennemann, the military commander and the policeman. They could deal with the business end of it. It was out of his hands, wasn't it? It had been out of his hands from the start. From the moment the stupid BDM bitch came to him with the story, it was already out of his hands. As he looked across at the crowd, he wanted to turn away. But he didn't. It wouldn't look good if he did.

He couldn't see who was pulling the rope as Anselm Ebbers rose up under the stone arch, almost out of the press of people it seemed. He was gasping and choking. The sounds were screams and cries of pain, but the noose was too tight to let them out. There were shouts and roars from the onlookers. Arms shot up in the air. The cry 'Sieg Heil' rang out. But there weren't so many arms. Oskar Mommsen noted that. The body, and now it seemed somehow a body although Anselm was not yet dead, kicked and jerked and gasped for several minutes. There were people walking away from the scrum. And the shouting had stopped, quite suddenly. The body hung limply now. It was done. And the crowd had thinned. They had got what they came for and some were less satisfied than others. Oskar Mommsen walked down the steps and across the marketplace to the gate into the hotel overlooking the lake. He needed a drink.

There was no one in the hotel when Mommsen entered. He walked behind the bar and poured himself a large glass of schnapps. It was his hotel, so it was his schnapps. He drained the glass and poured another. He looked up to see Rainer Becker. The soldier looked a little wild and flushed. But his job was done. He, at least, was satisfied with the point that had been made so forcefully. The mayor poured out another schnapps and pushed it along the bar. Becker drank it.

'More?'

'No, I've got work to do. But well done. You did a good job.'

The mayor said nothing. These were congratulations he did not want.

'Just leave the cripple hanging there, Oskar. Leave him till he stinks.'

*

The next day, Hauptmann Rainer Becker, as military commander of Ilsenburg, gave his last command. American tanks were only kilometres away. They had halted that afternoon, somewhere east of Goslar. And Goslar had surrendered without a fight. American planes had flown low over Ilsenburg that morning. There was nothing to stop them. There would be nothing to stop the tanks and the soldiers either. From the centre of the town, you could still hear artillery fire, but it was further away than it had been even days before and there was less and less of it. It was certainly a long way from Ilsenburg. Whether you wept and raged, or quietly rejoiced, or just wanted to get the bloody thing over with, there was no one who didn't realise the unbreakable Will they were supposed to have was broken, even among those who had shouted their final Sieg Heils as Anselm Ebbers's body was hoisted beside the lake only twenty-four hours ago. His last gasp had been the Will's last gasp, as brutal and pointless at the end as it had been at the beginning. But there was still a game to play in the debris. Hauptmann Becker still played it.

There was still resistance, said the captain. Resistance that would be unyielding and unrelenting. The forests and mountains of Germany would be turned into fortresses.

From there heroic Werwolf warriors would emerge to wreak destruction on the Allies and make the occupation of the country impossible. Even now, he announced, a detachment of Wehrmacht and Volkssturm commandos was making its way toward the high peak of the Brocken above Ilsenburg and into the Harz Mountains to continue the fight. He didn't have the men to defend the town. Reluctantly, he had to accept that. They were too weak. But they could still use what resources they had to give the Werwolf fighters time to reach the hills and lose themselves in the impregnable Harz. The American advance along the valley of the River Ilse could be delayed. Every day, every hour, counted in this new way of war. And so it was that Rainer Becker deployed his little army of old men and boys on the backroads and tracks into the mountains. They set off from Ilsenburg, carrying little more than rifles and a handful of the precious Panzerfäuste rocket launchers that might, given more luck than judgement, disable a US tank.

Erich Schröder, Klaus Voss, Johann Koch, and Poldi Neumann headed out of town along Mühlenstrasse, heading for the forest road that would take them to the small bridge over the River Ilse that they were to hold against the Americans for as long as they could. Truly every day, every hour, counted. The more time they bought for the commandos, the stronger the fight back would be. Maybe Ilsenburg's military commando did believe in the Werwölfe. Maybe he just said what he felt he had to say. His own actions, after all, had given him an intimate knowledge of the rewards of defeatism. But whatever he knew, or didn't, there was no commando army gathering in the mountains. The soldiers who had left Goslar without even attempting to defend it, like more and more troops in what remained of Germany, were simply fading away. They were dumping their weapons and heading home, or looking for a safe place to surrender, or walking somewhere, anywhere, that took them away from the fighting. It was true that some of the SS men who recently abandoned the Luftwaffe camp outside Ilsenburg had made their way into the mountains. They did so in civilian clothes and their aim was to disappear. However, such details were not Rainer Becker's concern.

When the Hauptmann called into the hotel by the lake to see Oskar Mommsen that afternoon he wasn't wearing his uniform. He came on a bicycle he had just requisitioned, since he didn't have one of his own. He came, he said, to say goodbye. It was important that he wasn't captured. The implication was that he was determined to carry on the struggle, somewhere, somehow. But he left that hanging in the air. He didn't have the gall to say it. He didn't relish the look the mayor might have given him if he had. He had never liked Oskar Mommsen, but the man was no fool. Little more was said. The two men had a beer together, almost in silence. They shook hands. Then the military commander of Ilsenburg left, cycling not towards the mythical mountain fortress of the Harz, but like so many, going somewhere else, anywhere else. A place to keep your head down.

Oskar Mommsen stood on the terrace that looked out over the lake, watching Rainer Becker riding away from the town, a slightly ridiculous figure now, on a bicycle he was too big for. He reflected that the Hauptmann was now one of the people Anselm Ebbers had addressed in the townhall. Yes, now he knew it was over. They all did. But didn't they all know as they dragged Ebbers out to his death? Didn't he know himself? Of course he did. But you did what you had to do. And now, as he turned back into the bar, he knew what he had to do next.

Propped up by the reception desk was the white rag, posing as a flag of surrender, which had flown over the Marienkirche to be pulled down by Erich Schröder and his friends. It was no more than a piece of a torn bedsheet. It had been brought from the townhall, along with the defeatist leaflets Wachtmeister Vennemann found in Ebbers's house. It was evidence, after all. Someone thought it should be kept. And since Oskar Mommsen was the chair of the tribunal, that someone assumed it was his business to keep it. He had no intention of keeping it, however. He had not got round to consigning it to a dustbin, that was all. But now he found himself looking at the flag and hearing the words of Anselm Ebbers again. Over. Well and truly over, in fact. He picked up the flag. He let it hang in front of him for a moment. He shook his head. Its day had come. Twenty-four hours was a long time. Twenty-four hours would have turned Anselm Ebbers into a prophet. He put down the flag and walked behind the bar. He took a heavy, serrated kitchen knife from a drawer. Then he went into the office behind the reception desk and came out carrying a small step ladder. It would do. He would be able to reach the noose. It was time to cut Anselm Ebbers's body down. Time to forget about him.

Krista Friesack hadn't left the Yellow House since she walked home from the townhall after giving her evidence against Anselm Ebbers. It irritated her that it was still in her head. There was no need for her to think any more about it. She had to keep telling herself she was right, though. It wasn't as easy as it should have been. The anger had drained away quite quickly. That changed things. There was no reason why it should. What had happened to Anselm was the only thing that could happen. He was a traitor, wasn't he? She had been taught there could be no pity for those who betrayed the Führer and the Nation. She believed it utterly. It was a sacred truth. But she still didn't want to walk into the town and see him. She didn't want people looking at her, even if the looks were of admiration and approval, as they should be.

But she wasn't even sure about that now. She had seen people on her way back from the townhall, people she knew well, people she had known since childhood. They looked away from her. She wasn't sure suddenly, though she couldn't grasp what she was unsure about. She felt drained. None of this should have happened. Defeat was impossible. She knew it was impossible.

Her mother had not spoken to her since the trial. That didn't matter much. They rarely spoke anyway, at least about anything that mattered. When she came home her mother looked at her for a long moment and then walked out of the kitchen. She went to her bedroom. Krista went to hers. That night she heard her mother crying. That didn't matter much either. She often cried, usually when she'd been drinking. She drank a lot. She struggled to put food on the table, but somewhere she found the money for wine and schnapps. In the morning, when Krista went downstairs, her mother went out to the garden and worked at the vegetable patch. When Krista walked outside, her mother came back in and went to her bedroom again. And so, the two of them sat in the two upstairs rooms in the Yellow House. There was only silence. Nothing seemed to break it. The street was empty. Even the gunfire from far away had stopped. There was only the sound of the river from across the road, below the mill. And for some reason, even the familiar, gentle noise of water she had known all her life made Krista uneasy.

It was late in the afternoon when she heard laughter, out in Mühlenstrasse. And then she heard her name called, loudly and cheerfully. She went to the window and looked down. Klaus and Erich and Johann and Poldi stood below. They were in the ragtag uniforms of the Volkssturm. They all carried rifles and they pushed a handcart that bore one box of ammunition and three Panzerfäuste.

'We're going into the mountains!' called Erich.

'We're going to fight! The fight back starts with us!' shouted Klaus.

'I'll be back for a kiss, don't forget!' said Erich, grinning broadly.

She laughed.

'And who says I'd give you a kiss?'

'I mean it, Krista!'

'We'll see. You'll have to earn it, Erich.'

Poldi Neumann raised his arm high.

'Sieg Heil! One dead Yank for every kiss – how does that sound?'

There was a moment of silence before they all laughed again. Something real had been said, something too real. And when they did laugh again, the laugher stopped short. The boys felt uncomfortably like the children they still almost were, heading off on one of the small adventures along the Ilsetal that once made up so many summer days in their younger years. And for Krista, trying to reach for a kind of pride in her friends that she couldn't quite touch, however much she wanted to, they looked like boys again, too. They all waved, Klaus and Johann and Poldi, and moved away, pushing the cart. Erich stayed for a few seconds more, looking up at her. And then he ran off after the others. One of the boys had started singing. Krista leant out from the window, listening till their voices faded away.

'We hear the final call to arms,
We all stand ready for the fight!
The Führer's flags fill every street,
The dawn of freedom is in sight!'

*

The tanks came first. Behind came the lines of infantrymen. The tank traps that had broken up the roads into Ilsenburg did nothing to hinder the American advance. The tanks went over them or round them easily enough and so did the soldiers. The streets were empty. Some people looked out at the unfamiliar uniforms and helmets. They wanted to see what an American looked like. Were they all Jews? Were they all black? What were they? Most people sat in their homes and stayed away from the windows, for now. They had made their statement. They had made their surrender. Hanging from the windows of shops and houses were white bedsheets and white pillowcases and white tablecloths and torn white clothes. The mayor had given his instructions the night before. A sea of white. It was easier than he thought it might be. Having made his choice, he expected his town would be safe. And everyone else, whatever they thought and whatever they felt, did what they were told. They had, at least, had twelve long years to get used to doing that.

Oskar Mommsen stood in the marketplace, at the gates of his hotel. He held the white flag that he had almost consigned to a bin. It felt as if there was something lucky about it. He had forgotten the acts of two days earlier. Next to him stood the policeman, Vennemann, along with the hotel's hall porter and barman. The last two were unsure why they were there, but they too did as they were told. The mayor knew that it would be unwise to overdo the welcome committee, but some kind of welcome was called for. It was the best he could do.

There were two tanks in the marketplace and groups of soldiers were threading their way through the surrounding streets. No one said anything to the four Germans. There was a curt nod from an American who climbed down from the turret of one of the tanks and one simple instruction in German. 'Stillstehen!' They stood still. In fact, they stood still for almost half an hour, just watching the movement of troops and vehicles around them. And then a jeep pulled in from the road along the lake. Two officers got out. One of them spoke in good German.

'Who are you?'

The man was looking at Mommsen.

'I'm the mayor of the town. We have surrendered, as you see.'

The German-speaker spoke to the other officer in English.

'Name?'

'Mommsen. Oskar Mommsen. I'm the proprietor of the hotel.'

The German-speaker took out a notepad.

'And you? You're a policeman?'

'Wachtmeister Jürgen Vennemann, sir.'

'OK. That'll do. We'll be looking to you two for some help at some point. In the meantime, you will need to get inside and stay inside until you hear different.'

Oskar Mommsen thought he would venture a little more.

'We can offer you a drink.'

The German-speaker smiled.

'We'll take you up on that at some point, I'm sure. Not yet.'

The other officer spoke to the translator.

'Maybe get some more details from these guys. Thanks for their cooperation and all the usual guff. Tell Mr Mayor there is a curfew in operation as of now. No one on the streets at all. That goes for the whole town. From now until tomorrow morning at nine. We'll see how things are then. If the place is secure. But there'll be a curfew every night for the time being. Let him know breaking curfew will have consequences. At this point lethal consequences. Give him some time to get that message out. Maybe an hour. Tell him he'll be questioned in the next few days. We need a list of who's who. Say we're relying on him for straight answers.'

'Yes, sir.'

At no point had the officer addressed Mommsen directly. He had barely looked at him. He gave him a curt nod as he climbed back into the jeep and the driver pulled away. The German-speaking officer took out a packet of cigarettes. He flicked at it from the bottom and held it out. The four Germans all took one.

'Any of you speak English?'

They shook their heads. The American started to translate.

Early the next morning Krista Friesack stood at her bedroom window again. As she looked down at Mühlenstrasse she saw a line of half a dozen American soldiers walking slowly along. They were doing nothing in particular. A patrol. An abundance of caution. One of the men glanced up and saw her. He nodded and smiled. She didn't respond but she didn't move from the window. They looked very ordinary, these people. Young men in a different uniform. It troubled her. She wanted them to look different. She turned her head as she heard the metallic rumble of tank tracks on the cobbles. It came from out of the town, the direction of the Ilsetal and the forest. There had been tanks and armoured cars and trucks travelling up and down through the night. She lay awake listening to them, as most of Ilsenburg's population must have done. She cried the first tears she could remember crying in many years. But there was nothing to do. There was nothing to say. Young as she was, she did know that. It was why, when her mother came to her room to take her Deutscher Mädel uniform, she did nothing, absolutely nothing. Her mother told her she was burning it. She said she was burning all the shit. Party cards, books, pictures, her own crappy uniform too. The more shit they got rid of the safer they would be, both of them. 'Do you understand that, you bitch?' That's how she ended the conversation, such as it was. It was all her mother had said to her in days. She was drunk, naturally. What else would she be? There should have been a row, wild and screaming. There should have been a fight. But there wasn't.

The tank Krista was looking down at came slowly, and behind it soldiers, grubbier and more dishevelled than the ones she had seen in the street. They must have been fighting, she thought. Somewhere there was still fighting. There was a truck following behind too. It was open at the back. She saw a figure sitting on the bed of the truck. She knew it was Klaus at once. He was on his own, looking small and fragile. He was covered in dirt and something else. She knew that it was blood, though it was dry blood that was as black as the dirt. He gazed ahead, staring at nothing. And as the truck passed the window, she saw what lay behind Klaus. Three bodies. If she hadn't already known who they must be, she might have found it hard to identify them. She didn't need to. Erich, Johann, Poldi. For a moment there came into her head a day, really only a moment in a day. By the river. They were swimming, all of them. The sun shone through the trees. She could feel the warmth of that distant memory of sunlight on her face. And then it was gone.

2

AN TRÍDHATHACH
THE TRICOLOUR

Bavaria, Babenhausen, April 1945

I don't know whether ambassadors always carry their country's flag with them, on the basis that you never know when you might need one, but His Excellency Cornelius Cremin, Ireland's Minister to the Third Reich, did bring a tricolour with him when I drove him out of Berlin at the end of February in 1945, south through the shrinking corridor that was still German Germany, as the Allies squeezed it tighter and tighter between them, the Russians in the east and the Americans and British in the west. I'm not sure what was in Con Cremin's head as we moved through Austria and then back into Bavaria. I don't think he knew. He could still beat the drum for the virtues of the neutrality of the Irish government because that was his job. He knew all the reasons, but he also knew there was no one left to hear them outside Dublin. At times he seemed to feel that as long as there were Irish citizens in Germany he should stay. I would say that did matter. He was no use to them, though. If he still thought he might be, it wasn't borne out by anything I'd seen during my months in Berlin. There was a sense of duty that probably he owed no one now, except himself, and a dose of solid Irish bloody-mindedness. So, Con Cremin stood on the burning deck, whence all but he had fled. And I stood with him, anticipating the end. I had no great sense of duty myself and nothing to be bloody-minded about. Still, I was paid to keep Con in one piece until it was over. I had managed to do that since leaving Berlin. I was still doing it, even as we heard the American army was making its way towards the town of Babenhausen, where the Irish legation to Germany was making a final stand in two rooms in its castle.

For those of us who were waiting for the end of the war to find its way to us, the trick was to do that without getting shot or blown up. We were hardly alone. There were millions desperately trying to do the same thing. In Babenhausen, sitting at the bottom end of Bavaria, south of Ulm, not much had happened. There was nothing to bomb. Yet suddenly there was hard fighting, and it wasn't far away. We had heard big guns for several days, tanks and artillery, but what was around us now was machine-gun and small-arms fire. It didn't feel like much of a threat. That's to say it didn't sound as if it was heading in our direction. And after all, we had protection. Of sorts. I was less impressed by it than others.

I don't know who thought the way to keep Schloss Babenhausen safe was to fly an Irish tricolour from the battlements, but that's what the owner, who was some sort of prince or count, imagined would offer salvation. If the Irish Minister had little to offer anyone Irish who was caught up in the Third Reich's last gasp, the idea that diplomatic niceties meant American and German soldiers, engaged as they were in slaughtering each other, would skirt round Babenhausen's castle and continue their killing elsewhere, became an article of faith, not just in the castle, but in the town below its walls.

After the green and white and orange of the Irish flag was hoisted up to replace the red and white and black of the swastika, a crowd of townspeople arrived with a plan certain to keep the hostilities at bay.

Before long there were large painted signs on all the approach roads to the town, declaring that the Irish legation was based there. They were written in German, French, English and even Irish. The town council felt some Irish would give the signs an added authenticity, since our two bedrooms at the Schloss Babenhausen must surely count as Irish sovereign territory. Con Cremin, more amused than anything else, gave them something Irish for copying. And shrugged. I did the same. Neither of us shared the belief the townspeople had in the protective power of the tricolour, let alone the signs and a *cupla focal as Gaeilge*. In Berlin, I saw for myself what the Nazis thought about diplomacy. And I had my doubts that the Allies cared much more, especially under fire. But if it wasn't going to do any good, at least it couldn't do any harm. It didn't quite work out that way.

The flag on the battlements and the signs on the roads into Babenhausen had been up for several days before the battle came close to the town. It was close enough that most of us at the Schloss, the prince and his family and staff, and the odd collection of waifs and strays sheltering there, including Con Cremin and me, spent the night in the cellars. When we came up in the morning, the guns were much further away. The fighting wasn't over but it had shifted, and somewhere, east or north, the big guns were in action again. We all stood in the entrance hall, smiling with relief that for whatever reason the danger had passed us by. It was at that moment that the doors burst open and a group of German soldiers walked in. They were filthy. Their uniforms were torn and stained. They were also drunk. The man at the front held a machine gun. He came in slowly, puzzled as he took us in.

I imagined we looked oddly neat, clean, cheerful and even well-fed.

'What's this place?'

I took in the man's uniform. He was Waffen SS, a sergeant I thought.

'I said, what's this place! Give me a fucking answer!'

The owner of the castle, Prince Wittke, stepped forward.

'This is the Schloss Babenhausen.'

'And these people? Who are they?'

'My family, my staff, my guests.'

The words came quietly and calmly. The sergeant still seemed puzzled. He turned to the men closing in behind him. There were maybe a dozen or so.

'Take some men and see if there's anyone else. And find some food.'

'We can give you what food we have, Sergeant,' said the prince.

'What's the flag up there?' The soldier jerked his finger upwards.

'It's an Irish flag. The Irish ambassador to Germany–'

'And the signs? What are these signs on the roads?'

'The Irish ambassador to Germany is sheltering here. That means–'

'I don't give a fuck what it means. There are German soldiers dying out there, dying in the fucking dirt. And you have some other country's flag flying over your bloody castle, is that right? And signs all around the town, not just German in what . . . English, French some other shit-arse language? What is it? It could be Jew-talk for all anybody knows. And there you are, asking Germany's enemies in, is that the game? Open house! Come on in boys, but don't hurt us, will you? Don't hurt us because while you're killing our countrymen, we've got some foreign fucker here. So, who is this ambassador, then? And whose side is he on?'

The Schloss's owner shook his head.

'Sergeant, Germany has a responsibility towards foreign diplomats . . .'

'That's bollocks!'

The soldier raised the machine gun.

'You're fucking traitors. You stink of it.'

Con Cremin moved past me. He glanced at me and shrugged.

'I'd better say something, Stefan.'

I didn't think that was a good idea.

'I'd leave it, sir.'

The Waffen SS man had already seen him step forward.

'Who are you?'

'My name is Cremin. I'm the Irish Minister to Germany. I'm the ambassador Prince Wittke is talking about. He's just doing what he can to shelter a diplomatic mission that the German government would naturally offer protection to anyway.'

'So, you wrote these signs, did you?'

'No. But the signs only say there's a diplomatic mission here.'

The sergeant stared at the Irish ambassador for some seconds, then he started to laugh. He turned to the soldiers behind him, holding up his machine gun.

'I can't work out which fucker to shoot first. The prince or the ambassador. What do you think, boys? Who'd have believed we'd be moving in such exalted circles? One minute you're crawling in shit with your comrades bleeding to death all round you and Yanks pumping bullets into you, and the next thing you know you've left all that sweat and blood behind! Brush yourself down, boys, we're in high society.'

The laughter from the other soldiers was quiet, even threatening. I could see the anger they carried with them. It could lead to action. They were on the edge.

'I'm sorry, Sergeant . . .' Con Cremin wanted to keep going.

'It's not helping,' I said quietly. 'Just stop.'

The sergeant spun round, hearing my words.

'Was that English, my friend? English?'

I didn't reply. I wasn't helping either. I took my own advice and shut up.

'Is that the language here?' continued the Waffen SS man.

He wasn't looking at me now, or at the Minister. He let his eyes move round the room. The look of bewilderment was back. But somehow there was less energy about him. As if he didn't know what to do. I felt all that mattered was that no one did anything, no one said anything, no one moved suddenly. The man could have pointed his gun at anyone there and just pulled the trigger. Or he could have turned around and walked out the way he came. Yet something was changing in his face.

Silence. Then the silence was broken. From a corridor the men who had been sent to search the castle appeared with bread and sausage, wine and brandy.

'No one else, Sarge. But there's plenty of this. They do all right.'

The sergeant nodded. The moment of anger was gone, or at least it had faded into the background. What his soldiers needed wasn't more violence. It was food.

'Bring what you can get.'

The order was for the men behind him. They followed their comrades back into the castle. The Waffen SS man looked smaller. All that anger had subsided. What was left was more like pain and deep weariness. His shoulders dropped. He shrugged. His body seemed to say, what does it matter?

'Where are your officers, Sergeant?' The prince walked towards him.

'What?'

'Your officers . . .'

'Dead . . . the decent ones anyway.' He smiled. 'The others . . . gone.'

'Gone where?'

'Who knows? They pissed off. That's all . . . just pissed off.'

The sergeant slung the strap of his machine gun over his shoulder. He walked across to one of his men, now holding up a bottle of brandy. He took the bottle and pulled out the stopper. He held it to his mouth. He drank, deep and long.

Barely half an hour passed before the Waffen SS sergeant and his men had gone, as abruptly as they came. They took as much food and drink as they could carry. They shuffled away in an aimless, straggling line. Whether they left to fight or flee, no one cared. Certainly, no one knew. I doubt they even knew themselves.

*

I knew a number of German cities when I was young. At least I visited them or passed through them. Hannover, Brunswick, Magdeburg, Göttingen were the ones I remembered best. Each one was different, and each one was something wonderful in its own way, even for the eyes of a child. But when I drove the Irish Minister south from Berlin, all the cities we touched were the same. And they would have been the same everywhere in Germany. There was only the wreckage of what was there before. In Berlin, in Leipzig, in Nuremberg, in Munich, I had seen all there was to see. Years of bombing had turned every city into one wasteland.

It was my mother's determination to keep something of Germany in her life that brought me there in my youth.

Why my great-grandfather found his way to Dublin was never very clear, despite a family mythology that was full of tales of what he did when he got there, most of which consisted of small lessons in the rewards of hard work and perseverance. But he hadn't left Germany behind, and neither had my mother, several generations on. Just as we Irish hold fast to our Irishness, wherever we settle in the world, my mother held her Germanness tight. In fact, I think it was that part of being Irish that made her work so hard at being German. That was why I was brought up to speak German, whether I wanted to or not, and why, despite the fact that our German relatives were now second and third cousins, several times removed, my mother kept old lines of communication open. That was why I had known those distant cousins once.

All that was a long time ago, though not quite as long as the years of war made it seem. I had no idea where they were now. We heard of one of them dying at the start of the fighting, but after that, nothing. It didn't take much to imagine that among the gang of boys I knew in Ilsenburg, a small town at the edge of the Harz Mountains, others would be dead too. I hadn't thought of that much during my time with the embassy in Berlin. When I did, it seemed far away. I had some fond memories, if I chose to look for them, but I didn't share my mother's sentimental fixation on a past that existed mostly in her head. Even the real past wasn't a place I wanted to revisit. My last journey had been the year Adolf Hitler came to power. Some of my cousins and their friends were concerned about that. They didn't think it was going to end well. However, most people couldn't contain their enthusiasm. I watched what was going on with interest, but not much. I had other things to think about. My wife, Maeve, had only recently died, drowned at thirty. I had a two-year-old son to bring up without a mother. I went to

Germany to escape some of that for a short time. It wasn't surprising that I didn't. There was less comfort in the Harz Mountains than I'd hoped. The cousins I hadn't known well anyway were caught up in their own lives. So was I. The thought of trying to find them again in Germany did come into my head. It went straight out again. After ten years and a war, what would there be to say to them, except to tell the survivors that the ones who didn't think it would end well, had been right?

All that, or several versions of it, went through my mind as I had driven through the ruins of Leipzig in February, fleeing Berlin with Con Cremin. The last time I'd been there was 1933, with my cousin Annaliese and her husband, Reinhard. A concert. I remembered Haydn, maybe Haydn, and Mendelsohn. Definitely Mendelsohn because during a meal afterwards the two of them started an argument about music that shouldn't be played that lasted all the way back to Ilsenburg on the train. I barely understood the row was about the fact that Mendelsohn was Jewish, or partly Jewish, or Jewish enough anyway. It felt slightly daft and oddly unpleasant. It seemed so daft that I assumed it was one of those rows couples have that mean nothing in themselves but stand in for everything else that's wrong between them. Before I left Ilsenburg, I forgot the daftness. Only the unpleasantness remained. I last saw Reinhard in a hospital bed, recovering from a beating he received from the town's Hitler Youth, who didn't like his taste either.

After leaving Berlin, the Minister and I went to Salzburg. It was meant to be safe, away from the fighting, either west or east. But it proved less of a refuge than Con Cremin anticipated. I think he pinned too much on old memories of the city's Baroque facades, snow-capped mountains, and a bit of Mozart playing in a coffee-house. The mountains were still there. The Bristol Hotel was still grand and hadn't been hit by a bomb yet. But if the bombs that dropped on Salzburg didn't fall in the numbers we were used to in Berlin, they fell nevertheless, and since air-raid shelters were in short supply we ended up, with half the town, in the woods beyond. Mostly the bombs fell during the day. There was no Luftwaffe to stand in the way. And every day, when we drove back to the hotel after another raid, one more piece of Salzburg that had been there a few hours earlier was reduced to rubble. We were only there because the Swiss consulate could offer help and support if the time came when there was no choice but to cross the border. However, that border was still some way off. Daily trips to the safety of Salzburg's forests were using up our petrol ration, and it wouldn't be long before there was no way to reach Switzerland. And war was coming closer all the time. The Russians had Vienna under siege. When it fell, they'd come west. If nobody asked questions about what was left of the German army, it was because it didn't matter. There was one question. Would the Yanks reach Salzburg before the Russians did?

Con Cremin decided on one more move for the ever-shrinking Irish legation. The Swiss consul in Salzburg provided a list of high-end boltholes within easy access of the border and with luck, he believed, out of the line of fire. Of course, nobody knew where that line was from day to day, or even hour to hour. He pointed us in the direction of a small castle west of Munich and south of Ulm. A town called Babenhausen, an hour's drive from the Swiss border. Away from the bombs, at least if the Minister still chose to stay in German territory. The consul knew Prince Wittke, the owner of the Schloss, personally. The prince would be happy, he was certain, to give the Irish legation refuge. No Nazi, Prince Wittke, he added. The last words were said in a mock whisper. I thought, as I heard them, that it wouldn't be long before no such whisper was required. There would be no shortage of people, princes or paupers, who were 'No Nazis'. Not on your life!

The Schloss Babenhausen was definitely an improvement on Salzburg. The prince took us in cheerfully enough, to join an odd collection of refugees he had gathered together. There was nothing very ragged about them. They bore no resemblance to the hoards I'd seen walking Germany's roads with their few belongings on handcarts, or the women and children camping in the ruins of the cities we drove through. Some of the prince's guests had lost their homes, I'm sure, but probably not their money. It felt strangely like a sort of country house party where, at any moment, a dead body would be discovered in the library. But it seemed safe. The bombs that did drop, dropped a long way off. There were no guns to be heard, at least at first. And if no one wanted to comment on fighting elsewhere, since the Party faithful still stalked the streets of the quiet town below the Schloss, the bets were firmly on the Yanks arriving soon enough. There was no shortage of information on how fast they were moving. Prince Wittke was happy, with a nod and wink, to pass on the gist of what he was listening to on the BBC. Con Cremin's decision to remain on German territory didn't seem such a bad one, though I'd had enough. Maybe my mother left too much of the German in me to be comfortable with what was left of Germany. I wasn't at all easy with the smell.

The days passed and slowly the guns did come closer. Then, with the Irish tricolour flying over the Schloss Babenhausen, to add diplomatic certainty to the sense of security the inhabitants felt, the war did break in on us. It broke in then it left us behind. The German soldiers who looked as if they were going to kill us, any of us or all of us, with more disdain than they would have felt for a platoon of Allied infantrymen, left as quickly as they came. They stayed in my mind, though. They still do. Everyone else forgot them by the next morning.

And two days later, it was finally finished. The Americans were in the town. No one rejoiced. There were tears, and I could see they meant many, conflicting things. But mostly there was war-weary relief. It was enough that it was over.

It was early afternoon when an armoured car and a jeep pulled into the courtyard of the Schloss Babenhausen. There was a group of us waiting. The prince had been watching from his battlements. Position has its privileges, and I assumed the soldiers who got out of the jeep must be aware of that. There was a colonel. He was flanked by two other officers. The prince looked pleased, relieved as someone whispered the rank in his ear. He hadn't known what to expect. A colonel was good, very good. He walked forward with an outstretched hand. The colonel nodded stiffly but didn't respond. He looked through the prince and up to the battlements at the Irish flag, at least that's what he seemed to be doing. Prince Wittke let his hand drop. Not so good after all. But then the colonel grinned.

'An trídhathach!' he said in passable Irish. 'Sin iontas.'

He'd expressed his surprise at the tricolour, and surprised his own men too, who had no idea what he was talking about. He had also exhausted his *cupla focal*.

'I'm told the Irish ambassador to Germany is staying here. Is that right?'

The Minister stepped forward, surprised himself, even puzzled.

'I am indeed, sir.'

The US colonel stretched out his hand. Con Cremin shook it.

'I'm pleased to be the man to liberate you Mr Cremin. Colonel Jack Carberry. A while ago, as you may tell from the accent, but still a Limerick man.'

*

A week had passed in Babenhausen and very little had happened. The US troops who had, for a few days, filled the town were mostly gone. They had moved south and east into Austria to join up with other units and mop up what needed mopping up. We knew nothing about that. In some places there was still fighting, at least that's what we heard, but no one believed it amounted to much. There was more than war-weariness now. There was a quiet sense of hope. No one thought things were going to get better quickly, but it was possible to think about living rather than dying. What would happen, no one knew. What the Allies would do once they had all of Germany, no one knew either. But the choice between life and death was at least there, however uncertainly. Those who wanted to die could fight. Those who wanted to live could choose not to and survive the choice.

A small garrison of Americans remained in Babenhausen, soldiers and military police. There were still two tanks in the town square. There was still a curfew at night. And there were Field Intelligence men who arrived when the army had moved on and began to work their way through the town. At first, people were unsure what they wanted. It was clear enough to me when they came to the castle to take names and check identities and take the first statements. As a Special Branch man, I knew the practitioners of my trade when I saw them. They wanted a picture of the whole town, including the Schloss and its not-a-Nazi-by-any-stretch-of-the-imagination prince. They wanted to know who the Nazi leaders were, who the Party members were, who the police and the SS men were, who the teachers and doctors and lawyers and councillors were, and which ones held Party cards. The whole Nazi structure of the community was being examined in minute detail, as it was all over Germany.

I didn't know any of these people. I certainly didn't know the names I heard whispered in the castle corridors, with concerned head shaking, of those who had been arrested and interned for further questioning.

None of the American Field Intelligence officers came near the Minister or me. The two rooms in the Schloss Babenhausen that served as living quarters, and a makeshift office in which the Irish legation's remaining documents and papers were piled up in cardboard boxes and packing cases, were left alone. The Intelligence men had a right to search wherever they chose, but they didn't choose us. There was, it seemed, tacit recognition that the diplomatic immunity the colonel from Limerick assumed still belonged to Con Cremin, would be maintained.

If nothing much had happened for a week, the end of that week brought an event that felt as if it meant the final end of the war. Adolf Hitler was dead. He had killed himself in his bunker in Berlin as the Red Army closed in. It wasn't the end, but it was almost the end. It had to be, even as we listened to a crackling voice on German radio, telling the German people to carry on fighting to the last German. Victory in death, something like that. It didn't need to make sense. It never had before. But there wasn't anyone to listen to all that. I could feel there was shock, even in our castle full of wealthy people who had always abhorred the Nazis. I knew they had because several of them told me. I think they were hoping for character references. Yet still, the news of the Führer's death brought a kind of mystified silence to Babenhausen. If American soldiers were laying into the beer in celebration, even those Germans who wanted to celebrate were quiet. The end of everything, but maybe, just maybe the beginning of something. Taking it in was hard, that's what I saw. It was easy to forget how recently this man's invulnerability had been a truth of German life, even for those who hated him.

Several days later I watched from a window as a military jeep drove up to the castle. The soldiers were British. They were the first British troops we had seen. I don't know why I immediately thought they had something to do with the ambassador, but that's what went through my mind. I saw an officer get out of the jeep and head to the front doors of the Schloss. He carried a briefcase. I noted that though the men with him were armed, he wasn't. Intelligence. I could smell it.

I walked backed to the room that served as Con Cremin's office and my bedroom. I didn't have to wait long before I heard the clipped sound of army boots on the stone of the castle corridor. The boots stopped. There was a rap on the door. I opened it to see the officer I had watched getting out of the jeep in the courtyard.

'Mr Cremin?'

'No, not Mr Cremin.'

I didn't offer any more.

'Then you'll be Gillespie, is that right? Inspector Gillespie?'

He spoke as if he was dragging some idle piece of unimportant information that he barely remembered, from the back of his mind. He wasn't; of course not.

'That's right.'

'Can I come in, Gillespie? I'm looking for Mr Cremin.'

'You might as well, Lieutenant.' I had his rank. I also had his accent. There was no reason it should have surprised me, but it did. The North, maybe Belfast.

He followed me in. I pointed to a chair in front of the desk.

'If you want to sit down, I'll find the ambassador.'

The lieutenant stretched out his hand. I shook it.

'John Mackay.'

'Stefan Gillespie.'

'Special Branch?' It was a question, but he knew the answer.

'Intelligence?' My question didn't need an answer either, but he nodded.

'I'm attached to US Intelligence.'

My turn to nod. I left him and went along to Con Cremin's room.

'Who is he?'

'A lieutenant in Field Intelligence. The same mob that's been questioning people in Babenhausen, but he's British. I say British, he has a thick Belfast accent. Says he's attached to the US operation. Obviously true, as far as it goes.'

'And where does it go, Stefan?' Cremin grinned. 'You seem to know.'

'Whatever about his attachment to US Intelligence, he's here for us, especially for us. When I say "us" I mean you. He comes well prepared and well briefed, for whatever it is he's here for. He certainly knows who I am already.'

'So, what is he here for?'

'Information. That's the long and short of it.'

'About what?'

'You'll know when you hear his questions.'

'I don't have to answer any questions at all. He must know that.'

'Well, if you want to know what the man's after, you'd be better off letting him have his say. You can choose when you tell him you're not playing. It won't take long to find out why they've sent him. Then you'll know more than he does.'

'And why not,' said the Minister, laughing. 'It'll liven things up.'

I returned to the office with Con Cremin. I did the introductions, and we took our seats round the desk, hemmed in by boxes and packing cases. I got the impression that Lieutenant Mackay was expecting me to leave them to it.

That seemed all the more reason to stay. He started with some niceties about the castle and the countryside and familiar observations about the war being over in weeks if not days. He moved on to a bit of more focussed small talk and a few more questions the Intelligence man would already know the answer to. Testing the water, maybe.

'Have you managed to get in touch with Ireland, Mr Cremin?'

'No. I hope a message got to our embassy in Switzerland. I'm waiting to hear. Obviously just now we depend on you, the Americans anyway, for communications. If my note has reached Bern, Dublin will know we're safe.'

'Do you have any instructions on your next move?'

'At some point I'll be crossing into Switzerland myself, I guess . . . and whatever arrangements the Department of External Affairs deems appropriate . . .'

The Minister spoke slowly, letting his words trail away. I knew what was in his head. He was under no obligation to answer questions from anyone, let alone a British Intelligence officer. I could see he was weighing up when to say it.

'I don't know how easy that is at the moment. You'd know better.'

'You'd be wise to wait a bit. It's pretty chaotic at the moment, as you can imagine. There are a lot of people who'd like to find their way into Switzerland . . .'

'I already have Swiss visas, Lieutenant.'

'You'd be surprised how many people do.' The Intelligence officer smiled. 'Though yours probably has the rare distinction of having your real name on it.'

Mackay took out a packet of cigarettes. He made the process of tapping one on the desk and lighting it a theatrical pause. He opened his briefcase and took out a manilla file. He leafed through it then smiled again. Now the small talk was over.

'I have a few questions, Mr Cremin. Just a few. You said your main aim in staying on here was to offer what help you could to Irish citizens still in Germany.'

'I've said that, certainly. It's my job.'

It was hardly an unusual thought, but I remembered, as the Minister clearly did, that it was last said in a conversation with Colonel Carberry over a glass of Irish whiskey from the last, precious bottle, a few days earlier. Obviously, the file Lieutenant Mackay had in front of him contained an account of the conversation. I didn't believe the idea that this was no idle visit needed any confirmation, but if Con Cremin had thought otherwise, I now assumed he thought that no longer.

'Of course, there wasn't a lot you could do.'

The spoken words were polite enough but behind the shrug that accompanied them was something more like, 'There was fuck all you could do!' The Minister didn't need an interpreter. He answered with a shrug of his own.

'There may be more you can do now. Citizenship and documentation are going to be important matters as the country is occupied. Even more so when the surrender comes. False papers and false identities are already everywhere. Displaced people may have lost all record of where they come from. Most of this won't involve your citizens, I'm glad to say. Our assumption is that there aren't very many Irish nationals left in Germany now, occupied or not. A lot of those may have a claim to British citizenship anyway. But the more information we have, the more helpful we can be to those we encounter. Your cooperation will make that task much easier . . . especially when it comes to sorting the wheat from the chaff.'

Con Cremin looked at Lieutenant Mackay with a smile. I found out what was coming moments later, but the Minister was ahead of me. He leant forward and made a gesture in the direction of the Intelligence officer's cigarette packet.

'The inspector and I finished our last decent cigarettes in Berlin . . .'

'Help yourself, sir,' said Mackay.

Con Cremin took two cigarettes. He passed one to me. Mackay produced his lighter and we all paused cheerfully. The Intelligence officer thought his business was going well. It wasn't. I sensed Con Cremin was just taking a breath.

'Tell me about the chaff, Lieutenant.'

Mackay turned several pages of his manilla file. There were lists of names. He turned the papers round, so that they were facing the Minister across the desk.

'These are all Irish citizens who may or may not still be in Germany, whether in occupied territory or what's left of the rest. They're people we have reasons to want to speak to. You'll see some addresses, but who knows what they're worth. You will have more up-to-date information on some of them.'

Con Cremin scanned the list of names.

'I don't know how many of these people you'll know . . .'

The Minister picked up the file and handed it to me. There was no reason why he shouldn't have done, but something about the move unsettled Mackay. I think it was no more than the silence that accompanied it. I looked at the names. Some I knew, most meant nothing. I didn't know how I was supposed to respond.

'You've got a better memory than me, Stefan.'

I kept reading. My job was to remember what I could.

'It's hard to know where to start, Mr Mackay.'

Cremin drew on the purloined cigarette and shook his head.

The Intelligence officer glanced at me. He didn't much like the way I was studying the list of names in front of me. He was no fool. Something had changed.

'Let's start with someone we do know about. Francis Stuart. He's high on the list of people we want to talk to. For reasons you may well understand . . . sir.'

'I'm not sure I do.'

It wasn't the answer the lieutenant was expecting. The shift in tone made him less easy. Con Cremin's voice was as courteous as before, but it still felt distinctly less cooperative. Mackay stood up abruptly and reached for the file I was reading. I handed it back to him without a word. But I smiled. He sat down again.

'Do you know where he is?'

'Should I?'

'You met three weeks ago at Bregenz, close to the Austrian–Swiss border.'

'You seem very well informed, Lieutenant.'

'He wanted his passport renewed in order to apply for a Swiss transit visa.'

'I think he did, yes. I'm afraid all I could give him was lunch.'

'So, he still has no valid Irish passport?'

'That's not really your business.'

'It is the business of Allied Intelligence. Stuart has spent the war working for Nazi radio and broadcasting Nazi propaganda in English. There is evidence he was involved in smuggling German agents into Ireland and in attempts to get arms to the IRA, with a view to either insurrection in the South or sabotage in the North.'

'I see. Well, certainly with regard to evidence of any activities directed against Ireland during the Emergency, I would be grateful for the opportunity to pass that on to my government. However, I assume your superiors have their own direct connections to our Intelligence services, so it's unlikely to be necessary.'

'I think you misunderstand your position, Mr Cremin.'

The Minister stubbed out the cigarette and stood up, still smiling affably.

'My position is that I am a representative of the Irish government, which maintains a neutral status in this war as you, and the people you work for, know well. I have no intention of collecting Irish citizens for you to interrogate, whatever the reasons. If Mr Stuart, or anyone else, needs to answer for actions here or in Ireland, it's Ireland's business. For the rest, my passport states clearly who I am. As a diplomat, you have no right to question me. And that, Lieutenant, is that.'

The Intelligence officer stood up himself as Con Cremin spoke.

'Thank you, Mr Cremin. I did tell them. But we all know what the British are like.' He gave a quiet laugh. I had watched him pass through several stages of idle banter, uncertainty and irritation. He had arrived back at the start. And it didn't surprise him so much after all. 'It takes an Irishman to know what to expect from an Irishman.'

'We all have jobs to do,' said Cremin. It seemed an amiable conclusion.

I stood up myself, assuming it was over. It wasn't, quite.

'When I say you misunderstand your position, sir, I'm only passing on what's been said to me by my boss in Göttingen, and presumably his bosses all the way up to wherever it stops . . . you never do know where that is, do you, eh?'

He looked at me. It was the policeman-to-policeman look. It meant something like: We know more than they think. We know they're all arseholes.

'I'm sure when things have calmed down, you'll find your way out, whichever way that is Mr Cremin. But you might take hold of the fact that you're not the representative of anyone to anyone. If there's a fag end of government in what's left of the unoccupied Reich, it's now a criminal enterprise.

Like every other bastard in Intelligence, it's my job to find the criminals . . . the crooks and the murderers and the SS men and the collaborators . . . well, you can take a thesaurus down from the bookshelf and make your own list. Germany has only one real government now, the Allied Forces. As far as the top brass are concerned, you're an Irishman in the wrong place who needs to go home. It'll be done courteously, as long as you don't stray into the Russian Zone. But as jobs go, you don't have one.'

Con Cremin took this in without losing the wry smile he had at the start. That didn't mean he didn't hear the truth of at least some of what had been said.

'Is that what they told you to say?' asked the Minister.

'No. But they didn't need to. You haven't had any news for a few days?'

It was an odd change of tack. But I knew it wasn't a return to small talk.

'We haven't been outside the castle, so no,' said the Minister. 'We got the news about Hitler's death. I guess everyone got that, but since then, nothing.'

'Yes, everyone got that. They certainly got it in Dublin.'

Mackay took an envelope from the back of the file he was holding. He handed it to Con Cremin. He put his papers back into his briefcase. He shrugged.

'We've had some newspapers in from Britain and reports from the US. De Valera's made quite a splash. If you feel the courtesy isn't holding up as well as you'd like, Mr Cremin, you will find you don't need to read between the lines . . .'

The Intelligence officer nodded a curt, businesslike nod, and walked out.

The Minister sank down in his chair.

'You were right, Stefan. Our own, dedicated Intelligence officer. Anyway, at least he had the sense to see he was wasting his time. What was the rest about . . .?'

He opened the envelope Mackay had given him. He took out a collection of cuttings from newspapers, typed pages and telex sheets, marked and underlined.

'I'll leave you to it,' I said.

Con Cremin held up his hand, gesturing for me to stay. He said nothing. He read through the papers in front of him in silence, with a kind of growing intensity.

He put them down on the desk, still gazing at them. He shook his head as he spoke.

'Jesus, you wouldn't think it was hard... just to do nothing.' He looked up, finally, with a face that seemed to express only disbelief. 'Courtesy might well be in short supply. You might as well start with this. The American ones are the worst.'

He handed me a telex. It was a section from an article in the *New York Herald Tribune* of a few days earlier. The headline read: 'Neutrality Gone Mad'.

'In this time of the breaking of nations when the stream of history becomes a rushing millrace, there is much to arrest the world's attention. But, despite all the preoccupation with greater events, there is still time to glance and gasp at the spectacle of the prime minister of Eire marching solemnly to the German legation to present his condolences on Adolf Hitler's death while the pious Dr Salazar places the Portuguese flag at half-mast to mourn the passing of the enemy of the human race. If Mr de Valera and Dr Salazar believe their tears for the late unlamented Hitler – whether those tears are sincere or of the diplomatic crocodile variety – will either be forgiven or forgotten, they are more naïve than men in their position have any right to be. Obviously, for all the colourless connotations of the word, neutrality can go rancid when it is kept too long. Has the moral myopia the neutrals imposed upon themselves in the face of danger blinded them to all ethical values? Or has a mere preoccupation with protocol atrophied their emotions?'

'Jesus, indeed,' I said. It was all I could find. I heard the anger.

'And the Americans, as Dev never used to tire of telling us, are our friends. They don't get better. Why the hell . . . whose bloody idea . . . do they have no clue what's been going on here? All he had to do was sit on his hands and say nothing!'

The portfolio of furious press cuttings and articles that Lieutenant Mackay had delivered as a final gesture certainly didn't improve with reading. He had extracted nothing from Con Cremin in the way of the cooperation British Intelligence wanted. If there were Irishmen in Germany they were interested in finding, it was their business. In reality he knew better than to expect much, and he got less, but I think he took some pleasure in the envelope that left the Irish Minister to Germany's high horse looking more like a knackered old nag. He did it deftly. By leaving us to it the parting shot was stiletto-like in its application, but he was still pissing on all the diplomatic protocol Con Cremin clung to. I really do think that somewhere in Con's head, he believed he could stay on in Germany, for a time at least, and help the Irish citizens caught up in the mess. When he'd finished reading the reactions to the Taoiseach's expressions of condolence on the death of The Führer, he was left in no doubt that he was kidding himself. The Allies were showing him the door and the choice he had was to walk through it. Éamon de Valera's visit to the German ambassador in Dublin was frontpage news, and it sat there alongside articles about the horrors of the concentration camps being revealed, day after day, as the Allies took control of the Reich. Even Prince Wittke and the other Germans at the Schloss Babenhausen, couldn't get their heads round why anyone outside Germany would bother to do anything more about Hitler's death than shrug. If it didn't help Ireland, it certainly didn't help them.

Once Con Cremin had absorbed his astonishment and anger, he had little to say. He had a job to do. If the state he served fucked up, he still had to get on with serving it. All that amounted to now was making arrangements to leave. But it wasn't quite over. The stone Dev had chucked into the pond was bigger than he realised, and a ripple found its way to Babenhausen. It was a ripple that responded as much to an excess of German beer and schnapps as to indignant newspaper articles and American Forces Radio broadcasts, but it still hurt. At least it hurt me.

It was a couple of nights after John Mackay's visit that I was woken by the noise of shouting and laughing in the courtyard of the castle. My window looked out that way. It was a warm night. I had it open. The voices were American, and it didn't take much listening to work out the men were drunk. I got up and looked out. There were half a dozen soldiers there, all gazing up and pointing. There were other voices, above me, two I thought, calling down. Someone had climbed up onto the roof and the battlements that ran along the front of the Schloss Babenhausen.

'Get the fucking thing down!'

'I'm getting it down!'

'Chuck it down here, Danny!'

'I've got to get up the fucking flagpole. I can't reach!'

'Can you get it alight?'

'What?'

'Have you got a lighter? Burn the fucker where it is!'

'It's not that easy . . .'

'Get it down here so I can wipe my arse on it!'

That's what I heard. It was interspersed with snorts of laughter.

Someone started singing 'When Irish Eyes Are Smiling'.

'Fucking Irish bastards!'

'I've got it. I've got the rope!'

I didn't know what was going on above my head. The Irish tricolour that had been run up in an attempt to keep the castle safe from the guns of the approaching Americans was being torn down by a bunch of drunken American soldiers. I didn't immediately find any reason for that, except that they were drunk. I was never a great man for singing 'Amhrán na bhFiann' and weeping into my Guinness when someone launched into 'Follow Me Up to Carlow' after a few too many, but it pissed me off. If I like to think I carried my Irishness lightly sometimes, I was Irish enough for that. What the fuck did they think they were doing? We'd already had one band of drunken soldiers who wanted to shoot someone for putting up the tricolour. At least they had something to resent. These were just ordinary arseholes. I didn't know what they intended to do, or why, but I pulled on some clothes and headed downstairs. Maybe I'd spent too much time in Con Cremin's company. It was his tricolour, after all. It mattered to him. Maybe I just thought fuck that.

I came outside as the flag came fluttering down from the battlements. It was a big thing, meant for a flagpole or flying over a building, and it had spread out in a light breeze. The soldiers roared and cheered. Two of them moved forward to pick it up. I looked behind me to see the two men scrambling down the heavy drainpipes at the front of the Schloss. No one had noticed me standing there yet.

'Are we going to burn it?'

'I'd say we are guys . . . I'd say that's exactly it.'

A man pushed past and stood in the middle of the flag.

'I tell you what I'm going to do first. I'm going to piss on it.'

He started to undo his fly.

'Come on! Piss on it!'

There was more laughter.

'Come on lads, you've had your fun.'

As I spoke, I had to admit I wasn't impressed. It was a lot of years since I'd cleared a Dublin pub of drunks. It must have been a knack that too many years in Special Branch had knocked out of me. The Yanks weren't very impressed either.

'Who are you?'

'He's one of the Irish embassy guys. A cop, they said.'

'What do they call you, Paddy? Constable or Your Excellency?'

More laughter.

'We're sorry for your loss. Dear old Adolf. It's a shame.'

It was only now that I realised what this was about. I did have a line on all that. I'd heard Con Cremin try it out. The words neutrality, diplomacy, protocol and respect were in there in various combinations, along with a distinction between the German government and the German people. It didn't convince him. I smiled. No, I didn't think it was going to convince a gang of drunken soldiers. I reckoned simple actions would do more to defuse the situation than a speech. I stepped forward and lifted one side of the tricolour, as if I was about to fold it.

'Just leave it, eh? Everyone here's heard all this.'

I thought the more sober men would take note.

'A bunch of fucking Jerries and some Paddy arse-lickers? So what?'

I kept folding more of the flag.

'Drop it! We haven't finished with it!'

The man who was still standing on the flag opened his trousers and started to piss. There was a cheer. And more laughter than ever. I should have heard there was a bit more menace in it, at least from some. But I didn't. I lost my temper.

'You stupid fucker!'

I stepped forward again. It was only to grab more of the tricolour, but I was held from behind by one of the soldiers who had climbed down from the roof.

The soldier who had just urinated walked towards me, doing up his fly.

'You fancy some, do you, Paddy?'

'Get out of here. You think your officers are going to –'

I didn't finish the sentence. The American swung his fist and smashed it into my face. I was still held tight from behind, my arms pinned back. I tasted blood.

'I was in Belgium in December. I don't know where you were. Toasting Adolf over your Christmas dinner? The war. Did you hear there was a war? That was our Christmas. They had us on the run for a time. I was lucky. The Jerries captured some of my platoon. They put them out in a field and turned their machineguns on them. Maybe you read about it in your Irish papers. We've all been around since then. A tour of Europe. Seeing the sights. All expenses paid. Two weeks ago, we were in Dachau. Now that was some sight, Your Excellency.'

The American soldier shrugged. Then he hit me in the stomach. Very hard.

I dropped. The man who was holding me let me go. I fell to the ground.

It was suddenly very quiet. Their energy had gone. There was no more laughter. And if none of the men were sober, at least some of them were no longer drunk. I think it was the man who had been holding me who took control. I was only aware of feet around me, someone looking down. My eyes were swimming.

'It's enough, guys.'

'Is he OK?'

'He'll be pretty sore, but he's OK.'

There was more shuffling of feet.

'Let's get out of here.'

I guess no one argued, though I think I passed out for a few seconds. That blow to the stomach carried all the American soldier's convictions. I wasn't aware of the Yanks leaving, but suddenly, lying there, I knew I was on my own now. I took a deep breath. It hurt. I needed to get up. I tried to lift myself. It hurt even more. I stayed where I was. Then I heard voices. German voices. And someone was bending over me. I closed my eyes. If I moved, I knew it would hurt all over again. Then, for a moment, all I could think was that my face was wet. Of course it was wet. Well, wasn't I lying on an Irish tricolour in an American soldier's piss?

3

DAS ILSETAL
THE VALLEY

Ilsenburg, July 1923

They knew all that stream, and the steep valley of the Ilse, the Ilsetal, that started where Ilsenburg ended and the houses that lined Mühlenstrasse thinned out and the beech and oak thickened and grew taller along the riverbank. They knew all the river's noises. They knew the churn and rush of the race that fed the watermill that sat beside the river between the Yellow House where Annaliese lived and the house with three stories and a high, red-tiled roof and its smart optician's shop at the front that was Clara's home. They knew the insistent pulse of the stream and the slow lapping of deep water behind the weir at night. They had known those sounds when almost the only other sounds they knew were the voices of their mothers quietly singing them to sleep. And later, through all their young years, they knew the valley and the falls, and the waters tumbling over rocks and surging through narrows and roaring over the drops, as the Ilsetal made its way up through the trees towards the high peak of the Brocken where it had its source. They knew how the sound of the stream changed abruptly, when the oaks and the beeches stopped and the pines rose up, thin and straggling on the open heath of the mountain slopes. The noise of the water was thin as well. And where the woods below were full of what felt like an infinite variety of bird song, on the Brocken heights there were only crows and the occasional screech of a buzzard overhead, and often there was only the wind to accompany the gurgling of the streams. And they knew, too, how all the sounds of the Ilse changed again, from busy confinement as it made its way through the streets of Ilsenburg, to the high peak where it barely dribbled out of the rocks to start its journey, when the snow came at the end of the year and the whole steep valley was white and shining and silent.

Annaliese Hoffman and Clara Bloch grew up with the Ilse. It was theirs from the beginning. They shared it, naturally enough, with all the other children of Ilsenburg and the surrounding villages, in numbers that came and went, increased or shrank, with the shifting alliances and changing interests of childhood and adolescence. They shared it, too, with the walkers and hikers who came to the Harz Mountains in search of something the children of the Harz breathed in every day and never thought about for a moment. Annaliese and Clara took it for granted simply because it was the air they breathed. They had no more reason to reflect on that than the Ilse's trout had to notice that they swam in water. They took each other for granted, too, and for much the same reason. But born as they were, within only a few weeks of each other, within only a few metres of each other, they were through all their childhood and youth, inseparable. They were always the Mühlenstrasse girls. The girl from the Yellow House and the girl from the Optician's. And they still were, though now, at almost twenty-one, they didn't much like the word 'girl'. No one seemed to take them as seriously as they felt they should be taken. Their families lumped them in with their various siblings and cousins as 'the children'. And when Annaliese's cousin from Ireland came to stay, a very distant cousin she pointed out to her parents, she wasn't at all pleased that the task of entertaining him fell on her. She had only seen him once before and she hardly remembered it. She must have been eight or nine. If he was seventeen now, that would have made him what, five, six? Could they even explain exactly where he fitted in as a cousin anyway, without resorting to a family tree? Wasn't there anyone else who could do it? It seemed there wasn't. And besides, she'd be ideal. He spoke good German apparently. It wouldn't be difficult. He was seventeen, after all. It would be fun. And interesting, surely! It wasn't as if she was being asked to mind a child. Annaliese didn't see it that way. Seventeen, for God's sake! Minding some spotty, adolescent kid she didn't know from Adam, was not what a woman of almost twenty-one years old was likely to find either fun or interesting.

When her cousin Stefan arrived with his mother, Helena, the best thing she could find to say to Clara was that at least he didn't have acne. As for his German, she couldn't tell whether it was good or not. He seemed to be struggling to say anything at all. Whether that was because he couldn't understand what anybody was saying to him or because he was stupid, she wasn't in a position to know. All she did know was the ten days he was going to be staying at the Yellow House were going to pass very slowly. Clara, who was maybe a little bit wiser than her best friend, had a clearer perspective on the boy from Ireland. At best he was terrified of his cousin Annaliese, but it was probably worse than that. The reason he was too afraid to open his mouth except to say something incoherent and immediately go a shade of red that wasn't far off beetroot, was that after only two days at the Yellow House, he thought Annaliese a vision of beauty like nothing his seventeen years on earth had ever seen. He was smitten. Clara thought it wouldn't be a good idea to point this out to her friend. It wouldn't help. Not at all. But she did take charge of things. Stefan's mother had gone on to see a friend in Vienna, and with everyone at the Yellow House out working or away at school, it was the two of them, the Irish boy and the German girl. Three, Clara felt, was going to work better. She decided on the trips and excursions they would take, and she made sure that she was at the Yellow House to make the evenings pass more quickly. There were walks to take and there was trout fishing and there was the castle and the cloister to visit and boats to row on the lake by the hotel, and a trip to Hannover to more castles and churches and a concert. He liked music and he liked walking. Surely that would do. And in the evenings, there were card games and board games and more music, because Annaliese didn't altogether mind demonstrating her prowess at the keyboard. He couldn't be unaware of that. He wasn't, though Annaliese didn't realise her piano playing wasn't the real source of his admiration. But it could have been worse. However, he did speak reasonable German. He was talking now but, thankfully, not too much. If Clara found what he had to say more interesting than Annaliese did, that helped. They had stopped staring at each other in silence. And it would soon be over. The days were ticking down.

As the Irish cousin's stay at the Yellow House was coming to an end, Clara's final plan was a long day following the Ilsetal, from the outskirts of Ilsenburg, where the woods began, up past the waterfalls to the high plateau that led to the Brocken. They would take him to the top of their world. They would picnic there and then take the little narrow-gauge train that ran down the other side of the mountain to Wernigerode. At Wernigerode, Reinhard Friesack, who was a great friend of the Mühlenstrasse girls and a teacher at the school, would collect them in his father's car. There would be a ride in the car, which was a rare treat for them all, and a meal and beer at the hotel in Ilsenburg. There would be trout from the lake and a bit too much beer. It would all be very German, at the end of a day that would let Stefan, who had finally emerged from being just about tolerated by his cousin, Annaliese, to being almost liked, touch something that was special to all of them. It would be a fitting end to a visit that had worked better than expected.

It was Reinhard Friesack who had given Stefan a copy of Heinrich Heine's book about travelling through the Harz Mountains in the nineteenth century. If Annaliese and Clara took the countryside they lived in for granted, they were happy to pay the same compliment to its great poet. A little bit went a long way, and at school, not so many years before, there had been a lot more than a little bit. But the Irish cousin read Heine's chapters about the Brocken and the Ilsetal with fascination and even a little passion. The passion was less for the poet himself than the mood of romantic expectation he filled the landscape of the Harz with. One passage in particular, Stefan kept coming back to. It was a legend that saw the Ilse as a radiant princess who lived high among the rocks of the Brocken where the river has its source. From there all her beauty and her abundance poured out into the valley and the waters of the stream, clothing her in silver light and flashing diamonds, brought life and laughter to the mountain and the valley below it. This was a vision that would have amused Clara and probably disturbed Annaliese. She might have realised her piano playing didn't have to be so very exceptional after all. And it has to be said that as the Irish youth eagerly looked forward to the trip along the Ilsetal, he might have wished there were only two of them, not three.

*

Dublin to Holyhead, the Mail Boat. Holyhead to Euston. Victoria to Dover. Dover to Ostend. Ostend to Hannover on the Warsaw train, and then on to Goslar for the last connection to Ilsenburg. It was a solid thirty-six hours of trains and boats, though only in London was there a long morning hanging about for the Dover train. It was a journey Helena Gillespie had made many times in her youth, before the century turned, when the family connections with Germany were fresher. Her father was determined to keep those connections alive, and she had done her best to do the same, though she knew they were fading. Time and distance and the dark hole of the War, and the constant erosion that came from the ordinary business of leading ordinary lives. She had brought up her son, Stefan, now seventeen, to speak German as easily as he spoke English. He did. She had brought him to Germany as a child of six and left full of plans to come back often and bring his cousins to Ireland. There would be long summers when they would all remake the family bonds she had formed herself as a girl. But then the Great War came and with it another war in Ireland, small and brutal and vengeful, whatever its aspirations, that only got worse when the Breaking of Nations was done. And when Ireland's war was done, and some grudging freedom had been wrung out of a surly British Empire, it wasn't really done at all. There was room, after all, when the British and Irish had stopped killing one another for the Irish to kill each other, in a civil war that was small and brutal and vengeful as well, whatever its aspirations.

Everyone paid some price for war in Ireland. You paid a price at some point for the side you took. You paid a price if you took no side at all. There were times when trying to stand aside was as dangerous as picking up a gun. Helena's husband, David, had almost paid the final price for that. He was a very ordinary policeman doing an ordinary job in the Dublin Metropolitan Police. After years of pounding the beat in a city he had always loved, he moved up the ranks to sergeant, and an orderly mind and retentive memory gave him a role that put those qualities to use, creating a system of records and cross-referencing that made his meticulous handwriting of his card indexes familiar to every detective in CID.

It was crime he dealt with, and it was in solving crime that all his links and connections and networks of informants and apparently unrelated facts found their purpose. But that started to change. First, after 1916, when he found himself filing names under new headings, which included not only political organisations but Gaelic Athletic clubs, Irish language classes and even teachers of Irish dancing and fiddle playing. If he was already uncomfortable, the mood became darker when the War of Independence finally broke out, following the election of 1918.

Unlike the Royal Irish Constabulary, the Dublin Metropolitan Police had always been unarmed, and unlike the RIC, most of its men wanted to try to take a neutral stance in the fighting that was breaking out across Ireland. But it wasn't an easy road. Dublin Castle, where David Gillespie worked, was suddenly full of British Intelligence officers and RIC detectives who had no qualms about the fact that what they did had nothing to do with the law they were supposed to represent. They all needed information and David Gillespie had plenty of it. They also wanted his ability to make unexpected and unlooked for connections at their service. His system impressed even the men from Military Intelligence. But when people started to think he was being obstructive about what he did and didn't choose to deliver, the atmosphere in Dublin Castle was strained, even threatening.

And on the other side, Sergeant Gillespie's instincts, sharper than most of the Intelligence men around him, told him that there were DMP men, friends as well as colleagues, who were passing Dublin Castle information to the IRA.

The idea of leaving them to it had been in David's mind for a while. He had already moved Helena, his wife, and his son, Stefan, down to his parents' farm on the western edge of the Wicklow Mountains. He no longer felt safe. DMP men were not often the target of assassination like RIC officers, but they weren't immune. And at times he didn't even know where the danger lay. There were men in the Castle who were suspicious of him. Making a point of not taking sides was taking a side for them. Then he witnessed what he had determined to avoid seeing, an officer he worked with copying material from his records and smuggling it out. He knew he would say nothing, but as far as the IRA spies in Dublin Castle were concerned, a line had been crossed. He knew too much. They gave him a choice. He could resign. It was in his head, wasn't it? But if he stayed, it would be on the same terms as Michael Collins's other spies. He would work for the IRA. They would be happy with that. He was useful. No third option was discussed, but David Gillespie knew there was one. If he became a risk to others, he would be silenced.

So, Sergeant Gillespie hung up his uniform and went back to Wicklow, to the small farm where he had grown up. Only Helena knew what had finally driven him out of the police. She was content at least. She had her husband and her son; that was all that mattered. If David had only told her part of what was happening in the cellars of Dublin Castle, she made her own connections with what she heard and what she read and even between what her husband said and what he was silent about. When a dozen British Intelligence officers were shot on a quiet Sunday morning in Dublin, he didn't need to tell her some of them were men he knew. And when she heard stories about men being taken into the cellars of the Castle for questioning, only to be carried out with their bodies so broken that no relatives were allowed to see the bodies before burial, she knew those cellars lay beneath David Gillespie's office. But all that was gone. They had their lives back. That's how it felt. And the peace in which to live them. So that's what they did. There was little money. The farm struggled to support them all. That, with all the rest, was yet another reason why Helena hadn't found a way to visit Germany again.

She sat on the train now, looking out at the first signs in German as they crossed the border from Belgium. It had been twelve years. Twelve years in which war, war in Europe, war at home, had made up much of the background to life. Twelve years in which parents had died who had only years before seemed healthy and strong and invincible. Twelve years in which she had moved from being in a Dublin flat and an imminent move to a smart, suburban house, to a farm whose rocky, unyielding fields stopped where mountains started. Twelve years in which friends she once knew in Germany in her youth had become mostly just names on Christmas cards. The wherewithal to pay for the trip came from a scrap of land in the hills that an uncle had left David. It didn't fetch much when it was sold and there was no shortage of things they needed the money for. But David wanted her to go. He knew she wanted to take Stefan, to try to keep something of her past alive in him.

'It's a real home from home, Ma!'

The boy who sat opposite Helena in the second-class sleeper laughed. The sleeper was a luxury she had argued with her husband about, though she knew he expected her to give in. And she did, having protested, she thought, enough. David knew, as she did, that it was unlikely there would be another trip like this. It wasn't said. It didn't need to be. For what it was, he would do the best he could for her.

'What's that, Stefan?'

'The soldiers.'

The train was crawling through a station it wasn't stopping at. Among the passengers were several soldiers moving along the platform. They had rifles slung on their shoulders, but one had his cradled in his arms, pointing forward not, perhaps, aggressively, but making the point that aggression could be provided if required. It was a familiar sight to both mother and son. Men with rifles at Dublin's railway stations, and even at small halts down the country sometimes, had been part of travelling by train in Ireland for years. You could take your pick who they were, depending on the date. British army or Black-and-Tans, IRA men and Free State soldiers. They all watched, sometimes nervously, sometimes with a dose of arrogance that was more or less convincing, but always with an eye for intimidation. Stefan Gillespie recognised their swagger, even through the train window. He also recognised the helmets that announced who the soldiers were.

'French, aren't they? Did you see the helmets?'

His mother had seen them. She shook her head.

'You'd have thought . . . five years on . . . there'd be an end to all that.'

Helena Gillespie sat back as the train picked up speed. Not much of a welcome. She had nothing more to say. She had put such things out of her mind at home, day after day, year after year. She kept putting them out of her mind. That was the only thing that made any sense. And now that the Civil War seemed over, really over, she had every hope she could put them out of her mind for the last time. She didn't want to begin her pilgrimage with more of it. But her son had been catching up on events in Germany. Now he saw what he had read about, for real.

'I can't see it's going to achieve much. France and Belgium send their troops in to take over the Rhineland because Germany's not paying its war reparations and in the one place the country's got any chance of making any money to pay war reparations . . . the factories stop working and all they can do is shoot people for going on strike. There's a lot dead, I think. So much for passive resistance.'

Helena nodded, looking out of the window. It wasn't a conversation she wanted. None of that was the Germany she knew when she was young. It wasn't the Germany she had come to touch again. He was right. Too much like home. Everyone knew about resistance in Ireland, passive and not so passive. And as far as passive resistance went, it couldn't surprise anyone, anywhere that passive was never the word for the response it provoked, whoever it was aimed at. But she was in the Germany she was in. That was the Germany Stefan was looking out at now.

'No,' she said, 'if there's no money, rifles won't make any more.'

'You saw the marks we got?'

Stefan got out his wallet and took the German banknote he had from it.

'Did you look? A million marks!' He laughed. 'Isn't that crazy?'

Helena smiled. He was fascinated. It was all new and, yes, a little crazy.

'I only changed a pound, Stefan. That's what Marie said to do. No more than a pound at a time, maybe even just ten shillings. That million-mark note could be ten million in a week's time. If you don't spend it, if you just hold on to it, it's only worth a fraction of what you started with. But the pounds will keep their value.'

'Well, at least I'll be able to say I was, briefly, a millionaire, Ma . . .'

She smiled again, but she wanted to talk about something else.

'You do remember, Marie, and Annaliese, her daughter?'

'Well, a bit . . . I'm sure when I see them . . .'

The truth was that Stefan Gillespie remembered almost nothing. It was over twelve years ago. There was a memory of the journey. That stuck in his head more than the people at the other end. There were some older boys, and there was a girl, but he didn't have a picture of her in his head at all. He was six then, now he was almost eighteen. At that age, the years between were like long, distant lifetimes.

'There are the boys too, Kurt and Bertolt. They're quite a bit older and I'm not sure they'll be there. But Annaliese's only three or four years older than you. I think she's twenty-one or twenty-two. Close enough, so. I know she's looking forward to seeing you. Marie wrote to say she does still remember her little Irish cousin.'

Stefan laughed, but he didn't warm to his image as the little Irish cousin.

'I know Marie will make you very welcome. My trip to Vienna's only a few days. I'm sure by the time I go, you'll be settled. You'll be like one of the family.'

Helena had a lot of faith in old family ties. They were always stronger in her head than they could ever be where decades of distance had pulled the threads further and further apart. Stefan was less sure. If he was fascinated by what was around him now, and the idea of Germany, he was less easy about the relatives waiting for him. They were strangers, however often he heard their names on his mother's lips.

'So, the woman in Vienna . . . Dorothea . . . is that right?

'Yes, Dorothea.'

The name still didn't have a face for him.

'Don't you remember her? She came to stay with . . . just before the war.'

Stefan nodded. That was a clearer memory.

'She played the violin. And you played the piano with her.'

Helena nodded, smiling. It was an even clearer memory for her.

'She's not a relative?'

'No. My father, your Opa, sent me to Germany when I was ... eighteen or so ... so about your age. I was here for six months. I stayed with Marie's parents in Hannover. And I went to the Hannover Conservatory to study piano. It was a kind of present from my father. There was a little bit of money then, and I wanted to do more with my music. I was ... well, I wasn't so bad then. I could hold my own.'

'You always say that, Ma.' It was dutiful, perhaps, but sincere. 'You play very well. You don't play enough. You should play more. You know you should.'

'Well, I'm good enough to give a few lessons.' She laughed.

'And you always say that, too. We all know better.'

'Well, maybe it did look different a long time ago. I thought I was good enough to find a way to earn a living. I thought I'd go on from the Conservatory and study back in Ireland. But that wasn't what Opa had in mind. Those six months were a gift that wasn't repeated. Piano playing was a fine accomplishment for a young lady, and he felt, after what he'd spent, I was quite accomplished enough.'

Helena smiled, but Stefan heard the regret. It wasn't something his mother often talked about. He had never noticed before that it was more than fond memory.

'It was different for Dorothea. She was my great friend. And she was a very good violinist, exceptionally good. And she did play with orchestras. She played in Vienna for a time, at the Volkstheater. That's why she ended up there. And then she did ... what I always wanted to do. She opened a little music school. For children, mostly. In a town outside the city.

You can imagine Vienna wouldn't be the worst place to do that, of course. I doubt I'd have done as well in Dublin.'

Stefan had never heard his mother say this.

'I didn't know about that, Ma.'

'There's nothing to know. It didn't happen. Before we left Dublin, I did a lot of piano teaching. It made extra money. I kept it up after we came to Baltinglass, you know that. But there are only ever going to be a few children to teach.'

There was silence for a moment. Stefan knew that his mother had hoped he might do something with music. He had laboured at the piano with little enthusiasm. If he had inherited a love of music from Helena, he didn't inherit her facility, let alone the passion she had once had. It was a topic better avoided.

'It was a plan I had, for when your father became an inspector. We were going to move out of the city. We had just enough to look at a house in Terenure. It would have been big enough to have a music room and maybe a small grand piano and I thought I could take on more students, start teaching more seriously, and even think about doing more. I knew people who taught violin and cello and it could have been the beginning of something. A beginning, but with somewhere to go and something to aim for . . . then, well, everything changed, didn't it? Your father had to leave the police. That life was done with, and we had to start again.'

Helena turned away, gazing out through the train window into the darkness. Night had fallen. And as the Nord Express rumbled through another station there were two soldiers on an empty platform, leaning on their rifles and smoking. A picture, if Helena Gillespie needed one, of where that change came from and what it had meant. It wasn't that the life she led now didn't bring its own satisfaction and its own contentment. She was a woman who didn't carry her regrets around on her back. Her husband and her son and the farm at Kilranelagh had become her life. And it was rich enough. It had never been difficult for her to find the riches that were around her because they were always there to be found. Sometimes, even often, in abundance. But there might have been a different way to find them.

'I'm going to bed, Stefan. I won't sleep much, but I'll give it a try.'

He saw Helena was tired. It was their second night on a train. But he could also see that she wanted to stop talking. The direction her words had taken her was better put away. Memories could be very fond and yet still be unsettling. And as she drifted off into the kind of fitful half sleep that goes with the rattle of rails and swaying carriages, her son sat looking out at the night and the shifting patterns of light and dark that were all he could see of Germany for now. For a while, the idea of his mother as a young woman with small dreams that were all her own was in his head. It had never occurred to him that the woman he had known all the nearly eighteen years of his life as his mother was someone he barely knew at all.

The train that brought Stefan Gillespie and his mother from Goslar, on that last, short leg of their long journey, arrived at Ilsenburg when it was still quite early on in the morning of what was the third day of travel. They were now at the northern edge of the Harz Mountains, and Stefan could see for himself the beauty of the landscape his mother so often talked about. The low hills and the round-topped mountains beyond were not the jagged, monumental heights of Germany's Alpine frontiers further south, though in winter the Harz was also a wilderness of snow and ice. But now, in summer, everything was green. In many ways the shapes on the horizon, seen from the train through half-closed eyes, were not very different from the hills that started to rise up behind the Gillespie's farm at Kilranelagh to lead the way to the mountains of the Wicklow heartland. But fully open eyes took in only the difference. Instead of the bare slopes of thin grass and heather and the black bog turf and the stands of bracken, there was thick forest everywhere, full of light and shade, rich and variegated, except at the very tops of the highest hills. Lower down, the farms were bright and fronted with flowers and the meadows were green and lush by the standards of West Wicklow, where stone was never far below soil that was always too wet or too dry. The towns and villages they had passed through after leaving Hannover certainly benefitted from the morning sun that had chosen a good day to shine very brightly in a clear blue sky, but they didn't need sunshine to show themselves at their best. There were houses painted in every colour, in pastels and bright shades, with their timber frames marked out by any number of geometric patterns. It seemed somehow that everything was old yet looked almost new. The red and brown and grey tiles of the steep roofs made their own patterns too. And the cobbled streets, in which every house was a different shape and a different colour, seemed to make up a picture in which everything blended into a perfectly disordered harmony, framed somewhere by the encroaching forests and the green hills that were never far away.

So it was at Ilsenburg, as Stefan and Helena walked from the station to the Yellow House in Mühlenstrasse. However, even before they had passed the lake at the centre of the town, and the hotel that took its name from the red trout that could be caught in it, and the old town hall and the castle with its ancient monastery that looked down from the hill on the other side of the River Ilse, and even as the great hump of the mountain that was the Brocken was pointed out to them, Stefan found himself suddenly somewhere else.

It was unexpected, instant and undeniable. In a place that was at one and the same time a source of deep discomfort and wonder.

They were met at the station by Marie Hoffman and her daughter, Annaliese. Marie was a widow of more than enough years to be comfortable with the absence of Herr Hoffman. She had two sons who were much older than Annaliese and no longer at home. They would drop in, of course, but for now the Yellow House, which was just the kind of old–new, brightly painted timber-framed house that made its own picture, surrounded as it was by a garden full of summer flowers, had plenty of room for its familial guests. For Helena and Marie, who had once been friends as well as cousins, the years were disposed of within seconds of an embrace on the station platform. They walked ahead of Stefan and Annaliese, talking over each other and laughing, as if they were just catching up on the gossip of weeks before. And again, Stefan found himself looking at his mother in a new way. There was a friendship here, an easy bond between the two women that clearly had nothing to do with passing time. It had to be said that there was no easy conversation between Stefan and Annaliese as they trailed behind, carrying the suitcases. It hadn't started well. Marie had forced an embrace on Stefan and her daughter that neither of them wanted. 'They are going to be great friends', she announced, 'just as they were when they were children'. Stefan still couldn't remember Annaliese from that first visit. She remembered him, though it was probably no bad thing he didn't know she remembered him as a snot-nosed brat who was too stupid to understand German and had to be dragged around everywhere she went with her friends. If Stefan's German was a lot better now, nothing else had changed much as far as Annaliese was concerned. She went through the motions of asking a few polite questions about the trip from Ireland, but when all she got in return were hesitant, monosyllabic answers, she decided she'd done enough. Was he still stupid? They walked on in awkward silence.

It wasn't stupidity that had got Stefan Gillespie's tongue, however. It was worse. Annaliese Hoffman didn't have a bad opinion of herself, it should be said. She had known the effect she had on boys, now young men, long enough. That wasn't something that concerned her in her seventeen-year-old cousin from Ireland. He was a boy. She was a woman. There might only be four years between them, but that was a gulf that put him in a different world. As the two cousins walked along Mühlenstrasse, Annaliese's thoughts were on the tedious week ahead. The thoughts that reduced Stefan to embarrassed incoherence were very different. By the time they reached the Yellow House, he wasn't just smitten, he was in love.

*

The trip to the top of the Brocken began with sunshine and with more good humour on Annaliese Hoffman's part than the first excursions with her Irish cousin earlier in the week. She had discovered that if he didn't say very much, what he did say was more entertaining than she'd expected. He wasn't stupid, in fact he had managed to make her laugh, even, quietly and almost without her noticing, at herself. And Clara had kept them going when the conversation flagged and the Irish boy seemed to plunge into awkward incoherence, as he did at intervals. She laughed at everything and she made a joke of everything that was tedious or difficult. It worked better, too, when the three of them were out of sight of Annaliese's other friends, who were all older and apparently wiser, with the sophistication that came from twenty-five or twenty-six years on earth and a disdain for anyone older or younger. Annaliese possessed, as should have been obvious to anyone who had a passing acquaintanceship with her, more than her share of such sophistication, and it was one of the things that made trailing around with a seventeen-year-old boy hard. When Ilsenburg's smart set were out of sight, it was easier. And Clara, well, Clara was Clara, and she avoided her best friend's friends with gusto. The town's smartest returned the compliment. The two young women shared a great deal, but socially they went their very separate ways.

As they left the road out of Ilsenburg and turned on to the forest path that led along the Ilse, the talk was mostly of the way they would go. The sun filtered through the beeches and the oaks and the tumbling water was sparkling. It was already warm. It would be a hot day. For Stefan, simply walking beside Annaliese was enough to make the day bright. Everything else was a bonus. And she was notably cheerful and talkative. He knew Clara had been doing a lot of the heavy lifting when it came to keeping conversation going. When she went home in the evenings and he sat on his own at the Yellow House with Annaliese, it had been harder. His tongue seemed to stick to the roof of his mouth and when he said anything, he felt he sounded like an idiot. Often, much as he longed to talk to his cousin, he buried himself in the book by Heine that Reinhard Friesack had lent him.

But on this new morning, even Heinrich Heine was on his side. He mentioned the journey the poet had made along the little river, through the same woods they were walking, mostly because he wanted to say something and couldn't think of anything else that wouldn't have immediately added to the list of inanities during his stay in Ilsenburg. Annaliese in particular had done little more than raise her eyebrows when Stefan had buried himself in Heine before; now he had something to say. Walking through the wood, she had room for what the world-weary sophistication of youth had told her was very old and very dull. Stefan was enthusiastic. He loved what he had read and he loved what he was looking at. And as he found it easier, unexpectedly, to talk, so, finally, did she.

There were few people about. A party of determined hikers passed them at speed and disappeared among the trees. They were still close enough to the town to meet neighbours of the Mühlenstrasse girls walking a variety of large and small dogs. But the way through the woods was quiet. It felt like they had it to themselves. They crossed the river over a footbridge and came out of the trees to see a wall of dark, moss-covered rock in front of them. Annaliese took Stefan's arm.

'He should see our cave, shouldn't he Clara?'

'I guess he should, though he won't see much. I've no torch, have you?'

'That doesn't matter.'

Annaliese pulled her cousin off the path and through some sprawling holly. In front of them, at the base of the rock wall, was an opening, blacker than stone.

'It goes right into the hillside . . .'

They bent slightly as she pulled him into the cave. Clara followed.

'You can see a little way back.' Annaliese was whispering. 'We won't go far in but if you look up, you'll see it's high. If we had a light, the rock sparkles . . .'

'I can see a bit,' said Stefan, 'but then it's just black.'

He was whispering too, though only because Annaliese had been. He looked up and there was no roof to see, only darkness, then he looked back into the cave. He could see it opened out, but then, as the light coming in through the entrance dissipated, there was only darkness in front, just as there was only darkness above.

'Annaliese, I know what you're . . .' That whisper was Clara's.

Annaliese stifled a giggle, then clapped her hands loudly and screamed. The noise was very loud in the silence, echoing back even louder from the rock walls. Stefan looked round, startled, to see his cousin laughing, and then he turned again. There was a noise in the darkness, like a rushing, whistling wind coming towards them, and then, where there was light, the sound was a cloud of darkness coming out of the darkness, coming towards them at speed. And then it was all round them, filling the air, a living thing that was a thousand living things. It passed over them, and almost through them. But Stefan felt only the breeze it made. Nothing touched him. And then it was gone, bursting through the entrance into the daylight outside.

There was complete silence. Then Annaliese's voice.

'Isn't it wonderful!' She was laughing.

'I knew that was coming,' said Clara. 'That was her favourite trick when she was little and she wanted to frighten the life out of someone littler. She wasn't nice, at all. Well, some people say she's still not very nice. They do have a point.'

'You bitch!'

They were both laughing.

'I have seen bats before,' said Stefan. 'Maybe not that many.'

He grinned. He couldn't say he wasn't surprised, but not frightened, and he knew, from looking at Annaliese's face, that frightening had not been part of it. Not much anyway.

She put her arm through his.

'But it is wonderful, Stefan, isn't it? I'd forgotten how wonderful. They never touch you. Everyone thinks they will... get in your hair and your clothes. But they don't. They're all round you. They're millimetres from you, hundreds of them, but they know... they fly past you and they'll never even brush your skin!'

*

The path along the river rose up slowly at first. It was a gentle enough walk, with a few rocks to scramble over and some steep slopes to stretch the legs and quicken the breath. The way was always up, though with high trees all around, flanking the twisting, noisy Ilse, there was never much to see ahead except more trees. The high hill they were aiming for would be invisible until they were almost halfway up it. But as morning passed into afternoon, the slopes became steeper and the rocks they had to negotiate got bigger. And the friendship that had waited, or hung in abeyance, almost to the end of the holiday, was suddenly there. The three of them talked more easily than they had and whatever it was that was different and distant between them disappeared. Helena, certainly, would have been pleased.

They talked of the things that they hadn't talked about before. Their childhoods, which had not been so different at times. The farm at Kilranelagh had its own valley and its own stream and its own hills. And the things they did when they were younger were the same things somehow. For Annaliese, especially, it was a long time since she felt she had put away childish things, and this day, somehow a little out of time, was a moment to enjoy remembering them. They talked of what they were doing, too, with an easy sense of having no real plans but enjoying what was left of the time before such things became necessary. Stefan had just left school and would be starting his degree in English at Trinity College when the summer was over. His life was changing. Annaliese was at a college in Magdeburg training to be a secretary. Her life was changing too. Her dream was a flat in the city. Independence. It would come next year when she got a job. Clara was in Leipzig, training to be an optician. Unlike the other two, her life was planned out. She would get her qualifications and work in her father's shop, and one day, when he was old, she would take over and the shop in

Mühlenstrasse would be hers. As for what else might go with all that, it couldn't be that sort of conversation. If Annaliese had a number of Ilsenburg's finest catches on lines, the lines were long, and she was happy to keep it that way. Clara had a life of her own that she kept very much her own. If the two of them discussed men they made little of it, however firm their friendship. It was a place they avoided. No one would have said Clara Bloch's family was so very Jewish; still, it was Jewish enough. But that was in another world, and one Stefan Gillespie could not then have conceived of. As for love, of all the things that he and Annaliese and Clara filled the long day talking about, as if making up for the time that had been wasted in awkward silence, love wasn't there. At least not outside Stefan Gillespie's seventeen-year-old head.

The three wayfarers didn't make their picnic until well into afternoon, only suddenly realising how hungry they were. They were not far from the point where the trees gave way to the bare slopes high on the Brocken. Stefan could see the mountain now, rising above the trees. They had left the path and crossed half a dozen small streams that fed into the Ilse, to find a waterfall that, like the cave and the bats further down the valley, was special to Annaliese and Clara. It wasn't the most spectacular of the waterfalls, but it was off the beaten track, so it was theirs.

They sat above the waterfall and ate dark bread and ham and sausage and pickles and drank the bottle of white wine that was Annaliese's particular contribution to the picnic. It wasn't because she had brought the bottle that she drank the best part of it. Perhaps it was only a habit that went with the excess of sophistication she had, and Clara and Stefan didn't. Perhaps it was just that she was having a far nicer time than she expected and her enthusiasm got the better of her. Either way, her cheerfulness and her ebullience grew as they looked down at the spout of water crashing on the rocks below. She recalled how often they sat there as children, a whole gang of them that spent summer's endless days roaming the Ilsetal. She remembered the great dare that was jumping from one side of the fall to the other, right at the brink where the water poured over. She had always been the best, better than any of the boys. She always jumped furthest. She never even got her feet wet. She could still do it, she said, with a childlike lack of modesty that didn't normally go with her almost twenty-one years . . . even after half a bottle of wine.

Stefan was laughing, enjoying being there and feeling close to Annaliese. Clara, as she saw that her friend was about to prove she could still jump across the waterfall, wasn't sure it was a good idea at all. And it wasn't. Her few words of caution were barely out of her mouth before Annaliese was standing up and stepping back from the water to take a run at it. She had some speed, certainly, and it was almost enough. Her first foot got to other side, but it landed on a smooth, wet rock that the leather of her shoes couldn't grip. She couldn't pull the leg forward. She slipped and fell, over the edge of the fall into the water below.

The cascade wasn't so high and there was a little pool below it that was deep enough to break a fall. As Stefan and Clara crawled to the edge and looked down, the shock they felt was almost immediately replaced by laughter. Annaliese was floating in the pool, soaked through from head to foot, now entirely sober and feeling stupid. She scowled. Stefan stopped laughing. If it had to be good to laugh *with* his cousin, her affections would never be engaged by laughing *at* her.

'Shall we come and get you, Liese!' Clara didn't stop laughing.

'I can manage, thank you.'

Annaliese stood up in the pool. As she put her foot down, she screamed.

The pool was deep enough to break a fall, but it depended how you landed. Annaliese had landed on one leg and that had taken all her weight. It wasn't going to take her weight again for some time. If it wasn't broken it was badly sprained.

Stefan and Clara scrambled to the bottom of the fall. They half pulled and half lifted Annaliese onto the rocks at one side, but there was no way to get her to the top and back to the path short of carrying her. From the pain she was in, it did look more like some kind of break than a sprain. She was stuck. They needed help.

The summit of the Brocken was not far away. And at the top there were people. There was a café and there was the station where the railway ran down the other side of the mountain. Clara knew the way back to the main path and she knew the way on from there. She would have to go. Stefan would stay with Annaliese. And so he did, while Clara made her way through the trees to the mountain. For a long moment, as they watched Clara climb back to the top of the fall and hurry away, neither of them spoke. Annaliese shifted her weight as she lay on her side. She gave a cry of pain, followed by a German word he knew, but had never used. She looked up at him and as she saw his face, so very serious and concerned, she laughed. It didn't do her much good, though. She grimaced again.

'You know, when I first met you, I thought you were a bit of an idiot.'

It wasn't exactly what he wanted to hear. He shrugged.

'But you're all right, Stefan,' she continued. 'I'm the fucking idiot!'

He smiled at her. Despite fond dreams that had passed through his head during his week at the Yellow House, he didn't expect his feelings for his cousin to be requited. Still, she thought he was all right. That would have to do.

★

Help didn't take long to arrive in the end. Annaliese Hoffman arrived at the summit of the Brocken not as she had planned, ready to show Stefan the Harz Mountains laid out before them in the evening light. She came on a stretcher, trying hard not to show the pain she was in. She was, of course, embarrassed, apologetic and feeling a lot less sophisticated than she had when she set off from Ilsenburg earlier that day. The last train down the mountain took them to Wernigerode, where instead of being met by Reinhard Friesack in his father's Wanderer Puppchen, an ambulance was waiting. It was a fracture, but not much of one, and by the end of the day Annaliese was at home with her leg in a cast, coming to the odd conclusion that despite everything, it had been a good day. It was a day to remember. And she would remember it as the years went by, though she would also try to put it out of her head, along with a lot of things she didn't want there.

The meal at the Landhaus Zu den Rothen Forellen didn't happen that night, but on the last evening in Ilsenburg, when his mother had returned from Vienna, Stefan and Helena sat on the hotel terrace as the sun went down over the lake and the mountains beyond, with Marie Hoffman and Annaliese, cast and all, and Clara. All the connections that meant so much to Helena had been reforged. That was why she came. There were plans made for more visits, to Ireland for the girls and to Germany again for Stefan and Helena and it wouldn't be wrong to say that the more beer that found its way to the table, the more ambitious the plans became. It wasn't that way, of course. None of it would happen. Annaliese would never go to Ireland, let alone with Clara. Helena Gillespie would never see Germany again either. A lot of years would pass before Stefan Gillespie would return to Ilsenburg, and when he did, it was to find everything had changed. It had changed utterly.

4

DAS TREIBGUT
FLOTSAM

Babenhausen, June 1945

The war was over. It had been over for several weeks, but nothing had changed at the Schloss Babenhausen. There was still a sense, as there had been since the first Americans arrived in the town, that we were waiting for something. But what we were waiting for had come and gone. The end. For the Germans around us, at the castle and in the town it felt like a slow exhalation of breath. Relief. Simply that. For those who mourned the passing of what went before, whose souls raged over great betrayals, it was their lot to maintain the kind of silence their dreams-turned-to-nightmares had inflicted on everyone else for so long.

We played no part in the celebrations we read about in the papers and even heard on the radio. That was it, apart from a couple of days in which the small American garrison drank its way through whatever alcohol they could find in the town. Prince Wittke produced a couple of bottles of brandy from his cellars and we gathered in the dining room the night after the surrender and drank a toast to the fact that it was over. That was as much as he said. It was more solemn than celebratory. As if we had waited for the end and somehow missed it. It felt like there was something to wait for. A beginning presumably, though what that meant, nobody could imagine. The not-yet-resolved end hung in the air. It hadn't shaken off the smell of decay.

However, as far as Con Cremin was concerned, one end brought another. Ireland's diplomatic mission to Germany was over. In the weeks that followed the surrender, he did what he could to pursue the interests of Irish citizens who might need help, and he tried and failed to make contact with the honorary consul he had left behind in Staffelde, outside Berlin, now firmly in the occupation's Russian Zone. But the Irish minister had no status now and since the American and British forces had not yet created any real administration, there was no one to address letters to other than army generals who almost certainly didn't read them. There was no one to even attempt to speak to. Con was stuck at the bottom end of Germany, out of the way of the centres of Allied control, and he had no permission to move from the area. He could travel south to Lindau and Bregenz and the Swiss border. That was the way the Irish legation-that-was would leave Germany. And the only real freedom the minister-that-was had was to make arrangements for departure. Naturally enough, his departure meant my departure too. Thank God.

I drove Con Cremin to the Swiss border and left him to cross over and take the train to Bern. He would be back in three days and when he arrived we would finally pack up and leave. We still had the car and the US army had even given us the privilege of a chit for two jerry cans of petrol. It was no mean feat to get petrol and it had taken me nearly a week of begging and badgering to do it. But if I was tempted to feel pleased with my negotiating skills, the Minister's wry smile put me right. All the extra petrol was to get him out of Germany, sooner rather than later. It wasn't for our benefit.

So, after dropping Con Cremin at the border, I took a long diversion to pick up the fuel from a US base at Lindsberg. It meant driving halfway to Munich before turning back to Babenhausen. I hadn't thought much about the journey beforehand. It was irritating that I had to go so far, but getting the petrol at all was an achievement. World-weary jokes about military bureaucracy were standard banter for any conversations with soldiers. It was the couldn't-organise-a-piss-up-in-a-brewery theory of the military hierarchy and if there was something in it, why would the Americans be any different. The US corporal, who filled up the embassy car and then handed over the two extra jerry cans, fully subscribed to the theory.

'Why the fuck did they send you here? Wasting your time, buddy.'

I smiled as if to say, well, that's the army for you.

'I guess Babenhausen's a small garrison . . .' I shrugged

'And they're so short of gas they can't fill up a fuel tank? Why's there a garrison there?' asked my new friend. 'Why's there a fucking camp there at all?'

I smiled the same kind of smile and added a shrug.

'It's a fuel dump. They've got more gas than we have. Nuts!'

'Sounds like nuts,' I agreed.

As he put the last jerry can into the back of the car and shut the door, he took the chit I had brought with me, pulled out a pen and scribbled a signature across it.

'I'll take the top copy. You keep the carbon.'

He tore off a piece of paper. Then he laughed.

'I get it. I get it now.'

I didn't make anything of the laugh until he continued.

'You expect shit for the birds from the brass, but the specialists are these fellers!' The corporal stabbed at the docket. 'Intelligence! You're signed off for the gas by a Field Intelligence officer. We got no shortage of ninety-day-wonder officers who can't wipe their asses without a diagram, but these guys knock them out of the water. Intelligence? They couldn't find a fuck in a whorehouse! You're lucky they didn't send you to Berlin to see if the Russkies were giving out gas.'

The American slapped me on the back, laughing again.

'Still, you get to see some of the countryside!'

He walked off, whistling cheerfully, pleased, I think, to confirm the idiocy of the officer corps in general and, so it seemed, Intelligence officers in particular.

I drove out through the gate onto the road for Memmingen. I had just abandoned my equally cheerful, Fred-Karno's-army approach to the tour of southern Bavaria the need for petrol had taken me on. My pursuit of fuel in Babenhausen had involved a number of US officers. There was a helpful but ineffective captain. Then a very unhelpful lieutenant who said he could offer a gallon of diesel I didn't want but it was more than his life was worth to dole out petrol to civilians. Next a Master Sergeant Spinelli, who said he'd find me petrol if I could get a couple of crates of the 'good stuff' out of Prince Wittke's wine cellar for him. It wasn't a route I was prepared to take and virtue, very occasionally, is more than its own reward. A couple of days later Sergeant Spinelli was taken in for questioning by the Provost Marshall's Office. Then suddenly, the helpful captain reappeared, this time with a chit for petrol, which was now available for only the inconvenience of a very long drive. No, not for our benefit.

I didn't examine the piece of paper except to establish that it did what was needed. It gave us what we wanted. Even if I'd looked harder, I wouldn't have registered that it hadn't come from Babenhausen's garrison commander but from an Intelligence officer in Ulm. I knew now, though. And it wasn't difficult to work out why American Field Intelligence had taken Ireland's ex-Minister and I under its wing. The docket wasn't signed by Lieutenant John Mackay, but I had no doubt the British Intelligence man was behind it. He would know I was taking the Minister to the Swiss border. He would know my return via Lindsberg, to collect the petrol, would mean spending the best part of the day away from the Schloss Babenhausen. The visit he paid Con Cremin, in search of whatever information he could get, hadn't been a success. I'd assumed that would be that. It couldn't be very important. But the man was a stickler. He was the bloody-minded sort. Or perhaps what I got a whiff of, even at the time, was more than that. I had put him down as RUC Special Branch. Maybe that wasn't right. He had a political bent that he couldn't quite disguise. It was too much a part of him. He wore a uniform but that didn't mean he wasn't MI5 or MI6. In that case, you couldn't be surprised he wasn't content to leave the result of his inquiries at a no-score draw. Driving now towards Memmingen, I knew Lieutenant Mackay was in our rooms at the Schloss Babenhausen, searching for something, or nothing, but surely searching.

There was no sign of John Mackay at the castle. I didn't expect there to be. He had given himself enough time. I walked upstairs and looked at my room and Con Cremin's. I wouldn't have known anyone had been there. I wasn't sure I could see anything that told me the rooms had been searched. Maybe in my room, where most of the documents and boxes of papers were, I could feel things had been moved and replaced. Even that could have been my imagination. I was certain the man had been there. I wanted to see something that proved it. But he was good at what he did. Better at what he did than disguising who he was, I thought. Smugger than you might expect from a hard-nosed Ulsterman. But then maybe he'd spent too much time in British Intelligence. Superintendent Gregory always said smugness was a speciality of theirs. British agents had a reputation for it. They carried it with them. In Ireland, once, that cost some of them a lot more than their reputations.

It struck me that I could be falling into a little smugness myself. I was maybe a bit too sure of my ability to read Lieutenant Mackay. Maybe a bit too certain that if I thought he had been at the castle, then he must have been. But it didn't take much to find out I was right. All he wanted to do was to get at the Minister's records when there was nobody to stop him taking time to examine them. If the job had been meticulous, he didn't care who knew he'd been there. So, when I went downstairs and saw the prince's housekeeper coming up from the kitchens with a basket of laundry, I simply asked her if the English officer had got what he wanted from his visit. I smiled as I said it, but I got no smile in return.

'I'm sorry, Herr Gillespie. I did tell the prince he was here . . .'

She stopped. If she was embarrassed, I thought it was more for the man who employed her than for herself. After all, Mackay was a kind of policeman, wasn't he? The habit of doing what any species of policeman told you, or anyone in a uniform for that matter, was something they had lived with for a long time.

'There was nothing he could do,' I said. 'That's the way it is.'

She nodded and smiled, then turned away. All embarrassment had gone. It hadn't been about what happened. It was about me finding out.

I found Lieutenant Mackay in the hotel the Americans had taken over in the middle of the town. The bar there was the officers' mess. For now, all fraternisation between Allied soldiers and German civilians was forbidden. It would take time for distance and antipathy to fade. Weeks away from war, there was still suspicion and anger from the men on the ground. Many of the Allied dead hadn't been dead very long. The same could be said of the German dead. But then defeat is defeat. And the determination that this defeat must be grinding and unrelenting had been hammered into the invading troops so ferociously and for so long that it wasn't going to be moderated any time soon.

The only Germans in the hotel bar were collecting empty glasses and mopping the floor. And from the reception I got, I felt I wasn't much more welcome myself. But the officers' mess was where I'd tracked Mackay down to, and he came out to find me at the front of the hotel. He greeted me like an old friend. Naturally, he knew why I was there. I could see it amused him. Whatever else his job entailed, this Irish diversion was a bit of a game. I think he was pleased I was going to let him carry on playing. Smug, definitely smug. But that was only part of it. Old habits and old prejudices die hard. I had no doubt that as an Ulsterman of the red-white-and-blue variety, the game was more satisfying for being played against the fag end of Ireland's diplomatic mission to the Third Reich. The scent of humiliation. And if there was an obligation to treat Con Cremin with some courtesy, the same wasn't true of me.

Still, for now, as the lieutenant grinned amiably, we were almost comrades in arms.

'Come in and have a beer, Stefan. I might as well call you, Stefan, if that's all right. Two Irishmen in unfamiliar waters. I almost feel I know you . . .'

'I'm sure you've done everything you can to do so, John.'

He laughed as we entered the bar. I was playing along and he liked that.

'Two beers!'

He snapped the order in the direction of the barman and walked out through some glass doors on to a terrace. It was a bright evening. American officers sat in the sunshine. There was a record playing. It might have been 'Moonlight Serenade' or it might not. Whatever it was, it seemed to be the only record they had. I wasn't listening to it, but at some point a voice threatened to get a gun if it came on again.

'Did you find anything useful?'

'I wouldn't say so, but you never know, do you? All I do is pass on the crap. It's up to other people to shovel through it to see if there's any real shite. It was difficult to resist the message your Mr Walshe in Dublin sent Mr Cremin . . . my boss passed it on. When you pack for Switzerland . . . don't leave any secrets.'

If I needed a reminder that Lieutenant Mackay was something other than a lieutenant in Field Intelligence, he didn't seem bothered about proving the point.

'Anyone can read the Irish codes, you, the Yanks, even the Germans could. Joe Walshe knows that. Maybe just a bit of craic . . . for whoever it is you work for.'

'I never heard Walshe was a great man for the craic.'

'Maybe he never had anyone to take the bait before.'

The beer arrived. Mackay offered me a cigarette.

'It doesn't look like your Minister's got much left to pack. It's not my speciality, but I guess if there were any shite worth shovelling, between your embassy being flattened by bombs and whatever you destroyed before you left Berlin, it's long gone. In fact, if Mr Cremin has a final bonfire before he crosses the border, you'd almost say there'll be hardly any evidence left that Ireland was ever in the Thousand-Year Reich at all. Well, apart from a few stains on the flag.'

He raised his glass and grinned.

'That eye of yours still looks a bit rough. Will you get a medal?'

I raised my glass and smiled in return.

'There are probably a lot of people out there you can impress with what you know, John. There'll be a good few you can intimidate. Don't waste your time on me. Wouldn't you be better off looking for some Nazi bigwigs? Isn't that what you're supposed to be doing? I thought you'd be more worried about them slipping into Switzerland than an Irish diplomat and his bag-carrier. Or maybe not. You can take the RUC man out of Belfast but getting Belfast out of the RUC man, is something else, isn't it? You've had your fun, Lieutenant. I'd say move on.'

Mackay turned away and called for two more beers.

'I'm not really interested in His ex-Excellency the Irish Minister. No one is. But there are all sorts of people to look for. Not all of them were last seen strutting around in SS uniforms. There's a list of traitors, British traitors. Some of them won't be hard to find. Some of them will take a bit of ferreting out. And some of them will be hiding very handily behind a bit of blarney and an Irish passport.'

'Then some of them won't be traitors, will they? Not to Britain . . .'

'Come on, Inspector, don't give me that bollocks. I expect it from Cremin and Dev and all the other fuckers in Dublin. You know better. If these fellers need hanging, a bit of paper with a harp and a Saorstát Éireann stamp won't save them.'

Two more beers arrived, very cold. Somewhere they could get ice.

'That depends what they're being accused of, doesn't it? And whoever they are, do you think Con Cremin's got their addresses stashed away somewhere in case he needs to tip them the wink? Or maybe anybody Irish would do. Is that it?'

'Whatever it is, it would do Ireland no harm to be more cooperative.'

I drained the beer. It was very good, but I wasn't staying for a third.

'They should get you back hunting for Nazis, John. You probably spent a lot of happy years beating up Catholics in the Falls Road, but you need to leave it behind, mo chara, if you want to stay in Intelligence long enough to get a pension and an OBE. When I say beating up, I'm just being polite. But thanks for the beer.'

I thought it was insulting enough to stick. It wasn't. He laughed.

'You could be right, Stefan. It takes an Irishman to know an Irishman.'

I assumed that would be the last I saw of Lieutenant Mackay. I told Con Cremin about his visit to the Schloss Babenhausen, but he was neither surprised nor concerned. He showed no inclination to complain or protest. Someone somewhere up the chain of military command might have produced an apology, but in the absence of any diplomatic status, the now ex-Minister's consciousness of that made him decide to ignore it. There were no secrets. There was nothing that mattered. There was nothing the British wouldn't know anyway. And was the fact that the Irish presence in Germany was just fading away such a bad thing? I knew Con felt it wasn't. And no one at home would thank him for a row that would eventually find its way to London and would have to be pursued to the top, for no purpose other than adding a bit more to the pile of bad feeling on both sides.

However, the Minister wasn't finished with John Mackay or British Intelligence. It was the last night in Babenhausen, his last night on German soil, and the last bonfire of, by then, trivial and unimportant documents. There was still the car to be packed, mostly with personal belongings and the few last diplomatic trappings. We sat on a wall as the sun was setting, watching the embers of the fire and the white ash drifting up from it in a gentle breeze. It was quiet.

'They're sending me to Lisbon,' said Cremin. 'I thought I'd get home, but no. When I've sorted things out in Bern, we'll go to Paris, now the embassy's back there. Pat wants to catch up with old friends. She didn't take to Bern. I guess she was worried about me. That's it. On to Portugal. Exchanging one dictator for another. Joe must think I'm the expert. Still, the best you can say for Salazar is that in the dictator stakes, he's an amateur . . . at least if you put him beside the last one.'

It was meant to be a joke, but it came out darker than he intended.

'Getting across Europe's going to take some time. With one thing and another I'm allowing a fortnight. I don't know what the trains are like in France. You can do it quicker, but I doubt you'll be home in less than a week or ten days. And I know you've had enough. The good news is I've found you a faster route.'

'It doesn't matter,' I said. 'It's bound to take time.'

'It'll save you time.' The Minister smiled. 'But it's not all good news.'

'I see. That's to say, I don't see . . .'

'You'll be going to Hannover courtesy of our friend Lieutenant Mackay. He'll get you on an RAF flight there. A couple of hours to London. Then home.'

'The second part sounds better than the first.'

Con Cremin took out a cigarette. He laughed as he gave me one.

'And there's me thinking you two must have hit it off.'

'I'm surprised he's feeling so helpful,' I said.

'I had a chat with him . . . I thought I'd let him know I wasn't interested in pursuing the matter of his visit to the Schloss. I'd say he was pushing his luck, whatever the bluster to you. I think there's as much bluff as bluster to Mr Mackay and I don't know that his superiors really asked him to break in. They don't give a cuss about something as trivial as the Irish legation departing with its tail between its legs. My job is just to shut up shop and go quietly. Another row between London and Dublin is surplus to requirements. I'm no mean bluffer myself. The lieutenant decided I was doing everyone a favour by letting it ride . . . and especially him.'

'So he owes us a favour?'

'I wouldn't overstate it. But I do have one more job for you that comes with the benefit of an easier way back to Ireland. I can't get access to anyone. A few local US commanders, that's all. I suppose I hung on in the hope that I could do something in a consular capacity but that would mean going north and finding someone in whatever kind of administration they've come up with who'll talk to me. But there's only one place they'll let me go. Straight across the Swiss border . . . and out of Germany. I was probably kidding myself. You do these things, don't you? But if there was even a chance they'd let me stay on with some limited diplomatic role, I'm afraid Dev's I'm-sorry-for-your-trouble call on the German embassy . . . put the lid on it.'

'So what can I do?'

'You're not a diplomat. There's no political point to make by not allowing you to take whatever way out of the country you can find, and no reason not to let Lieutenant Mackay help you find it. Along the way, you can deliver some messages. They may achieve nothing, but they may get something moving. If they come via Mackay's bosses in Intelligence, at least they stand a chance of getting to someone who counts. Once I'm in Switzerland, I'll be able to contact Dublin and I can make sure there's some pressure on London from that end. That's probably what's going to matter, but if there are people in Germany who know what it's about . . . it might make a difference. If it sounds like I'm flying a kite, I am.'

'Who do I need to get to?'

'Mackay's based in Brunswick, that's where he's heading. So, whoever runs the Intelligence set up there. I don't know what the rank is, a captain, a major. The point is that it gets passed up the chain. And since you know about some of it, if they've got questions, you can answer them, especially when it comes to Charlie Mills. I left him in Berlin as Irish consul, for what it was worth, and I haven't heard from him since. I need to know he's all right. That's the main issue. When I left him in Staffelde, there was a German government. Now he's in the Soviet Zone. The Russians don't even have diplomatic relations with Ireland. If neutrality hasn't endeared us to the British and the Americans, I get the impression Comrade Stalin's approach is distinctly hostile. Charlie's a German citizen. I can do nothing. British Intelligence could find out what's happened. They do talk to the Russians.'

'Do you think they could get him out?'

'I don't know. I'd like to think so . . . it's over three months since . . .'

Con Cremin shrugged. He took out another cigarette.

'It's not good in the east,' he said quietly. 'I shouldn't have left him.'

He stood up and walked towards the bonfire that was now burning out. He looked down at it for a long moment. He turned back, shaking his head slowly.

'I think I persuaded myself there was something I could do in Germany. There was neutrality to defend, of course. That was the main point of being here, wasn't it? Well, I did that. And maybe I did it for longer than I should have done. Was that diplomacy or bloody-mindedness? I've never had any doubt that neutrality was the best option we had, but I wonder if there wasn't a time to get out before the end. I was still trying to do something. There were people I thought I could help. You remember me hammering away at those lists of Jews Ireland was prepared to take. Meeting after meeting. And all the German Foreign office ever did was tell me, with diplomatic grace, to fuck off. I was still hammering away when we left. But they were all dead, weren't they? And we all knew it. As for ensuring no one forgot we were neutral, well, I did that. It seems no one has.'

Cremin's shoulders dropped. He smiled, but there was a sense of defeat.

'At the end of March, when we were still in Salzburg, I got an invitation to lunch in Berlin. Hosted by von Ribbentrop himself. All the ambassadors. I don't know how many of us there were by then. Nuts! If he'd left it any later the Russians could have joined us for dessert. I sent the Wilhelmstrasse a very polite note, to say that if they could arrange transport, I'd be delighted to attend. They replied with equally polite apologies to say transport wasn't available at that time. Not so surprising as Berlin was almost completely surrounded by the Red Army.'

I didn't know whether he wanted me to laugh. A shrug seemed better.

'I don't think it was neutrality by then. I don't even think it was diplomacy now. I was making it all normal . . . making what was long past normality, normal.'

Con Cremin threw his cigarette end into the cooling ash.

'Still, tomorrow, it's done, Stefan. We depart Germany as we arrived . . .'

'How do you mean?'

Turning away from the fire, he did find something to laugh at.

'They used to call us the cheap legation. Well, whatever about the rest of our reputation, Joe Walshe is going to make sure we hang on to that. My instructions on reaching Bern are to put the legation's car up for sale and get what I can for it!'

*

The journey north from Bavaria was slow. The roads were full of military traffic and full of people too. Displaced Persons could mean almost anything but they were everywhere. And wherever they were going, most of them were walking, because walking was all there was. They might be forced labourers from every corner of Europe, trying to find their way out of Germany. They might be men and women from the camps, just strong enough to walk away, but with nowhere to go, doing little more than move from one DP camp to the next, leaving one concentration camp to find shelter in another that had just been cleared of bodies and the bulldozers had buried the dead. Among the lines of people walking, there were always the striped rags that were all some of them had for clothing. It was hard not to feel the roads at times were full of people who had no idea where they were going. But some did. Groups of men who couldn't get out of the habit of marching, even though they'd dumped their uniforms for whatever else they could find. They were heading home. So too were others, older men and younger women, often with children and cartloads of belongings. Heading home or heading somewhere friends and families might make another place better than where they'd come from. All this I would keep seeing, over and again.

I took in all these people for a time, but it wasn't long before they all looked the same, just as the roads full of army vehicles looked the same, and the wreckage of the towns we went through looked the same. Somewhere American uniforms and trucks became British uniforms and lorries. The shade of khaki changed along with the accents of the military police at the checkpoints that stopped us endlessly.

Lieutenant Mackay was in an amiable mood, much as he had been at the officers' mess in Babenhausen, but he'd parked his sarcasm, which made the conversation less like hard work. Maybe he thought he was off-duty, or maybe he'd just exhausted whatever interest he'd been told to show in an Irish diplomatic mission that had now ceased to exist. Much of the time he didn't bother with conversation at all, and I was happy with that. It was going to take us two days to get to Brunswick, with a stop at some army base along the way. The route wasn't difficult to follow. We were on main roads and they were already well-signposted in English. It was clear Mackay wasn't used to driving. They'd sent him to the American Zone on his own, but normally he had a driver. I took the map. It was something to do and it kept what conversation we had mostly focussed on the journey.

We stopped at an army camp somewhere beyond Würzburg. I don't know where it was. It seemed to be nowhere in particular, just a collection of khaki tents and some barbed wire at a road junction, next to yet another checkpoint. I was a novelty, and all the more so because there were a couple of Irish officers, but Mackay ended up sitting on his own. It could have been that Intelligence officers simply weren't popular, the way a Special Branch man, even one as affable as me, could kill the conversation stone dead in a pub full of Guards out on the razzle. Or it could have been that John Mackay wasn't a good fit for his fellow officers. They all drank that night, but he drank more and he drank mostly on his own. Where the rest got louder, he didn't change. If they drank for pleasure, he drank only to drink.

When we set off the next day, I was taken aback by where we were going. I shouldn't have been. I'd been looking at a map the whole of the previous day, and Mackay had rattled off the route enough times, ticking off towns aloud as we went. I knew where Brunswick was, though I'd never been there. I did know Hannover a little, where I would end up, and I guess it had been in my head that we would be skirting an area I knew a lot better, the Harz Mountains. I realised we would be going through Goslar. The train from Hannover to Goslar and then the last leg, Goslar to Ilsenburg. That was how the long journey from Ireland ended. I saw myself on the platform with my mother, and then years later, standing on my own, very conscious of what it meant to be on my own. It was suddenly all very vivid.

I almost began to say something to John Mackay. But I stopped. I don't know why. It wasn't any awkwardness about having a family in Germany. I think it was a different kind of awkwardness. I felt uncomfortable with myself. I had thought about them during my time in Germany. I had wondered how they had coped, Annaliese and Reinhard and the baby I had only seen at the christening, and the others I didn't really know except by name. Coped was a weak word, not much more than a euphemism. Survived was more to the point. At least one of Annaliese's brothers hadn't, and even that news was old news now. I decided none of that was a conversation I wanted with a stranger, or with myself either. But as we drove towards Goslar, I was in a place I knew better than I remembered. We were in the mountains. And Mackay started talking about them. I wasn't listening.

'You look at all this beauty . . . what the fuck went wrong, eh?'

He looked at me and shrugged. He didn't want a reply.

As we drove on there was a vehicle ahead. It had pulled off the road. A couple of soldiers stood beside it and there were two more further on, one looking through what looked like a theodolite and another peering at a map. I did clock that the small, open-backed truck wasn't like anything I'd seen before and coming closer the grey uniforms were unfamiliar. Mackay slowed down as we approached.

'Well, there they are, doing whatever it is they're doing.' He laughed. 'Comrades in arms . . .'

'Are they Russians?'

'Your first? Plenty more where they came from now.'

We pulled out to pass the soldiers. Lieutenant Mackay gave a wave, which was reciprocated by the man with the map, who must have been the officer. However, the soldier who had been gazing through the theodolite had, with some speed, abandoned it for a camera. As we passed he was taking photographs of us.

'Let's repay the courtesy. Why not?'

The Intelligence man stopped the jeep a few yards along the road. He reached into the back and produced a camera of his own. He took half a dozen pictures in quick succession. He drove on again with a farewell toot of the horn.

'I didn't think the Russians were anywhere near here.'

'They're not, not yet anyway . . .'

'So what are they doing?'

'Surveying. The MPs have been told to let them get on with it. You see these crews almost every day now on this stretch, I imagine. I'm sure they do send a few engineers along to see how much barbed wire they might need and a feller who knows which way up to put the theodolite, but most of their men are in my line of business.'

'And what's the point?'

'Germany was carved up into occupation zones long before any of us got here. Churchill and Roosevelt and Stalin stood round a map and drew lines round the bits they'd take. We're north and west, the Yanks south, and the Comrades are in the east. The French got a bit too, just to shut them up. But where we all ended up, doesn't match the lines on the map, at least not Uncle Joe's lines. There's a whole chunk of Germany, east of here, that should be in the Russian Zone but isn't. The Yanks moved quicker than expected and we pushed on further as well. When we all met up to pat each other on the back, the line of contact was all over the place. Take Leipzig. The Americans have it now, but it's two hundred kilometres east of where the Soviet Zone border was supposed to be. Stalin wants Leipzig and every single one of those kilometres. As agreed, he says, and it was.'

'So what happens?'

'Negotiations. Nearly done they say. Uncle Joe's dug his heels in. The theory was some give and take. My bet is we give the Russians what they want, the British and the Yanks, and they take it. That's why they're here. Surveying a new border. We'll be out by the end of the month. They already know they've won.'

It was twenty minutes later that we stopped at an army checkpoint. There was a string of barbed wire, an empty armoured car, a building with broken windows that might have been a shop or a restaurant. Three men in military police uniforms sat outside on deckchairs. One smoked, one read a paper, one was asleep.

'Lieutenant Mackay?'

The MP on duty asked the question before Mackay got out his papers.

'Yes.'

'We had a message to say you'd be coming through here this afternoon . . .'

'I didn't know I was so popular, Corporal!'

'Can you talk to my CO in Goslar . . . on the phone?'

The MP gestured at the building behind him.

'Stretch your legs, Stefan.'

Lieutenant Mackay walked off and went into the building. I got out and lit a cigarette. The duty MP went about his business as a line of khaki lorries rumbled up to the checkpoint. By the time I was stubbing out the fag, Mackay was back.

'A detour. You're going to see a bit more of these mountains... and I hope your map-reading skills are up to it, because all I have is a map reference... here.'

He handed me a more detailed map than the one I'd been using.

'We take the next turn off this road and head for a place called Braunlage, then off that road... there's an inn here... then a turning after that... on to some fucking backroad up a mountain... that's what it sounds like... ending up here.'

A red line had been scrawled on the map, showing the route.

'Why here?' I laughed 'This ends in the middle of nowhere...'

'What do you care, old son? Do you think you can follow the map? All very well drawing a bloody line... there'll be no signs. This looks as clear as mud.'

'I'll get you there, Lieutenant.' I smiled. 'If we come out of Braunlage where I think, we should be just above Wernigerode. That's not such a bad road.'

I thought Mackay was about to accuse me of taking the piss.

'You know where we're going?'

'As a matter fact, I do... more or less. It's been a few years, though.'

A brief account of my family history got us to Braunlage, and it was only there, as we moved higher into the Harz, that I learned why we were making the journey.

'The endpoint is the scene of an accident. That's why we'll know it when we see it. That's what the feller in Goslar said. Not that he's seen it. A lorry's come off the road. Nasty business, though. Two men killed I think. The MPs are up there now. It happened sometime this morning. They were only found by a farmer . . .'

Mackay didn't offer more. He just stopped.

'What have you got to do?'

It was as I asked the question that it occurred to me there was an odd sort of urgency about all this. But I was only making conversation. It wasn't my concern.

'It was an Intelligence Corps lorry. It was carrying a load of documents to Nordhausen. It's a camp, labour camp, concentration camp. The Yanks are there, but it was a factory where the Nazis churned out rockets. Anything to do with that is all hush-hush stuff. VIP guff. In this case Very Important Papers, I presume. My CO in Brunswick doesn't want anything touched till someone from Intelligence gets there. He certainly doesn't want MP oiks rooting around. I was the nearest. I called in last night, so they knew where I was. A bit of scrambling about and phone calls and they found me. Now and again Intelligence works! So, muggins gets the job!'

'Left here, John,' I said. At this point I didn't need the map.

Mackay spoke more quietly.

'I'm not sure anyone need worry about these docs, though. Whatever they were, the CO in Goslar said the Bedford went up in flames. Burnt to a cinder.'

We drove on in silence. I did know where we were. I remembered a drive, with Reinhard Friesack and Annaliese and their new baby, and a drink at an inn we'd passed. It was 1933. From here, the road led higher into the mountains, not far from the Brocken. It was a long, winding, rising road connecting a few hamlets and farms and coming out somewhere close to Wernigerode. It wasn't on the way to anywhere directly.

'Do you know where this lorry was coming from?'

'It came from Brunswick, that's Intelligence Corp HQ for this area. It's my base. But you know that anyway . . . it's where we're going. Detours aside, that is.'

'How do they end up here . . . for Nordhausen? It's main road all the way.'

It didn't seem so odd to the lieutenant. He didn't know the place.

'I guess one wrong turn leads to another wrong turn . . . it happens.'

I nodded. It had happened. Obviously, it had. And with lethal consequences. But it stuck in my head that it had happened, for no reason I guess other than that I had nothing else to think about. It must have been hard work to make it happen.

We came out of a belt of trees where a downhill stretch of straight road turned sharply. And there was what we had come to find. There was a jeep, a motorcycle, a Bedford lorry and a smaller army truck with a red cross. Most of the men who stood around were military police. There were perhaps a dozen of them. No one was doing anything as we arrived, except smoking. By this time, it was obvious there was nothing more to do. Behind the other vehicles was a second Bedford. The front was buckled and crushed, the windscreen only a few fragments of glass at the edges. It was black and burned. Smoke still drifted from the back where a canvas awning had disappeared, leaving the skeleton-like frame that had supported it. Blacker fumes hovered over engine and cab. There was a sour, acrid smell in the air carrying petrol and oil and somewhere too, the clean scent of pine.

John Mackay stopped his jeep. The patch of grass where the other vehicles stood was edged by stands of pine trees and beyond and below was a steep drop. A rocky slope led down thicker trees and a forest that spread out across a hillside. For some seconds the lieutenant sat still, looking ahead at the burnt-out truck. He got out as a military police lieutenant walked towards him. I got out too. There was no reason to imagine anyone would care who I was, but surrounded by uniforms, I stood out. Nobody did ask me who the fuck I was, but I think I was expecting it.

The MP nodded at Mackay.

'You the Intelligence chap?'

'Yes, John Mackay.'

The MP nodded again. 'Dick Robinson.' He glanced at me.

'Just a passing Irish policeman, Dick. You know how it is. Ignore him.'

I smiled. The MP officer frowned. He wasn't in the mood for jokes.

'What happened then?' asked Mackay.

The two men began to walk towards the wrecked Bedford.

'He must have come down that hill at a hell of a lick. I don't know if he didn't see the bend coming or if he didn't brake in time. It's hard to see why he wouldn't have. There are no signs, but it's broad daylight. Who knows? Whether he saw it or not, he hit it too fast. He came off the bend, straight over the edge.'

Mackay and the other lieutenant were staring at the truck. Mackay turned away and took a few paces to the edge of the drop and looked down. It wasn't so far, but it was steep enough. At the bottom was more smoke, rising from the pines.

'They smashed into the trees. That did in the engine and the cab. You'd hope the impact killed the buggers because it must have burst into flames straightaway.'

Lieutenant Mackay just nodded.

'What about the bodies?

Lieutenant Robinson walked round the front of the truck. On the other side two bodies lay on a tarpaulin. They were burnt and charred, faces unrecognisable.

'They didn't get out of the cab. Like I say, you'd hope they were . . .'

'Is there any ID?'

'Nothing you see, but we know where they were. Intelligence Corps.'

'Yes, that's what they told me.'

Robinson took a notebook from his pocket.

'Sergeant Sullivan and Corporal Anstey. Do you know them?'

'Yes, Anstey was my corporal. He was also my interpreter.'

'I'm sorry.'

Mackay didn't respond. After a moment he turned away.

'They were driving from Brunswick to Nordhausen, that's all I was told. You probably know more than I do about that. I was told to wait for someone from Intelligence. And not to touch anything. I don't know what they had in mind.'

He shrugged, looking at the wreckage.

Lieutenant Mackay walked away from the bodies to the back of the truck. I walked behind him. Nobody was taking any notice of me. It seemed best just to stay near Mackay and say nothing. He looked in at the lorry's flat bed, framed by its smoking, skeletal metal bones. There was nothing to see except caked, solidified ash, dark and pungent, and crushed, black steel that could have been anything, from ammunition boxes to jerry cans. It had been some fire, clearly.

'How did you get it up,' said Mackay, not looking round.

'Our Bedford. You saw the drop. It's not so far. Should I have left it?'

'No, it doesn't matter. Is there anything left down there?'

'What do you mean?'

'Any of the cargo . . . what they were carrying?'

'I don't know. Nothing I saw. That fire wasn't going to leave much behind. I can't see that they were carrying very much. They must have had a lot of spare fuel, though, to go up like that. Maybe some of the jerry cans burst when they crashed.'

I walked away, back to the drop. I lit a cigarette. Mackay had climbed into the back of the truck. When I looked again he was squeezing himself through the concertinaed door into the cab. A moment later he was beside me, looking down.

'You knew one of them,' I said. 'That's hard.'

'It's no way to go, is it.'

He stepped to the edge of the slope then started to work his way down towards the site of the crash. It wasn't so steep that it was hard to do. I watched him until he reached the bottom. There was a bit of debris and the stumps of a couple of smouldering trees. He was rooting around but there seemed nothing to see.

'Is he going to be long?'

It was Robinson who spoke.

'I don't know Lieutenant. I'm only a passenger.'

He looked slightly irritated. He shouted down to Mackay.

'I want to clear this up and get out, Mackay. I've already had men waiting here for two hours. Do you even need me here now? We should do the decent thing with the bodies, shouldn't we? They are your chaps! Where do you want them?'

Lieutenant Mackay was now clambering back up the incline.

'Are you finished?' said Robinson more insistently.

'I don't know, Robinson.'

'Well, I'm sending my men back to Goslar. I'll hang on, is that OK?'

Mackay nodded. As the MP walked off, the Intelligence man looked at me.

'What do you think of this?'

'What do you mean?'

'You're the bloody policeman?'

I laughed.

'Do you need a bloody policeman?'

'Perhaps. You'd say some fire, wouldn't you, Stefan?'

'It seems so, yes.'

'Is that what you'd expect? Like a fucking bomb went off?'

'If they were carrying a lot of petrol . . .'

'I saw a couple of jerry cans below. Pretty mangled, but recognisable for what they were. Two, three cans. We might find more. I guess if they exploded . . .'

'It's not impossible.'

'No, it's not. How likely? It's not impossible he came off the road either, but how fast could you really go, coming down that hill? Could you really miss that bend?'

I looked back along the road we had driven down.

'You'd have to be some arsehole of a driver.'

I nodded. He had a point. And all of a sudden, he had kicked me into gear. I had taken no notice of any of what I'd seen, except to feel for the two dead men and to hope, as Lieutenant Robinson had, that they were dead before the flames engulfed the cab of the Bedford. But even thinking of that, it really had to have been some fire.

'The reason I'm here,' continued John Mackay more quietly, 'isn't because of two dead Intelligence men, it's because of what they had. I mean in the lorry.'

'Well, whatever it was, it's gone up in smoke.'

'It doesn't matter what it was. They didn't tell me. But what they did tell me was that it needed an eye kept on it until another truck arrived to transfer it all to Nordhausen. I'd guess it was paper. But a lot of paper. Boxes of the fucking stuff. Now you might say, paper burns, old son. Tough luck.

Would you say what's in the back of the truck looks like a bonfire on that scale? And crates, wooden crates?'

I shook my head. He was right.

'And why were they here, on a glorified mountain track? You know this area. That was your question, unprompted. Why the fuck would they end up on this road? How did they get lost? I knew Corporal Anstey very well. He was a smart soldier, very smart. They came from Brunswick this morning. I gather they picked the load up en route. And after that they were on a straight road to Nordhausen . . .'

The military police Bedford was pulling away now. Robinson came back.

'The ambulance might as well take the bodies. The sooner–'

Lieutenant Mackay cut him off.

'Where's the nearest medic . . . or a hospital? Preferably a hospital . . .'

Lieutenant Robinson frowned. I could see he was on the verge of telling John Mackay that it was a bit fucking late for a hospital. He exercised patience.

'There's a field hospital in Goslar, that's where the ambulance–'

Mackay cut him off again.

'Good, that's close enough. I'll follow. If you can find me a doctor . . .'

'I'm sure I can find you one, Lieutenant. What exactly for?'

'An autopsy.'

'An autopsy.'

'Am I missing something Lieutenant Mackay? What are you looking for?'

'No fucking idea.' Mackay grinned. 'If I knew, I wouldn't need an autopsy.'

Dick Robinson produce a steely look that said his orders were to cooperate with Intelligence, but that if he could find an appropriate reason to tell Mackay he was a cunt, he would take considerable pleasure in doing so. For now, he kept his powder dry and walked away to instruct the ambulance crew to load the bodies.

'So, Inspector, I'll ask you again. What do you think?'

It wasn't my business, but I couldn't help it being the business I knew.

'It's a pity they've completely buggered any tracks. Too late now.'

'It's funny you should say that . . .'

Mackay pulled a piece of metal from his pocket. It was black and bent almost flat, but it had a conical shape and a wire protruding from one end.

'What's that?'

'I'd say it's part of a headlamp.'

He handed it to me. I nodded. That's what it was.

'It was down below.'

He walked to the front of the burnt-out truck as the ambulance men lifted one of the charred bodies onto a stretcher. He watched for a moment. I knew he was wondering whether it was the body of the man he knew. It was impossible to tell. But then he turned back to the crumpled bonnet of the Bedford. He pointed.

'Knocked about a bit, of course, but both headlamps still in situ.'

The lieutenant handed me his piece of metallic flotsam.

'It's certainly not from a Bedford anyway. Far from it, I think.'

I looked at the thing more closely. There was a fragment of glass at the front of the lamp, still in place, just at the base. I held it closer. There were some letters.

'Where does it come from . . . how did it get there?'

'Do you see anything, Stefan?'

'I can see an M in the glass, and a P, is it? I can't make out the next one . . .'

'What if I said the P isn't actually a P, it's an R?'

I screwed up my eyes and moved the lamp to catch the light..

'All right. Then the third letter's . . . like a Greek F . . .'

'Not bad, Inspector. But it's not Greek, of course, it's Russian. How it got here, well, that's the hard question. But one way or another, it came via Moscow.'

5

WINTERREISE
WINTER JOURNEY

Ilsenburg, March 1933

Maeve was dead. Six months had gone by. It was supposed to be enough. At least it was enough for most people to feel it could be decently and sympathetically put aside. There would be the first anniversary to come, and that would be hard, but still, everything had to move on. Stefan Gillespie had no great desire to stop anyone moving on, as long as they left him to stay where he was. He didn't find what people had to say helped him, even when it came from those he loved. It was no bad thing when that stopped. He and Maeve had little more than four years. The year after they met and the years they were married. And for two of those they had their son, Tom. It was still hard to take in how much very ordinary happiness they had known in that time. Too ordinary even to notice. And then it was taken away, in little more than a moment. A holiday in the Wicklow Mountains, in a place they loved. A bright, almost lustrous morning when he slept and she swam in a lake. And it was finished. Then and there, in an instant. She drowned. No how, no why, simply the body Maeve's life had left behind. However many questions there were, they were the same question, repeated endlessly, aimlessly, helplessly. Years later, Stefan Gillespie would find there was a how and there was a why, and it would not be a way to understand. It would only be a way to turn back into the darkness. But now, there was the empty space that could not be filled. And the need, inside, to stretch those few years they had a little further, a little longer.

The idea of going to Germany again was his mother's. It didn't look that way, but he knew it came from Helena. There had been letters from Germany, after Maeve's death, along with all the other letters. There was one from his cousin Annaliese, and cards from her brothers, though he had barely met them ten years earlier. There was a letter from his mother's friend in Vienna, who talked more about music than she did about the dead woman she had never met, and yet touched him more than almost anyone else.

The return to Germany, planned on the last night he and his mother spent in Ilsenburg, along with the trip Annaliese Hoffman and Clara Bloch would make to Ireland, had been long forgotten. But Helena kept the links alive, as always. Now that something so bleak as her daughter-in-law's drowning had broken in on her life, she reached out to her family, because she still found something to hold on to there. She held on to it with a bloody-mindedness that occasionally irritated Stefan. He wondered sometimes if it didn't irritate the German cousins he had so little in common with and so few memories of. But Helena didn't let go. She had reasons to hold on harder. There was another generation to teach that Irishness was not its only possession. There was a son who needed air and something to fill his head that wasn't home.

Stefan Gillespie had taken what time he could away from the Gardaí and Pearce Street in Dublin where he was now a detective sergeant, and when it turned into more time than he wanted, he wasn't sorry to get back. To be alone was one thing, and perhaps that was what he wanted most, but being alone was harder at home than it was in a city police station. Too much care and too much love, even when it has the sense to say nothing, was a pain that could make other pains worse. The chaos of other people's lives that flowed in and out of Pearce Street from the streets of Dublin, and constant attrition he had no choice but to immerse himself in, was an easier place to be at times. And a city where no one cared who he was or what had happened to him wasn't a bad place to be alone, unseen and unregarded. He found a strength in all that, that helped him find another strength he needed. He was a father. Maeve had gone, but something of them remained that was more demanding, more challenging at first than what was in his head. There was Tom.

Stefan had no choice but to do his job. It wasn't just about a wage. He needed to do it. If it couldn't help him move on, it kept him moving. Tom would do more than that in time, but in the beginning there was more anguish than comfort. At two, Tom knew his mother more than anything else that came within the horizons of his small world. He was too young to comprehend her absence. Only time would do that. He knew his father, of course, but he also knew the farm at Kilranelagh and his grandmother and grandfather. It was there, with Helena and David, that he would live. It was there that time would do what was needed. It was there that the small boy and the wounded father would find their way to one another.

There was no thought of Germany in Stefan's head when the letter came from his cousin Annaliese, a letter he knew without need of investigation, had been prompted by Helena. There was a baby, born to Annaliese just before Christmas. A first child and a child that had been a long time coming. News from Germany didn't come often, but Christmas usually provided cards and letters that gave the highlights of the preceding year. There had been several years of disappointment for Stefan's cousin. Pregnancies followed by miscarriages. But that was over. There was a girl, Krista, and Annaliese and her husband wanted Stefan to be one of the godparents. It was unlikely they had plucked this idea out of the air. It was ten years since Stefan had seen Annaliese. His mother must have planted the seed.

Stefan's first response was irritation. He didn't want to reach out to these people he had only known briefly, years before. He didn't want his mother imposing her half-forgotten family on him. The time for that had gone, surely. And Annaliese's half-joking hope that Tom and Krista might grow up to be friends seemed faintly ridiculous. His mother's assumption that being a godfather to anyone was something he would want to do, let alone do at the remove of a thousand miles and more, pissed him off. He had no god whose interests he wanted to represent. At nearly thirty, that was still an idea Helena simply laughed at. And as that thought came into his head, he laughed at himself. If his mother treated him like an adolescent at times, he wasn't beyond responding to her like one. He looked at his cousin's letter and read it again. And somehow it felt different. He remembered her as a young woman of twenty-one or twenty-two, and he remembered the simple, heartfelt letter she wrote when Maeve died, and he felt a tear. He didn't know what it was for. Perhaps a little for the past, a little for his own present. His mother had told him, only days before, that when people reached out, you couldn't always turn away. What also came into his head, was the memory of another place and the motion of getting there, of trains and boats and other towns and other hills. Another place, another air, people who weren't a part of home, even the best of it . . . maybe it wouldn't be so bad.

*

There was still snow when Stefan Gillespie arrived at Ilsenburg. He had travelled for two days with none of the interest and excitement of ten years earlier. Being nowhere, being in transit, wasn't unpleasant, but though he watched what was going on beyond the windows of the trains, nothing really stuck. He was conscious of the flags. From the moment he crossed into Germany from Belgium the colours were everywhere. Black, white, red. The crooked cross. Fluttering and flapping, draped from windows. On station platforms and townhall balconies, on schools and shops and factories, and even isolated farmhouses glimpsed on wooded hillsides, and on houses. There were the uniforms too, brown and khaki, with armbands of the same black and white and red. They weren't everywhere, but they stood out. Every station platform seemed to have its uniformed men, hanging about. They seemed to do nothing except that. Hang about. But as Stefan Gillespie saw the men in baggy brown, again, he felt a kind of purpose in their idleness.

He spoke barely any words to anyone. He wasn't looking at Germany in the way he did at seventeen. He had no great desire to see or to understand. Absorbed in himself, there was no space for it. All he did sense was a kind of busyness and activity and engagement. That, at least, was very different from the sombre mood he felt in 1923, when money was worthless and a kind of surly resentment seeped through the carriage window. There was more bustle now than Stefan was in the mood for.

At Ilsenburg, Annaliese's husband met him at the station. Stefan remembered him from before. Then he had been a friend of the Hoffmans, whose father owned the hotel by the lake and who had a car. The car was to provide a final evening jaunt for Stefan and Annaliese and her friend Clara. The jaunt didn't happen. Annaliese's broken leg happened instead. At the time, Stefan hadn't noticed anything that suggested a romance between his cousin and the rather serious, spectacled man with the car. It could be that Stefan's fleeting passion for Annaliese blinded him, and he smiled as he walked through the town past the lake, remembering. Reinhard Friesack had seemed older, much older, though there were only six years between him and the woman who was now his wife. The years were longer then, thought Stefan; with time they shrank. But the town was the same. He liked this place. Its colour and its quiet. There were swastika flags to be seen, but not so many. There was a large photograph of Adolf Hitler in the booking office at the station, dressed uncomfortably in lederhosen. It was a look that no German would find absurd, but as Stefan saw it he smiled, hearing his mother's opinion of the Führer. He didn't take the interest in Germany she did but he listened to her often enough.

She used to call him the man with Charlie Chaplin's toothbrush moustache and her joke was always the same joke. 'Put him in a bowler hat and you wouldn't know which one was funnier!' Helena didn't make the joke now. Germany's Chancellor still had his moustache but she couldn't find anything to laugh at anymore. She was worried by what was happening in the country she cared so much about still. All the more so because many of her Irish friends found Germany's new leader a great tonic altogether. The world, and Ireland itself, could learn from him. If Stefan Gillespie instinctively shared his mother's dislike of the man with the toothbrush moustache, that was all. It was an exaggeration to say it meant much to him. He heard applause for the New Germany too from many of his colleagues in the Gardaí. They knew nothing about Germany, of course, but they could get the scent of a man who hated the English, even at a thousand miles.

On the walk from the station to Mühlenstrasse, the conversation was about Stefan's journey and Ireland and his family. Reinhard Friesack knew little about Ireland and probably less about the Gillespies, but he had made it his business to know enough. He asked about the farm and Stefan's mother and Tom, and he talked about Annaliese and his baby with an enthusiasm Stefan felt the warmth of and the pain of too. There had been a time when he and Maeve . . . He put it away, for another time and he smiled and nodded and found his own enthusiasm. He liked the German immediately. He was easy to talk to. They had barely met on his last visit and that meeting revolved around the Brocken and Annaliese's accident, and so, as the two men walked into Mühlenstrasse, almost the first thing Stefan recognised was Bloch's optician's shop and the house where his cousin's best friend, Clara, lived. The shop looked a little bigger, maybe even smarter.

'Is Clara still there?'

'She is,' said Reinhard. 'Her father retired, and she took over.'

'Is she married?'

'Yes, ever-practical Clara, do you remember?'

Stefan laughed.

'More practical than Annaliese, anyway . . .'

'Well, when she got her degree as an optician, she sensibly married an ophthalmologist technician, or whatever the word is, and they opened another shop . . . in Wernigerode. So, I suppose she's done well . . . very well really . . .'

Stefan heard only the words. They were ordinary words. He didn't hear the bit of space at the end that made it sound as if the woman whose home and business was only minutes from where he lived, was a long way away.

'Does she have any children?'

'Yes, two. One in my class, in the school I teach at. Max. He's nine.'

Stefan didn't hear hesitancy, but the change of subject was abrupt.

'I don't think you'll find the Yellow House much altered. Annaliese's mother, Marie, left it to her. We had a little apartment before. We moved in two years ago. I know she loved it as it was. So did I. Which was a good thing, as it means we don't have to spend money we don't have on things we don't need!'

Reinhard laughed. They rounded the bend to see the Yellow House, looking as bright and welcoming as it had once before, cheerfully surrounded by too many trees and bushes, as Stefan remembered it. And there was the sound of the weir and the river across the road, suddenly loud, just as it had been when he heard it before.

If Annaliese looked older to Stefan, it wasn't much older. She was still striking, though maybe if he had looked for a word now he might have chosen elegant rather than beautiful. He was conscious of how little he really knew this woman. There had been a few days of awkwardness between them ten years earlier, and a silent unrequited passion from him, and then something more like friendship that had lasted hardly long enough to see out the ill-fated adventure along the Ilsetal. Now, they were little more than strangers, held together by not much more than the letters their mothers had continued to send each other, until Marie Hoffman's death.

But it wasn't awkward and it wasn't difficult. Annaliese seemed genuinely delighted to see him and they talked easily, about nothing in particular and nothing that mattered much. The baby did matter, of course, and how much she mattered, to the new father and the new mother was self-evident. He watched Krista and as he did, he watched her parents watching her. He expected it to hurt, but the warmth that was there somehow soothed that away. He did think about Maeve and about Tom. And he found something to hold on to in that. If he wasn't a great believer in Helena Gillespie's faith in the bonds of family, even at a distance, he thought of her faith. Perhaps she was right. This would matter to her.

Having hardly slept for two night, Stefan slept well in the small room at the front of the Yellow House where he had slept at seventeen. The river lulled him to sleep and the river woke him up. Over breakfast the conversation was about the baptism, which would happen the next day. He learned more about Reinhard, who was not only a teacher in Ilsenburg, but a deacon at the Lutheran church, the Marienkirche. The joke was that he didn't want to be a teacher, but a pastor. If she didn't keep him on a tight rein, said Annaliese, he'd have us living on nothing and he'd be off doing a degree in theology somewhere while I scrubbed floors. Being a deacon was one thing. And it carried some kudos, there was no doubt about that. For a moment Stefan caught a wink from Reinhard. He thought Annaliese was on the point of saying something like, 'Every man should have a hobby'. She managed to avoid it. Reinhard joined in with a few wry barbs of his own; Stefan recognised what must be familiar husband and wife banter, but he also saw that Annaliese's husband was a serious man. He had a suspicion that though Reinhard Friesack probably didn't intend to put his wife to scrubbing floors, he might have his mind set on being something other than a schoolteacher.

Stefan also discovered there were two subjects that didn't lend themselves to the easy-going atmosphere of conversation in the Yellow House. There was talk of an expedition to the Ilsetal. It was, after all, what everyone who came to Ilsenburg wanted to do. Maybe not the Brocken itself. There was still thick snow up there. But a bracing walk and a way back that involved a stop at a country inn. It sounded good and it was a thought that led Stefan, naturally, to recall the disastrous expedition of ten years earlier. Maybe Clara could come. And bring her family.

When he thought back, Stefan couldn't remember how Reinhard shifted the conversation to the baptism and the order of service and what it was that would be asked of the godparents and what it was the godparents would have to say in return. But they were deep into that within seconds. Annaliese had disappeared to see to the baby. Not unreasonably, but with great haste. It was delicately done, but this time Stefan knew Clara Bloch was not a welcome topic at the Yellow House. Nor was another memory of Stefan's last visit. Almost the only thing he knew about the man who was now his cousin's husband was that he was something to do with the hotel by the lake. Didn't his father own it? If he missed the ill-ease that came with Clara's name on his walk from the station, the other unwelcome topic couldn't have been clearer as they passed the Landhaus Zu den Rothen Forellen.

'Does your father still have the hotel?'

The answer was clipped and uncommunicative.

'No.'

'I remember the last evening there . . .' continued Stefan.

'It was sold.'

There was silence for almost a minute. Then Reinhard was talking about the excavations at the monastery and the work that was going on to rebuild the organ there and how so many women in the town had knitted clothes for Krista that they could probably open a shop. And everything was easy again and he was laughing.

At the end of Sunday's Divine Service in the Marienkirche, the family and friends of Annaliese and Reinhard Friesack gathered at the font for the entry of Krista Marie Friesack into Christ's community of believers. Most were believers after their own fashion, though not all breathed in the quiet, sacred air that was filled, as they waited for the pastor to begin, with the organist's quiet improvisation on Bach's cantata 'Christ Our Lord Came to the Jordan'. For some it was only duty.

Annaliese's brother Kurt had made a point of wearing his baggy brown Sturmabteilung uniform. He had been in the SA since 1924. He was an officer, a Hauptsturmführer. And now that his time had come, he didn't tire of advertising his importance. The fact that Reinhard, his brother-in-law, considered a church no place for a uniform that no amount of laundering could entirely cleanse of the bloodstains earned in years of street-fighting, was an even better reason to don it.

Annaliese's other brother, Bertolt, was also now a Party man, though he had come to it late as he saw the wind was blowing only one way and nothing would stand in its path. And he had already discovered the benefits of a Party card and a crooked cross in your lapel. His printworks in Leipzig had been a modest success before, but since joining the Party he had become a wealthy man. Even before Hitler's chancellorship, he had doubled and trebled his turnover as he picked up more and more Party contracts. And now most of his competitors had gone out of business. Social democrats, communists, Jews, well, whatever they were, that was their own business. Bertolt's business, recently, had been acquiring their premises and equipment for almost nothing (only some machinery had been wrecked). Overnight, it seemed, he became not just rich, but powerful. It really was, as he often reflected, a new Germany. He was never a great churchgoer, though he turned out at Christmas and Easter and tagged along when his mother was alive and he went home to Ilsenburg. Now, he didn't bother at all. His brother Kurt was a wise owl when it came to getting on in the Party. Bertolt took his advice: Fuck the church. But while Kurt observed his niece's baptism in tight-lipped silence, Bertolt did mumble Luther's hymns. When he wasn't looking down at his watch.

Stefan Gillespie had met Krista's other godparent for only a few minutes that morning. She was a cousin of Reinhard's and had, for a time, shared a flat in Magdeburg with Annaliese, in her secretarial-college days. Whether Saskia Oberg had been a little wilder in those days, she had an air of matronly seriousness about her that made her seem older than Annaliese, though there were only months between them. Frau Oberg, certainly, was to be counted among the believers, as were, she assured Stefan, her husband and her four children. She quizzed him briefly about his own bona fides in that department and seemed less than satisfied that the Church of Ireland was up to scratch. She wondered what its relationship with the Church of England was. When he laughed and said that was a complicated question, she sniffed disapprovingly. He felt he didn't pass the test.

The pastor faced the godparents. Annaliese stood by them with Krista.

'It is your privilege and responsibility, after Krista's baptism, to remember your godchild in your prayers, and whenever possible, to support her in mind and heart, especially if she should lose her parents, so she may be brought up in the true knowledge of God. Do you gladly and willingly assume this responsibility?'

'Yes, with the help of God.'

'You also have the privilege and responsibility of praying for this child and helping bring her to the Lord. Will you keep Krista and her family in your prayers, and support her, so that as she grows, her faith and love for the Lord grows too?'

'Yes, with the help of God.'

The congregation prayed, with exceptions. Water was sprinkled. Krista watched and didn't cry, to great approval. A last hymn of Luther's was sung.

'A baby, helpless, meek at birth,
Now lies in Mary's breast,
A child whose power sustains the earth,
And makes us ever blessed,
A child whose radiance has come
To shine upon our night,
To show the way and bring us home
As children of the light.'

After the service they all walked through the town to the hotel by the lake and along the way people came out and wished the baby well. There was a meal and there were toasts. When Reinhard spoke, Stefan Gillespie thought he was funnier than he'd expected. What he said about his child stuck in Stefan's mind, so much so that he knew it was something he would take home with him. Reinhard was probably a good teacher. He wouldn't be a bad pastor either. His little speech set a tone for the celebration that held steady until people began to depart, with a lot of back-slapping and embracing, and ever more good wishes. It was cheerful and light, and if it was helped along by the Red Trout's good beer, it was only helped.

Stefan walked out onto the hotel terrace to smoke a cigarette. He was thinking about the evening he spent there with his mother and Annaliese's leg in plaster and Clara. It was just before he began his short-lived career at Trinity College. That was what lay ahead of him. It was no small thing. But it turned out to be smaller than he had imagined. He didn't fit. Despite his Protestant upbringing, he felt too Irish to belong in a place that still shut much of Ireland out at the college gates. But following his father's footsteps into the police was something he hadn't thought about since childhood, when it went with driving trains. Even now he didn't know where it came from. There was a new police force in a new state,

An Garda Síochaná. Something made him walk into a police station and ask about it. Something made him join. Maybe because he had to do something, anything, maybe because his mother was furious he'd abandoned the education many sacrifices had given him, maybe because, without realising it was in him, there was something his father had been denied that needed finishing. Whatever the reasons, whatever about the haste, within a year of that trip to Ilsenburg, he was in uniform.

Annaliese found the idea that Stefan was a policeman, a detective even, a source of quiet amusement. It made her smile to think about it. He imagined that somewhere in her head, whatever he looked like now, he was forever seventeen. She wasn't the only one who couldn't quite take him seriously. His mother was the same. Looking out at the lake now, he saw Reinhard Friesack gazing across it too.

'It's always at its best when evening's on its way, Stefan.'

'Yes. I was just thinking back . . . a meal here . . . a summer night.'

'I miss it sometimes,' said Reinhard. 'You know I grew up in the hotel?'

Stefan didn't reply. He remembered it was a subject best avoided. But not today. Reinhard was happy to talk about it suddenly. Perhaps he even wanted to.

'I'd be hopeless running it, though. And I'd hate it. My father loved it, maybe a little too much. He was hopeless too, I'm sorry to say. For different reasons . . .'

Reinhard looked back at the lake. He shrugged.

'It's no great secret. Drinking the profits is an occupational hazard.'

'I'm sorry.'

'You should know some of our secrets!' Reinhard laughed. 'As Krista's godfather, I mean. Not all of them, but at least the ones people gossip about.'

'I'm not a great one for gossip, Reinhard.'

'It wasn't all about that. He made some bad investments. When it all went crazy with million-mark, billion-mark, trillion-mark notes . . . you were here, weren't you? And it got worse. Pa lost all his money. He borrowed to keep the hotel open. And when it picked up, it was too late. The only way he could hold on was to bring in a partner. Oskar Mommsen. Now the owner. You met him when we came in.'

Stefan didn't remember. He had shaken a lot of hands.

'So he bought the hotel?'

'In the end. Oskar had to, really. Pa was a dead weight. He got the money to clear his debts, with a little bit over. Just enough for him to drink himself to death.'

'I'm sorry, I didn't know he was . . .'

Reinhard Friesack shook his head.

'No, it's a work in progress. He's in Hannover. He wouldn't come today. He won't come back to Ilsenburg. He doesn't want to see the hotel . . . he loved it too.'

Somewhere in those words was the reason Reinhard was saying this. And saying it to a man he hardly knew. There was no one else to listen. He wanted his father there when there was a moment of happiness to share. It hurt that he wasn't.

'Krista is a miracle, you know.'

The past was pushed away. It was this moment that mattered.

'She is,' said Stefan, laughing.

'You're allowed to laugh, Stefan. I doubt you believe in miracles. But I mean what I say. I do believe. I'm not sure I'm supposed to, even as an ordained deacon. Maybe especially as an ordained deacon! It's not sound theologically. The age of miracles is not our age. Well, I won't have it. Annaliese . . . we both thought it would never happen . . . and here we are. A family . . . the family we prayed for . . .'

'Reinhard! People are leaving . . . get back on parade!'

Annaliese stood in the doorway to the bar.

'On my way . . .'

He moved on, humming something that could have been sacred or profane. He gave his wife a sharp salute. She walked out. She put her arm through Stefan's.

'He's very happy,' said Annaliese.

'And why not?'

'When they're all gone,' continued Stefan's cousin, 'I'm going to go back to church to put some flowers on Ma's grave. I thought maybe you'd want to come.'

'I do. My mother wanted me to take some flowers . . . for her.'

'Yes, I thought she would. Half an hour?'

'That's grand.'

Annaliese walked back into the bar. Coming out as she went in was Oskar Mommsen, the hotel owner, now a man of substance in the town. He had just become mayor, not long after becoming a newly-minted Nazi. He was what Stefan had already learned to call a March Violet. The flowers had bloomed in their thousands all over Germany since Adolf Hitler came to power, and people flocked to join the Party. Mommsen's hurried application had cemented his mayoral appointment. No election was necessary. He approached Stefan with a glass of beer and thrust it at him. Stefan only vaguely remembered an earlier handshake, but Herr Mommsen had placed him.

'So, my Irish friend. How is your Emerald Isle?'

'Green, Herr Mommsen. What else can I say?'

The hotel proprietor laughed. He was ready to laugh at anything.

'It's Oskar, Stefan. Oskar!'

'Cheers, Oskar!'

'I think we have a lot in common, don't you think?'

Stefan didn't feel it was likely he had much in common with Oskar. There are people you like at first glance and people you don't. It doesn't always make sense, but that's how it is. Mommsen, for Stefan, came into the second category.

'We all admire how you showed the English the door. And shoved the bastards through it with the application of the boot and the bullet, to speed them on their way. If we failed to do it when we had the chance, well, everyone knows why. The stab in the back. I need say no more about that . . . enough said, I think.'

Stefan sipped his beer. It was more than enough, it was plenty.

'But that's all over. I'm sure you've seen for yourself. We're back! And now we're back, well, we can bide our time. When our boots are all polished up . . . England beware!'

Oskar Mommsen winked and laughed loudly again. It didn't take much.

'You need to be careful with boots.'

The mayor of Ilsenburg grinned, then frowned. It didn't make sense.

'The thing with boots, Oskar . . . is you don't want to get too big for them.'

Stefan drained his beer. He winked at Mommsen as Mommsen had winked at him and then walked away. The mayor wasn't sure how insulting the insult had been, but he did know he was a lot less enthusiastic about the Irishman than before.

In the cemetery that lay between the Marienkirche and the path that wound up to the castle and the monastery on the hill, Annaliese and Stefan stood over the grave of Marie Hoffman, Annaliese's mother and Helena Gillespie's old friend. The flowers they had both placed there were snowdrops from the garden of the Yellow House. Annaliese closed her eyes in prayer. The prayer that went through Stefan Gillespie's head was not really his own. The words were words he thought his mother might have said. If a memory mattered, if a thought was fond, if there was something still to find in a moment of reflection, it had to be prayer enough.

Stefan and his cousin walked past the church. She pushed the pram in which Krista lay asleep and he helped her lift it down the step to the road. It was there, as Annaliese started to push the pram toward the town, that he recognised Clara Bloch. He hadn't seen her. All he knew was that she ran the optician's that had been her father's and was now Frau Something-or-Other with two children.

Clara stopped as they walked towards her. Stefan didn't see his cousin's face tighten, but he did notice that she was gripping the pram handle tightly. It was obvious to Stefan that they would stop. He slowed down, smiling. Clara stood waiting for them. It seemed strangely silent to Stefan and he could feel that Annaliese wanted to keep on walking. It was only a feeling, but he was puzzled.

'Hello, Clara. I hope you recognise me.'

'Of course I do, Stefan. I heard you were here. I saw . . .'

She didn't finish the sentence. She must have seen him walk past the shop. It was in his head to call in, but if he hadn't it was only because he assumed he would see her anyway. The awkwardness when she was mentioned hadn't fully hit home.

'I hope you're well, Stefan. Your mother too.'

It was stilted, almost cold. She was looking at Annaliese.

'I hope today went well, Annaliese.'

'Thank you. It did.'

Why wasn't she there, thought Stefan? Surely she should have been.

'I haven't had a chance to congratulate you . . . about Krista.'

Krista was four months old. Yet Clara hadn't even seen her?

'I would have brought a present. I thought you wouldn't want me to.'

'Thank you for the thought,' said Annaliese.

That was it. The conversation was over. The two women looked at each other for a moment longer, then Annaliese pushed forward with the pram. Clara walked on the other way. She gave Stefan a nod, so slight it was barely there.

Annaliese and Stefan crossed the bridge over the river to turn into Mühlenstrasse. They walked in silence. Stefan's instinct was to say, 'What the fuck was all that about?' He didn't know his cousin well enough to do it. This day had brought them closer, but not so close that her business was his business. He did know that she wouldn't want him to say anything. It was in the way she walked almost, looking down at the baby asleep in the pram. Don't say anything. Nothing happened. Nothing at all happened. He was meant to have seen nothing. And perhaps it was nothing. Friends fall out. Sometimes they fall out very badly. Yet that wasn't it. Something dark had passed, momentarily, over the happy day.

*

In his classroom, Reinhard Friesack stood at the blackboard, pinning up a map that he had drawn himself, with great care and even love, years earlier. It came out regularly for this particular lesson and at the edge it showed its age. At the top of the map was Ilsenburg, with a sketch of its castle and its lake. A blue line edged with green curled its way south to the high hill with the word 'Brocken' in bold, Gothic letters. Dotted about, less prominently, were circles that represented other peaks in the Harz Mountains, along with towns and villages. Next to the map was a black-and-white print of a young man with long hair and a heavy coat, who seemed about to set off on a journey a long time ago. Like the map, it was curled and torn at the edges. It showed all the signs of being much used and much loved.

The class of eight and nine-year-olds chattered quietly, half watching their teacher and half watching each other. Reinhard turned to face them. This was the kind of thing he enjoyed. Even with children so young it could be more like a conversation than a lesson. And if they weren't interested in poetry, they were interested in where they lived. That was the place to start at any rate.

'So on the map you can see where Heine went. And the main point, where he's aiming for, is the Brocken, and that means he comes here, to Ilsenburg. He's writing about our town. It's a hundred years ago, but it's our town and our river and our mountains. When we read what he says, we have something no one else has. This is our home and that's where Heine comes on his journey. And it's a kind of adventure. He's telling a story about all sorts of things, but mostly about what he feels, about how he loves this place, and how he loves Germany, because I think when he comes here, and sees our town and our valley, he's seeing all of Germany in a way. And when he has to leave Germany, when he's living in another country, in France, he thinks about Germany and I imagine – it's not very hard to do – he thinks about the trees along our river. That's why I asked you to learn the little poem he wrote, *In Exile*. Those oak trees he remembers, I'd say we only have to walk a little way along the river, towards the first waterfall, and we can see the same trees. So, who did learn that poem? Did anyone? Who can I catch out . . . who?'

Laughter. Several hands shot up. Some faces were eager, others sheepish.

'Who do I choose first . . . not you, Richter. I'm sure you've learned it, but we've all had enough of you showing off. Why not let someone else show off?'

More laughter. Reinhard walked along the front row of desks.

'Not anyone with a hand up . . . too easy. Come on! Only eight lines . . .'

He looked down at a boy who was gazing fixedly at the top of his desk.

'Strauss, what about you . . . do you know it?'

Max Strauss was Clara Strauss's son. He was a quiet, nervous boy, and Reinhard had a soft spot for him. His silence hid a thoughtful, reflective mind.

'Did you like the poem?'

'Yes, Professor.'

'Did you learn it?'

The boy finally looked up. He nodded uncertainly.

'Give it a try, eh?'

Max stood up. He started to speak and stuttered.

'*In Exile* . . . Ex . . . Exile by . . .'

'He doesn't know it! Try me, sir!'

'All right, Richter! Go on Strauss . . .'

'*In Exile*, by Herr Heinrich Heine . . . Exile . . . I had a shining homeland once. There by a stream...The oaks grew up and violets gently bowed. It was a dream . . .'

There was a loud rapping on the door. Max Strauss stopped.

'Carry on,' said his teacher. 'That can wait.'

The door opened. There was no waiting. Three boys in their late teens walked in. They wore the uniforms of the Hitler Youth. One of them carried a pennant, with the red-white-and-black insignia. One had a piano accordion.

'Good morning, Professor Friesack!' called one of the youths bullishly.

'Don't you wait before you come in?'

'Aren't you expecting us?'

Reinhard remembered that he was expecting them. The headmaster had told him the night before. He had forgotten, or maybe chosen to push it out of his mind.

'That doesn't excuse your manners, Lehmann. Knock and wait?'

There was a shrug and a surly silence. Reinhard Friesack knew these teenagers. He had taught them but he didn't want them in his class. He had been told they were coming. He could not welcome them, but he had to accept them.

'Finish the poem, Strauss. As you were interrupted, start again.'

Max Strauss was still standing, but he didn't want to speak.

'I'm sure these lads know the poem. They're not that long out of school!'

There was laughter from the class, but it wasn't like the laughter before. But there was no laughter from the boys in the Hitler Youth uniforms, not even a smile.

'I had a shining homeland once . . .' Max Strauss hesitated, uneasy under the gaze of the three teenagers. The reassuring smile from his teacher pushed him on and he found a stronger voice. 'There by a stream . . . The oaks grew up and violets gently bowed. It was a dream. It kissed me there with German words . . . How good they seem . . . In memory . . . those words that said: "I love you!" It was a dream.'

There was silence. Max sat down.

The teacher went to his desk. 'You'd better get on with it, Lehmann.' He sat down and did something he had almost never done in his class. He lit a cigarette.

Fritz Lehmann stepped forward. He raised his arm and barked a command.

'Heil Hitler!'

The class leapt to its feet and responded, arms high, voices higher.

'Heil Hitler! Heil Hitler!'

Reinhard stayed where he was and drew deeply on his cigarette.

'You may remain standing! I see there are just four Deutsches Jungvolk in this class. Four Deutsches Jungvolk and two girls in the Jungmädelbund. That's a pathetic effort. But it's going to change. You only have a few years before you're ready to serve the Führer in the Hitlerjugend itself. You need to prepare. Everyone has a part to play now, however young. We are here to take names. You will all follow the flag! Your parents expect it. Your teachers expect it too. Heil Hitler!'

Again the class responded. The accordion player sounded a chord.

'Now you can sit!'

The children sat at their desks. Lehmann walked up and down.

'How many Jews here?'

There was silence, then a few whispers.

'You heard me. How many Jews?'

Reinhard Friesack put out his cigarette. He stood up.

'I know you.' Lehmann laughed. 'Strauss, Mandel, Korn. Stand up!'

No one moved.

'Stand up!'

The three boys stood.

'You will go to the back of the classroom and you will stand facing the wall. While Germans speak to Germans about serving the Führer in Germany's great crusade, we want no Jewish eyes on us, do we? So, dogs and Jews to the wall!'

The pennant carrier and the accordionist laughed. Some of the children were laughing too, pointing at their Jewish classmates. The laughter was spreading.

'I think that will do, Lehmann.'

Reinhard's voice was quiet as he walked forward. The laughter ceased.

'If the children want to join your . . . club . . . they can do it elsewhere.'

'I don't think you understand, Professor . . .' The last word came out as a sneer, in a tone the Hitler Youth leader made no attempt to disguise. 'We have permission to be here, from the headmaster. We have his authority. And we have more than that. We have the Party's authority. We have a job to do, all right?'

'You don't have my permission to behave like a thug in my classroom. As for your authority, it stops at my door. These are my students and in this room, no one will insult them or humiliate them. You can get out. Do you understand? Out!'

No one spoke. Lehmann's comrades shifted uneasily.

'I have a lesson to teach. That's my job, gentlemen.'

Fritz Lehmann wanted to argue. He was flushed and furious. But he didn't know quite how far he could push this. The face of the man who had once been his teacher, determined but still calm, was something he didn't yet have the confidence to take on. He was deflated. He summoned up a parting shot, though.

'This won't be the end of it.'

'I think it'll do for now, Lehmann, don't you?'

Boy and man faced off. If the boy's words felt empty, the man was far from certain they were. It might be the end of one thing but what would come next?

As the Hitler Youth troop, with drooping pennant and un-played accordion, moved towards the door, Lehmann had one more chance to make his point. He saw the print of Heinrich Heine, pinned on the blackboard. He stepped across to it and ripped it down. He scowled at his old teacher with something of his ego reclaimed.

'You won't be teaching this fucking Jewish garbage much longer.'

The door slammed shut. In the silence that followed, Reinhard Friesack bent down and picked up the torn print. He slowly, carefully re-pinned it to the board.'

'So, Heinrich Heine. Where were we?'

It was late in the afternoon when Reinhard Friesack left the school. The day had ended with a long and fruitless conversation with the headmaster. It achieved nothing. The headmaster didn't want his school turned into a recruiting station for the Hitler Youth. He didn't want the Nazi Party telling him what to do and what to teach. But he had no intention of arguing. The writing, as he told Reinhard over and over again, was on the wall. It was on the wall in letters as high as they could be. No one could change that. There were a few Jewish children in his school. There were only a few Jewish families in Ilsenburg, after all. But he had been told what was coming. Before long there would be no Jewish children. It wouldn't be allowed. It didn't matter to him. He had nothing against them. But the government was the government. And if there were new laws, then what could you do? You had a duty to obey them. There were reasons for what was happening. There must be something in what they said about the Jews. These people had to know what was best for the country, after all. And he didn't want to get involved in politics. He just wanted to run his school and keep his job.

The end of one thing, but what would come next? The words went through Reinhard's head in the classroom. Now they came back. They wouldn't go away.

He was too preoccupied with his own thoughts to see that ahead of him, standing round a bench at the edge of the town's lake, was a group of teenage boys in Hitler Youth uniforms. Rolf Lehmann was with the two others from the school. There were three more. They were watching him, and as he came closer they moved across the path. When he looked up, he knew they were waiting for him.

*

Kurt Hoffman was undecided about how he should deal with his brother-in-law. He was angry, of course. He was angry with the Hitlerjugend clowns who had failed to show the discipline they should have done. He had no particular objection to putting opponents of the National Socialist Party in hospital. In Hannover and Magdeburg and Leipzig, with brown-shirt comrades, he had done his fair share of work. But it wasn't the way to deal with a schoolteacher in Ilsenburg, and not only a schoolteacher, a deacon at the Marienkirche. He was angry, maybe angrier with his brother-in-law. The man was a fool, he knew that already, but how much of a fool, he couldn't have anticipated. It would have to stop. Reinhard Friesack's stupidity would certainly do Hoffman no favours in the SA. You were easily tainted. Any sign of weakness in your family rubbed off on you. Besides, he loved his sister. He certainly wasn't going to see her on the receiving end of the kind of treatment that was reserved for the families of communists and social democrats and assorted purveyors of anti-German rubbish who had to be expunged from the new order, one way or another. Association was enough to foster suspicion and suspicion stuck. Once that stink was on you, like dogshit, it took a lot of scrubbing off. But all things served a purpose. It struck the SA man that whatever about the ill-discipline shown by the boys of the Hitler Youth, it might be no bad thing that his brother-in-law got his deserts the way he had. Argument, he knew, was wasted on Reinhard. He'd given him plenty already and he'd watched it wash over the teacher's bland, supercilious features. He did listen but he had no intention of hearing. Did he hear now, perhaps? Better this way, than if he chose deafness.

'You'll be all right. Nothing broken after all.'

Standing by the hospital bed, Hoffman was easy-going, cheerful, his voice a knowing wink. He chose not to wear his SA uniform. Affable, that was the way.

'No, nothing broken, Kurt.'

'Exactly.'

The word was a lid. Reinhard heard it going down.

'Exactly? Is that it then?'

'Best if it is, probably. I wouldn't make too much of it.'

Reinhard Friesack began to laugh, but the pain stopped him.

'I know who did it. I know the boys. I taught them, for God's sake.'

The SA man moved closer. He spoke more quietly.

'Now it's their turn to teach you. I know what happened at the school. Reflect on the lesson you've learned, Reinhard. If you want to keep your job.'

'What are you talking about?'

'I'm talking about the Party drawing a line under your behaviour. Because if you make a fuss, if you make a complaint, you're going to draw a lot of attention to yourself. And by the end of it, you won't be teaching anything, anywhere. I'm not defending their response. They'll be told more discipline is expected. But what you did . . . no one's going to blame the lads for a bit of horseplay that went too far.'

Reinhard Friesack was struggling to take this in.

'They come into my class . . . they scream and shout . . . they try to throw pupils out of the room while I'm standing there . . . and when I send them packing, they wait outside the school and knock the shit out me! That's a bit of horseplay?'

Kurt shook his head. He spoke more slowly.

'You need to take care of your reputation. It goes before you . . .'

'What?'

'Reinhard, Reinhard, for an educated man . . . you're very dumb.'

'Along with half of Ilsenburg. Do you think everyone believes your crap?'

'Some people can't see what they want. In time, they will.'

Reinhard's brother-in-law smiled again. It was a smug smile.

'You'll learn to work with the Hitlerjugend, my friend. You'll learn to work with the Party. If it all feels new, it is . . . very new. And this is only the beginning.'

The last words hit the teacher harder than what went before. If there was a threat between the lines of everything Kurt Hoffman said, here it didn't need any ferreting out. This threat wasn't directed at him. It was for everyone. He heard the future chime in it.

Then the SA man was smiling more broadly.

'It's no big deal. You need to embrace it, that's all.'

'The Hitler Youth?' Reinhard didn't disguise his distaste.

The other man shrugged and carried on speaking, smiling again and resuming his hail-fellow-well-met tone. He was a believer. He lived these words.

'Whatever, my friend. The children in your class, all the children in the school . . . all children everywhere . . . they're all going to be in the Hitler Youth and the League of Girls. Well, apart from the children who aren't going to be in your class or any other class much longer. You can forget them. The fact that they're there at all is an insult to German parents. And you're a German parent now, happily. You have a wife, a baby, and a job. And what a responsible job it is. You have the privilege of shouldering that responsibility and teaching the Germans of tomorrow. In times like these, that's something. But keep up with the times, eh? It's all you have to do. For Annaliese, for Krista . . . for yourself. Is that so hard?'

The affable tone didn't change, but Reinhard Friesack was in no doubt what energised them. It wasn't horseplay. This was his wife's brother, who thought that when a gang of youths set about beating him up and putting him in hospital, he was only getting what he deserved. Not only that, wasn't there an invaluable lesson in it? Keep up with the times. That's all he had to do. If he wouldn't, his brother-in-law's now beaming smile informed him, it was not going to work out well at all.

Kurt Hoffman reached out and patted Reinhard gently on the shoulder.

'For now, least said, soonest mended, eh?'

He chuckled, anticipating a chuckle in return, as if this was all a bit of sport that they both understood and would soon laugh about over a beer at the Red Trout. Reinhard looked at him for long enough to show his brother-in-law what he thought of him. The SA man shrugged. He knew. If Reinhard didn't like him, the feeling was fully reciprocated. Even when the Friesacks had money, Kurt didn't think much of his sister marrying the man, but it was a reason of sorts. With the money gone, she had ended up with a husband who still thought he was better than any of them but couldn't even give her a child she didn't miscarry, repeatedly, year after year. It seemed self-evident to the SA man that this must be the fault of his soft-arsed, over-educated, holier-than-thou, brother-in-law, who spent more time reading his bloody Bible and saying his prayers than was decent for any man who was a man. The fact that Reinhard Friesack returned from the Great War with an Iron Cross, to go with lungs permanently damaged by gas, wasn't something his brother-in-law gave any attention to. After all, it was only fucking second class.

*

Stefan Gillespie was sitting on a chair in the corridor when Kurt Hoffman came out of Reinhard Friesack's room. Annaliese's brother nodded stiffly. He didn't know what to make of the Irishman. He had no interest in him. He hadn't known him when he was younger. He didn't know why his mother had cared about a woman in Ireland she never saw. And now that she was dead, he couldn't see why his sister had brought this man two thousand kilometres across Europe to stand in the Marienkirche and spout bollocks. Still, that was up to Annaliese. He had been polite after the baptism, but Stefan was altogether too pally with his brother-in-law. He had said nothing that made Kurt Hoffman suspicious of him, but Oskar Mommsen didn't like him. The mayor thought he had some odd ideas about Germany, though he couldn't exactly say what they were. And he had little to say about the English. That couldn't be right in an Irishman. Just because Stefan had a German first name, didn't mean he passed the SA man's smell test.

'I think he'll live, Stefan.'

He laughed as Stefan got up. Stefan smiled. He hadn't heard most of what was said between brother-in-law and brother-in-law moments before, but the door was open and the bed just inside the ward. He wasn't so far away that a few words, especially those of the SA man, hadn't drifted his way. He got the gist of it.

'I'm sure. I wanted to see him before I go.'

'You're off, right.'

'Tomorrow.'

'He likes you, wouldn't you say, Stefan?'

It was a question, but it somehow wasn't looking for an answer.

'I don't set much store by all that godparent stuff, do you?'

This question didn't seem to demand a reply either. Stefan gave one anyway.

'I don't know that I have a simple answer for that, Kurt. I don't know what I can do to help or how I should go about it . . . I guess I'll do what I can.' Stefan smiled. 'The long and the short is that I haven't worked it out myself if I'm honest. I think that maybe . . . it's just a way to try and ensure we don't all lose touch . . .'

'Let me put it this way, my friend. Annaliese is my sister. Krista is my niece. I can't see you'll have much to do with her. Water was sprinkled and words were said. That's that. You're on the train. But I'm going to see her grow up. But maybe there is one thing you can do to help. Since Reinhard takes God and presumably baptism and godparents very seriously, you can do him and his daughter a favour.'

'And what would that be?'

'I have told him myself, but the problem is, he thinks I'm a cunt.'

Stefan said nothing. After all, he had got enough of the conversation between the SA man and the teacher. On Reinhard's part, his view of Kurt sounded fair.

'I wouldn't give a fuck about him, except that he's my sister's husband and now he's my niece's father. The thing he needs to do for his daughter, is leave behind whatever shitty ideas he's picked up and see the light. He's had his fun. Now he's in the real world. That's our world. Krista's world. He can join it or take the consequences. Next time he plays the arsehole, we might not all be laughing.'

Stefan Gillespie sat by Reinhard Friesack's bed. The bruising on the face was bad. It would be bad where it couldn't be seen too. As a policeman, Stefan was as good a judge of a beating as most doctors, and in terms of some of the niceties maybe better. He could certainly see the differences between kicking and punching, and on Reinhard's face it was kicking that had done the damage. And that told its own story. He had been on the ground and the boots that kicked had kicked very thoroughly. Nothing broken, had been Kurt Hoffman's cheery observation. Stefan had registered the amused indifference from the corridor. If it was true, Reinhard was lucky.

'Thanks for coming.'

'I only knew you'd been hurt. Annaliese didn't make much sense when she got back from the hospital. I couldn't work out whether it was worse than she said or better. I thought I'd come and have a look . . . and say goodbye as well.'

'I had hoped we'd do it over a beer, Stefan.'

'Me too.'

'Still, let's look on the bright side. You won't be shedding many tears about leaving . . . and leaving us to it. It's not been quite the baptism we'd all hoped for . . .'

A wry smile began the words. They ended with an empty shake of the head.

'You were talking to Kurt.'

'I was. He asked me to give you a message. I don't think it's very different from the one he gave you himself. Though he framed it in terms of my role as Krista's godfather. That seems to give me the duty . . . I think that's what he had in mind . . . of telling you to shut up, do what your told and "join the Party".' Stefan spoke the last few words in English. 'I know you've enough English for that. It'll be some party in the Party, right? Well, I imagine you've already found that out.'

'I have the message. Loud and clear. Never mind. We plod on . . .'

Reinhard looked away. There were tears in his eyes. He tried to wipe them away, but when he turned back to Stefan, they were still there. His head dropped.

'This is only the beginning . . .'

He said the words to himself, quietly.

'However seriously I took it, you know I really didn't believe people would take it in... that so many would take it in... there's a kind of joy everywhere I look... not everywhere, no, that's not true, of course it isn't. But where there isn't joy... there's something else. Even a few months ago it felt as if there was a fight, yes, but a fight that could be won. That feeling has gone. Suddenly, it's vanished. It's hard to explain... I think... that's to say I doubt you can see it like that at all. You'll see things you don't like... you have seen them... but not the helplessness.'

'I don't know, Reinhard, maybe I'm beginning to...'

'Kurt's right. No more jokes. No more arguments. What did you say, shut up and do as you're told? Yes, that's what I have to do now. All I can do. Because they can do anything. There's nothing to stop them. Most people probably didn't think it would be like that but now it's happened overnight... and what are they doing?'

Stefan shook his head. He could only feel some of this.

'Singing, dancing, cheering... rejoicing. I can't quite do that...'

He gave a smile that had only emptiness in it.

'But I can shut up. I can do what I'm told. Then I can close my eyes tight.'

Next morning, when Stefan Gillespie left Ilsenburg, he got up early. The train he needed for his connection at Hannover was early, but not that early, He had something to do. He walked along Mühlenstrasse to the white-boarded house with the high red roof and the shop next door that had the old sign with a pair of giant spectacles and the name Bloch. The blinds were down in the shop, but he could see through the door that someone was inside. He knocked gently, then harder. A bolt was drawn back and Clara was there. She looked puzzled at first, then she smiled.

'I'm sorry I didn't come before. I don't know why . . .'

'It doesn't matter, Stefan. Come in.'

He followed her into the shop. There was little for him to say and there seemed to be even less that she wanted to say. He didn't speak about Annaliese because he knew Clara wouldn't want him to. He asked about her husband and her children. He said he had a boy of his own. She didn't know about Maeve. She asked his wife's name and he simply said it. That was enough. There was a lot of silence, even though he was only with her for a few minutes, yet it was not an awkward silence. He saw there were tears in her eyes. He felt them in his own eyes too. Perhaps those damp eyes were the conversation they couldn't have any other way. He embraced her and she held him tightly. It mattered that he had come.

Annaliese and Stefan barely spoke as they left the Yellow House to walk to the station. She knew where he had been. She was furious. Or something like furious. He wasn't sure where to put it. Anger, embarrassment, irritation, resentment. All those things. And maybe none of them. Maybe what she felt most was his intrusion into her life. He didn't understand. He had no right to interfere. She didn't know why he was really there. Because of her mother, because of her mother's old friend. Reinhard had been all for it. But she should have left it alone. Who cared? The past had no currency now.

'You had no right to do that.'

She spoke as they reached the town square and the lake.

'To do what?'

'I don't need to say it, Stefan!'

'You do. I said hello to a friend. She was a friend. Maybe not for long . . .'

Perhaps he didn't mean the words to sound like an accusation against her.

'You know what happened to Reinhard. You were at the hospital. It was because of Jews, Jews in his class. It was because he believed . . . helping Jews . . .'

Stefan couldn't help laughing.

'I see. Some kid in his class . . . it was his fault . . . not the morons who waited outside the school and beat the shit out of him. Jesus, Annaliese, that's some stick!'

'She's a Jew . . . you don't understand.'

'I'm a simple man,' said Stefan. 'But you know what, when I was here ten years ago, and Clara was the friend you had known since you could hardly walk . . . and we had that great day together that was still a great day when they brought you back from the hospital with your leg in plaster . . . I didn't even know she was Jewish. You seem very concerned I should know that vital information . . . now.'

'Those were different days, Stefan.'

The anger had gone. She was quieter. But her voice was still hard.

'I think they were.'

'These are the days that matter,' said Annaliese. 'All that's gone. And thank God for it. There's a future now. It belongs to Krista. That's what Adolf Hitler has given us all. A future for our children. We've come out of the dark into the light.'

'Did you get that from Kurt? I didn't know he did whole sentences!'

'Wherever there are Jews, there's trouble. Everything that went wrong with Germany came from the Jews. What happened in the war . . . all the fighting afterwards . . . everything we lost . . . everything that was taken from us. You don't see it because your eyes are closed. You have your independence . . . I know all that . . . my mother loved those stories. But what is it all worth? You're not so free, Stefan, whatever you may think. English Jews, American Jews . . . everywhere.'

'Jesus, Annaliese, and I thought Clara's shop just sold glasses!'

'It's not about Clara.'

'Oh, I thought it was.'

'The Jews don't belong in Germany. We have to separate ourselves from them. And you can't play games with it. Look what happens . . . look what happened to Reinhard. He doesn't see it. I know he doesn't. But he has to. For all our sakes. Kurt knows what's happening. We're Germans. We have to follow the Führer's lead. If we don't . . . can't you understand? I have to protect my family.'

There were tears in Annaliese's eyes now. Stefan said no more. He didn't know what the tears meant. He didn't know if she really believed anything she had just said. But he doubted that mattered. She didn't have to believe it. If there was passion in her voice there was somewhere, something else driving that. Fear.

The train pulled away slowly. Stefan looked back to see Annaliese watching. As she saw his face at the carriage window, she turned sharply and walked, almost stalked away. She didn't want him to see she had stayed on the platform. Then she disappeared. He looked out at the last straggling houses of the town and then up, beyond them to the Brocken, still capped with snow. The first night at the Yellow House there had been a plan to walk up through the Ilsetal, along the river, if not to the peak at least part of the way, retracing the summer expedition of old with a winter journey. At the time, he hadn't noticed how little Annaliese joined in. It felt like there was enthusiasm, but it wasn't hers. It came from him and from Reinhard. But they never walked beyond the town, even to the end of Mühlenstrasse where the woods began. It was forgotten. As for the rest of it, he wondered how much he would tell his mother. Some, yes, but not all.

He wouldn't tell her that almost everything that happened was best forgotten. He wouldn't lie, but he would leave the gaps in what he said for her to do with as she would. Whatever she chose to hold on to in Germany, he would not be coming back here. The winter journey had seemed no bad thing. He thought it promised something, even if it was no more than a way to stop, even briefly, standing so still. But it was a mistake. The fond memories of another time were gone. He wasn't invested in this place the way his mother was. He didn't have much to lose. But however little it was, he had lost it.

PART TWO

DIE KONTAKTLINIE

THE LINE OF CONTACT

ЛИНИЯ КОНТАКТА

It should be brought home to the Germans that Germany's ruthless warfare and the fanatical Nazi resistance have destroyed the German economy and made chaos and suffering inevitable and that the Germans cannot escape responsibility for what they have brought upon themselves . . . Germany will not be occupied for the purposes of liberation but as a defeated enemy nation.

Directive to Commander-in-Chief US Occupation Forces,
May 1945

Henceforth the great banner of freedom and peace for all peoples will fly over Europe . . . Comrades, Our Great Patriotic War has concluded in our complete victory. The era of war is at an end and the era of peaceful advance has begun.

Josef Stalin, May 1945

6

DER DRITTE MANN
THE THIRD MAN

Goslar, June 1945

I knew Goslar only as a railway station. It was the last leg of the journey from Ireland to Ilsenburg, or the first stop on the way home. I had never been into the town. I didn't see much of it when I arrived there with John Mackay after two more hours picking through the debris of the crash in the Harz Mountains. I started off watching him do what, in a different place, I might have done myself, but in the end I joined him. He was more Intelligence man than policeman. I was better at it.

The search produced nothing, except another fragment of glass from the Russian headlamp. That didn't add anything. It merely confirmed something that was unexpected. And the unexpected has its problems. It might be everything or it might be nothing except random chance. If it really is nothing and you make it everything, the only thing ahead is a dead end. There wasn't much else. John Mackay's attempt to read the tyre tracks at the crash site took a lot of time but neither of us could do anything with them. The point where the Bedford went over the drop was clear enough, though what it said was less clear. It didn't read right, that's all you could say. He was no expert, and neither was I, but it didn't feel like the lorry had been going very fast, yet too much speed had to be the explanation for it coming off the road in the first place. Long contemplation of the Bedford's front end asked similar questions. The fire had been devastating, but however long you pondered it, the engine compartment looked less crushed than it should have been, even for such a solid piece of machinery. As far as any other tracks went, there was, at second and third glance, as at the first, just too much traffic overlaid.

At Goslar there was another night to spend before Brunswick and Hannover and my way home. Lieutenant Mackay wanted the results of the autopsy he had asked for and he had orders from Intelligence to look into the crash further. I don't know whether it was the prospect of the paperwork that pissed him off, or the sense that what really mattered was providing a full explanation of how the documents in the lorry were lost to shut the Americans up, since they were going to be very unhappy. The loss of the two Intelligence men was less of an issue.

Coming into Goslar, we passed the station and drove through the town. It had escaped bombing and there it stood, in all its wood-framed medieval beauty on a bright summer evening. Another place where, for a few seconds you might have forgotten the devastation that was round every bend. But that was all I saw of Goslar. The British garrison was outside the town on the site of a small factory. It was some kind of storage depot. There weren't many soldiers, some Royal Engineers and Army Service Corps men, and a military police platoon. My mind was on getting home and I didn't much care what they all were or what they did, but since there was nothing to do except sit in the factory canteen before finding a camp bed in one of the looted offices, I showed enough interest to pass the time. There was a doctor and a few medics attached to the place too, and that was what preoccupied Mackay. All he was there for was his autopsy.

The next morning he got me up to see the bodies. Faced with the scene of a fatal accident and some odd circumstances the previous day, familiar instincts did kick in. I had been a detective too long not to produce a Pavlovian response when something puzzling was dangled in front of me. But I was only visiting. However, John Mackay, now my friend it seemed, had decided that in the absence of anyone else to pursue his investigation with, I would have to do. I've seen too many bodies to be overly troubled by mortuary slabs, but this wasn't something I had any desire to see.

Still, the lieutenant had decided I was going to see it, whether I wanted to or not.

'There's no obvious cause of death for either of them.'

It was the army doctor who spoke.

'If they didn't die in the crash, obviously the nature of the fire...'

He let that thought fade away. Mackay and I had been there too.

The bodies lay on two steel tables. The chest cavities had been opened up and a small area of the skull had been removed. Everywhere the skin was black and red and where it was wet with pus, the ooze was sticky as if the bodies had been daubed with tar. In places the black bone showed through where the skin had burned away. The faces were, like other soft tissue, charred, almost melted flesh.

'There is very little bone damage as such. I mean fractures, breakages. I don't know how far the lorry fell, but from what you told me about the way it came off the road and down this hillside... I'd have expected more. But I'm not really in a position to judge. I'm talking off the top of my head. This is the kind of thing I've seen before . . . so I'm looking at it in terms that may be . . . inappropriate.'

'What do you mean,' asked Mackay.

'I could compare it with what happens when a tank catches fire . . . whether that's from a shell or even a flamethrower. I saw that in North Africa, from both ends. What happened to some of our crews . . . and some of Rommel's. It's not something you want to think about. Some of them can't get out. If they're lucky they pass out from fumes, but a lot of the time . . . anyway, these two look a bit like that. But of course, they weren't just sitting there, were they? Hadn't they rocketed down the mountain and landed right against the forest fence, as you might say?'

The lieutenant nodded. The same question again.

'This was some fire,' continued the doctor. 'Did they have fuel in the cab?'

'It's possible. There could have been jerry cans in there.'

'If the fire took hold that fast . . . the fuel tank went up . . . any cans up front could have exploded. I'm still thinking about tanks. Short version. I don't know.'

'But no bones broken, no head injury, damage to organs?'

'No. Organs . . . it's such a mess it's hard to say There are a couple of head injuries that might suggest they hit something . . . when the windscreen went or some of the frame broke away. You'd need someone to examine the Bedford. It is at least some evidence of real impact, though whether it had anything to do with the cause of death for either of them, I've no idea. The only thing you'd hope is that perhaps it was enough to stun one of them before . . . so, if you look closely . . .'

The doctor pointed at the head of one of the dead soldiers.

'I've scrubbed the skull here . . . you'll see a small hole, just around the temple. It's very soft there, so it doesn't take much . . . and it goes right through.'

Mackay bent down to look. He stood back and gestured to me. I looked down too. It was simply a small hole, piercing the side of the head. Everything round it was black and the hole was black. That was it. The doctor was now at the other steel table. He picked up a scalpel and pushed a flap of pus and tar-like skin aside. He let the scalpel point at a hole that was hard to see. The muck around it had been scraped away, but the bone and what was left of calcified skin and blood and hair had fused. It wasn't as defined as the first hole, but it was similar.

'This one's head must have hit something very hard. It's driven in through the bone, which is much harder here. A bolt, a part of the cab that sheered away. As I say, you'd have to look at the cab, though from what you describe, the fire can't have left much to see. It's one thing that does suggest a pretty solid thump.'

Lieutenant Mackay nodded. He looked at me. I nodded too. I think he was expecting more. He looked slightly disappointed as he turned back to the doctor.

'Maybe that's something.'

I saw he wasn't satisfied. No answers, only more questions.

I stood outside the factory smoking a cigarette with the Intelligence man. I already knew we wouldn't move on that day. He hadn't said anything, but he'd been on the phone. He had orders and I guessed they meant more digging around. I was hoping it would be different. The fact that I recognised this place, that I was so familiar with the mountains we had driven through the day before, didn't make me easy. Inevitably I found myself thinking about the people I knew here. I didn't much want to think about them. I wished I hadn't come this way. What was gone was gone. There could be nothing left. I didn't like the thought. It made me feel cheap.

'I have a few things to sort out, Stefan . . .'

'I thought you would,' I said.

'I have a couple of fellers coming down from Brunswick. My German's pretty useless, so I need an interpreter for starters. They want a report upstairs. You know this stuff was on its way to the Yanks . . . they'll want chapter and verse. They will be mightily pissed off at Nordhausen. I can make a guess what it was about . . .'

He dropped his cigarette and stubbed it out. The last few words weren't addressed to me. I didn't know what it was about. I couldn't have cared less.

'If I'm stuck here longer than a day, I'll see about getting you a lift, but since you've got nothing to do . . .' Mackay grinned. 'You can earn your keep.'

'Do I hear a bit of Gilbert and Sullivan coming on, John?'

'What?'

'When constabulary duty's to be done . . .'

'Why not? You'd only be sitting on your arse. And for fuck's sake, you know this place. I want to sniff around. There may be nothing to sniff, but I've got to have something to put in the report, haven't I? You know the routine. Fill half a dozen pages with guff that smacks of elbow grease and grey matter, and it'll pass. If you can't find any answers, just make a long list of all the questions you asked.'

I stubbed out my cigarette. No choice. I was going anyway.

'So, Torfhaus. That's where they picked up the load. You know it?'

'I don't know the name. I was only ever here for a few weeks . . .'

Lieutenant Mackay walked over to his jeep and pulled out the maps.

'Between Bad Harzburg and Braunlage. The road we were on yesterday.'

'OK. I know where that is.'

'Of course you, do Stefan.' Mackay laughed. 'Weren't you sent by God?'

I needed the map from time to time, but once I had my bearings Torfhaus wasn't hard to find. It was on the main road. It was little more than a few houses and scattered farms. There were more inns than the place warranted, but it sat at the edge of the mountains. Walking in summer and skiing in winter. In another time it must have earned its extra money that way. Now it was empty and quiet. And just outside it, emptier and quieter, and marked on Mackay's map with a series of visual instructions, was a disused farm. It was close to the road, hidden behind a belt of scrubby trees. Probably it hadn't been empty for more than a few years. The garden was overgrown, but you could still see where the flower beds had been. Windows were broken and the front door had been smashed in. It must have been looted, maybe weeks ago, months ago, or even years ago.

On the way John Mackay told me what he thought I needed to know. I couldn't work out whether he believed I could be useful or had brought me along as some kind of lucky charm. I doubt what he told me amounted to anything the average American or British soldier in the area couldn't have worked out, but in the game we were both in, I'd say he wasn't as careful as I think his superiors might have wished. I had the impression that if he thought a secret wasn't much of a secret, he didn't care what he said. Or maybe irritation with the powers that be made him mouthy.

'Everyone knows Nordhausen was producing flying bombs and rockets. V1s and V2s. You only need to drive past the camp. It's like Flash Gordon's breaker's yard. You know about all that stuff... doodlebugs... and Adolf's Wunderwaffen?'

'I've read about them.'

'So, it all ended up at Nordhausen . . . underground. And it's the rockets that matter. That's what we want. That's the next big thing. So, the Yanks want to get everything they can out of Nordhausen before the Russians take over, equipment, documents, the lot. Because it's all done. Give it a week and it'll be in the Soviet Zone. The Yanks'll be out and so will we, north and south of the Harz Mountains.'

'That's happening then?'

'Yes, the news is it's definite now.'

'And what's that got to do with an empty farm in Torfhaus?'

'It's not only about bits of rockets and blueprints.' Mackay laughed. 'It's about the mad fucking scientists who made them. We want them too. And some of them have gone to considerable lengths to make sure we don't leave them behind for Uncle Joe's lads . . . or put them on trial for their industrial-relations methods.'

'What does that mean?'

'It doesn't matter.'

Mackay said nothing for some minutes. It did matter, at least to him.

'Insurance policies.' He started speaking again suddenly. Whatever it was that had troubled him, it had been pushed aside. 'Someone buried a lorryload of documents from Nordhausen under the floor of a barn in Torfhaus. I don't know when. I don't know who. An engineer, a general, a manager. Why? Belt and braces. One, to keep on the right side if the Nazis had miraculously found a way to keep on fighting. Wishful thinking, but there was plenty of that. Two, to have something worth trading. Maybe to save his life, maybe just to get him out and set up somewhere else. Anyway, whoever the feller is, he must have cashed his chips.'

Following the map I directed Mackay off the road as we came out of Torfhaus. The farm was there and behind it stood a large stone barn. Inside, there was damp, mildewed hay everywhere. It must have covered the earth floor. In the middle, the loose hay had been cleared away. A deep, square trench had been dug.

'As this area's under British control, the Yanks pointed us here and some Army Service Corps chaps arrived to hoist it all up. The Bedford came down from Intelligence in Brunswick to take it to Nordhausen and let US Intelligence have it. My elders and betters imagine that when the Yanks have got all the Jerry rockets and Jerry rocket plans and Jerry rocket makers across the Atlantic, they'll call His Majesty's government and offer to let our boffins loose on it all. Don't bet on it.'

The Intelligence man stood looking into the trench. He was even less careful about what he was saying than he had been. There was a warning bell in that. I couldn't know what it was that gave John Mackay an edge of resentment in his voice. But he had it. He definitely had it. A resentful Intelligence man, whatever the reasons, was unpredictable. Unpredictability was dangerous. If he wasn't being careful, I needed to be. Whatever his intentions, I would want to keep my distance.

'This is a big hole,' said the lieutenant with a wry smile.

'Big enough,' I said.

'And that confirms what the RASC men told me at Goslar. The Bedford was packed with boxes. If there'd been any more, they'd have been hard pressed to get them in. Do you see all that burning to a bloody cinder? Some fire, everyone says, but it wasn't going to atomise the fucking lot, eh? So, there's just one conclusion.'

He waited for me to offer up that conclusion. I left it to him.

'When it went over the edge . . . whatever it was carrying . . . had gone.'

We walked back to the jeep. I stopped as Lieutenant Mackay got in and started the engine. It was only then that I saw where I was and what I was looking at. Eastward was the Brocken, sharp in the sunlight, somehow picked out from the hills around that looked dark under passing clouds. I'm sure it only stood out in my head because I knew it. I didn't ever remember seeing it from that side.

'Never mind the view!' called Mackay.

'I went to the top of that,' I said, as he drove away.

He wasn't listening.

'The RASC lads left first. They went straight back to Goslar. Anstey and Sullivan followed. They were behind the Army Service lorry before it turned off.'

I had opened up the map again.

'After Oderbrück, where we came out just now.'

'Yes. The Bedford carries on to Braunlage heading for Nordhausen. It's going to take them . . . What? An hour and a half, give or take. The road winds about a bit round the mountains, but it's one road. Point A to point B. Yet for some reason the buggers turn off this road at Braunlage and head for the fucking hills!'

John Mackay drove on. In Braunlage he crawled slowly along the town's main street. There was nothing to see. Houses, a few shops. There was a large British Army signpost: Nordhausen, Leipzig, and a white arrow pointing ahead. It couldn't be any clearer. At the junction where the two Intelligence men must have turned off, and where Mackay and I had done the same, there were no signs. We had just left Braunlage's last houses behind. All that was left, opposite the junction, was a small inn. It was a scruffy, rundown place. There was a petrol pump that had a painted sign hanging from it: Kein Benzin. The words were barely legible. It was evident there hadn't been any petrol for a long time. We turned in.

There was a blue truck. It was a petrol tanker and the blue made it RAF. Two men in overalls sat at a table drinking beer. They looked up as Mackay stopped. For a moment they seemed nervous, but then they smiled and carried on drinking.

'Carry on lads,' said Mackay. 'I haven't seen an MP all morning.'

'Thank you, sir.' One of the RAF men raised his glass.

The lieutenant got out of the jeep. I stayed where I was.

'Where are you going?'

'Brunswick, sir.'

'Do you know this road?'

'A bit.'

'Were you here yesterday?'

'No, we just came from Göttingen.'

Mackay turned to me.

'Fancy one, Stefan?'

We went in. It was dark. The smell was sour. It wouldn't be the best beer.

'The rules are very tight still,' said Mackay. 'No fraternisation. No chirpy chat, no eyeing up the frauleins, and definitely no stopping off at the pub for a pint, at least not till we've sorted the nice Nazis from the nasty Nazis. Still, orders are only there to give the men something to ignore. Ah, here comes our genial host . . .'

The innkeeper reflected his inn. Scruffy and rundown and sour.

'Vom Fass für meinen Freund und für mich . . . eine Flasche . . .'

My beer from the tap, Mackay's from a bottle. He asked for the bottle.

'Close enough,' he said. 'I think the same . . .'

'The same as what?'

'There was broken glass in the footwell of the Bedford. Not from the windscreen, from a couple of bottles. No labels, black as hell, but bottles. They could have come from anywhere, of course, but anywhere might include here.'

That was good. He was a better policeman than I thought. Maybe he was a better policeman than Intelligence officer. I tried to claim that distinction myself.

Lieutenant Mackay had more German than it took to order a couple of beers, but not a lot more. I really wasn't there for the ride. I would have to earn my keep.

It was soon clear that Mackay's nose was worth following. There had been a British lorry yesterday. There hadn't been much traffic. A column of armoured cars and the usual military police jeep that went through Braunlage a couple of times a day. The lorry did stop. One of the soldiers brought two bottles of beer to take with him. The officer wouldn't let them stay for a drink. That pissed him off.

For a few seconds I was confused, and so was Mackay as I translated back into English. The sergeant wanted to get on. Corporal Anstey wanted a drink. But the word wasn't sergeant, it was officer. Two men left the farm at Torfhaus in the Bedford truck, but ten miles on there were three men. Sergeant, corporal, officer.

The story didn't get any clearer. The officer was there before the lorry. A good half hour before. He was on a motorbike. He didn't come into the inn. He stopped opposite the road junction and sat there, waiting. It wasn't such an odd thing. Sometimes you'd see a couple of MPs sitting in a jeep in the town for no apparent reason. The innkeeper grinned. Maybe for no more than a smoke. It was only when the lorry came that the innkeeper saw that the man on the motorbike was waiting for it. He was looking out through the window. The officer stood in the road and directed the Bedford in. Two soldiers got out. The three men stood looking at a map. The officer got on the motorbike. One of the soldiers got into the Bedford. And then the other soldier ran across to the inn. He bought two bottles of beer. I asked the man if anything more had been said. The innkeeper chuckled.

'He had good German... well, his swearing was top notch.'

Lieutenant Mackay didn't need a translation.

'Anstey.'

'There was an accident,' continued the innkeeper. 'He told me the road to Nordhausen was blocked. I don't know what happened. I never heard about any problem. He said the military police were coming, and they'd set up a detour. The officer, well, the cunt of an officer if you want me to be precise... he didn't like him, I'd say... was going to show them and put them back on the main road further down.'

'Was that it?'

'Yes. The horn was blasting on the truck. And he went...'

'They followed the motorbike?'

The German nodded.

'Der Offizier... könnten Sie ihn beschreiben?'

The last question was Lieutenant Mackay's.

'No. I've no idea what he looked like,' said the innkeeper. 'Tall, that's about all. He never came in. I don't know if he even got off the bike. He had a helmet on and goggles, and a red scarf... never took them off, so there was nothing to see.'

I sat in the canteen at Goslar with a cup of tea and a cigarette and a week-old copy of the *Daily Sketch*. I'd read the paper the night before and it didn't get any more interesting the second time round. John Mackay had said almost nothing on the drive back to Goslar from Braunlage. When we arrived he disappeared. In pursuit, I knew well enough, of the man on the motorbike and the blockage on the Nordhausen road. He was asking questions, looking at military police logs, and presumably phoning Intelligence HQ at Brunswick. There had to be a simple answer to the third man who left Braunlage with Corporal Anstey and Sergeant Sullivan. Well, that's what he kept saying when he did speak on the way back. But I think he felt, because I felt it myself, that a simple answer, possibly an answer of any kind, was not going to be forthcoming. The more he examined what had happened to the Bedford lorry on a mountain road, the more questions piled up.

And I had my own question now.

It didn't hit me in the makeshift mortuary, gazing at the charred corpses of the two Intelligence men. Even when I bent down to look at the two, pencil-like holes in their skulls, I just saw two holes. I thought about pieces of metal and sheered-off bolts. And I winced, thinking of what that might have meant. But as we drove to Torfhaus and peered at a hole in the ground and drove to Braunlage and heard the innkeeper's peculiar tale, I kept seeing those skulls and the holes in those skulls. Behind the muck and the tar, I had seen this before. It was a long time, but I could put myself there, in a much cleaner, sweeter-smelling mortuary in Dublin.

I went back to the doctor and back to the bodies. I asked the medic to find a photographer. Pictures of the skull, pictures of the holes, that Mackay could get enlarged. I didn't really think I was right. There would be another explanation. A closer examination of the cab might produce one. But then maybe it wouldn't. I don't know why I couldn't leave it alone. There were two dead men. Something had happened to them that wasn't an accident. I knew that was the nagging thought deep in John Mackay's head. I knew those worms. And he put one in my head too.

Lieutenant Mackay slumped down in the chair opposite mine.

'Wild goose chase.'

He shook his head.

'Invisible fucking man.'

So, no simple answer, maybe no answer at all.

'The CO here's looking at me like I'm a candidate for the trick cyclist. And I'll probably see the same expression on Captain Battersby's face in Brunswick. He's cracked.'

'No officer on a motorbike then?'

'No officer on a motorbike. No accident on the way to Nordhausen. No blocked road. No detour. No MPs running round directing traffic. I'm glad you're here. Otherwise they'd be sending someone from Brunswick with a straitjacket.'

'Did you get any more on your Russian headlight?'

'That's definitely what it is. It's off one of those trucks we saw. There's plenty about. Now the deal's done and we're going to be pulling back west, along with the Yanks, they can go where they want . . . in theory they need to wait, but there's no point our MPs chasing after them to hear the Russian for "fuck off".'

There were good reasons to stay out of this. I heard them. I ignored them.

'Ten years ago I investigated some murders in Dublin. There were missing people and dead people. Nothing so unusual there. Except that something held together what happened . . . at the time and years before. I didn't know what I was looking at, but a very good pathologist did. You know what a captive-bolt is?'

'For killing pigs?'

'Pigs and whatever else . . . in this case, it was a man and a woman.'

'I don't see . . .'

'You'll want to find out if there was anything in the Bedford cab that could have made those little round holes in your soldiers' heads. If you think they didn't die in the crash . . . or in the fire . . . there's one more question to add to your list.'

I watched Mackay taking this new thought in.

'Where the fuck is this leading us? I can't see it . . .'

'Find an explanation and you can tick that off and blame the crazy Irish cop. Think about it. One hole you can't explain? OK. But the same hole . . . in both skulls?'

I should have anticipated what came next. It was one of the reasons I gave myself for shutting up, even though I didn't in the end. It was too late anyway. If there was a crime, I was a witness now. I'd been at the crash site. I'd helped Lieutenant Mackay search it. I'd been at the inn to hear the story of the motorcyclist who never was. Not only that, in the absence of an army interpreter, I was the one who got the story out of the innkeeper. At a minimum they'd want statements. If it went further, they'd want to question me to confirm what other people said. Now, unable to keep my mouth shut, I'd thrown a captive-bolt pistol into the works.

'We will need you to stick around now, Stefan . . .'

It was apologetic, but not very. He wasn't offering a choice.

'I know the drill . . . "Never volunteer", isn't that what they say?'

'You don't need to do any more. My men will be here later anyway.'

I don't know whether the thought that was now at the front of my mind had been there all the time, maybe ever since I saw the Harz Mountains in the distance, heading north. If it was there, I left it alone. It wasn't practical, or even possible. That's to say it hadn't been. Now, it was both. It felt too wrong not to act on that.

'You know I have some family in Ilsenburg . . . it's only a train ride . . . at least I did have some family. I told you. If I'm here . . . if I have a few more days here . . . if I can get to Ilsenburg . . . I'd like to see if they're there . . . they may not be . . .'

'You can't go wandering around . . .' John Mackay looked unsure.

'I'm not in your army, John.' I grinned. 'Maybe I'm allowed to fraternise.'

The lieutenant shrugged. The look shifted from unsure to why not?

'There's a military police post in Ilsenburg. If they know you're there . . .'

The next day Mackay dropped me at the Landhaus Zu den Rothen Forellen. It was now a barracks for a platoon of MPs. I had a military pass to stick inside my Irish passport, signed by the very suspicious CO at Goslar. A Lieutenant Foxe, who looked like he might have been better off finishing school, greeted me with something like enthusiasm. For five minutes, I was a novelty. I found out almost immediately that someone was still in the town. Annaliese Friesack was on the list he waded through. He shook his head and sniffed, a little less enthusiastic now.

'This Friesack women is your cousin?'

'Yes.'

'A close cousin?'

I didn't know why that mattered. I don't imagine he did.

'Not close at all. In the nth degree and many times removed . . .'

The MP ran his finger along the lines of a typed sheet.

'Annaliese Friesack was a member of the Nazi Party. She is listed for denazification. But she's in Category IV, which means there are a few restrictions, but not much. Information on her is still being processed, which probably means not worth bothering. She has a daughter who was BDM, Hitler Youth girls, but they all were. And she wasn't that long out of the Jungmädel. The husband was arrested two years ago. Missing presumed . . . whatever. There's a note from Intelligence. Frau Friesack may end up Category

V. Bottom rung if you get what I mean. Not that it matters much now. It's all change for the next train to Moscow.'

'Here?'

I knew all that was close but I hadn't connected it to Ilsenburg.

'The border with the Soviet Zone comes just west of here. We'll be out in a few days and they'll be in. Of course they have a different denazification system. Shoot a few to show you mean business, stick a few more behind the wire in any old concentration camp you happen to have handy, and offer the rest an irresistible deal on exchanging their membership of one party . . . for membership of another. Probably means less bloody paperwork.' The lieutenant shrugged. 'Anyway, you carry on, Mr Gillespie. Your bona fides come from Lieutenant Mackay, so that's fine. Just let me know where you are . . . and when you're going back to Goslar.'

Walking through Ilsenburg I was startled by how little had changed. I had no idea what had gone on here, but the war, at least on the surface, had left it alone. The houses were maybe a little more ragged round the edges than I remembered, but that was it. Mühlenstrasse looked the same. It sounded the same. The River Ilse gurgled behind the buildings on one side. I saw the window of the shop I stood in twelve years earlier, holding Clara Bloch. My heart quickened. I almost smiled. But the smile didn't come. There were glasses on show in the window, but there was a different name on the door and a different sign above it. I didn't think any more then. Perhaps that was easiest. And next, rounding the bend, the Yellow House.

I saw a girl, a teenager, bending over a row of potato plants, earthing up the black-green stems. She was raking hard, and I could feel something almost intense. She raked as if she was working off anger or frustration. I watched her for a moment. She was unaware of me. As she straightened up and wiped her brow, I thought, absurdly, that the tall, graceful figure was Annaliese. The hair was Annaliese's as I first saw her. It was a memory, only that. I knew who this was.

The girl was aware of me. She turned. I saw how much younger she was than she seemed bending over the potatoes. I smiled. She didn't. She scowled.

'Hello,' I said. As an opening, it lacked imagination.

'I'm looking for Annaliese . . . Annaliese Friesack.'

The scowl was now a look of suspicion. Idle visits were out of fashion.

'Who are you?'

'I know who you are . . .'

'I said who are you?'

'I don't know how best to answer that, Krista . . . the name, well, you might not know it at all. Probably not. I wouldn't be surprised. Last time I saw you, you were four or five months old . . . no weight at all. I held you, in the Marienkirche.'

She was still suspicious, but now mostly puzzled. This was nonsense.

'The visit's maybe overdue, but for better or worse, I'm your godfather.'

167

7

EIN NEUES TESTAMENT
A NEW TESTAMENT

Ilsenburg, April 1943

Prayer was harder than it had been for Reinhard Friesack. It wasn't that he expected simple answers to his prayers, indeed answers at all in terms of consequences he could measure or see. The business of prayer was understanding. You prayed for other people, of course, for those you loved and those you wanted to find a way to love. You prayed for the world and everything that was wrong with it. You prayed in hope of the hope you needed to find. But in all that, you were looking for the light that would show you the way. The gift of prayer was the grace to understand. Sometimes that grace might let you hear the still, small voice in the darkness, sometimes you had to accept that there was grace too in God's silence. But as the years passed, and the darkness thickened, and Reinhard encountered that silence more and more, he found it harder and harder to accept. Prayer became more painful and more distant. His head knew prayer was not God's balance sheet, but his heart demanded results. Something, anything other than the cloying silence. And as he knelt before the altar in the Marienkirche, looking at the figure of Christ on the cross on many mornings, there was no calm in him, only anger. He strove but could not pray. The silence was raging inside him. He walked out.

It was not chance that made his inability to pray that morning about Clara Bloch. He felt that strongly. If there were times he didn't think about her, she always came back. And when she did, she asked him the same question. Who was he? What was he? His answers never satisfied him. He was the pastor of the Marienkirche now. He was the husband of Annaliese and the father of Krista. He was a man of faith. He was a man who cared about his town and the people in it. He was a man who knew his limitations but tried to live a life that was good and decent and generous. He was a man who closed his eyes. Like everyone. And now Clara Bloch was asking the same questions, even more insistently. She was still Clara Bloch. She was always Clara Bloch after all the years she had been Clara Strauss. Always Annaliese's friend to him, after all the years that had separated the two women. They were still the Mühlenstrasse girls, in his own fond memories of youth. And now, as he came across the Schloßstraße bridge and stood at the corner of Mühlenstrasse, he almost heard the two girls' laughter. He almost felt that if he turned his head, he would see them again, running together as they used to run. He was looking at the house where Clara still lived with her husband and her children. There was still an optician's shop next to it, but it was no longer hers. It had been bought a long time ago, when the law told her she could no longer do her job or own her business, and her husband could no longer make the glasses she would have prescribed. It had been sold for almost nothing. The house followed. With nothing else to live on, that too was sold for only a fraction of its value. The little two-roomed apartment behind the house that had been her husband's workshop was all they had left. Their children had gone somewhere, anywhere. No one knew and no one asked. They lived somehow on almost nothing, like the half dozen other Jews in Ilsenburg. They came out very little. When they did they went unseen and unregarded, except for a few people who refused not to see them and refused not to regard them. Reinhard Friesack was one of those still.

Clara never asked for anything. In all the years that stripped everything from her, she never looked to the people who had once been her friends and neighbours. She stood her ground in her own way, as the little piece of ground she had shrank to nothing. But now she had asked. She came to the Yellow House, that as a girl had been her second home, and begged Reinhard's help. She begged him to remember the past. She begged Annaliese to think of what they once were to each other. He said he would try. He said he would do whatever was in his power. And as he stood on the doorstep, knowing how little that power amounted to, Annaliese turned away. She said nothing. He found her crying, but he felt his own tears lasted longer than hers. Long ago she had steeled herself to the way her real world was.

'There's nothing you can do,' she said. 'Except to damage us.'

There probably was nothing Reinhard Friesack could do but he had no choice but to try. Even the chance that he could make a difference was worth something. It was still possible to act. People did still stand in the way, quietly perhaps, but it could be enough. Couldn't Clara just be left alone? All it took was for someone to look the other way or put a piece of paper back in a file and forget it. It did happen. In this small place, so far from everything, why did she matter?

Reinhard found Oskar Mommsen in his office at the Landhaus Zu den Rothen Forellen. Oskar had several offices now. As well as the one that went with his ownership of the hotel, he had an office in the townhall that served his mayoral duties and another in the Little Brown House next door that he occupied as the head of Ilsenburg's Nazi Party. If the pastor of the Marienkirche was a man of almost no importance now, Oskar Mommsen's power, in his tiny fiefdom, was everything. And while he bowed to the Gestapo and the SS, he had a long leash.

'Ah, Pastor, good morning!'

The word pastor was not quite in quotes, but it came with a wry smile. The mayor had once been a regular communicant at the Marienkirche. He now came only occasionally when there was some civic purpose or other to be served by his presence. He liked a bit ceremony if the ceremony was his. He didn't treat the church with contempt, but he let Reinhard know he didn't take it very seriously.

'And what can I do you for today?'

'You did say you'd look at the case of Clara Strauss and her husband . . .'

'I thought we'd done with that, Reinhard.'

'I can't just be done with it, Oskar.'

'It's police business, Reinhard, Gestapo business. There are still a number of Jews in the town. They have to go. The instructions don't come from me. I have a copy of the order but the decision isn't mine. It's political. It's policy. It's not for me to interfere. They need to take whatever they've been told to take and report to the railway station . . . whenever that is. I can't remember. And it doesn't matter.'

'It's tomorrow.'

'Then tomorrow it is.'

'You can delay that, Oskar. You can stop it . . .'

'For all of them or just for the couple of Jews you have a soft spot for?'

'Why not for all of them? Half a dozen people. They're doing no harm.'

'I think you know better than that . . . they're Jews. That's harm enough.'

'Oskar, I'm not going to argue about any of that. You said it doesn't matter. It doesn't matter if they go, it doesn't matter if they stay. All you have to do is tell the police to leave it alone . . . leave it for now. Nobody wants this. Do you want it?'

Mommsen took out a cigarette and lit it.

'You are the one who should leave it alone, Reinhard.'

The words were harder. Reinhard Friesack felt it. He had lost.

'You should take care, my friend. Look after yourself. You have a history, you know. These things are not forgotten. And it's not all history, is it? Your associations in the church don't go unnoticed. There are people you'd be well advised to steer clear of. I get reports on many things, not just flushing out Jews. So never mind the fucking Yids, Pastor . . . you need to watch your own back.'

*

The call that eventually brought Reinhard Friesack to the priesthood didn't come in the way he would have wanted. It was barely a call at all. Except that something made it happen. In a way it was like his marriage. It wasn't that he didn't love Annaliese, but they came together in a way that had no great passion in it. There was familiarity and friendship first, and fondness and then out of that something that became love, or if love wasn't the right word straightaway, that grew from the commitment they shared and the life they lived together and the child who was so long coming. Surely it was love by then. He knew it was no different for his wife. They moved towards caring and from caring, being together seemed right. There was need in it too, for both of them. They found each other because they needed each other. They were older by the time they decided to marry. Past dreams of love and unreasonable expectations of what was on offer in life. It was enough for them, more than enough. It wasn't such a bad place to stand. Life needed that. And when that other decision came and Reinhard took the road to ordination, he was past any dreams of a vocation that came with a shining light and a clap of thunder. It was true that the idea of becoming a pastor had been in his head sometimes. Becoming a deacon had been the first step, after all. But that was enough too. Now there was a plan. The position of headmaster of the school in Ilsenburg was his if he wanted it. He only had to wait. Professor Schultz would retire before long. A few years. 1935, 1936? The school board already knew who the job would go to.

Then the world changed. Other people had other plans.

He did stick it as long as he could. After that day in 1933, when a gang of boys he once taught put him in hospital, he went back into his classroom and told himself it wouldn't be so bad. There was only so much that could change. The town was the town. The mountains were the mountains. Learning was still learning. There would always be a way to teach in the light, even when the light was dim. He had Annaliese and Krista to think of and he had his students and his school. He would do what he could, holding on to what mattered without any fuss. People had to do that, didn't they? If things got bad, they would get better in time. He would offend no one, except occasionally in the privacy of his own head. There would be hard gruel to swallow, but he would swallow it and find a way to keep a candle burning in his window. The idea that there was a limit to how bad it could get was a simple one. But it was a false hope. It got bad, and it kept getting worse.

It wasn't long before almost anything he cared about had disappeared. There were more and more things he couldn't talk about and more and more things he had to talk about that he despised. The list was a long one. It started with Heinrich

Heine and it never ended. Heine's books weren't burned in Ilsenburg's square, but they were gone from the school and the library, and there were no concerts where his lieder were sung. All his love for the Harz Mountains was turned to hate. It was only one small thing, people said. When it came to what was degenerate, you couldn't pick and choose. You certainly couldn't expose children to it. It wasn't as if there was any shortage of new poetry. Reinhard's students had plenty to learn.

'Clear the streets for the brown battalions,
Clear the streets where the storm troops fight!
The swastika carries the hopes of millions,
The dawn of freedom and bread shines bright!'

He didn't leave when the last three Jewish children left, but it was soon afterwards. It wasn't directly because of them. He hated the school now. He hated it profoundly. He didn't hate walking through the gates as much as the Jewish boys whose fathers had no jobs and whose mothers were shunned by people who had been their friends only yesterday. But then they didn't just hate it, they feared it too. They could expect humiliation from their teachers on a regular basis now, and beatings in the playground that no one made any attempt to stop unless there was blood. Some days they were left alone, but even then there was enough degradation in what was taught to keep them going. Blood and race was the daily fare and their very existence was a sour lesson in what bad blood was and what racial purity was all about. Reinhard did what he could. He had some authority left. He was still respected. A popular teacher and a deacon at the church. Most people in Ilsenburg assumed he would be the new headmaster soon. But there were those, and Oskar Mommsen was certainly among them, who already knew better. Whatever Reinhard kept in his head he wasn't as popular as he had been. Not a troublemaker, no, but not entirely reliable. Soft on Jews.

And however hard he worked at shutting his eyes and getting on with it quietly, the other teachers began to keep their distance. Most of them were Party members now. He wasn't, though the National Socialist Teachers League sent him the membership form at regular intervals.

Then, when one young teacher went into the army, Albert Werner arrived. Herr Werner didn't wear a Party uniform every day, but he made his presence felt with or without a brown shirt. There was still no law to keep the three Jewish boys out of the school. Not yet. There were only three of them. But Werner had them out within a month. He had the elderly Professor Schultz out within three. Early retirement. And by then Reinhard Friesack already knew that he would not step into his old mentor's shoes. Albert Werner would be the school's next principal.

That was it. There was no real surprise. Annaliese made a show of surprise and indignation. But it was a show. If she still believed the old plan had any chance of giving Reinhard the job, it was because he no longer talked about what he thought or what he felt or what he did or didn't do at school. They didn't talk much about anything now. All he said was that he couldn't stay on. He was resigning. He didn't discuss it with her. He simply said he was leaving. And when she asked him what the hell he thought he was going to do, he told her he was going back to college. Once upon a time he dreamed of being a pastor. Now he would do it. He said it before he thought it. He wouldn't even try to look for work as a teacher. He couldn't do it. He didn't ask for his wife's approval. She laughed. Then she shouted. What about Krista? Where would the money come from? He didn't listen to Annaliese's objections. He made the decision then and there, blindly. He had to do something. She expected something. He had to shut her up. And his decision did. So there it was. No great light. No thunderbolt. No voice from heaven. No burning bush. One more place to stand. Or was it even that? Was it a place to hide?

Annaliese Friesack saw the sense in what her husband decided to do. She had no interest in the reasons. What she knew clearly, as the shock and consternation subsided, was that the further he was from the day-to-day business of life around him, the better. He wouldn't oppose anything then. He would express no political views. He didn't need to speak against the laws of the new Germany. He would do as her brother Kurt, now an officer in the SS, had told him and continued to tell him. Shut up. No opinions. No questions. That would just about do. But in a small town where everyone knew everyone, Reinhard Friesack couldn't hide the fact that he didn't fit. He couldn't pretend to fit. Silence was not enough.

As a teacher even silence was increasingly seen as dissent. You couldn't just say the words they wanted said, you had to believe them. Going through the motions wouldn't do. If it wasn't enough to bring him to the attention of the police or the Party or the Gestapo, it was still too much. Reinhard's presence nagged at Annaliese, even when he seemed to do nothing. He never felt safe. Leaving the school behind wasn't a bad idea. And maybe the church wasn't such a bad idea either. It was one thing that made him happy. Prayers and masses and weddings and funerals and Bible reading and vestments and conducting the choir. Surely nobody gave that any attention. Some people liked it and some didn't. Some people needed it and some couldn't care less. But it was its own world. Every Sunday was the same. The old pastor at the Marienkirche still delivered the same sermons Annaliese heard him deliver as a child. They didn't mean much then and they meant less now. If there was a safe place left where you could just go through the motions, where going through the motions was your only purpose, where you might be congratulated for going through the motions, it was in front of an altar.

So it was that Reinhard Friesack said goodbye to his school, having stayed to the end of the year to make it clear he was leaving to pursue his vocation, not because of any friction between him and the new headmaster. He began his journey to the Lutheran priesthood at the Theological Faculty at the University of Halle with four other men, all of them older. There were more important things for young German men to do than go into the church. War was two years away at this point, but all Germany knew it was coming, however often all Germany told itself it wasn't.

Halle wasn't far from Ilsenburg. Reinhard was at home most weekends. He was determined not to separate himself from Annaliese and Krista. But as time went on, it was sometimes true to say that he was more comfortable in Halle with his books and his lectures and his fellow seminarians than he was in Ilsenburg. It was equally true sometimes that life at the Yellow House felt easier for Annaliese when he set off for the train to Halle on a Monday morning. Neither Reinhard nor Annaliese truly recognised the distance between them, but it had become part of their lives. She gave him support without question. The little bit of money she inherited from her mother helped them through the time he brought no income home. She went out to work too, for the first time in years. Oskar Mommsen gave her a job at the hotel as receptionist and secretary. She started reluctantly, because they needed money, but she enjoyed what she did. It felt like a new, brighter life. She felt secure too. However it started, the change in their lives was for the better. Reinhard was doing what he wanted. Krista was growing up. They were all safer.

However, Annaliese Friesack knew almost nothing about the church. She knew what happened on Sundays. Sometimes she went to a wedding, more often a funeral. She helped with collecting for charity. She liked carols at Christmas. But the church, like everything, was caught up in the turmoil that wasn't so much part of the Führer's Germany as its drive and purpose. It wasn't as safe as she thought.

Reinhard Friesack knew about the battle that was going on in the Protestant churches, but like millions of others, clergy and laity alike, he saw it going on at the fringes of the normal life of God's community. It didn't stand outside faith, but faith required no engagement with it. If the new regime got what it wanted, a unified Reich Church, it could be a positive thing. Unity was good. If that didn't happen, well, nothing had changed. Unity wasn't everything. As for the life of the church, it was lived in the life of the nation. What was good for Germany would be good for God's German people. And if some things were difficult, the man who was now the nation's leader made no apology for that. It would be difficult. The chaos the country was fighting its way out of demanded that. Nothing could be perfect in an imperfect world anyway. Adolf Hitler was Germany's leader. Every Christian had a duty to accept that and follow him. The words were St Paul's and they brooked no dissent: Whosoever therefore resisteth the power, resisteth the ordnance of God . . . Render therefore to all their dues: tribute to whom tribute is due; custom to whom custom; fear to whom fear; honour to whom honour. There was no argument. All that was necessary was to obey the law and support the state. If conflict in the church couldn't be ignored, it could be prayed away. The people who called themselves German Christians and demanded every element of Nationalism should find its way onto the altar were not going to prevail. They made the loudest noise, but faith was not a Party rally. The people who called themselves the

Confessing Church not only defied St Paul and rejected what faith insisted was God's ordnance, they failed as patriots, they didn't put Germany first.

No one needed to join that battle. The centre would hold. Reinhard Friesack believed it. For the most part. He put new doubts where his old doubts were stored. And as the warehouse of doubts filled up, he still told himself prayer would empty it.

Pastor Reinhard Friesack was ordained in the great Gothic space that was the cathedral of Saints Maurice and Catherine in Magdeburg. The war was only two months away. Like most people, he felt it was imminent. Like most people, he prayed it wasn't. He wouldn't have the space to look away when it came, but he would have the space to stand outside. That's what he hoped. He had worked hard for it. He had kept away from conflict and dissent. He had kept his heart as well as his mind in the Gospels. That's where he would find his strength. If he had come to the priesthood in uncertainty, he had grown to believe that a call did come. It just took its time to arrive and find its own way to bring him home. He did have a sense that he was safe where he was. And Annaliese felt the same. The uneasy relationship he had with the new regime in Ilsenburg had been forgotten. Even his brother-in-law, SS-Untersturmführer Kurt Hoffman, who regarded Lutheran pastors with contempt, like any other mumbo-merchants in frocks, thought he was in the best place. Nothing could be less interesting than what a priest had to say.

Safety had come at a cost, though, and not one that Reinhard saw coming. He had spent more time away from home than he anticipated during his training, when the Theology Faculty at Halle closed and he had to move to Leipzig. The distance between him and Annaliese increased. There was no hostility, but she had become more independent. He had seen too little of Krista, growing up, and he played a smaller part in her childhood than he realised. He didn't ignore that childhood world, but he never quite became a part of it. It was as if he assumed being her father was enough. He didn't see that it needed work. He didn't know her. And she didn't know him. Her small world revolved around the children of Ilsenburg, as his once had, but it wasn't the same world. Soon Krista would join her older friends in the Jungmädelbund, on the beginning of her journey through the girl's section of the Hitler Youth. It was all she wanted; all she dreamed of. She already had a uniform, though she wasn't old enough to join. The night before her father's ordination she cried herself to sleep because he wouldn't let her wear it.

If ordination was the end Reinhard desired, it was not the beginning of reuniting him with Annaliese and Krista. He had a job, at a parish in Magdeburg, but he went alone. Annaliese had her own life now. So did Krista. They would not leave Ilsenburg. It wasn't what the newly minted pastor expected, but his wife was immovable. And she was right, as it turned out. When the old pastor of the Marienkirche retired, the parishioners were happy to have a new pastor who was one of their own, who had been a deacon there, who even sang in the choir as a boy there. He wasn't in hock to the Nazis, like some. Few wanted that in a priest. But he would get on with them. They all wanted that. The Nazis might not respect Christ's cross, but they would respect a pastor with an Iron Cross, just like Hitler.

All that was still to come. It would put some of the things that were wrong between Reinhard and Annaliese Friesack right, at least for a time. For now, Reinhard's journey to becoming a priest had reached its conclusion. There was a sense of joy in the cathedral in Magdeburg as he made his vows to God. For a moment, maybe just one moment, Annaliese felt closer him. She even felt proud.

'The Church in which you are to be ordained confesses that the Holy Scriptures are the Word of God and are the norm of its faith and life. We accept, teach, and confess the Apostles', the Nicene, and the Athanasian Creeds. We acknowledge the Lutheran Confessions as true witnesses and faithful expositions of the Holy Scriptures. Will you therefore preach and teach in accordance with the Holy Scriptures and these creeds and confessions.'

'I will, and I ask God to help me.'

*

When Clara Strauss and her husband left Mühlenstrasse for the last time, in April 1943, with the one small suitcase each was allowed to carry, the policeman who walked to the station with them was a man Clara knew as a girl. Wachtmeister Vennemann delivered them to an SS man and two Gestapo officers. She didn't know them. They had come from Goslar and they would accompany the Strausses and Ilsenburg's only two other Jews to the collection point in Magdeburg. A special carriage attached to the Magdeburg train had already picked up Jews from other towns and villages around the Harz Mountains. At Magdeburg they would join a transport that would take them onward. Where wasn't immediately clear. There was a lot of paperwork. Clara and her husband had signed various pieces of paper and received ever more documents in return. The SS man at the station checked that all the yellow stars were visible. And still nothing they signed and nothing they were given told them where they were going. East. That was all.

Pastor Reinhard Friesack didn't go to the station. He spent a sleepless night praying for guidance. None came. But there was nothing he could do on a railway platform. It would help no one. His duty was to his parishioners. It wouldn't take much to put that at risk now. It was too easy to put yourself on the wrong side of the Party. If one thing had been truly constant over these years it was that everything kept getting worse, everything kept getting harder, everything became more dangerous. The war was getting worse. You couldn't say it, but it was obvious. The dead and the missing grew in number all the time. And at the Marienkirche prayers for the dead were long, even in such a small town. They lasted far too long to fit with the chatter that followed the Sunday service, that was still all about the war being won on every front and the enemy being rolled back everywhere. And if Ilsenburg had avoided the bombers, there was no one without dead friends and relatives in every city for a hundred kilometres around. But you had to be careful about saying anything negative. Oskar Mommsen was right, as ever. It only took a few careless words to set the Gestapo on you. Reinhard Friesack knew that. He disliked living by those rules, but he did. What was the point of standing at the station to watch the Gestapo write your name down? For what? There was no point at all. Yet, Reinhard knew he had failed. He wasn't meant to be guided, he was meant to guide.

It was a week later when there was a rap on the front door of the Yellow House. A rap and then a slow, repeated thud. It was night and it was late for visitors in times when no one went out after dark anymore. Reinhard went to the door. He switched off the lights. Blackout habits were instinctive now. But there was enough light from a sliver of moon over the castle hill to see a thin, grubby figure leaning on the wall to the left. A man, clearly weak and shaky on his feet.

'Reinhard . . .'

The pastor didn't recognise the man for some seconds. The face was dirty. The overcoat was torn. If it had fitted once, it now hung like a shapeless sack.

'The suit's still at the cleaner's . . . this is the best I could do.'

Reinhard recognised the smile.

'Hugo!'

'I was just passing . . .'

The man coughed heavily. One joke too many.

'Come inside. What's happened to you?'

The man came in. The door closed. Reinhard put the lights back on.

'Come into the study. There's a fire. I'll get you some . . .'

He wasn't sure what he would get. He didn't know what was happening.

'Who is it, Reinhard?'

Annaliese stood in the doorway from the kitchen.

'It's Hugo Weiss, darling. He's had . . . is it an accident?'

'After a fashion, old man.'

'You remember Hugo? We were at college together . . .'

Annaliese was puzzled, more than puzzled.

'That's the thing, Frau Friesack, an accident.'

She didn't believe him. This wasn't right.

'It's a few years, isn't it,' said Weiss. 'Sorry to burst in like this . . . didn't we last meet at Reinhard's ordination? That'll be it. I've been travelling . . . on foot . . .'

There was a sound from the stairs. Weiss looked up. It was a look of fear. And then he laughed, quietly, to himself. He was close to delirious.

'You must be Krista. You see, I remember. At your father's ordination . . .'

'Go to back to bed, Krista. Herr Weiss has been in an accident.'

Annaliese's voice was sharp. Krista looked for a moment and then went.

Reinhard led the man into the study at the front of the house. Annaliese stood where she was. When Reinhard came back she spoke in a hard whisper.

183

'What's going on?'

'I don't know. I'll find out. You remember Hugo . . . you must do.'

'Yes, I remember him. What the hell does it matter whether I remember him or not? What does he want? You haven't seen him in years! The state he's in . . .'

'I'll find out what's happened, Liese.'

'I suggest you don't.'

'What?'

'Whatever it is . . . we don't need to know. Get him out of here!'

'Don't be ridiculous. He needs help.'

'Just get him out!'

Reinhard watched her. She was frightened. She always had better instincts than him, but he wasn't going to listen to her now. She would have to listen to him.

'I'll put him in the study. Can you get him some coffee . . . and something to eat. I'll get some water and a towel. If he's cleaned up . . . some food, some sleep . . .'

Annaliese didn't move.

'Please,' said Reinhard. 'He was my friend.'

She turned back into the kitchen.

A coffee and a brandy and some clean hot water made a great difference to Hugo Weiss. Chicken soup improved things even more. Annaliese did what she had been asked to do, but that was it as far as she was concerned. She went upstairs to bed.

'She's right,' said Hugo quietly. 'She has a nose for trouble.'

'What's happened?' asked Reinhard.

'I never did learn to do what you're so good at, old man . . . you got a fag?'

Pastor Reinhard produced a cigarette and lit one himself.

'Shut up and pray and say God Save Germany . . . whatever the shite.'

'Is that what I am?'

'No, of course it's not. But you could keep your mouth shut. I couldn't. But then I didn't have the option, did I? Jewish father . . . nothing I can do to get that old bastard out of my blood. I lost my parish three years ago. I'm not saying no one helped. They did. But they can only go so far . . . and even the ones who wanted to help . . . well . . . one good Jew, even the good Jew who's your fucking pastor . . . doesn't change what Jews are. It doesn't mean they're not lying cunts who want to rape your daughters and burn Germany to the ground. I got through Kristallnacht. And for my sins, I locked the door of my church and cried. That's it. I cried. They burned the synagogue down. Two streets away. I shut my door. That's all I did.'

'What else could you do?'

'I get less and less comfort from knowing that's true.'

'The truth isn't there to give you comfort, Hugo.'

'Ah, you speak from experience. That's something . . .'

Reinhard poured more brandy.

'I hung on,' continued Weiss. 'What else? Then it was over. The parish couldn't protect me. The Gestapo were sniffing around. I asked for it. I was talking to people who were protesting . . . who were trying to take them on. When they started arresting pastors in the Confessing Church, I hid some of them. I helped a couple of them get to Switzerland. I went underground. But I kept working. Well, you can only last so long, can't you? You do know they've arrested Bonhoeffer?'

'No, I didn't.'

'Last week.'

'They came for me in Leipzig. Someone told. Someone always will. I got away. I was in Magdeburg for a few days. I had to get out. I got as far as Wernigerode on the train.

I was trying to get to the monastery. I thought they'd give me a couple of nights anyway, but the Gestapo were there. I've been walking since. In the mountains. No food. Nowhere to go. I knew you were here . . . I'm sorry. Desperation. I'm so sorry, Reinhard . . . if you give me a night, one night . . .'

Hugo Weiss dropped his head. He was crying silently.

Reinhard Friesack nodded. The words beneath his breath were a prayer. It came with unfamiliar ease.

The next morning, Reinhard gave Hugo Weiss new clothes. He gave him some breakfast. It was still early. Annaliese was upstairs. Krista was in her room too. Neither of them would appear, Reinhard knew that. It was better that way. He started the car and drove it out the road. He still had a car as a pastor, though the petrol ration was barely enough to make it worth using. What was in the tank would get him to Goslar and back. It would have to do. From there Hugo could get to Hannover. Big enough to disappear in. And if he reached Berlin, even better.

The two men hardly spoke. All the talking had been done.

Reinhard dropped his old friend as the train for Hannover arrived. That was the best way. On to the platform, on to the train. No waiting. No one to see you. He couldn't know whether Hugo would get there. He had done all that he could. He drove back to Ilsenburg. This wasn't what he wanted. But he had made his choice. And as he pulled up at the front of the Yellow House, he knew what that meant. There was a car outside. A black Mercedes. An SS man was standing at the gate, watching him as he stopped his car and got out. They knew. They already knew.

8

DAS BROCKENGESPENST
THE BROCKEN SPECTRE

Ilsenburg, June 1945

I don't know what I thought I was going to say to Annaliese. If I'd thought at all it was only to change the subject in my head and think about something else. I was there because chance brought me there. And something like guilt. The fact that it was easier not to take the road to Ilsenburg was something to do with why I took it. I had plenty of excuses not to. But Lieutenant Mackay was happy to leave me there because chance had made me useful. For now, what I did and where I went depended on him and his superiors. I had to go along with it. And going along with it meant the excuses for ignoring the Ilsenburg turning looked thinner than they had done. It was a long time since I'd found myself worrying about offering my mother poor excuses for anything. But this would piss her off. She had great faith in what was meant to be. As a child, it impressed me. I was even in awe of the idea. Until I came to the conclusion that everything that happened, good, bad or indifferent, happened, and if it helped you to say it was meant to be that way afterwards, good luck. And she did pick what was meant to be, of course. Too many things had happened to me that shouldn't have happened for me to join in. Yet, stuck on the edge of the Harz Mountains, looking across at the Brocken, when I should have passed it by with no more than a fond or not so fond glance en route to Hannover, it did feel as if something had conspired to bring me there. If I didn't really believe that, I still couldn't ignore it. Or maybe I couldn't face the argument, or worse, the disappointment when I got home. So, I arrived at the Yellow House, with nothing to say to someone who would probably have nothing to say to me. 'How's it going?' It didn't sound like enough, even in German. But what would?

Annaliese stared at me, uncomprehending, and I think struggling to recognise me. I'd say that was as much disbelief as anything. We were both in our forties. We had changed. I wouldn't say time had withered Annaliese, but there had been a cost. Maybe my face said the same thing, I don't know. Her frown lasted a few seconds. Then she laughed. I did too. There was something absurd about it. And that's what you do sometimes if you don't know what to do. Laugh. The laugh didn't last any longer than the frown. There were tears. She had her arms round me. She wasn't sobbing, but there were tears. My eyes were wet too. We stepped back, looking at each other again, and not knowing what to say.

Practical politeness took over. Krista was dispatched to make some coffee, or whatever barely drinkable black liquid passed for it. I was used to that. It was all there was everywhere. Then food. She talked about food and offered apologies. Apologies were useful. They were something to say to fill the empty spaces. They had soup, potato and cabbage soup, and she could heat that up. It wasn't bad. By then we were in the kitchen. She was still talking about soup. I was pushed into a chair. The same kitchen. Same stove, same furniture, clock, same plates and cups.

'I don't need anything, Annaliese . . .'

'Of course you do, Stefan!'

'Maybe later . . .'

She nodded. She breathed more slowly. She sat down.

'Where have you come from?'

'I'm in Goslar . . . I was . . . I'm supposed to go to Hannover.'

'Are you with the British?'

'I was with the Irish embassy in Berlin. The ambassador left . . . like everyone . . . we were down by the Swiss border . . . when the end . . . it's not so easy getting out of Germany . . . my boss went one way and I came this way. The British will put me on a plane to London . . . and I'll get home . . . it's been a long time.'

She didn't really take this in. But I think my voice felt good.

'I got held up in Goslar . . . and they let me come to Ilsenburg.'

'It's very hard to believe,' she said quietly. 'I'm not sure I do.'

She laughed again. Then she looked down at the floor.

Krista brought the mugs of bitter, black hot water.

'I don't know what to make of Krista,' I said, with a cheerful predictability. 'It's hard to take time in, isn't it? But there she is. And all the years in between . . .'

I thought these were the kind of words any long-lost godfather anywhere might produce. I could have added something about where did all those years go? But enough of the obvious. Krista was already looking at me as if I might turn out to be an idiot. She was at an age where that's a reasonable response to any adult.

She sat on a chair across the room, nursing her mug, looking hard at me and then looking away. She said nothing then, and as the evening wore on, she kept saying nothing. She answered a few questions I asked, though usually when prompted by Annaliese. In fact, I didn't have many questions for either of them. Every question led back to things that weren't going to make good conversation.

There were a lot of silences. I found myself doing most of the talking, but even what I had to say kept bumping into where we were. There was Ireland, of course, my mother, my father, my son, the farm. That was safe ground, but there was something hanging over it, said or unsaid. We were lucky in Ireland, lucky not to be involved. Annaliese said it and when she finished saying it, the thought was still there. Luck couldn't have been a word anyone used much. As for the war itself, and the years before the war, I knew as soon as I walked through the door that she wanted to say nothing about any of it. It was over. It was done. For better or worse. Thank God it was finished. She had a few variations on that, but she was uneasy even with the platitudes. I could see that Krista was even more uneasy. Eventually she got up and went, silently. I saw her through the window, working in the garden again. I thought it was probably where she went to escape.

'It's very hard for her . . .' said Annaliese. 'She can't take it in . . .'

'It's very hard for you too, Annaliese.'

'I can take it in,' she said, smiling. 'I'm glad to take it in.'

'The town doesn't seem to have been damaged.'

She shrugged. I think the word stuck in her head. Damaged.

'You've been in Berlin, Hamburg too?'

I nodded.

'You're right. Here, we haven't had that . . . I know how . . .'

She stopped. This wasn't what she was going to talk about.

'The officer . . . at the hotel . . . said Reinhard was arrested . . .'

Annaliese didn't speak for a long moment. The tick of the clock seemed louder. I guess she had been waiting for this question, or for some version of it.

'Yes.'

She was silent again. I had to say more. I needed to know.

'I know when I was last here, there were problems at the school.'

'Yes, there were problems. It wasn't easy for him.'

'No.'

'He didn't make it easy.'

She looked away as she spoke. I'm not sure the words were for me. It felt like she was telling herself.

'He left the school. He became the pastor, at the Marienkirche.'

I couldn't help smiling.

'Isn't that what he always wanted?'

'I don't know what he wanted. I tried... I tried to do everything I could just to keep things the way... just to be like everyone else and live the way everyone lived... just a family, just the three of us. I don't know why that wasn't enough. It wasn't so hard here, it really wasn't... I don't know what he did. What he said. He wasn't with us sometimes... that's how it felt... then something happened. The Gestapo came. One morning they took him away... I didn't see him again.'

I suppose I had no reason to think this wouldn't be painful, but as the words came out, it felt less painful than it should have done. There was a kind of matter-of-fact tone. As if there was little to say. I didn't take in how vague it all was.

'What happened?'

'They started arresting people all the time... as the war...'

'Was he in prison?'

'There was a trial. In Magdeburg. They sent him to a camp...'

'Did they tell you where?'

'He was in the gaol in Magdeburg. Then Nordhausen . . . it's a labour camp . . . when I did try to ask . . . I was told I shouldn't ask again . . . they told me to forget . . .'

There was silence again. The clock ticked. Annaliese was looking in my direction still, but not at me. Her eyes were empty, stuck in the space between us.

'Where is he now?'

She shook her head.

I assumed she meant he was dead.

'I don't know where he went, Stefan. They moved all the prisoners from Nordhausen before the Americans came. I heard that. Nothing else. I don't know where they took them. North, to other camps, that's what people said. I don't know if he was even still alive then . . . that's how it was. You didn't get any information about anything. You still don't.'

'Do you think he is dead?'

'I don't know. How can I? I think . . . I think probably . . .'

It must have been obvious that I expected something more in her voice. I don't know what it was. Maybe urgency, maybe determination. At least concern.

'You know enough, don't you . . . about these places . . .'

Annaliese's words sounded not just beaten but beaten down.

'The Allies must have names, surely. What about the Red Cross?'

She smiled a smile that was as empty as her eyes had been earlier. She spoke without conviction.

'Do you think if I go to the hotel and ask the lieutenant, very politely, if the British Army will find my husband for me, they'll be off across Germany to scour the DP camps for him? I'm not allowed to leave Ilsenburg, even if I could find somewhere to look. I'm on a denazification list. Did they tell you that, Stefan?'

I nodded. She shrugged. She had no more to add.

'Can you stay tonight, Stefan?'

'If you can put me up.'

'The same room,' said Annaliese more warmly. The other conversation was over. 'The soup will be better than the coffee. And I have a bottle of wine and a little schnapps hidden away. If we can find a way to talk about better times, we should try. If we can't, there is the piano. You used to like to listen. So why not that?'

We stood up. She went out to the hall to take me upstairs. The mood was lighter. She wanted to make it lighter. I wanted to help her do that. It cost me nothing. Why else was I there? But as we walked past the sitting room, the door was open. I glanced in and I saw the dark, polished wood of the piano. I remembered the first time I was in the Yellow House. I remembered watching Annaliese play. I remembered a boyhood passion that should have made me smile. I also remembered the other girl who was at the piano, turning music for her best friend. I knew I would not ask about her. Not for Annaliese's sake, for my own.

The evening at the Yellow House ended with music. There was Schubert and maybe Schumann. I knew some of it. I might have known it years ago in the same room. Or as many years ago, and more, when my mother still played because she enjoyed playing. Either way it felt like something being pulled out of the past to shut out the present. I think that's what it was. It hadn't taken long to fill the space Annaliese and I had to talk in. She couldn't talk about what mattered and she was still too close to all that to talk about what didn't matter. Something like that. I thought I might do better with Krista. I tried just talking about Ireland. I didn't do a good job. She was suspicious of me, that was obvious and maybe not surprising. People who spoke English had been the enemy only months before. I guess it was no surprise that she didn't find my explanation of neutrality interesting, even with some half-arsed jokes. She didn't say much. I'm not sure she said anything. The idea that Ireland didn't take sides, when all she had known most of her life was her side against the rest, bewildered her. Annaliese did me a favour and stopped me rambling. The more I said, the more I saw Krista's eyebrows rise.

'She doesn't really understand what neutral means, Stefan.'

'It's bit like transubstantiation.' One last joke. 'A mystery . . .'

Annaliese didn't bother to smile. Banter wouldn't cut it. She wanted another break in trying to talk. By then I think both of us were wondering what would be the earliest time it wasn't impolite to say the night was getting on and everyone must be tired. Krista gave up abruptly. She said goodnight, which was something. Annaliese played on.

The next morning an MP arrived with a message to say Lieutenant Mackay was coming over from Goslar to collect me. His CO had come down from Brunswick and he wanted to talk to me. It wouldn't take up much time. I didn't mind. I'd told Annaliese I'd stay another night, but a break was no bad thing. She could sort out some new piano pieces. When I first came downstairs, there was a door open into another room off the hall. I remembered it as Reinhard's study. That door had remained firmly closed the previous evening and I hadn't thought about it. I hadn't remembered the room. Now I looked in. The floor was stacked with wooden crates, full of vegetables. Mostly potatoes packed in earth, but cabbages, carrots, leeks, onions, kohlrabi. Annaliese was pulling a bunch of carrots from a box.

'The garden has been a godsend. We've had hardly any meat for months, and we're getting ready for what's to come.

A long winter. Food's scarce now . . . and it won't get better. Now they're here, I don't think they will want to feed us!'

She shook her head.

'But we have something here . . . in the cities . . . it won't be good.'

'No.'

It was all I had to say. No, it wouldn't be good.

I stood for a moment, looking past her to the rows of books that lined the walls. Everything else I remembered had gone. There was no desk. There were no armchairs by the fire. Whatever about the books, it was a storeroom for vegetables. But the books still had a presence. I felt it. The ghost whose room this had once been. As I looked and Annaliese watched me looking, I knew that she felt it too.

I drove with John Mackay to Goslar. He was quiet. He said he had too much to do and his CO was pushing him to get it done. What he meant was he had a lot to do that wasn't about the burned-out Bedford and two dead Intelligence men. He wasn't getting anywhere with that. All his superiors wanted was a report. He kept throwing up questions that meant it couldn't be signed off. It seemed no one cared except him.

'The thing is, we fucked up. Major Battersby fucked up. It was a job for American Intelligence, so who cared? Stick it all in a lorry, drop it off, and Bob's your uncle. Escort? Bugger that! Let the Yanks do their own bloody removals.'

I lit a cigarette. He wanted to sound off. Why not?

'But now it's a cock-up. Worse, it's embarrassing. The Yanks won't give a fig about two dead soldiers. Where's our stuff, you English bastards? I don't doubt the major got a number-one bollocking. A bollocking for the embarrassment . . . and that'll be forgotten quickly enough. But if there's something else going on . . . if we didn't just lose their documents . . . if they're heading for Moscow . . . then that's a bollocking that's going to go all the way up. A lot higher than Major Battersby . . .'

'Haven't you got enough questions about that already?'

'No one wants any answers. I had to write two letters last night. I was Dick Anstey's lieutenant. There was a letter to his parents and a letter to his fiancé. It's not the first time I've written those letters. You don't always say exactly what's happened. Sometimes you don't even know. But I'm not used to saying something I don't believe is true.'

He said nothing more till we arrived at Goslar. I took in his words. I understood how he felt. Most policemen care about the truth. Most policemen, at some time or other, have to ignore it. Sometimes they have to spit in its face and smile as they do it. You can feel a lot of anger about that. But nobody else gives a toss most of the time. John Mackay was angry. He was just in the wrong place to do anything about it.

Major Battersby was young, cheerful, and effortlessly polite. And very helpful. Probably more helpful to me than to his own lieutenant. Likable enough if you don't have an Irish nose that can sniff out what lies beneath. Any Irish nose will do. You don't have to be any particular variety of Irishman. You might be from the wilds of the West, or the bog of Allen, or the Walls of Derry, or the Glens of Antrim. You might be a Fenian Catholic with a hurley in one hand and a statuette of the Sacred Heart in the other, or you might be a raging Presbyterian damning the anti-Christ in Rome and waving your Union Flag at the Twelfth of July bonfires. But you'll know that special sort of Englishman. You'll know the only reason he doesn't say he thinks you're a feckin' idiot is because it's not worth the effort.

'I can pass these letters from your Mr Cremin on, Gillespie. I don't know what use that will be . . . but at least I can get them to the right desks at this end. But some of this is government to government stuff, isn't it? I'm sure Mr Cremin knows that.'

'I think he felt . . . in all the . . . confusion . . .'

'Chaos, you mean.' Battersby laughed. 'Absolute chaos!'

'He felt a bit of a push on the ground . . . might move things along, sir.'

'He has a point. The wheels grind very slowly at the top. I'm sure there'll be an answer on the Irish seamen . . . that should be information we have. It's in the British Zone. Were they in a labour camp or were they POWs? It's not clear.'

'Labour camp . . . Bremen. The Minister was trying to get them to a POW camp.'

'I'd be surprised if they're not on their way home . . . some of these other questions . . . well, I'll be blunt. If some of these people come our way . . . I mean the way of Intelligence . . . I'm afraid that's our business. It may not be diplomatic to say so, but I doubt anyone's going to care much about citizenship at this point. As regards this chap in Berlin . . . Staffelde, is it? Your what . . . honorary consul?'

'Charlie Mills.'

'I'm sure the Irish government is talking to Whitehall. And things will speed up. Along with establishing the borders of the Allied Zones, there'll be Allied Sectors in Berlin now. One British. That means some joint administration. If your man's stuck in the Soviet Zone, it'll be easier for us to get him out of . . . where was it again?'

'Schloss Staffelde.'

'Shame about his castle.' Battersby grinned. 'I imagine the Russians have confiscated that already. They do, of course. They collect that sort of thing.'

He passed cigarettes to me and to Mackay.

'Next thing is the bloody lorry accident. You've kindly offered your views on that, Mr Gillespie. For which, much thanks. Lieutenant Mackay's Brocken spectre. I assume as an expert on the Harz, Inspector, you're familiar with that.'

'I can't say I've seen one, Major.'

'Apparently they're impressive. A bloody great figure in the sky in front of you. You can see it but there's nothing there. Only mountains and mist and light and your shadow. Lewis Carroll wrote a poem about it, ghost hunting, I mean. "And I remember nothing more, That I can clearly fix, Till I was sitting on the floor, Repeating "Two and five are four, But *five and two* are six."". And that's it.'

Major Battersby was pleased with that. It had nothing to do with anything John Mackay had seen or said, but it told you his opinion in a way that, in advance, made you a fool for having a different one. I could see that the lieutenant thought it best to give his CO his moment of smug superiority and then carry on regardless.

'You have my preliminary report, sir.'

'Yes. All very thorough, but we need to move on. It's a bloody shame. Two good men. I know how well you got on with Anstey. But it does feel like you're trying to pull something out of the mountain mist that isn't there. Odd elements, there are some. Unpredictable and unexpected. That's the nature of an accident, Mackay. That's what it is. I appreciate your concerns, but to be honest, I need you out there sorting out the Nazis. That's what I'm looking at. Every day. Trials are coming up and some of these people are drifting away . . . evidence with them.'

'I still believe there are questions to be answered, sir.'

'Two scenarios, Lieutenant. One. A lorry gets lost, in an area the driver doesn't know. It happens all the time, all over Germany. They don't know where they are. There's a God-awful mountain road. The driver puts his foot down, hits a bend and comes off. Right where there's a drop. He can't stop. Maybe he doesn't see it. He goes over. They hit a wall of trees at the bottom. And the engine goes up. That's what I have from the MPs who found it. Mostly, it's what I have from you. Facts aplenty, then speculation. We'll go with facts.'

'I don't know about mostly. There's a lot more.'

'Scenario two. Sullivan and Anstey drive into the mountains for some reason. They pull over and stop. It so happens there are some Russians waiting . . . in a truck with a headlamp missing. The Russians shoot Sullivan and Anstey. Not with guns, but with something you'd use to kill a pig. They unload the Bedford, push it over a cliff and set in on fire. Your contribution is pigsticking, Inspector?'

Major Battersby turned from Mackay to me.

'I saw the bodies, Major. Those two wounds reminded me . . .'

'It's certainly a good tale, gentlemen. And evidence? A headlamp that could be from a Soviet ZIS. They're all over the bloody place. The border they're mapping out runs right through the Harz Mountains. You can't move for them. And if headlamps get knocked off, for God's sake, I don't suppose their drivers take any more care than ours do! Anything they can smash up, they will. On the basis of that, what am I supposed to do? Ask Soviet command if any of their chaps drive around with captive-bolt pistols, looking for Bedford lorries in the foothills?'

'There's also the motorcyclist . . . the innkeeper at Braunlage.'

'Man in pub looks out of window and sees chap on army m/c talking to a couple of soldiers in army transport. And that's the story. Come on, Mackay!'

'He's a witness.'

'To what?'

'I don't know, Major. But I know it doesn't make sense.'

Battersby closed the report in front of him.

'Tidy the thing up and get the paperwork in. I'm not ignoring this, Lieutenant. I have spoken to the MP Investigation Branch officer at Brunswick. I'll pass your report on to him. If they think there's anything more to do, they can take over. They do have Scotland Yard men on board . . . with respect, Inspector.'

Once more the major turned to me for his final dismissal.

'We are grateful for your assistance. You'll be off soon, I gather. At least you'll be going back to Ireland with a bit of a tale to tell . . . over a few drinks.'

I sat in John Mackay's jeep outside the MP post at Goslar. He lit a cigarette. He started the engine and pulled away from the factory and onto the main road.

'I'll drop you over to your cousin's. Another night and you need to be out.'

'All I'm waiting for is my lift to Hannover, John.'

'I'll sort it out. The Reds will be in Ilsenburg any time.'

'That's fast, isn't.'

'I think that's how they want it.'

'OK.'

'Anyway, you'll be glad you met, Major Battersby.'

'Ah, well, I shall have my tale to tell in Dublin's Fair City . . .'

'Don't be too hard on him, Stefan. He's like a lot of Englishmen, he wasn't born a cunt. He had a long, hard training to get there . . . and sure didn't it pay off?'

'But that's still a lid on your case. You did your best . . .'

'I think it's worth one more shout.'

'What do you mean?'

'If he's going to pass it to those Scotland Yard fellers in the Investigation Branch, I think it should be tidied up, as requested. And there is still a witness, whatever the major says. Our friendly innkeeper. There must be more to that.

More of a description of the man on the bike. And what sort of motorcycle it was. Did Anstey say any more to the innkeeper? We didn't really question him properly. Are you up for it, Stefan?'

'You've done all you can, John.'

It shouldn't have needed me to say there was nowhere to go. Or at least that no one gave a toss about going there. They were barely out the other side of a war. Maybe bodies just came too cheaply. It shouldn't have been that way, but it was.

'Ah, come on. Stay for the craic since we're a couple of Irish clowns!'

We drove back to the inn at the junction outside Braunlage. It was closed. There was nothing odd about that, even in the middle of the day. One look at the place was enough to see it wasn't much of a business. The innkeeper struck me as the sort of man who would open if he wanted to open and not bother if he couldn't be bothered. It didn't surprise me that not being bothered was likely to be an occupational hazard. John Mackay hammered on the door. There was no answer. But there was a sound. From inside. The radio was on. You could hear it. It was American swing, big band. Tommy Dorsey or Glen Miller. And loud enough.

'He must be having a party,' said Mackay.

The lieutenant hammered on the door again.

'Let's try the back . . . the bugger must be in there . . .'

We walked round to the side of the inn. There was a stack of beer kegs and a line of dustbins full of rubbish that looked like they'd been full for a long time. There was another door, at the end of a passageway. The wood was rotten. Panes of glass cracked or missing. Mackay pushed at the handle. It wasn't locked.

The smell of sour beer was strong, much stronger than it had been in the bar. The music was very loud now, probably coming from the bar. We were in a dark corridor that emerged suddenly into a hall that wasn't much lighter. There were several doors off it and a steep staircase rose up in front of us. The innkeeper was at the bottom of the stairs. Neither of us needed telling he was dead.

I knelt down. At first glance I thought his neck might be broken.

'It looks like he could have fallen down the stairs . . .'

I spoke, hearing how obvious what I was saying sounded.

'Yes, it does,' said Mackay. 'And isn't that handy? Very handy.'

The body had some elementary things to say. The limbs were a little stiff but they were coming out of rigor mortis, not going into it. The skin was red in places, but the red was changing to something more like purple. The policeman's guide to these things is more sundial than chronometer. I estimated he had been dead some time, but how long was just me taking a stab at it. Six hours, eight hours, ten. A number of things made the stab seem reasonable. The innkeeper was wearing what looked like pyjamas. Whatever happened, happened in the night. There was nothing in the way of bruising that was obviously significant. No wounds of any kind. But the way the neck was lying wasn't the way a neck should lie.

'There's nothing that suggests he didn't fall down the stairs.'

John Mackay was coming down the stairs as I stood up.

'Anything to see up there?'

'He lived in shite, that's about it. You have to walk round the rubbish and the empty brandy bottles to get across the bedroom. If you were looking for signs of a struggle . . . forget it. Even if there was one you'd be hard pressed to notice.'

'Any evidence of a break in?'

'No need. There's no lock on the door we used. And isn't it simple? Man who drinks too much falls downstairs in the dark.'

I smiled.

'The Major Battersby school of criminal investigation.'

'But you wouldn't disagree, Stefan?'

'At first glance . . . no.'

'You'd give a happy coincidence more than one glance, though.'

'I'd also ask why this man matters. To anyone. If someone wanted him out of the way, why? He's nobody. All he did was sell two soldiers bottles of beer.'

'No innkeeper, no evidence of a man on a motorbike. Gone.'

Lieutenant Mackay found a German policeman in Braunlage. The full extent of his interest in the innkeeper's death was to point upstairs, grin and cup his fingers in front of his mouth to mimic a bottle. The idea that the death might warrant investigation puzzled him. What would be the point of that? There were no detectives in Braunlage now anyway. His job was to do what the British army told him. Directing traffic, enforcing the curfew and arresting looters and black marketeers. I thought he probably didn't do much of any of that. There was nothing to loot and when it came to the black market, I saw how it worked in Babenhausen. The job of what was left of the German police force was to take its cut. The innkeeper was just another dead body. All he needed was burying. He had a brother in Sonnenberg who would to that. There was no one. The man's wife had been dead for years. His son disappeared at Stalingrad; in Russia anyway. He had a daughter who died in an air raid. The policeman didn't know where. Somewhere, anywhere.

We left the policeman in the bar, pouring himself a drink. He said he'd get the undertaker. We drove away. Neither of us had asked the innkeeper's name.

As we came close to Ilsenburg, along the road, at junctions, there were some heavy wooden drums wound with barbed wire. When we turned off towards Westerode, another roll of wire was being unloaded from the back of a truck. We got a cheery wave from the Russian soldiers as we passed. Mackay beeped the horn in response.

'As soon as we're out, the wire goes up . . .'

'And the point is?' I asked.

'The point is, it's theirs.'

'Who do they want to keep out?'

'Wrong end of stick,' laughed Mackay. 'It's to keep people in.'

Coming into Ilsenburg there was a straggling line of people outside the station. Men, women, children, loaded down with suitcases, queueing to get on to the platform. Queues of DPs with suitcases had been everywhere on my journey through Germany, but it didn't seem to fit here. They were local people, leaving.

'Last train to Goslar . . .' said the lieutenant.

'Is it?'

'Very shortly. There'll be trains I guess, but a stop at the Zone border. And Russian guards to tell you if you can cross it. Some people won't wait to find out.'

There were more Russians when we reached the Landhaus Zu den Rothen Forellen. An open-back ZIS truck stood at the front. A Soviet soldier sat at the wheel, sharing a cigarette with a British MP, both speaking pidgin German.

'He has got two headlights,' said Mackay, grinning, as I followed him in.

'More surveyors . . .'

'No, they're K for Commandant's Service. Making the final arrangements to see us off the premises. That's going on everywhere along the new line of contact. I told you. Two days and we're done. This lot probably call themselves military police but they're Intelligence. Well, secret police. But still our comrades in arms!'

In the hotel, Oskar Mommsen swept the floor. His sleeves were rolled up. He was going hard at it. Years ago, I had never seen him do anything like work. Now he did everything. He seemed to do it with enthusiasm too. He was making a point. I wasn't sure what it was. I glanced at him. A nod. A smile of recognition.

Lieutenant Mackay looked through the bar to the terrace and the lake beyond. Several men stood round a table, looking at maps and documents. One of them was the military police lieutenant I had already met. There was a Red Army officer there too, and a man in a dark coat that was oddly heavy for the weather.

'What the fuck is Foxe up to?'

'I'm going back to my cousin's . . .' I didn't care.

Mackay walked past me, irritated, to join the men on the terrace.

As I turned away, Mommsen was standing next to me.

'Annaliese told me you were here, Herr Gillespie.'

Oskar was big on deference now, I could see. Not the man I remembered.

'Herr Mommsen.' I repaid the compliment.

'You're with the British?'

'No, I'm not. You might say I'm in transit. I'm not with anyone.'

'That's the way to be,' he said. 'I think we all want that. No sides anymore. We had the Americans first, then the British. But they have to have people to run things . . . people who know the place. I've been useful to them you know. They have a very comfortable spot here. I keep it that way. And I do know the town...'

I nodded. I didn't need him to sell himself.

'There are problems, of course... what went before. But I think if you're useful... if they can find a use for you... even the Russians have to keep the wheels running smoothly.' The hotel proprietor lowered his voice. 'A worry. We all worry about the Russians. But they have one of our own with them. We'll be all right!'

He smiled a smile that wasn't as full of hope as his words. He walked away, shoulders drooping, and disappeared into the office behind the reception desk.

At that moment Mackay came back with the military police lieutenant. The conversation was in harsh whispers, but I heard enough of it to feel the anger.

'Get the fucking lists off the table, put them in a bloody file, and get them out of here when you leave. You don't hand your paperwork to the Russians!'

'Don't give me orders, Lieutenant. What the hell's secret about denazification files? They need to know who's who. We're on the same side!'

'Jesus, you need to catch up, Lieutenant. And I am giving you an order. Do it. You don't need to be polite. If they don't like it, tell them to fuck off. The only thing they'll be surprised by is that you didn't tell them when they walked in!'

Lieutenant Foxe looked uncertain.

'The feller in the coat,' said Mackay. 'Who is he?'

'He's a German... he knows the area.'

'I'm sure he does. He's a fucking spotter. Old communist party or new communist party, wherever he comes from, he's NKVD. And they're looking at names everywhere they go. They don't care that much who the Nazis are any more... they want to know who's on their side and who isn't. Do you get it?'

Now the military police officer appeared confused.

'I'll do it myself!' said Mackay.

The Intelligence man walked back to the terrace. Lieutenant Foxe followed. I didn't know whether I was supposed to wait or if I could do what I wanted. I assumed nobody cared. I went on out and headed for Mühlenstrasse. It was quiet. The streets were almost empty. Staying indoors, even during the day when there was no curfew, was still what most people instinctively did. I don't know if there was an atmosphere to pick up, besides the one in my head, but that was probably real enough. There might not be the desperate fear I saw when I left Berlin with Con Cremin. But there was fear. Ilsenburg had seen the Americans and the British. Everyone knew the Russians were different. How different?

As I walked towards Mühlenstrasse, I turned aside and walked to the bridge over the Ilse. I think part of me was delaying getting back to the Yellow House. I would be saying goodbye to Annaliese and Krista. If I hadn't known why I came in the first place, I had even less idea now. This past wasn't much of my past. Before I came back, it felt like almost nothing. A few fond memories and a few less fond. Stirring all that up didn't matter much in my life. I would forget it quickly enough, or at least I wouldn't think about it much. Or maybe I would think about it more than I cared to. The memories I did have of Ilsenburg would be more uncomfortable now. I couldn't feel I'd helped Annaliese by coming either. Once the surprise had gone, I wasn't sure anything else remained. I should have left it alone. I looked down at the river, the bright trees, the backs of the houses. It was still a beautiful place. That had been my first sense of Ilsenburg when I was young. I didn't really know what had happened since. And I didn't want to.

I left the river and I walked across the bridge. There was a man standing at the bottom of Mühlenstrasse. It was the man I had seen on the terrace at the hotel. The long coat. I only really took that in. He was Russian. No, a German who was with the Russians. John Mackay called him a spotter, whatever that meant. He was looking at me with his head to one side. There was a smile, but it came with an expression of something like wry bewilderment. As if he was puzzling out something that shouldn't be. He shook his head, laughing. I didn't know him.

'Well met, Stefan . . . I think. I didn't quite believe it.'

I knew the voice. And only then did I know the man. He was almost bald. His face was thin and lined. The lines were so closely packed together that they darkened the skin in a way that somehow changed the shape of the face. He wore round-rimmed glasses with thick, pebble lenses, yet he still seemed to peer as if he couldn't quite see. He didn't look obviously old, but somehow age hung on him.

'I still wonder if I'm really seeing you at all.'

Reinhard Friesack stepped forward and stretched out his hand.

9

DAS GERICHT
JUDGMENT

Magdeburg, April 1943

Reinhard Friesack had been in a cell in the police station in Magdeburg for three days. No one had spoken to him when he was taken from the Yellow House and driven away from Ilsenburg. They were searching the house. Annaliese and Krista had gone. When he asked questions he was told to shut up. No one had charged him with anything. No one had explained anything. They put him in a cell and locked the door. That was all. He was still in his own clothes. He had been fed. No one had hurt him, though at night he had heard sounds that told him there were other people in the cells who weren't so lucky. Maybe that would come, he thought. If it did, there was nothing he could do. He didn't know what to expect.

Now he would find out.

He was in a bare room that had little light. A dim bulb, a small window. He could hear traffic outside. They must be facing the street. He sat on one side of a table. On the other side was a man in a suit. A round, open-faced man who gave off a strange cheerfulness. It wasn't a hard face. He gave no name, no rank, nothing that identified him. He must be Gestapo, that was all Reinhard knew.

'You know why you're here?'

'No one's told me why I'm here. No one's told me anything.'

'But you know why you're here.'

'My wife ... my daughter ... I left them at home ... when I came back they were gone. Just your people ... police ... searching the house. I don't know why.'

'I'll stop asking you if you know why you're here. You do, so don't waste time pretending you don't. It doesn't help. But you needn't worry about your wife and your daughter. I'm sure they're safe at home now. In fact safer without you.'

The door opened. A man in SS black entered. He carried a file that he put on the table in front of the interrogator. He sat down on a chair beside him. He smiled.

'Ah, Walter, good.'

'I think you know Untersturmführer Laue ... Herr Friesack.

Reinhard thought he didn't. He shook his head.

'My dear Reinhard, surely I haven't aged that much.'

The name was there now. The face came with it.

'It's only five years ... maybe six.'

He did know him. Walter Laue. Fellow theology student. It wasn't much of a memory, and not a good one. He remembered arguments. No more than that.

'Well, we didn't know each other very well. Different circles. And I left in the second year. I wasn't cut out to be a pastor. More important things going on.'

'Herr Friesack doesn't know why he's here, Walter.'

The SS man shrugged and smiled at Reinhard again.

'Four days ago,' said the interrogator, 'in your home in Ilsenburg, you gave shelter to a man you knew was a criminal, a Jew, a fugitive from justice, wanted by the Gestapo ... on the run. You hid him and then facilitated his attempt to escape the authorities by smuggling him to Goslar and on to a train to Hannover. At that time, we might note, opening your home to an enemy of the Reich, a conspirator against the state, you were remarkably unconcerned for the safety of your family.'

'Hugo Weiss was a man I knew when I was training to be a pastor. I hadn't seen him in years. All I knew about him was what I knew as a student. He was a pastor, like me. We were ordained at the same time. He knocked on my door and, yes, he asked for shelter. That's all. Why wouldn't I give him shelter. I knew Herr Laue at the same time. If he knocked on my door, I'd invite him in . . . it doesn't matter that I didn't know him well. If he needed a bed for the night . . . why not?'

'That's very good, Friesack. Very Christian. But you knew the Jew Weiss better than that, I think. You knew he was on the run too. He told you, didn't he?'

'I knew he needed help. I gave him help. I didn't know—'

'Don't lie, Pastor,' snapped the interrogator. 'Think of your vows. We know. We know what he said. I have some of it here . . . you were overheard you see. And sadly, a German's duty to the Führer sometimes comes before . . . other things . . .'

The Gestapo officer shook his head, as if this really was a painful truth.

'What do you mean?'

'I'm sure you'll have time to work it out.'

The interrogator pulled the file Laue had delivered across the desk.

For a moment, in the silence, Reinhard Friesack had lost any sense of where he was. He was at home. He was in the kitchen with Annaliese. There was something they were laughing about. Maybe it was a long time ago. Maybe it was only days ago. Then he was back, looking at the man across the desk, turning pages in the file. Annaliese. He was telling him Annaliese went to the police.

'This is your file,' said the interrogator.

'I didn't know I had one.' Reinhard spoke quietly.

'You'd be surprised, Pastor . . . though I'm not sure you should be.'

Silence again. The Gestapo man turned more pages. He looked up.

'By the way, the Jew Weiss is dead. I don't know if it happened when he was caught, or afterwards. No matter. But if you think there's something useful to be achieved by protecting him . . . there isn't. What would be useful for you, however, is providing information. Since there was no opportunity to interrogate the Jew, the more names, the more contacts, the more detail you can give us . . . the more likely it is something may be said in your favour when you come to trial.'

In Reinhard's head there was still the image of Annaliese. Was it true? It needn't be true. These people would say anything. But how else did they know?'

'Information!' said the interrogator. 'Names! Do you understand?'

'No, I don't. I don't know what you're talking about.'

'You knew Weiss was a Jew?'

'I don't know that I did . . . when I first knew him . . . I suppose he said his family was Jewish . . . or some of his family. He was a student . . . a pastor. I hadn't seen him since I took over in Ilsenburg. What names? What do you mean, names?'

'Weiss was part of the Confessing Church.'

'Yes.'

'So you did know that?'

'I knew five years ago. I'm not part of that. I never was. I'm like most Lutheran pastors. What I do, I do for my faith. I have a church and a congregation. I try to do the work I think God put me there to do. And I take no part in politics.'

'Taking no part in politics isn't something to congratulate yourself on.'

'I don't believe the church and the state should be one thing. That's not an unusual position. It's what most of us believe. That doesn't question our patriotism.'

'It may be up to others to judge that, Pastor. Now, the Confessing Church. You'll know all about it. Anti-German, anti-Führer . . . some might say anti-God.'

'I have nothing to do with the Confessing Church.'

'Was that always the case?'

'Yes.'

The interrogator looked at the SS officer at his side. Walter Laue had done nothing and said nothing. He smoked a cigarette. He watched Reinhard Friesack with a little curiosity, but nothing more. Reinhard was aware of him, but not much more. It was the interrogator who counted. He had to focus on him. He didn't know what to say that would help him. He had to say nothing that would make it worse.

'I think that's true,' said Laue. 'But he had friends who did.'

'Friends you kept in touch with, Friesack, like Weiss.'

'He came out of nowhere. It's years since . . . I didn't even recognise him.'

'Things happen over the years,' continued the interrogator. 'Take the Confessing Church. It starts as a bunch of anti-German clowns who think they have some special dispensation to sit in judgement on Germany's future. They make a lot of noise. They insult their country, their race, and finally their Führer. But what are they? The shite on the shoes of your church. Mostly they can be ignored. Sometimes they need a lesson and we lock a few up. Then there's a war. And Germany's life is at stake. You'd think that would be the time to shut up. But it isn't. They have a mission. The mission now is to fuck their country, fuck their race, fuck their Führer. They're not just a pain in the arse, they're working against Germany. They're plotting with the Jews and the Bolsheviks and every enemy Germany has. Your friend Weiss the Kike is one of them. That's the filth you hide from justice. The cunt who sleeps under the same roof as your wife and daughter.'

Reinhard looked down. He didn't answer. There was no point.

'And it's nothing new is it . . . nothing new.'

The Gestapo man held up the file.

'Over the years, you'd be surprised how many reports have come in about you. There's no shortage of good Germans in Ilsenburg. Even in your congregation. Look at it. Jews seem to have been a speciality. You couldn't keep your job as a teacher because you always had something to say about some fucking Jewish runt. You think no one ever reported it? And you're still at it. You ask the mayor of Ilsenburg to interfere with a police action to clear the last Yids out of the town. How about turning a blind eye? They're not doing any harm. You think you know better than the Führer about where Germany's enemies are? Am I right?'

There was nothing to say. These weren't real questions.

'And what about those golden days studying theology?'

Reinhard didn't ask what it meant, but he looked at the SS man again. He looked only because the interrogator was looking at him too. His turn to speak.

'Well, you didn't choose your friends wisely, Reinhard.'

SS-Untersturmführer Laue gave a more-in-sorrow-than-in-anger shrug.

'I am no part of the Confessing Church. I never was.'

'But you did stand out. Reports come in from all sorts of people. Someone was concerned enough about the outline of the thesis you wanted to write, to send a copy . . . I don't know where . . . but it came my way eventually . . . I passed it on . . .'

Old words came into Reinhard's head. Weiss's words. 'Watch that bastard, Laue. He's a Party spy.' But so what? How did anyone spy in a theology lecture.

Walter Laue reached for the file. He leafed through it.

'Your proposal, Reinhard.'

He read from a typed page.

'Here it is. "The writings of Jewish teachers associated with the Pharisees and subsequently Rabbinic Judaism often have more in common with the words of Jesus in the New Testament than may be assumed. Could it be that although Jesus opposed the views of many of his contemporaries, Pharisaic beliefs varied so much that some were not inconsistent with, for instance, the Sermon on the Mount. I propose to look at similarities as well as dissimilarities between Jesus and other Jewish teachers, especially comparing New Testament and rabbinical parables."'

The SS man sat back and chuckled.

'Jesus the rabbi! Sidelocks? That's quite a thought.'

'That's all it is,' said Reinhard. 'A thought. Academic. Theological. It's not a thought nobody else ever had. In any case, that thesis was never written, was it?'

'No, because you were told to find something else . . . and what was that?'

'This is crazy . . . you're asking me about my theology degree. What for?'

'Luther . . .' Laue turned another page. 'You might think as you were about to be ordained as a Lutheran minister . . . you'd have some regard for Martin Luther.'

'And I don't? What are you talking about?'

The SS man returned to the file.

'You start with a quote from Luther. "Beware of the Jews . . . God's wrath has consigned them to the devil who has robbed them not only of a proper understanding of the scriptures but also of common human reason, modesty, and sense . . . when you see a real Jew you may with good conscience cross yourself and boldly say, There goes the devil incarnate." You go on to take everything Luther wrote in "On the Jews and their Lies" and declare that he is wrong, utterly wrong.'

'I compared what he said in his earlier writings about Judaism with what he wrote later. What he says is so different, that you have to decide where the truth is. There's nothing original in that. Other people have come to the same conclusion.'

Walter Laue shrugged and sat back. He wasn't there to argue.

'You also made a point of walking out of a lecture given by a prominent theologian, Ludwig Müller.' The interrogator was speaking again. 'Along with your friend Weiss and a number of others. You subsequently signed a document that refuted the law preventing Jews from keeping their positions as pastors. You also took a dozen copies of the New Testaments Professor Müller had presented to every student . . . and you deposited them in a dustbin outside the lecture theatre.'

'Why not? The whole church said they were blasphemous.'

'The whole church?'

'A Bible that dumps the Old Testament and removes every reference to it in the Gospels . . . and a man who stands in front of a class of theology students and claims Jesus wasn't Jewish at all . . . where are the pastors who really believe that?'

'Where have you been, Reinhard?' Walter Laue spoke as if he was truly concerned for the man opposite him. 'Do you even know blasphemy anymore? Martin Luther did in his time. Adolf Hitler certainly does in ours. What do you think would be left of your angels-on-the-head-of-a-pin little world if the Jews had free rein to act out their horrible blasphemies? But they won't. Not in Germany. No Jewish master-race here, old friend. And no fools like you to invite them in.'

For a moment Reinhard Friesack forgot where he was. He looked at Laue with a kind of wonder. This was a man who once sat across a table from him in a university library, reading Plato and Aristotle, Augustine and Aquinas, Descartes and Spinoza, Kant and Kierkegaard, reading above all the Books of Moses and the Gospels. Could Laue even believe a word of what he was saying? Before his mind brought him back into the bare-walled room again, the pastor almost pitied him.

The interrogator closed the file, slapping it down on the desk.

'I'm done with you Friesack.' He looked at the SS man. 'You, Walter?'

'I have nothing more, no.'

They both stood. Pastor Friesack looked up at them, bewildered more than afraid now. The direction the interrogation had taken seemed bizarre. It pulled things out of his past that he barely remembered himself. Where did all that come from? How was it that they knew so much about him, and so much about so little?

The Gestapo man gazed down. He took out a cigarette and lit it.

'Don't think that any of us have the slightest interest in what you fucking think, Pastor. What you think about anything. God, the devil, Jews, saints in heaven, choirs of angels, or Martin Luther and your country. That's just a game. That's just to show you we know who you are, exactly who you are. A traitor to your race and a traitor to Germany. In your head and in your Kike-loving heart. You'll be tried tomorrow. In a concentration camp the next day. So God speed!'

The interrogator walked out. Laue gave one last shrug and followed.

Pastor Reinhard Friesack bowed his head. He was trembling. It was fear now, but only in part. He hadn't really been questioned at all. They just spoke at him. The outcome had been decided already. It was a game. The man with no name was right. There was nothing he could do. No one expected him to do anything. Things would only be done to him. Only three days ago he had been at home. He heard himself saying Annaliese's name. Why, Annaliese? He put his hands together. He searched for a prayer. Not for the first time he didn't find one.

*

It was night when the truck arrived at KZ Dora, Nordhausen. Four prisoners sat under the tarpaulin with Reinhard Friesack. Two soldiers sat with them. The prisoners didn't speak. When they tried to exchange a few words, one of the soldiers would bark at them to shut up. There was no real reason for it. The soldiers talked cheerfully enough themselves, as if the prisoners weren't there. They were pleased with a number of things, but mostly with the good luck that had kept them where they were for several months. Girlfriends and food featured prominently. They were less cheerful about the fact that the clock was running down on their present posting. They didn't talk about their next posting, but it was coming. They didn't know where, and as Reinhard listened to them, he could almost hear the word that wasn't spoken in silences between the bits of soldierly banter. As long as it's not Russia. Please God, anywhere else but Russia.

He hadn't seen the other prisoners until he was pushed up into the truck with them. They came, as he did, from the cells in Magdeburg. He saw two of them had received the kind of interrogation he had feared. They were bruised. Their clothes were stained with blood. He had no idea what they'd done and he found he had no desire to find out. It was an odd feeling. He might be sitting beside someone who had done no more than say the wrong thing to the wrong person. He might be sitting beside someone who had done no more than he had in reaching out to help a friend. He might be sitting beside a thief. He might be sitting beside a murderer. It didn't seem to matter. They were all in the same place. They were all in darkness. The resigned nods the four men exchanged expressed only that. It was lesson one.

He presumed they had all been through the same kind of interrogation and trial. He hadn't expected the trial to be pleasant, but he was startled by what it was. Even after ten years of watching what his country had turned into, he couldn't take in the combination of viciousness and slovenliness that was served up across his ten minutes in the courtroom. No one he knew was there. He had no idea where Annaliese and Krista were. He had to believe they were all right. No questions he asked were answered. And he was still struggling with the one thing he had been told, if it was even true, if it wasn't part of the process of breaking him and humiliating him. Had Annaliese told the police about Hugo Weiss? Wouldn't she have known what it could mean? Despite all their differences, despite all the things that had driven them apart, despite her fear of not conforming, was that what it came to? He couldn't know now. For where he was, there was no space for truth. It was a world of lies.

Five minutes before he went into court Pastor Friesack was approached by a man in a black gown who said he was defending him. The man was drunk, even at ten in the morning, and told him his only option was to plead guilty and apologise. It might be a good idea to claim the Jew Weiss had threatened him and his family. Whether it would reduce the sentence or not was anybody's guess, but it was worth a try. When Reinhard asked what the charges were, the lawyer told him it didn't matter. There were a lot of them and since they were all versions of the same thing, it would only piss the judge off if they started quibbling. He was guilty before he walked into the courtroom, otherwise he wouldn't be there, so the worst thing he could do was to fuck with the judge. And that was it. That was the whole defence.

There was only one witness, the Gestapo officer who interrogated him. The man still didn't seem to have a name, only a rank, inspector. He outlined the arrival of Hugo Weiss at the Yellow House and Reinhard's part in hiding a Jewish enemy of the state. He referred to past evidence of political and religious (so-called) anti-German activities, which were outlined in the prisoner's statement. He was the prisoner already, not the suspect, and not the defendant. Since Reinhard had not given a statement, he told his lawyer he wanted to see it. The lawyer wasn't keen but eventually he did ask. The judge said as the statement was the Gestapo report, it consisted of a full record of Reinhard's interrogation. Why did he want to see it? Had he been lying? Or was he suggesting the inspector was lying? The response from the courtroom to that was laughter. No copy of the report was forthcoming.

When Reinhard was told to stand up, he thought he was going to be questioned and would have at least some opportunity to defend himself against the wilder accusations of conspiring with Germany's enemies. In reality, the trial was over. For the next five minutes he listened as the judge shouted at him. The short version was that he was a fucking disgrace to everyone, to his wife and daughter, his profession, his church, his country and his God. Men like him, overeducated, privileged, pampered, corrupt were a rot at the heart of all Germany held sacred. If he thought the fact that he had been given an Iron Cross in 1918 was something the court would take into account, he was mistaken. It only made his betrayal of his nation and his race worse. He was shitting in the face of better men who had died!

Reinhard Friesack was sentenced to imprisonment in a concentration camp. He wasn't sure how long the sentence was. The lawyer said these things were open-ended but with a bit of luck someone might look at it again in five years. Things would ease up once the war was over. As Reinhard was led to the cells his lawyer, who was anxious to get to a bar, told him to keep his chin up. It could have been worse. Under the circumstances, he really hadn't done so badly.

So it was that Pastor Friesack found himself making the journey to the labour camp at Nordhausen. No one told him that's where he was going, but he knew from the two soldiers who were guarding him and the other prisoners. It wasn't a long journey. He knew the town. He would be south of the Harz Mountains, but Ilsenburg would be there. That bright world would continue. He almost wished they were taking him further away. It might make the pain easier to bear. He would see the hills. He would know the mountain paths that led home.

The truck stopped and started as it went through several sets of gates. It was dark now. Reinhard could see little through the flaps of the truck's tarpaulin. Barbed wire and fence posts. Then the outline of wooden huts. Men in uniform. There was little noise. The voices of guards and soldiers. The barking of dogs. And then the four prisoners were being pushed out of the truck. There was an open door and a bright light in a hut's wooden wall. The pastor saw the shapes of other huts and then above them, high above, the white cliff-like face of a hill with a black opening below. It was there for seconds as he was shoved through the hut door.

Inside the hut were guards in several varieties of uniform. Some in SS black, others in Wehrmacht field grey. Two prisoners in stripes stood at a long table. The four men lined up in front of the table. A guard told them to take their clothes off. They hesitated, bewildered by the sudden light, unsure what was being said. The guard shouted again. Two of the men began to undress. Reinhard was barely taking in where he was, let alone what was happening. The voice he heard was just noise. His head was spinning. He didn't see the SS man who walked up to him until a hand slapped hard against the back of his head. He stumbled but he didn't fall.

'Strip, you fucker! Strip!'

The four men stood in a line, naked. The uniformed prisoners gave them each a set of the same striped clothing uniforms and told them to put them on. Behind the table an SS man with a clipboard shouted out the men's names, followed by a number. No one seemed to expect any response. Most of the guards in the hut took no notice of them. They sat on benches, smoking and drinking beer.

'Barracks!'

Three guards got up and walked across to the four men, now in the striped uniforms. There were no weapons, except in holsters, but they all carried sticks.

'Move it! Now!'

One of the guards stared hard at the prisoner who had clearly received a heavy beating in the cells at Magdeburg. The prisoner looked down to the floor.

'Kneel down!'

The prisoner seemed to be used to orders. He knelt immediately.

The guard took his pistol from his side. He held it against the man's mouth.

'Suck on that, cocksucker.'

There was laughter from the other guards.

'I said suck on it, queer.'

The prisoner opened his mouth. The guard pushed in the tip of the barrel.

'I tell you what I'm going to do, shall I? Every time I see you I'm going to stick this in your gob for you to suck. And one day, one day, I'll get so excited by what you're doing, that I won't be able to control myself. I'll have to pull the trigger. You will never know, as each day goes by, which day will be your last.'

There was more laughter and a round of applause from the other guards.

Then they were outside again. Reinhard was separated from the other men. He followed a guard towards one of the wooden huts that stood in rows on either side of a road. There was no light. Night in the camp meant strict blackout. The guard opened a door at the front of a hut. Reinhard walked in. The door shut behind him. For a moment he stood in complete darkness. There was a voice.

'Welcome, my friend. I'm glad you could join us.'

As his eyes adjusted, Reinhard could make out a man in the striped uniform that was now his own. There was a little light from the pale night beyond the windows. The man was short, thin, old probably, at least older than Reinhard. He walked into a space that was filled by rows of two-tiered bunks. Only the first few were visible, but they were all the hut contained, except for the men in them. The smell hit his throat. Bodies and filth and sweat and somewhere decay. Reinhard had smelled it outside but the night air and the cold stone of the cliff dissipated it. It was strong here. It was the smell of his new world. Soon it would be his smell.

'Here,' said the man. 'Nice position by the door. Handy for the shit barrel.'

The man walked forward and pointed at a lower bunk. Reinhard stood looking at it for a moment, then sat down on the edge. It was narrow and hard. All that lay on the bare boards were a couple of pieces of cloth that looked like sacks.'

'You won't sleep tonight. A few days and you'll sleep like a baby.'

The man walked away, through a door by the entrance to a hut. Whoever he was, he had a status of some kind. A few planks of wood gave him his own space.

*

In the dark hut, Pastor Reinhard Friesack could feel the men around him. No one spoke. Some were sleeping, but he could sense that many were not. He couldn't know how many men were in the hut, but a lot. There were snores and there were rasping breaths that told of sick lungs and there were sometimes cries, maybe from the kind of dreams that had to go with this place, maybe from men lying awake. He wouldn't sleep, the man was right about that. For now he couldn't imagine how he would ever sleep again. He closed his eyes and found some of the prayers that had eluded him for a long time. They came, perhaps, because he truly needed them.

'O my heavenly Father, God and Father of our Lord Jesus Christ, God of all comfort, I thank you for revealing to me your dear Son, Jesus Chris in whom I believe, whom I have preached and confessed, whom I have loved and praised, I pray, my Lord Jesus Christ . . . take my soul into your hands. O heavenly Father–'

Reinhard stopped. The man was back, crouching by the bunk.

'Time for a prayer, pastor? Is that it?'

'Don't worry, I'll keep them to myself.'

'For the people who put you here, no doubt.'

'I wouldn't say I'm up to that yet.'

'That's something.'

'Is it?'

'Prayer won't keep you alive.'

'I don't know. Hope might . . .'

'Pastor Reinhard Friesack.'

'Yes. You?'

'Hans Gürtner. You do know there is no hope, Pastor?'

'We'll have to disagree. It can always be found somewhere.'

Reinhard listened to his own words. He spoke them but did he speak them honestly? He knew Hans Gürtner didn't think so. He felt the man was testing him.

'I can hear your breath, Pastor. I know the sound. Not good. But not TB . . .'

'The trenches . . . gas.'

'It'll be harder then. Or does it matter? Are you here to live or die?'

'Why would I want to die?'

'Some do, some don't. I don't mean you don't care one way or another. That comes later. I was in Dachau before I came here. There's whole barracks of priests and pastors there. It's like a faculty of theology. Most of the ones I met just wanted to get out at the other end in one piece, but some . . . some arrived with a different end in view. They were there to bear witness and to carry that witness all the way to St Peter's pearly gates. It's not hard to do, but if you're one of those, get on with it and don't cause trouble for the rest of us. Equilibrium is survival. Those who seek death can have it, but I say unto you only the living bear witness for the dead.'

Hans Gürtner smiled.

'I'm not here to make some point,' said Reinhard, '. . . any point at all.'

'There is only one point. Living. If I keep repeating that, you should too.'

'Thank you, Herr Gürtner. Usually I'm the one who does the sermons.'

'I only give it once, Pastor . . . So, why are you here?'

'I gave a bed for the night to a man the Gestapo were after.

I won't say I wanted to. But I did . . . I didn't think anyone would even know . . . but someone . . .'

Reinhard left any more words unsaid. He still couldn't say them.

'Someone often does. And no . . . you never quite know who . . .'

Gürtner made Reinhard Friesack uncomfortable. He saw too much.

'That was it, anyway.' Reinhard kept talking, simply to move on from the thought he didn't want. 'They came the next day. And then . . . I realised I'd been watched for years . . . the smallest things I'd said . . . arguments with people I worked with . . . conversations I had at college, that I couldn't even remember . . . it wasn't just that I'd done something . . . broken a law . . . it was all about what I thought.'

'That was your first mistake, Reinhard . . . thinking . . .'

'Should I have seen it coming?'

'I'd say so, but I guess you shut your eyes to make sure you didn't.'

Reinhard didn't answer. That was true too.

Outside the dogs were barking. It was the only sound.

'Have you eaten today, my friend?'

'No, I haven't. It doesn't matter.'

'Eating always matters. It matters more than anything else. Whatever shit they throw at us, you take it. If it's bilge water with a lump of pork fat in it, take it. If it's bread so hard you need to break it up with your fist, take it. If it's a raw potato that's going to fuck your gut, never mind, take it. So take this. And eat it.'

The man pushed a piece of bread into Reinhard's hand.

'Mostly they feed us something. It's never enough, but it has to be.'

Reinhard bit into the hard, tasteless crust. It was sour in his mouth.

'But now you're here, Pastor, thank your God for your luck.'

'I'm sorry, Hans. It'll take me time to find a new sense of humour.'

'That too, but it's not a joke. You won't think so tomorrow when you walk outside and maybe they send us off to unload bodies for the crematorium, for this world has its hierarchy. You're at the top. The top of a dung heap is still the top.'

Reinhard struggled to swallow the grey mulch in his mouth.

'We're all dispensable, but not in quite the same way. The Jews are at the bottom. If we're here to be worked to death, they're not. They're here to die. It's that simple. That's why they're here. Most of them are in the tunnels . . . inside the mountain. You'll see it tomorrow. They're hollowing out the whole fucking hill to build factories for bombs and rockets and whatever. That's what it's for . . . there are caves and galleries for kilometres . . . all huge . . . I guess they started as mines . . .'

'Yes. I know the Harz. I'm from–'

'You're not from anywhere now, Pastor. You're only from here.'

Gürtner's words were sharper. Reinhard found himself nodding.

'The Jews are in the hill. They dig there. They sleep there. Mostly they don't come out, except as bodies. Every morning there's a cart full of them. Next up are the Poles and the Russians. The Russians are mostly soldiers. They don't die at the same rate as the Jews, but some of them are in the tunnels as well, so they cop it fast enough. Outside are the barracks. Like I said, all dispensable, but if you can keep up with the work, you've got a chance of lasting . . . as long as you can. Mostly you're talking about Germans. You've got thieves and murderers and conmen who weren't sharp enough to get into the SS, queers who didn't have friends in the Party, and an assortment of anti-socials, which just means people the police didn't like the look of. Then, sitting atop this unprepossessing shit heap . . . you have us.'

'And what are we?'

'Red triangle, politicals. When you've been here a while, Pastor, you realise what a privilege that is. Our shit food is just a little less shitty. Our shit jobs are just a little less likely to kill us. They even talk to us. But there's a price for privilege.'

'And what's that?'

'When they ask . . . we do what needs doing . . . to help them run the camp and make sure the wheels turn smoothly. You put on an armband and you're a Kapo. You keep people in order. You see work gets done when the guards can't be arsed to supervise it. We don't point out troublemakers unless we have to, but we find our own way to make sure there isn't any trouble. And with that comes the extra bit of food and even time off. You can even complain. Someone might listen. You watch a lot of people die. But in your head you bear witness . . . and you organise.'

Reinhard took in what he could. Yes, it was a whole world.

'You have a brain, Pastor. I like that. Use it to survive.'

'And what are you organising for?'

'The end. Because it will come. It doesn't matter who's alive when it does, it only matters that some of us are. Between prayers, you might want to think about all that. The nights are long, Reinhard Friesack. There is nothing to do but think.'

'You're right. I wish you weren't. Thinking will be the most painful . . .'

'No. The longer you last, the easier it gets. Learn the right lessons.'

'And what are the right lessons?'

'The first is hate. The second is hate. And so are all the others, Comrade.'

10

ZWISCHEN DEN ZEILEN
BETWEEN THE LINES

Ilsenburg, June 1945

I stood with Reinhard Friesack by the old bridge over the Ilse, at the town end of Mühlenstrasse. We stared at each other. I think we were still ghosts. Him to me and me to him. After the first words, we were both waiting for the other to speak. If starting a conversation with my cousin Annaliese had been difficult ten years on from my last visit to Ilsenburg, it was effortless next to finding something to say to her husband. Whatever journey had brought Reinhard home in the company of a lorryload of Russian Intelligence men, it must have begun in the concentration camp where he had spent the last two years of his life. How are you? That would normally have been innocuous enough, but under the circumstances it seemed to carry more weight than was helpful. How the fuck do you think? I might have been tempted to give that reply myself if I'd been through what he had. Not that I knew what he'd been through. I only knew that I probably couldn't even guess. Anything more specific would make me sound like an idiot. When did you get out of the camp? How was the camp? Was it hard? So, you made it out alive, anyway! However careful, however bland any real words I came up with might be, they would have begged every question and sounded almost as absurd as all the warnings in my head. I don't know why it didn't occur to me just to ask about Annaliese and Krista. He must have been to see them. That was now. That was positive. It should have been safe ground. I think somewhere, without realising, Annaliese's silence about him steered me away from that. But Reinhard saved me the trouble of finding something pointless to say. He snapped a question at me.

'What are you doing here?'

Not an unreasonable question, but definitely curt. I gave my briefest version of the Irish legation in Berlin, the end of the war in Bavaria, and my RAF flight home. He looked at me more quizzically than I expected. It was an explanation I had off pat by then. It didn't really amount to much. But he still seemed curious.

'It's very good of the British to let you play the tourist again.'

He laughed, but I got the distinct impression I was being quizzed.

'I was hanging about . . . they were glad to find me something to do.'

There was a smile and a shrug, a little bit warmer.

'I'm asking for a friend, you might say, Stefan. My captain wanted to know who you were. The Russians don't have a lot of time for neutrality . . . which isn't so surprising. An Irish embassy in Berlin during the war wouldn't be anything you'd want to say too much about. Captain Sokolov assumes you're something to do with British Intelligence. I'll tell him you're not, but he won't take any notice.'

'I'll be gone today, later . . . I'm only saying goodbye to Annaliese.'

'I won't see you again then. I have to get back to Magdeburg.'

We stood in silence. Out of words, it seemed. Reinhard gazed past me, along Mühlenstrasse. His face was softer, more thoughtful. I don't know if he was looking at the shop and the house that were once Clara Bloch's. Maybe he was.

'I have an office in Magdeburg. In the old police station. It's where the Gestapo took me when I was arrested. I don't like it but I like the point it makes.'

He looked back at me and laughed.

'Not a job I'd have seen you doing, Reinhard. Teacher, pastor . . . there are times I'd choose either of those over how I ended up . . . a policeman . . . whatever.'

'I just come under whatever, Stefan.'

The explanation, such as it was, told me he would explain no more.

'But it was good to see you. I mean that.'

He shook my hand. I don't know why he felt he had to say he meant it.

'You've seen Annaliese . . . and Krista.'

It was a statement of the obvious, but I wanted to end with something lighter, something easier. The conversation had been hard work. It wasn't lighter.

'I've seen them.'

The words were clipped and curt again. They came without a smile.

'Have a good journey home, Stefan Gillespie.'

He looked at me hard for some seconds, then turned and walked away.

The Yellow House was always quiet. There was no reason why it should feel exceptionally quiet now, but it did. That's to say even as I walked into the hall I was conscious of it, almost tangible. Maybe there was already a silence Reinhard Friesack had left in my head. If there was he had left it behind him here too. In the kitchen Annaliese sat at the table, staring into space. Her hands were clasped in front of her tightly, so tightly that her knuckles were white. She seemed unaware of me as I approached her. I felt no greeting was required.

'I've seen Reinhard,' I said.

Annaliese nodded. She looked up. She gave a smile that was almost wild and for an instant her face was nothing like her. I thought she was going to laugh.

'Yes.'

That was it. I don't know what I expected, but more than nothing. Her husband, the father of her child, a man she thought must be dead, had come back. I couldn't know what had gone on between them before he disappeared into a camp, but whatever problems they had would surely fade in the light of a kind of resurrection. Whatever was wrong before, even if it was still past mending, wouldn't Annaliese feel something like happiness and relief and thankfulness? Nothing. What I saw instead was confusion and fear and a sense of helplessness.

I drew up a chair and sat opposite her.

'He's with the Russians . . . in some way, working for them . . .'

'Yes.'

She reached across the table and held up a thick, folded cloth. Deep red.

'He brought this. That's all.'

Annaliese opened several folds. I saw a flash of yellow.

'He said we should hang it out of the window tomorrow.'

I turned down another fold and laughed.

'He's a lot more practical than I remember . . . it sounds like a good idea. I don't know what he does, but if he's around he'll make things easier in Ilsenburg.'

'That's what Oskar Mommsen told me, Stefan. We should all be relieved . . .'

Annaliese's voice was a kind of monotone. Words, just words. She certainly wasn't relieved.

'Look, whatever happened between you and Reinhard...'

'You think this is about some kind of marital tiff, is that it, Stefan?'

'That's not what I mean.'

I think it probably was what I meant, even if I imagined it being at the higher end of such things. Marriages went that way. I didn't say I thought Reinhard must have had a lot more on his mind than what he thought of his wife in a concentration camp, but I didn't. On that front, I couldn't have been more wrong.

'We have to get out,' said Annaliese, 'Krista and I.'

'What do you mean?'

She was looking at me now, talking faster.

'I just assumed it would be all right. I knew people were leaving, but where would we go? We have the house. That's all there is. Everyone's afraid of the Russians... we all know that. I've heard the stories. But it's done, isn't it? No more fighting. No more killing. Even the Russians... it won't be like that. Most people are going to stick it out. It's our town... and it's still here. And I have my papers... from the British... I was in the Party, but only because I had to be, because I had to be after Reinhard went. We had to survive then as well. I have my papers and...'

Annaliese took a folded sheet from her pocket and held it up.

'Category V. I got my review... my Category V!'

She thrust the document at me with a kind of desperation.

'He said it didn't matter. The Russians wouldn't care what it said.'

I knew she meant Reinhard, but that's all I knew.

'I thought he was dead,' she said coldly, 'because I heard nothing...'

I don't think it would have been fair to say that Annaliese wanted her husband dead, but whatever was wrong, dead seemed to be better than alive.

'Krista's terrified . . .'

'Of the Russians?'

'Not the bloody Russians. Him, for God's sake!'

The words were almost screamed at me.

'She won't come out of her room. I don't know what to do.'

'I'm sorry, Annaliese. You seem to think I understand. I don't.'

She sat back and took a breath. She needed to calm herself.

'He thinks I betrayed him.'

'When?'

'The man he hid . . . the pastor . . . the Jew. He thinks I went to the Gestapo.'

I don't know what she expected from me, but if my first response was surprise, my second was that I didn't know enough to know anything at all.

'You look as if you think that might not be a crazy idea, Stefan.'

'I don't know what to think, Annaliese. Should I say it is crazy?'

'It doesn't matter whether it's crazy . . . it's not true.'

'Then you need to tell him. And now you can.'

That sounded simple. Nothing about any of this told me it was.

'He's believed it for two years . . . two years in a camp. They told him it was me . . . the SS, the Gestapo. Where do I find someone to tell him they were lying?'

'He knows you. Isn't that where you start?'

'I don't know what he knows now. I don't know him, that's certain . . . We've only spoken for minutes and all I got was a wall. He came here to see Krista, that's all, though all he's done is terrify her . . . as for me, he just told me the Russians will start all over again . . . an investigation. The papers the British gave me . . . I might as well use them to light the fire. My investigation begins with me informing on him.'

I had met Reinhard Friesack only for minutes too, but I felt the wall. Whatever he believed lay buried behind it.

'So, we have to go.'

Annaliese stood and paced the room, purposeful now.

'This Russian border runs this side of Bad Harzburg. So close. It must be now. The British are moving out and they're moving in. This is the only time . . .'

She stopped, looking down at me.

'You have to help us, Stefan.'

I hadn't seen it coming. I should have done.

'I don't know what I can do, Annaliese. I've seen people going . . .'

'The trains have stopped now,' she said. 'There'll be no more until they have a checkpoint. The last bus went yesterday. They won't drive them back in case the Russians confiscate them. There's no one with a car . . . no one who would help.'

I stood up slowly, mainly for something to do. I was short on advice.

'But you have a way out, Stefan.'

'What do you mean?'

'You'll go with the British MPs, won't you? Or your Lieutenant Mackay. Isn't he going to take you back to Goslar? He must be a friend of yours by now.'

'I don't know that friend's the right word.'

I took out a cigarette. It wasn't easy. She thought I could do something.

'Oskar said the Russians are already stopping people and asking for papers. The British said it wouldn't happen till midnight, till tomorrow, but it's happening already. But they can't stop a British jeep. You can take us, can't you? It's easy enough. We'll bring almost nothing, I promise. Wouldn't the lieutenant do that? A favour. It costs him nothing. When we're across, we can get out. We can walk.'

Annaliese was smiling, talking fast, and persuading herself it was true.

'I don't know if it's that simple, Annaliese.'

'Why not?' She was pleading now. 'Not just for me, for Krista!'

'I don't know what they'll do . . . I don't know what Reinhard wants from me . . . but it's not nothing at all . . . please understand . . . there was hate in his eyes.'

I didn't have anything to say. How real were her fears outside her head? Part of me thought she was blowing it up too much. But what did I know?

'I'll go down to the hotel and find out what's going on.'

'You'll ask him, Lieutenant Mackay? I think he'll help . . . if you explain.'

She was still persuading herself. I wasn't convinced John Mackay would help. He had no shortage of regulations to say why he couldn't. As for explanations, I didn't think the story would appeal to him much. My cousin needed to get away from Ilsenburg before the Soviets closed the border because her husband, who had just survived two years in a Nazi concentration camp, believed she betrayed him to the Gestapo. They all told him she did. But it was grand because she said she didn't.

'I'll talk to him,' I said.

Annaliese sank back on to the chair, emptied. She hadn't persuaded herself at all. As I left, she was staring into space again and fingering the red flag.

At the Landhaus Zu den Rothen Forellen, the British MPs were moving house. It was happening quicker than they'd expected, but their orders were through. The Russians were there and if it was hours ahead of the deadline, it made no difference on the ground. A Union flag still fluttered over the hotel entrance but the half a dozen soldiers drinking Oskar Mommsen's beer in the bar were Russian. The MPs were loading up two Bedford lorries. Along with the crates and bags and tents and weapons and ammunition boxes, were several crates of the same beer the Russians were now consuming. I couldn't imagine either army paid him for it. As I came into the bar, the hotel proprietor was handing several foaming glasses to his new customers. He looked harassed. He took a cigarette and lit it as I approached.

'Is Lieutenant Mackay about?' I asked.

'He's with Lieutenant Foxe and the Russian . . . Sokolov . . . Solokov?'

I laughed. 'You'll get used to it.'

'Well, I've been questioned by the Americans, the British . . . now our Russian friends. I'm used to it. And they all need someone who knows the town.'

He turned back to the beer tap as another soldier demanded a drink.

John Mackay came in from the terrace.

'You ready, Stefan. We're going sooner rather than later. There's no point quibbling over the bloody deadline. They're here. Let the buggers get on with it. If you give me an hour . . . once our convoy sets off . . . we'll bid Ilsenburg farewell.'

I didn't think all that brusqueness boded well for extra passengers, but I was there to ask. I went outside with Mackay for a cigarette. I got the reply I expected.

'You think I'm running a fucking taxi service for Germans who don't much fancy the Soviets. That would be some job, old man, I can tell you. I'm afraid your cousin should have thought about all that earlier. It's bad enough driving you!'

He grinned as he said it, but it was no joke. There was no argument.

'And she's on the bloody denazification list! Do me a favour, Stefan.'

'Category V?'

'Never mind the category. No fraternisation. Them's the rules!'

I nodded. I didn't think the result would really surprise Annaliese.

'Are you waiting here?'

'I need to go back... pick up a few things... and say goodbye...'

'I'll pick you up, Stefan.' He shrugged. 'And I'm sorry, old man.'

He wasn't sorry at all, but he was polite, at least for an Ulsterman.

The atmosphere in the Yellow House had changed completely when I returned. The news I brought was no surprise. I was a vain hope, that was all. Annaliese had decided to act. Krista was in the kitchen, packing food into a rucksack. Her mother was looking at a map spread out on the kitchen table. She spoke brusquely now.

'Never mind. It didn't work. We can't wait. We're going.'

'You are?'

'No trains. Roads blocked. That's it, isn't it?'

'Pretty much.'

'But not all roads. This border they're giving us... it runs... I don't know exactly... but west of the Brocken and the Ilsetal. Bad Harzburg is in the British Zone, so is Torfhaus. So the road between the two is as well. Somewhere just east of that... coming out of the Harz... you walk across a field or through a wood or over a stream... I don't know... you've gone from one side to the other, right?'

'I guess so.'

'And from here . . . the Ilsetal . . . to there . . . nothing but woods and hills.'

I nodded. That was true.

'So we walk.' She turned to Krista. 'Don't we?'

'We walk,' said Krista, smiling. An uncertain smile, but still a smile.

Annaliese folded the map.

'And we know the way through the forest . . . every way there is.'

'Do you think you could do it?'

'Why not? I think we have to do it now. While they're all busy with each other. The Russians and British . . . doing whatever they're doing. Don't you think?'

'I think . . . if you want to do it, yes, sooner not later.'

Krista walked out. I heard her going upstairs.

'Why don't you come with us, Stefan?'

I laughed. It was unexpected. And it wasn't a joke.

'I don't think that's a good idea, Annaliese.'

'Probably not . . . but I . . . I'm only saying it's easy . . . I don't know . . .'

'There's nothing I can do,' I said. I didn't like the way that sounded. Yet, there was nothing I could do. They were her forests, her mountains. 'I'm sorry.'

'I thought you'd make sure the British didn't send us back.'

It was said with a smile, but it wasn't a joke either.

'You can be pretty sure they won't.' What did I really know?

'I don't know that I can be very sure of anything, Stefan.'

There was a blast from a horn outside. I knew it was Mackay.

'My lift.'

Annaliese nodded. She took my hand and kissed my cheek.

'Take care then, Stefan. I did think one more adventure . . .'

She walked to the hall. I followed her, picking up my case.

239

'Krista! Stefan is going now!'

After a moment Krista appeared and walked downstairs.

'At least you met your godfather . . . once.'

She laughed. Krista reached out her hand. I shook it. An odd gesture, but as this girl I didn't know smiled, there was at least something there. I thought of that Sunday by the font in the Marienkirche. Between then and now, nothing. I didn't think Annaliese ever believed there would be anything. A godfather was simply a role to play and be forgotten. Looking back it struck me that the only person who cared then was Reinhard Friesack. The man they were running from.

I dumped my case in Mackay's jeep. As he drove away, I lit a cigarette.

'They're going to make a run for it,' I said. 'Through the forest.'

'Very doable if they know it, I reckon.'

'They do. Both of them probably. Like the back of their hands.'

'They don't want to hang about, though . . .'

'My cousin knows that.'

The jeep approached the end of Mühlenstrasse and the house that stood as a reminder of Clara Bloch. It would be one of my last images of Ilsenburg. I don't know why that made me do what I did. If anything, it said something about my cousin Annaliese that was unlikely to make me feel like helping her at all. I knew that wasn't how Clara would have seen it. Even that shouldn't have been enough. But it was.

'Fuck it. Stop, will you John?'

'What is it?'

'I'm going with them.'

'Is that a good idea?'

'No. Probably not a good idea at all.'

*

It was night. It was black outside but it was even blacker in the cave beside the River Ilse. It was the cave where, once upon a time, Annaliese Hoffman took her Irish cousin and tried to frighten the life out of him by scattering the roosting bats. The bats came and went through the course of the night. I could hear them. They moved in dribs and drabs, with no more than a quiet twittering and a little movement in the air above me. The cave was Annaliese's idea but leaving the Yellow House that night was mine. It was hard to know what the next day would be like. There was still a curfew and being out in the streets before it was over was a risk. You would be stopped and questioned. With Russian soldiers on the street that morning, it would have meant an end to the journey before it had begun. It seemed sensible to leave in the evening, before the curfew, and to disappear. Nothing could be done at night, even by two people who knew the paths along the river and up into the woods and mountains beyond. But the journey could start at dawn. And it should start unseen, with no one knowing anything about it.

So before the curfew, Annaliese and Krista and I left the Yellow House, with little more than a suitcase and two rucksacks could hold. I left Reinhard Friesack's red flag hanging from a bedroom window at the front. It seemed likely it would be some time before anyone realised the house was empty. We crossed Mühlenstrasse and walked to the back of the mill. We followed the river out of Ilsenburg, avoiding the road. We walked beside the river and over the wooden bridge that led to the cave. In the cave, we sat in the darkness. We didn't speak. We waited for night, then lay on the ground and tried to sleep. I don't suppose one of us did. A long night. It was full of memories, comfortable and uncomfortable. I imagine it was the same for Annaliese, though she probably had darker places to avoid than I did.

As for Krista, she was a mystery. I had barely exchanged a dozen words with her since I got to Ilsenburg. When the dawn first showed at the mouth of the cave, and the last flights of bats came in to roost, we were glad the night was over.

We came out of the dark as it was getting light. We sat by the Ilse and ate some bread and an apple. It was an odd feeling. It must have been for Annaliese too. However many times she had walked this way, that day she walked it with me, twenty years earlier, had to be in her mind as it was in mine. There were three of us that day too. It seemed easy enough not to speak as we finished eating and set off. Krista was keen to get started. And she did speak now. She talked about the route we would take almost with enthusiasm. Suddenly she had something to say. It was clear she knew the valley and the mountains just like Annaliese knew them. It was a place she was at ease, at home. And now she wanted to be up and doing.

The sun came up quickly as we walked along the river. The aim was to follow the Ilse some of the way up towards the Brocken and then turn west, moving along the slopes of the mountains, through woods and pasture and heathland, following tracks that would take us from what was now the Soviet Zone into the British Zone, crossing where there were no roads or barriers or checkpoints. There was a map, but Annaliese and Krista didn't have to look at it.

For a while, our only words were about the way we were going. Few were needed. It was only when we stopped to turn away from the river that Annaliese said anything more. We knelt and drank from the Ilse with cupped hands and filled our water bottles, I think as much to carry some of the Ilse with us as because there wasn't water along the way. And then we walked away, leaving the Ilse behind. Krista stepped ahead, always in front, as if determined not to look behind her. Only Annaliese turned back to look at the river. I thought she probably had a prayer in her head.

As she caught up with me and we walked on, she spoke quietly.

'I know you're thinking about another time . . .'

'I guess it's hard not to.'

We moved on together. Krista was some way ahead, making a pace we didn't need, but I thought only because she was enjoying it. Even looking at her back, there was a difference. If she was quiet again now, there was something more alive in her today. This was her place, it didn't need saying, as it had been her mother's when I first knew her. And just as it was hard not to remember that other day along the Ilsetal, it was hard not to see Annaliese in Krista. Whatever Krista carried it seemed a lighter load. For the first time I heard her laugh, as if shaking off something dark. Leaving Ilsenburg didn't trouble her now. She wanted to go.

'I do think about Clara,' said Annaliese, not looking at me.

I didn't know if she was waiting for an answer. I didn't have one. For better or worse, her husband had come back from the dead but I knew enough to have no doubt that the best friend of Annaliese's childhood wouldn't. And so did she.

'It's not what I wanted . . .'

I didn't ask her what she meant. Adolf Hitler, the last ten years of her life, or everybody's life, the new world she believed in too, the rubble that was all that was left of it, a world war, cutting off her oldest friend, looking the other way at what happened to her, pretending nothing had happened, her husband disappearing into the camps, the fact that everything didn't go along the way it was meant to and she had to open her eyes. Maybe some of that, maybe all of it. Whatever was in Annaliese's head, she could have.

I was happier with my own memories of Clara, such as they were.

'No one could do anything, Stefan.'

'No.'

The sun on my face seemed to say that wasn't true. I think she felt it too.

'It all seemed right . . . we all believed . . . can you understand that?'

'No. I can't. But I don't have to. I'm glad I don't. Let's leave it at that . . .'

There was nothing else to say. If she wanted a few words of absolution, I couldn't offer them. But my own memory held me back from the judgement that could have come so easily. I was standing on O'Connell Bridge. Another river. And a woman I loved. Before the war, but not before I had seen some of what was happening in Germany. She had seen more, much more. She was Jewish. That didn't mean a lot to me then, though it had made a mark on my life that would stay with me. I took in only so much. She had taken in everything. So when she told me she was leaving Ireland, and leaving Europe, I wanted to make her stay. I still don't know if what she felt for me would have made her stay in different times. I always wanted to believe it might have done. She saw past love. A long way past.

'This isn't Germany,' I had told her. 'It never will be.'

'I don't know what it is, Stefan,' she replied.

'You're Irish,' I said. 'You don't mean that.'

'And you're a policeman. If they sent you to Clanbrassil Street in a few years, to fill a truck with Irish Jews and take them to a camp – would you do it?'

'That couldn't happen.'

'Couldn't it? You didn't answer my question.'

'I hope I'd refuse . . .'

I was trying to be honest. I think I didn't sound it.

'You hope?'

'I wouldn't do it. Don't you know that?'

'You'd walk away?'

I remembered those words. Walk away. She smiled as I said it.

'You think walking away would be enough, Stefan?'

I left my own uncomfortable memories where they were and looked out at the wooded valley that was as bright and green and full of light as it had been the first time I saw it. The river sparkled and gurgled as cheerfully as ever. There was a kind of energy that pulled us all on, I think. It wasn't my journey. I had nothing to run from. But my cousin did. And the further the forest paths took us from Ilsenburg, the stronger she seemed to get. I could feel it in the way she walked. I knew her own memories were far more uncomfortable than any I might have but the day seemed to be lightening her load too. The sound of birds and moving water, the patterns of leaves and sunshine, the air that had its own sharp scent. After the panic that filled the Yellow House, it was a peaceful walk to freedom.

We came out of a belt of trees to a patch of heath where several paths met. Ahead of us, Krista stood with two men, talking. So many hours had gone by without seeing anyone, that I felt the same shock that I knew Annaliese felt. We had left unseen. We had walked all morning unseen. It made us careless.

'I think she knows them,' said Annaliese.

'We should have been watching . . . she shouldn't have been so far ahead.'

'Let's see who they are, Stefan.'

Annaliese carried on. She had the confidence now.

The two men were barely men at all. They could have been seventeen or eighteen, not much more. And Krista did know them. Annaliese at least knew who they were. And they were doing what we were doing. There was a gang of them making their way towards Bad Harzburg too. The others were further ahead. I don't know what particular reason they had to leave the Soviet Zone, but they said there were more people making the journey. No one expected the new border to be a real border. Everyone was used to papers being checked and rechecked. That was how it was. It might be worse than before, and the Russians might have a reputation for being bastards, but one bit of Germany wasn't going to be any different from another bit of Germany five minutes up the road. Some people had already left, but few imagined there was much urgency attached to getting out if you wanted to. Now word had spread that it wasn't going to be like that. I knew from Mackay it was true. If you were in the Soviet Zone, the Russians had a view of Germany that was all their own. The Soviet Zone was where you would stay.

Meeting two friends had perked Krista up even more. The fear I had seen in her had been pushed away, at least a little. The journey had done that in part. Now the sense that there was a kind of adventure in progress energised her. The boys certainly echoed that thought. Why didn't we go with them? We could catch up with the others. They knew the way to go. The Russians would never see them. Krista was sold. I definitely wasn't. I could tell Annaliese wasn't either.

'I think we'll go our own way, lads . . . keep them guessing, eh?'

A joke felt like the best way to deal with it.

'Good luck!'

The two boys walked off, chattering loudly and cheerfully. The way the chance meeting had happened was a warning to us. If we had been invisible, we needed to stay invisible. There could be no doubt we were better off on our own.

'We should take any path . . .'

I looked at Annaliese. She laughed.

'... that's as far away from theirs as we can make it.'

She looked at the tracks that branched away through the trees. Above us, to the south, was the Brocken and the slopes of lower hills rising south and west. There was scrubby heathland around us, spreading on either side of the track the two boys had taken. A little below us was a darker, thicker stand of trees.

'The Mölkenhaus?' It was Krista who spoke.

Her mother nodded. She pointed ahead, towards the trees. We set off walking again. Krista stayed closer. Instinctively we moved more cautiously.

'What is the Mölkenhaus?'

'We used to camp there,' said Krista quietly. 'With the Hitler Youth and—'

'Never mind what happened then! Forget about it. It's done with.' Annaliese seemed to want past memories erased.

We walked on. A moment later Annaliese broke the silence.

'It's a barn ... that's on the other side of this wood. They used to bring the cattle there for milking when they were up on the high pasture. It's not used now. It's just a bit of meadow among the trees. It's nowhere in particular but there's a track to the road to Bad Harzburg. Somewhere that must cut across this border ...'

'Wherever that is,' I said. 'We can't see it, can we?'

'We keep on till we know we're in the British Zone. It won't be so far.'

It sounded simple. But I was uneasy. The presence of other people wasn't helpful. How many were there? Would they draw attention to themselves? I knew from John Mackay that the Russians were serious about their border. How far they would take that and how quickly they would move was the unknown.

'When you know we're close we'll have to rely on your instincts and keep going, as you say. What we don't know is what the Russians are doing. Roads are blocked already, we know that. But are they anywhere else? There's part of me that thinks once we get to where we cross, it might be better if it's dark. We won't be able to see, but if there's any kind of surveillance . . . no one's going to see us.'

'From the Mölkenhaus to the Bad Harzburg road isn't much more than a kilometre. That road must be in the British Zone . . . it runs straight into the town.'

I nodded. It had all gone very smoothly. The last stretch might not.

'If the place is empty . . . we could wait there till dark . . .'

We walked on for almost an hour. The brightness of the morning had gone. There was cloud over the mountains. There was a breeze now, cooler. The weather seemed to reflect the way all three of us felt. At least for me, the ease with which Krista had walked out of the trees and straight into two other people nagged insistently now. We couldn't take it for granted we were alone. And suddenly it became clear that we weren't. I heard the noise of an engine, close at hand.

I stopped and held up my hand. I saw Annaliese had heard it too. Without a word we moved off the track, into the trees, still thick and dark. We listened. There was the sound again. An engine racing. And voices. Men shouting. Not far, but far enough to be indistinct. Were the voices Russian or was that my imagination?

'The Mölkenhaus,' whispered Annaliese, 'I think it's from there.'

'We need to know who they are,' I said. 'Can we see . . .'

She nodded. She didn't like the idea any more than I did. She gestured to Krista to stay where she was, then moved forward, threading her way through the pines. I followed in her footsteps. We didn't walk far, but we walked so slowly that ten minutes had passed before Annaliese raised her hand, then crouched down, almost lying on the ground. I sank beside her. We inched our way forward.

We were looking out across a wide stretch of pasture, full of summer flowers. On the far side of the field was a big, high-roofed wooden building. In front of it were two vehicles. One was the now familiar ZIS, the other a truck. Russian soldiers were unloading boxes from the truck. No doubt about the voices now. Several men were standing in front of the Mölkenhaus, shouting and pointing upwards. I could see two soldiers on the roof, struggling to hold something up.

'Well, we won't be holing up there . . .'

'What are they doing?'

'I think putting up an aerial . . . some sort of lookout?'

We lay where we were for several minutes, watching. There was no point watching. I think we kept doing it because we didn't know what else to do. Then Annaliese started to slide back among the low branches. I did the same. We turned and crawled until we felt safe, then stood and made our way back to Krista.

We sat among the trees, subdued in comparison to the way we had set out along the Ilsetal that morning. Krista had already withdrawn into herself again. That indeterminate, almost painful fear that I had sensed in her from the beginning was there again. Not only there again, but deeper, I think because she thought she had escaped it. I was little help. I didn't know where we were. I didn't know which way to go for the best. We had negotiated a maze of tracks. Short of knowing we had to go west and keep going west I could offer nothing at this point. But Annaliese could. The presence of the Russians was a shock, but she absorbed it and moved on. They were in one place. They might be in other places. But they couldn't be everywhere. It was a statement of the obvious, but we needed the obvious stated. We were close to the British Zone now, very close. Wherever the line ran through all these forests and fields, it could be barely a kilometre away.

'We have to leave the paths. It's always a risk, even if you know the woods. When you get in among the trees it's hard to know which way to go. The thicker they get, the worse it is . . . you can go round in circles . . . but this is OK.'

'So where do we go?'

Annaliese took out the map. The first time she had.

'We want to get away from here, as far as we can . . . in the time we have. We use the trees to keep out of sight . . . and to guide us. Where we are now is near the edge of this wood. If we'd stayed on the track we'd have come to the Mölkenhaus. Not far from where we were watching. If we go the other way, we reach the edge further along. There's a long slope down to a stream. It's pasture. But the line of the trees runs along the top. I don't know how far, maybe three, four kilometres. We follow that. Open fields on one side but we can't be seen. Then somewhere, when we're far enough away, we turn . . . and we walk across those fields . . . and that's it. If it's best to wait till dark . . . we can hide among the trees . . . then do it.'

I looked at the map as if it told me what she said was right.

'A lot of empty space . . . if we keep out of sight, I can't see why not.'

A plan pulled us all together. We moved through the pines and within half an hour they gave way to thinner, brighter woodland. There were beeches again now and the way was easier. We had put distance between us and the Russian post. And then, as we emerged from the trees to see the green, open pasture sloping away, the sun returned, low in the sky. That was welcome. Less welcome was what we were looking at across the fields. If there was a question about where exactly the border between the Soviet and British Zones ran, we had an answer. Below us, several hundred yards away, stretched a line of barbed wire. It wasn't a heavy obstacle. Two strands of wire supported at intervals by timber tripods, but it was something to cross and it stretched along the valley bottom in both directions.

'That's quick work,' I said. 'They're not messing about, are they?'

'It's not so bad, is it? I mean not so hard to get over it . . .'

The words were for Krista, who was staring at the wire, shaking her head.

'No, it's not so bad. I'd say it's just been run along from the back of a truck. There's not much holding it up. We'll cope. And at least we'll know we're across.'

I thought that might get a smile of some kind. It didn't.

We followed the line of trees for another kilometre or so. Then we stopped. There was no sign of the wire running out but we were well away from the Russians at the Mölkenhaus now. And Annaliese thought we shouldn't go any further north. There were forest roads that way. We already knew the Russians were using them. This would do. This would have to be it. We would wait till it got dark. Then we would go. As Annaliese and Krista sat looking out across the fields I stripped boughs from the beech trees, as big as I could manage and as big as we could carry. They would be heavy enough, thrown across the loose barbed wire, to flatten it.

And when I'd done that, I sat under the trees too and watched the sun go down.

The darkness we were waiting for was coming but it didn't come in time.

The calm of evening and the emptiness of the fields below us lasted for an hour, perhaps a little longer. With my back against a tree I think I was dozing off. It wasn't that anxiety didn't still hang over us but we had been walking since just after dawn. I think Krista heard the dogs first. She stood up suddenly. Then we were all listening. It was hard to say how close it was. I thought not so very close. But what did that mean? And then I realised the noise wasn't only coming from one direction. Behind us, to one side? How far? Were they coming our way?

'Don't do anything yet,' I said. 'Wait . . .'

'Wait for what?'

'We need to go together, Annaliese . . .'

At that moment, further along the line of trees, hundreds of yards away, there were people running. Four or five, I couldn't see. They were racing down the slope towards the wire. Now there was an engine roaring. There must have a been a track because right behind them came a Soviet truck. It was already moving past them. It would reach the wire before they did and it would be waiting for them.

'Krista!'

Annaliese shouted. Krista was running. Out from the trees, down towards the wire. It was panic, blind fear. But nothing was going to stop her and nothing was going to stop her mother. Now we were all running, the three of us. I don't know if the soldiers in the truck were even aware of us. They were standing in a line, waiting for the runners who had now slowed to a halt, beaten.

Krista reached the wire and somehow she was over it. She fell for just a moment as she cleared it, then picked herself up. She looked back.

'Run!' screamed Annaliese. 'Run! Just go, Krista!'

And Krista turned and ran on.

As Annaliese reached the wire she stumbled. I was beside her. I took her hand and pulled her up. There was blood. From her arms, her legs, I don't know. But the wire was holding her clothes. As she struggled it held her tighter. I trod the wire down with my feet I grabbed her coat and tore at it, trying to pull it off.

'Get the coat off! Get the fucking coat off!'

'I can't, Stefan! I can't get . . .'

The dogs seemed to come from nowhere. There were two of them, black Alsatians. They stood in front of us, barking and growling. Daring us to move.

Two Russian soldiers were walking toward us. In no great hurry. One held a rifle.

'Hoch!'

We both raised our hands.

11

TODESMARSCH
DEATH MARCH

KZ Dora-Mittelbau, Nordhausen, April 1945

American guns, they said. Everyone said. Louder and closer every day. They weren't German guns, that was the joke. The German guns were fucked, they didn't have any ammunition, and the people they had left to fire them were fourteen-year-old kids. The jokes in the camp were more hopeful. The end wasn't just something to whisper about in the barracks at night, you could hear it. And you could see it on the faces of SS men. They walked around doing nothing, as they always did, but they carried their anxiety with them. Where they'd normally take a whip or an iron bar to a prisoner who stood still for even a moment when he should be working, they stood still too. And they listened to the guns as everyone did.

There had been weeks of work that went on even at night, loading trucks with the machinery that was being pulled out of the factories and the assembly lines inside the mountain. It was not often that Reinhard Friesack was inside the hill, but everything that could be taken away had to be dismantled, everything that could be kept from the Americans, every piece of machinery that could be used somewhere else to make bombs and rockets. The work was as pointless as it was backbreaking. The factory installations inside the hollow mountain were vast. Getting them out was almost impossible, however many men died doing it. And die they did, as they always had. But the V2 shells and the combustion units and the fuel tanks and the hydraulic presses and the gantries and the girders mostly stayed where they were, broken and battered, but immovable. As for what the scientists and the engineers got out onto trucks, the question wasn't so much how to get it all to its destination, as where the fuck that destination was. It was a joke even the Wehrmacht and SS drivers shared with the prisoners who loaded their trucks. The Americans and the British were pushing in from the west, the Red Army was racing from the east. The Thousand Year Reich was running out of Germany.

Suddenly there was no work. There were no more lines of trucks. The civilian managers and scientists and technicians who had been supervising the dismantling of equipment were gone. There seemed fewer guards outside the wire.

Bodies had been brought from the mountain that morning but they lay in rows beside the narrow-gauge rails that carried them out. There were no orders to bury them. There was a silence over the camp that Reinhard had never known during the hours of daylight in the two years he had been there. The only sounds were the different registers of thunder that came, ever louder, from different American guns.

An SS sergeant ordered Hans Gürtner and Reinhard Friesack to the camp administration block, through the inner gates to the outer compound where the German offices and the SS barracks were. As Camp Elder, Ältester, and Camp Clerk, the Schreiber, they were the two most senior prisoners. Gürtner was already expecting the news they received. Liberation would come but it would not be yet.

'Dora-Mittelbau is be evacuated. Your cooperation will be required.'

There were two men in the office. SS-Untersturmführer Merkle and SS-Hauptscharführer Brauny. It was Merkle, the lieutenant, who delivered the news.

'Can I ask where?' said the Camp Elder.

'It will begin today with the evacuation of Soviet prisoners. Other prisoners will leave in batches, from here and from the sub-camps. You will ensure that order is kept. You will appoint kapos to supervise the columns of men while marching and for the freight cars that will carry them to the final destinations.'

'Do we know where we're going, Untersturmführer?'

'It need not concern you Ältester.'

Reinhard watched the two officers. Did they even know?

'Other camps, though?'

'Yes. Destinations may change depending on the conditions . . .'

Hans Gürtner nodded and smiled. No more information. Conditions meant whether the tracks had been bombed, whether the camps had been bombed, whether the camps would even be in German hands by the time they got there.

'But there will be trains?'

'By train, yes.'

The SS man closed a notebook he had written nothing in. He was done.

'And what about food?'

The SS lieutenant shrugged.

'My concern is the transport.'

The other SS officer spoke.

'There will be something, Gürtner.'

'Something is always better than nothing, Hauptscharführer.'

The lieutenant walked closer to Hans Gürtner and Reinhard Friesack.

'Let me make something clear. The job is to get the prisoners to the other end. There will be a count on departure. You will keep that count, Schreiber.'

'Yes, Herr Untersturmführer,' answered Reinhard.

'If there are problems with the sick or there are those who can't keep up with the march, they will be dealt with as required. Those numbers you can remove from your list. Any attempted break-outs will be dealt with the same way. Clear?'

Reinhard nodded.

SS-Untersturmführer Merkle stepped back and addressed both men.

'Anything serious in the escape line will naturally incur more serious consequences. If men go missing from a column or a freight car, the kapo in charge will be shot. If prisoners try to escape in significant numbers, you will be shot, Schreiber, and then you, Ältester. Do your job . . . and there will be no problems.'

As the two prisoners walked back through the inner gates, Hans Gürtner stumbled. Reinhard caught his arm. The Camp Elder took a deep breath. He coughed as he leant up against the Camp Clerk, walking towards the barracks. Reinhard could see that the coughing was painful. It had been like that for weeks.

'You knew about this?' said Reinhard.

'I thought . . . maybe. I wasn't sure. Brauny said something . . .'

'What's the point?'

'How long have you been here?' As Gürtner coughed he laughed.

'I know,' said Reinhard. 'They don't need a point.'

The next day there were no jokes. The fact that the American guns were so close was hard to bear. Days. They were only days from the gates. The thunder, as it moved towards the camp, had let them hope. They should have known better.

A column of some four hundred men, marching four abreast, moved away from the parade ground that stood between the barrack blocks and the white face of the Kohnstein and out through the camp gates. Reinhard Friesack left behind the wire that had held him prisoner for two years. With him walked the man who had done more than anyone to keep him alive through those years, the Camp Elder, Hans Gürtner. They walked at the head of the column, just behind SS-Hauptscharführer Erhard Brauny, the Transportführer. Gürtner moved stiffly. He was sick. He had been sick for some time. But he still had to lead the way. Six kilometres. He could manage it. And then the train and the corner of a cattle truck.

The column was flanked by SS guards and kapos. Each prisoner carried a piece of bread and some meat paste, or something that had been connected to meat at one point in a long journey. The something that was better than nothing. Some had a blanket, though too many didn't. They wore the thin striped uniform that was all they had. And they tried to march as they made their way past the rusting carcasses of rockets and rocket engines and fuel tanks that lined the approach to the camp. The debris of the wonder weapons. You needed to show you were up to it. And for a short time at least they felt clean air. Beyond there were green fields and the Harz forests. Their first destination was a railway junction, Niedersachswerfen, six kilometres away. There was relief at that. With prisoners who had reached the camp recently from the east, as the Russians advanced, came stories of hundred-kilometre marches that distributed their dead along the way. But they had a train. The names of endpoints in the prisoners' heads were just names. Bergen-Belsen, Sachsenhausen, Neuengamme, Ravensbrück. Whatever the name, the same place.

There was no train at Niedersachswerfen. There were tracks and there was the mud that lay on either side of them. Heavy rain had begun not long after leaving the camp. The men were drenched. Somewhere ahead there was a station and a platform and maybe some shelter. They couldn't even see it. The prisoners lined up on either side of the rails and sat in the dirt. The rain continued to fall.

It was four hours later that the train arrived. The locomotive pulled a long line of open box cars. There would be no shelter. They would travel as freight. And when the train finally pulled up, they realised they would not travel alone. Of the twenty cars, fifteen were already full of prisoners picked up from the main camp at Nordhausen and sub-camps along the way. Only four were empty. And into those the four hundred men who had marched with Reinhard Friesack and Hans Gürtner had to fit. There was a lot of shouting from guards and SS men. Erhard Brauny, the senior Transportführer knew nothing about the extra prisoners. This was meant to be his transport for his prisoners. And when the argument finished, and the SS major he had been shouting at told him to fuck himself and left, it still was his transport. Except that now he had a thousand prisoners instead of four hundred.

Behind the engine, the first car was a closed cattle wagon. It carried Brauny and most of the SS guards. It had a roof and it had room. For the rest, including the wagon Reinhard Friesack was in with Hans Gürtner, there was neither shelter nor room. The prisoners were packed so closely together that they could only stand, crushed into each other. There was no space for the small privileges that could mean life or death in the hierarchy of the camp. Gürtner was now Ältester for the whole transport. It gave him the privilege of being shot if anything went wrong.

It was another hour before the train left Niedersachswerfen, heading west along the southern slopes of the Harz Mountains toward Osterode. By now it was dark. The rain had stopped, but every man was wringing wet. They propped each other up but could barely move. Reinhard held the Camp Elder up. It was hard to fall in the press of bodies, but if you did, it would be even harder to fight your way up. You would need strength if you weren't to be trampled by the other prisoners. Gürtner's breathing was heavy and rasping. He was shivering in Reinhard's arms. It seemed like he was sleeping at one point, but it wasn't sleep. He was falling in and out of consciousness. When he came to he was wracked with pain. He was struggling hard to breathe. Reinhard could do nothing but hold him.

'Take the food. In the morning. Pocket. Before someone else . . .'

'Tomorrow you'll eat the bloody food. If I have to force it down!'

Hans Gürtner laughed. For a few seconds the pain had gone.

'They'll let us out in the morning, Hans. Air! We just have to hold on.'

The Camp Elder's head slipped forward. He was unconscious again.

It was a long time since Reinhard Friesack had shed tears. They were one of the first things he learned to dispense with on his arrival in the camp. They served no purpose unless you wanted to devote the little energy you had to their cultivation. Where there was all too much to weep for, there was soon nothing to weep for. So it was almost with surprise, as a little light from the eastern sky crept into the freight car, that the Camp Clerk felt tears in his eyes. His eyes somehow knew the truth before his head grasped it. The man his arms were still holding up was dead.

*

Hate did not come easily to Reinhard Friesack. It didn't come when he entered the concentration camp. At first, if he felt something like it rising up in him, he pushed it away. He still had enough faith for that. But hate came eventually. And when it did it came as something else, or at least it became the foundation for something else. He would reflect in later years that however the words that ended that first conversation with Hans Gürtner stuck in his mind, and they always would, hate was simply a shorthand. It meant using what had happened to you. Using it to stay alive first of all. Using it to stop up the well of compassion that could have filled your being and neutered your will. Using it to harden your softest instincts. Using it to dispense with the idea that any sacrifice you could make was anything other than nothing. Using it to look forward not backwards. Using it to see an end and to know that end was worth living for. Using it to know that your survival was not essential, but survival itself was. Using it to wait, not for vengeance, or justice, or peace, but for the destruction that would make everything new. For the end that would be a beginning. For an apocalypse without God.

All that would take time. It started on his first morning in the camp As light came he saw that the building he was in was far bigger than he had realised. The rows of tiered bunks that filled it contained hundreds of men. And as loud voices sounded outside, they all got up and moved mechanically to the doors, now pushed open. There was little said. The routine had a soulless quality that Reinhard felt immediately, so strongly that he was already a part of it. He shuffled like everyone else. There were a few nods, a few curt greetings from those in the bunks around his. Then they were outside in a wide, flat expanse of beaten earth. He did what everyone else did. He stood in a line. All around similar lines were forming as hundreds of men emerged from the wooden huts that lined the parade. He took in the barracks and wire and the white cliff at one side, the Kohnstein, with a road and a narrow railway line disappearing into a high black hole cut into the hillside.

In front of each group of prisoners stood a prisoner in the same striped outfit, wearing an armband, most of them shouting continually. One of them peered at the ranks from Reinhard's barracks, screaming out the same commands as the others.

'Square up! Square up! Ready for the call!'

Reinhard looked at the man next to him. He whispered a question.

'What's the call?'

'Roll call.'

'Who's he?'

'Franck. Block Elder, for our barracks.'

The shouting stopped. An SS officer walked towards the massed ranks. Behind him were other German soldiers and SS men. There were dogs too, barking constantly. With the officer were two prisoners. The three men stood on a small wooden platform. Reinhard recognised one prisoner immediately as Hans Gürtner. Older than he had looked in the darkness the night before. Very thin and very tall.

'Hans Gürtner . . .'

'Camp Elder . . . our block, our man! We're the lucky ones!'

The other man grinned and winked. People laughed here, thought Reinhard. Would he ever? This world was real now. It would become his world. Everything terrible, and he knew there would be terrible things, would soon become ordinary.

The prisoner next to Reinhard tugged at his arm, pulling him aside. Through the ranks came two prisoners pulling a handcart. They passed Reinhard, heading to the front row. There were two bodies on the cart. They tipped it. The bodies fell.

'Died in the night. They have to be counted too. Quiet!'

It was only now, as Reinhard Friesack surveyed the lines of prisoners in front of other huts that he saw several more bodies lying in front of the first rank of men.

A call went out along the line, echoed and repeated.

'Stand to attention!'

The other prisoner who stood with Hans Gürtner and the SS officer stepped forward. He carried a heavy, battered book, like an accounts ledger. He opened it and started to call out names. As he shouted the names, the replies came. Some came sharply and crisply, some slower, weaker. And even as the long roll call began, some of the kapos walked through the lines of men in their charge, watched by the SS guards who were now walking up and down too. Every so often men were pulled out to the front. These, as Reinhard would learn, were prisoners who looked too sick or too weak to work. There was no privilege in being excused a labour detail. For most it was the beginning of the end. For Reinhard, all that was to come. He waited a long time for his name to be called. He would wait a long time every morning, every day in the slow years that followed, every day in every weather, in snow, in rain, in blistering heat, hour upon hour standing to attention. It was meant to take a long time. It was meant to humiliate and punish. And it did.

Food that first morning was more dry bread and coffee that was just dark, tepid water. His first job was to take the handcart and the two dead men from his barracks to the crematorium. It was a harsh introduction to his new life. He didn't know Dieter Franck was doing him a favour. This was light work. It wouldn't always be like that. The three men wound their way through the camp to a concrete building with a high chimney. They dropped the bodies outside. There was already a line of a dozen others. As they turned away a tractor arrived. It pulled a trailer that was heaped high with more dead bodies. Twenty, maybe more.

'Jews from the mountain,' said one of the prisoners. 'They have their own roll call. In the tunnels. Light load today. Still, at least they see a bit of sunshine.'

Reinhard realised he was meant to laugh. He felt a surge of anger. It wasn't what he was used to. He wanted to hit the man and hit him very hard. That was compassion. No good to anyone in this place. He would find that out, of course.

For the rest of the day, Reinhard was left with the other two prisoners and the handcart. They cleared rubbish and filth from around the barracks. They emptied the overflowing barrels that acted as latrines at night. They went back to the crematorium and took piles of prison uniforms to a washhouse next to the kitchen block. These were clothes from the bodies that had been burned that day. They were rags, filthy and lice-ridden, barely holding together, but they would be cleaned and used again. Reinhard touched the rags he now wore himself. They were thin and worn, clean now but with stains that would never wash out. The man who wore them before him would be dead. Dead when? Maybe only days earlier.

The days would get harder, much harder for a time, but as Reinhard Friesack hardened himself to that as best he could, in his head as well as his body, there would be help. The man he spoke to that first night, Hans Gürtner, the Ältester, the Camp Elder, would offer more than lessons in survival, he would be the reason Reinhard lived. There would be no compassion in that, no idle sentimentality, no energy wasted on life for life's sake. Hans Gürtner would have his own reasons for keeping Pastor Friesack alive. Eventually those reasons would be Reinhard's too.

As Camp Elder, Hans Gürtner was the most important prisoner in the camp. He sat at the top of a dung heap, of course, but it was still the top. He was the essential link between the Germans who controlled Dora-Mittelbau and the prisoners who not only filled it and provided the slave labour on which it fed, but also ran it. The SS delegated their system to the inmates. They watched it and wound it all up, but since the machine was there to break the people who lived and died within it, there was no better way to break the men you were working to death than to make them work each other to death. While you looked on, the Camp Elder facilitated all that. He was the managing director picked by the SS board. He chose his own management team. And all the way down the chain of managers, the first rank kapos and the second rank kapos and the third rank kapos did what they needed to do to stay alive longer than the prisoners below them. Those were the wages. That was the bonus. Some enjoyed doing what that involved, some didn't, but they all did it. And without realising it was happening at first, Reinhard Friesack became part of it. He climbed the management ladder. Hans Gürtner decided he should.

He had been in the camp for almost six months when the Camp Clerk died. He was already working as one of the Clerk's deputies by then and Gürtner gave Reinhard the job. After the Camp Elder, it was the most important role in the pyramid of prisoners. Paperwork mattered. The chaos of the camp was always ordered in its own special way and it was paperwork that brought that semblance of order. There were lists to be drawn and redrawn, every day and every night.

Lists of living and the dead. Lists of the work details. Lists of the tradesmen and the potato peelers and cooks and body burners. Lists of those who formed up each morning to work in the camp and those who went out to take the trek to the factories and the sub-camps. With the Camp Elder, the Clerk was the one who sat with the Camp Commandant and the SS officers and the factory managers who came in from outside to pay for their slave workers. It was the Clerk who instructed the kapos on the work their crews would be doing. It was the Clerk who counted the dead at the end of each shift and filled the gaps to keep the numbers up. He recorded those who went into the hospital block and those who came out. Very little paper was needed for the second list. Above all, the Clerk was the prisoner who stood on parade every morning and called the long roll of names.

It was also the Clerk who recorded what food came into the camp and how it was distributed to each hut. It was the Clerk who saw it disappear as it made its way to the people whose survival depended on how much or how little reached them. First, before anything got through the gates, the SS and the guards took what they wanted. Next the supplies were parcelled out by the Camp Elder and the Clerk to the senior kapos. And if the Camp Elder was fair in what he kept and what he passed on, there was little he could do to ensure the kapos did the same. By the time the rations arrived at the individual barracks, there was often less than the minimum that was supposed to keep a prisoner alive. And even that corruption wasn't there by chance. Venality was wired in. You couldn't challenge it. If the Camp Elder lost control of the kapos, he was replaced. If he lost his authority in the eyes of the SS, he would find himself back at the bottom of the heap, in a system where losing what power you had was unlikely to end well. The kapos had to have authority. Since they had whips instead of shovels, they had to be allowed to use them. If some used them more than others, so what? Brutality and corruption couldn't be checked where brutality and corruption were the cogs and wheels of the machine. If you had enough authority, as Hans Gürtner did, you might check it now and then. If there were kapos who took things to excess, you could find ways for them to die. That was easy enough. No one cared. And for a time the odd unexplained death might hold the worst of the worst at bay. But it was a fine line, and maybe a futile one, when the worst was just the ordinary business of the camp.

Reinhard Friesack, who had been a good teacher and not such a bad man of God, was a very good Camp Clerk. He earned what passed for respect from the Camp Commandant and the SS administration, who saw him as the man to go to to solve problems. And there were plenty of problems as the camp grew in size and turned from a facility for manufacturing bombs and weapons and aircraft parts into an underground centre for building the rockets and missiles, the V1s and V2s that were going to win the war, even as it was being lost on every front. That was what was happening inside the mountain. It meant more and more slave labour but also ever more civilian engineers and technicians. They all had to work together. The slaves whose lives were expendable and the valuable scientists and engineers. Managing that wasn't something the SS were very good at. They weren't very good at managing very much. Hans Gürtner and Reinhard Friesack turned out to be a lot better at it. They could manage the forced labour crews and dispose of the dead slaves in ever-increasing numbers. It was a growing task since more people died making the things than they ever killed. They could keep up with the demands of the Reich's scientists for more skilled workers too. And a bit of skill mattered. It could keep you alive. They also managed, quietly, a level of sabotage that made the already erratic wonder weapons even more unreliable and ineffective.

By this time the knowledge that wonder weapons or no wonder weapons, Germany was already beaten, was no secret anywhere, even in a concentration camp. And the point of surviving, that was about something other than simply staying alive, was suddenly more than a conviction. It was a real thing. The purpose that Reinhard Friesack had absorbed from Hans Gürtner was a living thing, or almost. And it was probably true to say that Reinhard had absorbed it rather than learned it. The Camp Elder talked to him a lot. But he rarely talked about his beliefs except as the fight that would come to make a new world. The old would have to be destroyed. What mattered was only that there were people who came out of all this with the determination to destroy it. The old world created this place. The camps were not some strange perversion of that old world, they were its foundations laid bare. Those who had tinkered at the edges, the social democrats and the liberals, were as guilty as the rest. Who cared what they cooked up with money and power and land to give a nod to something better? They handed Germany to Adolf Hitler as surely as the army and the factory owners. They were too weak to stop it. But how could they stop what they were always part of? For those who came out at the other end of a descent into hell, the way would be open to change everything.

Reinhard Friesack didn't lose God straightaway. He tried to hold on to his faith. At first he thought it was his faith that would keep him alive. And if it couldn't he wanted to believe that whatever sacrifice he had to make would be worthwhile. But something about sacrifice began to eat away at him. It was resurrection that mattered, not death. He knew that as a priest. But what was that resurrection? He didn't know now. He wondered if he had ever known. And then he wondered if it mattered. Because what did it do? What did it do in this place?

His faith was fading. It was painful but after a time he felt he didn't want to stop it fading. It was almost an impediment. There was a resurrection. Hans Gürtner saw it. In its own way maybe it did come out of death. The death of the old and the creation of the new. The fact that the Camp Elder was a communist was not something that troubled Reinhard when he told him. Why should it? He didn't have much time for communism, but he had no fear of it. And Gürtner never spoke about it much in the early days. But little by little Pastor Friesack came to feel that this man had a faith greater than his own. There was no God in it but there was something else. There was a reason to come out of hell alive and to do whatever it took to make that happen. To live in order to destroy the old and then to remake it. But that was still to come. Death hadn't finished with the men from KZ Dora-Mittelbau, even as the war was ending all around them. It was still waiting. It had snatched away Hans Gürtner now, after all his long years of resistance, and as Reinhard Friesack took his place on the transport as Ältester, he was in no doubt that death's work was far from over. All that darkness should have felt much further away by now. The Germans were on the run everywhere, weren't they? Wasn't there hope? Yet the purposelessness of the journey they were on troubled him. He didn't know what death had planned. He knew of no how or when or why. But Dora-Mittelbau had honed his instincts, like any hunted animal. He smelled it. Death was still very close.

★

UNITED STATES NINTH ARMY
WAR CRIMES BRANCH

GARDELEGEN INVESTIGATION

STATEMENT #12 REINHARD FRIESACK

19 APRIL 1945 RESUMED FROM 18 APRIL 1945

INVESTIGATOR CPT. SAMUEL G. WEISS

On the second night the train was attacked by American fighters. It wasn't heavy bombing. Maybe a parting shot after some more important raid. I think three SS men were killed and five prisoners. But the engine was damaged. We were stuck there. I don't know where. I think Brauny said somewhere outside Osterode. So we unloaded and sat there. Brauny went back down the line to find a phone and arrange for another locomotive. When he told me that, I think I must have laughed. He left me with the usual admonition. Tell the bastards anyone who tries to run will be shot. And if your kapos don't keep them in order, you'll be shot. I think it was the last time he said it. I don't know whether I was still useful to him or whether he was starting to feel he couldn't be bothered. Whatever it was he had as a heart, it was as if it just wasn't in it anymore. That didn't stop the killing, though. Because men took their chance. There weren't so many guards now. When dark came, escape looked easy. It never was. Doing what you were told was the way to stay alive. Doing it fast and doing it well. It didn't work a lot of the time in the camp, but it worked better than anything else. Even on the train, you could run and die or keep going and live a bit longer. How much longer?

Remarkably, Brauny did come back to say a locomotive was on its way from Osterode. It was hard to believe. He was surprised himself. 'They can't find the petrol to get soldiers to the front but they've got a fucking engine for you cunts!' And so we set off again. Most of the time I couldn't see where we were going, but I glimpsed a few stations through cracks in the freight car walls. Seesen. Salzgitter, Braunschweig, where we somehow passed through another air raid untouched. By now I was sure the Transportführer had no real idea where he was going. He said Sachsenhausen to his men. When he saw me watching him, he shrugged. He had to tell them something and Sachsenhausen was out there, east and north. It would do. But my senses cried out we were going nowhere at all.

Sometimes when the train stopped, they let us get out, sometimes they just left us in the trucks with the piss and the shit and the bodies. There were always a couple more. Enough men had died, just because they died, or because they were killed making a dash for it, that there was soon room to sit down in the cars. But there was no food. None for days. The weakest weren't crushed to death anymore, they starved. Hauptscharführer Brauny gave me the job of organising the burial parties. We buried the ones who died on the train and those who were shot trying to escape. There were more and more of those as we went along. When we stopped it was often in the middle of nowhere. There would be forest close to the tracks. A lot thought it was worth the risk. There it was, in front of them. Run and you might get away. But not many did. If they got out of range of the bullets, I imagine they believed they'd made it. Free. But they underestimated the German spirit. Out into the fields and the woods, from every holt and heath, came the shopkeepers and farmers, the teachers and town councillors, the old men of the Volkssturm and the teenagers of the Hitler Youth. They called it zebra hunting. And the zebras they didn't shoot or beat to death, they brought back to the train for Brauny's men to shoot. They were duly shot and I saw they were duly buried. By this time the Transportführer had ceased caring how many men he was going to get to the final destination. I'd say he already knew there might not be any final destination. He no longer asked me to number the dead men. But I had them all. I have them still.

The train had been travelling for six days when it reached a station called Mieste. It would be the final stop. We were unloaded for the last time. The tracks ahead had been destroyed. It was anybody's guess when the line would be repaired. We were disembarked. Soon after we arrived another train pulled in behind us. There were six cattle trucks. The smell that came off them, even before the doors were opened, choked us as we sat in rows along the track. And we were used to those smells. Our own freight cars had been our latrines for days on end now.

When the cattle-truck doors were pulled back, the prisoners who emerged were skeleton-like in their filth. We were healthy by comparison. They came from the hospital block of a Hannover labour camp. Some could only crawl out from the darkness, tumbling to the ground because they were too week to stand. I don't know if Brauny gave the command, or whether it was just an instinct for economy of effort that meant no order was needed, but even as prisoners fell to the ground, SS guards walked along the row of cattle trucks and shot those who couldn't stand up. The ones who could tried to stand to attention and hoped they looked stronger than they really were. We watched with the bitter equanimity we learned long ago.

An hour later I was directing the burial parties to dig in a field next to the station.

For two days we sat at the station. On the second there was food. The turnips were few but there was no shortage of boiled water. We buried more prisoners from the hospital train. Fifty of them. None of them had needed shooting.

On the third day Brauny gathered us together. I think we were around 1500 in all. There were more guards now. Along with the SS, a dozen Luftwaffe soldiers had arrived from a nearby base. We were lined up in columns and each prisoner was given a couple of potatoes. Those who couldn't walk were put on horse carts.

We marched along a main road. Brauny gave me the usual instructions for the kapos. Order. Straight columns and keep order. No one was to leave the line. If you needed to piss, you pissed as you marched. Our destination was the town of Gardelegen. 1 kilometre. There would be shelter. A roof over our heads. An empty army barracks would house us. We would be dry. There would be more food too.

I passed this on to the kapos, who passed it along the column. Some, I could see, felt easier. The pace of the march even picked up. I simply did what I had done for two years and followed the orders I was given. I didn't feel much easier myself. But I never allowed myself to think further than I could see. That wasn't very far.

There was shelter in Gardelegen. There was food, more food than any of us had seen in a long time, bread that was fresh and soup that had something in it. We were at an army cavalry school in the centre of the town. There were only a few soldiers left in it. We had the stables. The horses were long gone, but they left their hay and straw. It was the best shelter any of us had known in years. It was dry and warm, and we could barely remember softer beds than that horse fodder gave us. The word went round, I don't know where it came from, that this place, the Remonte School, now had the status of a hospital. A great red cross would be painted on the roof to let Allied planes know. When the town surrendered, as it had been agreed it would, American doctors would take charge of the cavalry school.

I saw Hauptscharführer Brauny twice in the first few days in the stables. When I told him the tale that was going round, he laughed, naturally. I didn't believe it either, but stories keep people going sometimes. Guns could be heard again, as we had heard them back in Nordhausen. Always only days away, sometimes only hours away. That's what everyone said. But never quite there. Not yet. There was even a song you heard whistled in the Remonte School. From some old American film. I had never heard it. Someone picked it up somewhere. And even though hardly anyone spoke English, a few words of it went round the place. 'Send the word, send the word . . . That the Yanks are coming, the Yanks are coming . . .' I gave my view when asked, but most wanted the end in sight. It was.

Days went by. Nothing happened. We stayed where we were. Only the guards changed. A few at a time, Brauny's SS men disappeared. I noticed but it didn't seem to matter. We didn't love them. Others took their place. Maybe no better, but surely no worse. There were the Luftwaffe soldiers from outside Gardelegen and paratroopers from the same base. There were Volkssturm soldiers, too, in their ragtag uniforms who didn't look remotely like they were about to put up last-ditch resistance to the American army. Sometimes a few Hitler Youth teens. We had no idea what was going on in the town. We were shut away in the cavalry school. We were fed. We were left alone. And every day people thought the Americans would be there. It was a better outcome than any of us could have hoped for when we left the camp. I heard that so much I began to believe it myself.

It had been five days since our arrival in Gardelegen. It was four in the afternoon. Another day of nothing. There had been a lot more toing and froing among the guards. You might have said there were more of them about. But there was nothing more to say than that. We only saw the stables and the stable yard. The gates into the yard were opened and a line of guards came in, the usual mix of Luftwaffe soldiers, paratroopers and Volkssturm. A Volkssturm officer, I think his name was Debrodt, had us all out in the yard and lined up in columns, five abreast. He said we were being moved to a building outside the town. He said something about security and the barracks being needed now. We were too used to this to think there was anything odd about it. And in the mood that had grown in the stables, some people felt it must be a good thing. The idea that we were going to be handed over to the Americans at some point was still solid. Was it happening?

Brauny was standing next to the Volkssturm officer. He seemed to have abandoned his connection with us. That's how it felt. It struck me that he should still be in charge. But it certainly didn't look that way. He looked like he was staring into space, but then he turned his head and my eye caught his. He looked away. The man called Debrodt finished his speech with an assurance that there would be a meal at the end of the march. It was hardly arduous. Ten minutes. He then ordered any German kapos or any other Germans to move out of the column. The German kapos looked along the line at me. I shrugged. It was an order. I stepped forward. They followed. Several other men who were Germans did the same. There weren't many. By now the column was a mix of any and every nationality. Russians, Poles, Czechs, French, Belgians, Jews from everywhere. The Volkssturm officer said that because of the shortage of men, any German could volunteer to act as a guard, rather than just as a kapo. Anyone who did would be given an army jacket and would receive privileges in food and accommodation. Again, the German prisoners looked at me. I nodded. A jacket instead of an armband. We were still kapos. The same job. It made no difference what we wore.

Two soldiers pushed forward with a barrow and handed out the jackets. Behind them another soldier pushed a second barrow. On this one lay a row of rifles. Brauny moved forward and lifted up one of the guns. He asked how many of the volunteers could fire a rifle. No one responded for a moment. The volunteers looked at each other uncertainly. It was unexpected. Then one put his hand up. Debrodt didn't seem happy with the response. He pushed past Brauny and said anyone who took a rifle would get schnapps and cigarettes. And they would no longer be prisoners. In effect, if you picked up the rifle, you got your freedom.

Out of the twenty men who now wore army field grey, a dozen hands went up. A dozen rifles were thrust into their hands. I was looking at Brauny. He held my gaze for a moment and I thought he shook his head. I wasn't going to take a gun. I didn't know what they expected, but on the journey from Nordhausen I'd buried hundreds of prisoners shot trying to escape. I can fire a rifle. Not for them. I didn't need Hauptscharführer Brauny to tell me it wasn't a good idea. But that's what he was doing. He knew what was coming, of course. I didn't. None of us did.

Suddenly the stable yard was empty. The column of over a thousand men had gone. The gates had closed. The only people left were the eight of us who had volunteered to act as guards, but minus rifles. I could still hear the tramp of feet. As I turned back to the stables, I saw that Brauny was still there, standing by the gates, smoking. He walked across to me and gave me a cigarette. It was the first time he had ever done it. I took one and he got out his lighter and lit it for me. He told me he was going. Leaving. I didn't get why he was saying it. He was a soldier, of sorts. He went where they sent him. But that's not what he meant. Then I got it. Once I understood, I could guess he wouldn't be in his SS uniform when he went. He said if I had a chance to get out safely, I should take it. Then he told me what was going on. The Nazi Party leader in Gardelegen had decided the prisoners in the Remonte School had to be killed. All of them. Every man. Too dangerous to be left alive. He said, so that's where they've gone. To be killed. He gave me his cigarettes and left.

I knew Brauny, as well as you could know any of them, I mean. He often took the rollcall at Dora. As Lagerschreiber I was directly answerable to him. There was a kind of ladder in the camp. I guess in all of them. At the bottom, the positive end you might say, were the ones who were more or less indifferent to what went on. They still believed in it, but they didn't overdo it. At the top were the ones who enjoyed it so much they couldn't get enough. Brauny was about halfway. He didn't mind killing for no reason at all, if the mood took him, but had to be in that mood. I doubt he was running because he had any qualms about what was happening. I'd say he saw that with American soldiers only hours down the road, murdering a thousand prisoners, even in the line of duty, was no longer the reasonable course of action it would have seemed to him a few days earlier. Anyway, now I knew.

I stood staring at the gate that had shut behind Brauny. It didn't feel like I'd been standing there for long. But an hour had passed, maybe a bit more. I looked down to see that I had smoked all but one of the cigarettes. The afternoon was still very bright. And it was still quiet. The big American guns were silent for now. Then I heard firing. Sharp, cracking, repeated shots. Not artillery. Machine guns, rifles, and then explosions that could have been grenades or explosives. Again, nothing big. It wasn't far away. And it wasn't a battle. Wherever the column of prisoners went, that was just outside Gardelegen, that's exactly where the shooting was now.

They sent me to the Isenschnibbe barn the next morning. The eight of us went with men from the town. The shooting had gone on most of the night. That's all we heard. They left us locked up. But the next day they wanted everyone they could find up there. And it was only when we got close that we saw what had happened. The smell of smoke and petrol was in the air even as we marched out of town and a great black pall of smoke hung over a little hill. On top of it there a huge concrete barn. It was burning. It had been burning since the previous afternoon. And as we got nearer, I knew the smell that was there beneath the fumes. I've spent enough time taking bodies to the camp crematorium. I knew too well what burnt flesh was.

I saw there were bodies all round the barn, even from far off. I could see that at one end, the bodies were piled high and there were people throwing more on the pile. There were still gunshots. And I saw that soldiers and Volkssturm and Hitler Youth boys were walking round the barn, looking at the bodies, making sure each one of them was dead. With them I saw two of the men who volunteered as guards and picked up a rifle in the stable yard. One of them saw me. He raised his rife and laughed. It was only as I climbed the hill to the top that I understood.

All those bodies in the smoke-filled doorway of the barn were burnt and blackened, burnt beyond recognition. The place had been an inferno. A thousand men were shut up in it and burned alive. I picked up the rest from what the men around me were saying. As the barn blazed, a ring of soldiers and Hitler Youth looked on and shot anyone who manged to get out. Now there were hundreds of us in the stench, men from town, schoolboys, and the eight of us who Brauny left in the Remonte School when the others marched away. We were there for something almost as mad as what had already happened. The dead were to be buried, a thousand charred corpses, so that when the Americans came, there would be nothing to see. Nothing. It would be invisible. That's how mad they were.

I see no point in saying anything else. I've told you my part in it. For what it was like that afternoon, that night, I think a few survived. They'll tell you. I won't speak for them.

*

It was the day after Reinhard Friesack finished his statement for the American war crimes investigators that he left Gardelegen. He had some good clothes and good shoes and some food. As he walked away from the town there was a long line of men, in columns, marching the other way. Each carried a shovel and a large white wooden cross. Armed American GIs walked beside them and a tank followed behind. They were the men of Gardelegen, marching to the Isenschnibbe barn to disinter the dead who had been hidden after the massacre and give them a proper burial, along with the bodies that still lay where they had been incinerated or shot. The American captain who took Reinhard's statement had asked him if he wanted to be there for the service that would accompany the burials. He said he had no interest in being there. He had seen it. That would do. Few things could be staler and more unprofitable than watching the people who made it happen bow their heads and push a few pieces of wood into the earth. The words of Jesus of Nazareth didn't often come into Reinhard's head now, but he remembered something that when he was a pastor, he never pretended to understand. 'Let the dead bury the dead.' He understood it now in his own terms. And as he left Gardelegen he took the road east. He did ask the Americans if they knew where the

Russians were. They laughed. He was the first German anyone had met who was looking for the Red Army. Keep walking east and you'll find them. And that's what he was doing.

12

КРАСНОЕ ЗНАМЯ
THE RED BANNER

Ilsenburg, July 1945

They say you make your own luck. Even the Germans do. *Jeder ist seines Glückes Schmied*. Not that they've ever excelled at it. But then the Luck of the Irish has never delivered on its promise either. Still, at least you can do something to give good luck a helping hand. Bad luck just comes at you. And it came at us on that stretch of Russian barbed wire in the Harz. We weren't the target. We hadn't been spotted. It was the others they'd seen. I think if we'd found the nerves to slip back into the forest and wait, we might have done it. It seemed that Krista did. Her blind panic beat bad luck, but it also put her mother and I into the hands of the Russians.

Within an hour we were back where we started, in Ilsenburg. The truck took us to the Landhaus Zu den Rothen Forellen, where the red, white and blue of the Union Jack had been replaced by the red flag of the Soviet Union. Now it really was the Red Trout. There were six of us going in. And there was one coming out.

Two soldiers were lifting a body onto the back of a cart. The German who watched them, holding his horse's head, nodded at Annaliese. I didn't know he was the undertaker until she told me. Now there was a man who could prove useful whatever flag might fly from the hotel's flagpole. The same had obviously not been true of Oskar Mommsen. He had kept on the right side of the Americans and the British, but the men from Moscow had been unimpressed. As the four other prisoners moved on into the hotel, Annaliese and I stopped, recognising the body.

'Friend?' One of the soldiers said in thickly accented German.

Annaliese shook her head and walked on. The soldier was looking at me expectantly. He clearly wanted an answer. My cousin's had been the right one.

'No. I doubt he had any friends.'

The Russian laughed. A hard call, but Oskar wouldn't mind.

'Nazi,' continued the soldier. 'Heart attack.'

The bruises on the hotel proprietor's face said something else.

In reception there was no ceremony. We were led upstairs and each locked in a room. The ordinary hotel rooms. There was a bed and there were blankets. The window in my room was open. There was nothing to stop me climbing through it. Not that I'd have considered anything as stupid as leaving without checking out. Looking down, the light from the bar lit the terrace and the edge of lake. I could see the Soviet guards patrolling the grounds, one with the familiar Alsatian. Oskar Mommsen's body made its own statement on what to expect from the new management at the Red Trout.

The next morning some bread and sausage and tea came to the room. The bread was hard. The sausage was rotten. I wasn't that hungry. The black tea wasn't bad.

Half an hour later I was sitting in a room opposite a Russian officer. I recognised him as the man I'd seen with Reinhard Friesack a couple of days earlier. Captain Sokolov. He already knew who I was. He may have remembered me too, but I knew Reinhard Friesack had been looking for information as well as conversation when he followed me to Mühlenstrasse. Whatever he got would have gone to this man. The Russians might be less affable than the British but they were all in the same line. And since it was my line at home, I knew how it worked. Whether they called themselves military policemen or Intelligence officers, this was some kind of Intelligence post. I knew the job. I knew the smell. And what a crappy job it was. Always. All I had to do was leave it alone. Why the fuck did I walk into it?

'You carry a lot of money. Dollars. Pounds.'

Sokolov spoke good German.

'I wouldn't say a lot. I have some funds from the Irish legation in Germany. It goes back to the Department of External Affairs in Dublin. If I use even a few dollars, it all has to be accounted for. Every penny and every cent. I'm a courier.'

The Russian nodded. I knew he wasn't interested in the fact that I had a money belt containing a hundred and twenty dollars and fifty pounds. It was part of the process. He was telling me everything would be taken to pieces. Everything mattered, however small. I had to know I couldn't guess what would incriminate.

'And who does this money go to? Who do you give it to?'

'It goes to nobody. It just goes back to Ireland. It's a diplomatic —'

The captain cut me off.

'I think we can leave the diplomatic claims aside, Herr Gillespie. The fact that your country had an embassy in Nazi Germany isn't a badge of honour. Quite the opposite. And you certainly have no embassy now. You're just a man who has committed a crime. So you need to tell me what sort of crime it was . . . all right?'

I could see if he wasn't satisfied with one crime, he would have others.

'So, let's start with why you're here at all.'

Sokolov must have already had this from Reinhard. I gave it to him again. But the usual caveats about answering questions applied. Keep it simple, so simple that nothing changes if you have to say it all again. Keep away from anything to do with Intelligence. Nothing about John Mackay asking questions in Babenhausen. Nothing about Irish embassy documents going to Switzerland. Certainly nothing about a very odd lorry crash above Wernigerode that had kept me in Goslar with Mackay longer than intended. Out of the well-known goodness of the British heart, I had been offered a quick way back to Ireland when I got stuck in the chaos of the war's final days. And when the kind-hearted Lieutenant Mackay got delayed, it happened to be close to where the German relations I knew in my youth lived. I hadn't intended to try to find them, but with two days to kill, I did just that. That was it. And once you removed the circumstances that brought it about, it was true.

'I know Reinhard Friesack works for you, Captain. He can confirm all that. The fact that I knew these people . . . I knew Annaliese Friesack . . . years ago. I was even godfather to Reinhard's daughter. He must have said that already, surely?'

'You know the Friesack . . . Hoffman woman's Nazi connections.'

'I know she had some . . . it's hard to imagine many people didn't . . .'

The captain gave me a look that suggested that wasn't helpful.

'I don't know much about denazification, but the British looked at that, didn't they? They put her in the bottom category . . . I assume that must mean . . .'

I stopped. The same look. And I didn't honestly know what I assumed.

'The British investigation failed to take a lot into account.'

I thought he must mean Reinhard Friesack's conviction that she betrayed him to the Gestapo. He didn't say it. It must have been there, but it wasn't all.

'You knew her brothers . . . when you were in Germany before.'

'I met them . . . at the baptism. I didn't know them. They were older . . .'

'One is dead. He owned a factory that manufactured weapons. He used large numbers of slave labourers. Common enough, of course. They all did. Happily he died in an air raid. The other one, Kurt Hoffman . . . was a high-ranking SS officer.'

'I remember him in an SA uniform, that's all. That was nineteen thirty-three.'

'What has Annaliese Friesack said about him?'

'Nothing.' I shrugged. I'd almost forgotten him until now.

'Does she know where he is?'

'She's never mentioned him.'

'We think he's in the British Zone. Where did she want to get to?'

'She wasn't trying to get anywhere . . . just away from here.'

'He's her brother . . . you knew him. Why wouldn't she talk about him?'

'The last time I saw the man, I was in a hospital to visit Reinhard Friesack. Beaten up by the Hitler Youth. I went to see him because I liked him. Because I cared, I guess. Kurt Hoffman . . . I couldn't have given a fuck about. He was a cunt.'

'That's true enough, Herr Gillespie. We want him because he was responsible for the murder of large numbers of Russian soldiers. I don't mean killing. I don't mean war. The murder of hundreds of men who were prisoners.'

I nodded. Understanding was enough. He didn't expect indignation.

'You see your cousin's connections, right? The brothers . . .'

'I didn't know. All I saw . . . I saw over ten years ago . . . for ten minutes.'

'Annaliese Friesack is under investigation. She was told that. And after she was told that, you made it your business to help her avoid that investigation, right?'

'I don't know about any investigations . . . any of that.'

'You don't know she worked for the SS herself then?'

'What do you mean?'

'I mean what I say. A simple statement. Do you know about that?'

'No . . . I don't know . . .'

I couldn't respond to this. I couldn't even guess what it meant.

'She worked in several factories in Magdeburg and Halle, including those the other Hoffman brother owned. Amongst other things, Frau Friesack directed what I think was euphemistically called the "employment" of slave labourers from the camps.'

Captain Sokolov intended to silence me with this. He did.

'If that's truly news to you, Inspector, I'll leave you to mull it over.'

I said nothing. I was in deeper than I'd realised. But was it even true?

'Reinhard tells me you're a policeman in Ireland. Your passport says so too.'

I nodded, my mind still on what he had just told me.

'So what sort of policeman are you?'

'What do you mean?'

'Do you direct the traffic? Do you chase bank robbers?'

He was smiling now. That's to say he was taking the piss.

'I'm a detective.'

'And what do you detect?'

'What do you mean?'

'I'm guessing bank robbers isn't quite it.'

I'd been here too many times myself. There wasn't any guessing going on.

'What the British call Special Branch. By any other name . . . Intelligence.'

Sokolov liked this. Still not enough crimes. Let's find some more.

'In Ireland. At home. My job here was to help the ambassador, that's all.'

'Come now, Inspector. We finally have something in common. Intelligence takes many forms. But it's always political somewhere down the line. And you can never quite get away from it. You travel with a British Intelligence officer. You come here with a British Intelligence officer. And when the area is absorbed into the Soviet Zone, you make a point of smuggling out this woman with her Nazi past and with a brother who is wanted for very serious war crimes. And all by chance?'

'Captain, hundreds of people have left this area in the last few days. If I'd walked from Ilsenburg to Bad Harzburg with my cousin twenty-four hours ago, nobody would have cared. It wasn't even clear the deadline had come and gone. The MPs that were here said it was midnight. You put up checkpoints before that.'

Captain Sokolov sat back in his chair and laughed.

'So, after all that, Comrade, your defence is . . . bad timing?'

I might have smiled myself. It wasn't great. And since it wasn't great for me, it was going to be worse for Annaliese, if even part of what the Russian said was true. I didn't know what I felt about that. I didn't know what was true and what wasn't, of course. I had acted without knowing enough. It was never a good idea.

That afternoon a Russian guard unlocked the door of my room. He had no German other than, 'Out, now!' So I followed him out. Captain Sokolov had decided to give us all some air. There were a dozen or so prisoners at the Red Trout now. Most of them seemed to know one other. Whatever they were there for, they were locals. I didn't know them but I nodded at some of them and they nodded back, as we all seemed to drift to the edge of the lake and look out at the water. Annaliese was there, smoking a cigarette. She held one up for me, one of those cardboard tubes with a wad of tobacco at the end They were permanently fixed to the lips of most of the Soviet soldiers. I lit it from hers. It tasted as bad as it looked. She smiled.

'The guard gave me some. I'm almost sorry he did.'

'Grim stuff.' It was, but I still smoked it.

'Are you OK, Annaliese?'

'I've been better.'

'Do you have any idea what's going to happen?'

'I'm under investigation. That's it. Whatever that means . . .'

'I feel I'm in something I don't even understand,' I said. 'Crossing this bloody border they've just put up, I guess there's a price to pay for that. But the rest of it . . . I don't know what happened here, do I? I don't know what happened to you. I don't know what happened to Reinhard. They seem to think you were involved in . . . it's not for me to say, is it? You hear the word SS and you think . . .'

'I'm sure I know what you think, Stefan.'

'Fools rush in.' I shrugged. 'Maybe cousins too . . .'

Annaliese drew hard on the cigarette, then dropped it and stubbed it out.

'When they took Reinhard, I was under suspicion. Because I didn't report him. Do you understand? I could have been arrested too. I think if it hadn't been for my brother, Kurt, I would have been . . . but I still had to keep going. I had to prove I was loyal. I did what he said . . . I joined the Party. I didn't do anything . . . just joined. But I had to live too . . . I had Krista as well . . . I had to have a job . . .'

I gave a nod. I couldn't know what it was like. I could guess.

'My other brother, Bertolt, came to the rescue . . . I suppose that's how it felt at the time. His factories were making parts for aircraft. He had one in Magdeburg, one in Halle, one in Hannover. He gave me a job as a secretary . . . and I started to deal with the wages and the workers. By then a lot of his workers came . . . from a camp, from Buchenwald. I was never in one of those places . . . I never saw one.'

I thought the job wouldn't have involved much work on the wages front. It didn't seem any time for cheap shots, though.

'I did send paperwork to the SS . . . and I sent the payments. Bertolt had to pay the SS for the people . . . I can't say I never saw how they lived, how they were treated, how Bertolt . . . I can't deny I did. But I was hardly in the factories...only sometimes. When workers died, I asked the SS for more. No one questioned that was how it had to be. How it should be. What could I do? Can't you see how . . .'

She let the words fade away.

'I don't know.' It wasn't an accusation, though it sounded like one. Perhaps it should have been. I couldn't see. If I'd been part of it, maybe I would have done.

'Bertolt's dead . . . they keep asking me about Kurt. I don't know anything.'

'What about Reinhard? Can't he help?'

'I'm not sure he could help now . . . even if he wanted to.'

'Do they still think you went to the Gestapo?'

'I think they believe me . . . I told them the truth. I had to.'

'What is the truth?'

'The truth is, I did turn a blind eye. I tried to lie about the man being in our house. If I could have protected Reinhard, I would have. They knew already. It wasn't me who told them . . . it was Krista. She went to her Deutsche Mädel leader.'

There was nothing for me to say. I thought of my son, Tom.

'That's it! Get inside! All prisoners back to your rooms!'

The Russian guards were rounding us up again.

'They'll let you go, won't they, Stefan?'

I shrugged and smiled a hopeful smile. No one had said it.

'I saw Reinhard . . . for a few minutes . . . he thinks so . . .'

'What about you?' I said.

She just shook her head.

'Will you find Krista, Stefan? The British must have her . . .'

'If I get out, I'll try, Annaliese.'

'Please, Stefan. Help her. There's no one to help her now . . .'

We walked into the hotel.

'You will, won't you? For me.'

'If there's anything I can do . . .'

'Take her away. Please. Take her away from it all . . .'

It was the last time I saw Annaliese Friesack. She walked down a corridor as I went upstairs. But those final words, a little mad I thought, were still in my head.

I couldn't tell whether Reinhard Friesack really knew anything about me. As far as the Russians were concerned, I assumed he was attached to some kind of Intelligence unit because he was useful, not because he was important. But he had seen Annaliese. He had said he thought they would let me go. It was a better place to be, at least in my head. The British must know something about where I was. Mackay would have expected me to turn up at some point. Whether anyone on the other side of the line gave a fuck was another matter. I was waiting to find out. I lay in the darkness of the hotel room, wondering how long I would have to wait. It was a conversation in my mind that was as pointless to continue as it was impossible to put an end to. It went round and round and all it did was stop me from sleeping.

I managed to scrounge a couple of Russian cigarettes and a box of matches. You couldn't say there was much pleasure smoking them, but it was something to do. I got off the bed and lit one. I walked to the open window and looked out at the lake. There was a bit of a moon. I liked this place once. I suppose I still did. There were voices below, on the terrace. I looked down. There was only a dim light from the bar but I could see Captain Sokolov sitting at a table with a beer. There was a man beside him. They were talking easily. There was some quiet laughter. I could only hear the buzz of the words. It was Russian, unsurprisingly, but as I watched the two men, with no real interest, suddenly there was a surprise. A soldier came out with two bottles of beer. The second man stood up and took them from him. He was in the light. I knew him. It was Major Battersby, John Mackay's Intelligence Corps boss. There was no doubt. There he was, British uniform and all, sitting over a beer with a man who must be, in some way, his opposite number.

I moved back into the darkness. There was no reason a British Intelligence officer shouldn't have a conversation with a Soviet Intelligence officer. Whatever about the border and the new Soviet Zone, they were allies. If Germany had been carved up between the Allied powers, they were going to speak to each other. There was a country to run. There was no reason either why a British Intelligence officer shouldn't speak some Russian. He would come from another agency, MI5, MI6. I had the clear sense that even Lieutenant Mackay had links with all that.

But I'd been at my job long enough to recognise what it was wise not to know. One way or another, whatever about Battersby and Sokolov, it was something to see ... and forget.

The next morning, when the bread and the inedible sausage arrived, Captain Sokolov came in with the guard. He was in a cheerful, even amiable mood.

'It's do svidaniya, Herr Inspector. Apparently, we don't want you.'

'I can go?'

'You'll be driven to the checkpoint. The British expect you.'

That was it. Half an hour later I was sitting in the back of a Russian jeep in the forecourt of the Landhaus Zu den Rothen Forellen. Two Russian soldiers sat in the front. I had my suitcase and even the money belt with the dollars and pounds that Captain Sokolov seemed to think proved I must be guilty of something other than making sure the Department of External Affairs could keep its accounts in order. The engine was already running as Reinhard Friesack climbed in beside me.

'I'll keep you company, Stefan.'

'Did you get me out of here?' I asked.

'I'm afraid I don't matter enough to do that. Someone smiled on you.'

We drove through Ilsenburg's square, out along the other side of the lake.

'What about Annaliese?'

'She's already gone.'

'Gone where?'

'She will be interned while her case is investigated, like anyone else.'

'Prison?'

'I believe they took her to Sachsenhausen.'

'I thought that was a concentration camp.'

Reinhard gazed ahead. He said nothing.

'Under new management, though.'

'I think you may spare us your lectures, Stefan. People made choices. I made mine. Annaliese made hers. And so did millions. Every choice has its price. With twenty million dead Russians, and never mind the millions of Germans who died for nothing . . . then the rest . . . you know about the rest . . . you know enough . . . don't be too surprised if no one cares about the judgment of the people on the sidelines.'

There was an answer, I know. I didn't have it to hand.

'It will be fair. If there's a sentence, she will serve it.'

'And is part of that . . . what you think she did to you? It isn't true.'

'I know. She told me . . . I'm sure that will all be taken into consideration. She let the Nazis have Krista, though. She never fought what they were doing to her. If I tried, it only ended in us hating each other. So I gave up. But none of it is about her or me. I don't matter in the least. None of us matter. The future has its cost. Our generation has to pay so that other generations don't. That's all. The personal is neither here nor there now. There is no room for the personal anymore.'

We were coming out of the town. Trees lined the road. Dappled light.

'What about Krista?'

Reinhard shrugged and kept staring ahead.

'Will you ask the British to send her back?'

'No.'

His voice was clipped, almost aggressive.

'Perhaps the Nazis had her too long. I don't think she will find the new life . . .'

He spoke coldly but the words didn't come easily.

'She must make her own way.'

Reinhard turned and smiled. The subject was closed.

'We'll be there in a few minutes. It's been a strange meeting, Stefan.'

I smiled too. There was no more to say and we said no more. I think abandoning Krista was the best he could do to help her.

At the checkpoint the barrier was up. On one side a red flag and half a dozen Soviet soldiers. On the other a military police jeep and the men in red caps. I got out. Reinhard Friesack took my hand. He gave me an envelope as he clasped it. Then he was gone and I was heading to Brunswick. Major Battersby's orders.

I opened the envelope Reinhard had left me. In it was a piece of paper I knew I recognised. It was faded and a little torn at the edges. There was a picture. Lilies and pink roses round an arched window, and in the window was Jesus, sitting under a tree, surrounded by children. The black letters declared that Krista Friesack had been baptised in the name of the Triune God. My signature was there. And when I turned the baptism certificate over, Reinhard had written the words I had spoken at the font in the Marienkirche. At the end he put a question mark. It seemed there was room for the personal after all . . . whether you wanted it or not.

*

I was driven into Brunswick, where the MPs deposited me at a building in the centre of the town. It was an office block of some kind, though it had the feel of a police station about it. My nose told me that. Above the entrance there was a great hole where stone and concrete had been beaten out of the façade. It wasn't bomb damage. The shape that still clung, ghostlike, to the hole in the wall was still just about recognisable as a swastika. I was taken to a canteen and given some food, then walked back to the front of the building and into a large office. Major Battersby was waiting for me, sitting back and smoking a black cheroot. He shook his head and gave me the kind of disappointed smile that he must have picked up from trips to his headmaster's study at whatever public school they sent him to.

'Well, that was a fucking stupid thing to do, Inspector Gillespie.'

He expected me to join in with this. I couldn't be bothered to, but I gave it a half-hearted shot.

'It'll definitely be up there with some of the others. Near the top, maybe.'

There was a bit more of that. His banter came in one size. Patronising. But he didn't have much to add. I was being tidied up. This was the dustpan and brush.

'I spoke to the colonel here after we heard you'd made a proverbial arse of yourself with the Comrades. I presume he made contact with his Russian counterpart. Whatever he said, it worked. My advice was to tell them we didn't really want you back, but we'd take you anyway and pack you off to the Emerald Isle, as they probably didn't want you either. Nobody needs any more international hoopla than we have already, that's the thing, especially when it's about a country nobody cares about. I did suggest the tried and tested excuse . . . an Irishman with too much drink in him who got lost en route to the next pub! Forgive the cliché.'

I didn't care about his clichés or his Irish jokes. He would have more. But I did care about his feigned ignorance. Whoever did the negotiating that got me out of the Soviet Zone, he was there. He was in Ilsenburg. Whatever he was doing, and however little I featured in that, it was inconceivable that

I wasn't discussed. But my own instincts had already told me I saw nothing. My job was to play the Irish clown. Have more than thou showest, speak less than though knowest. Not hard.

'To be fair, Major, eight hundred years of the English would drive anyone to drink.'

That got a laugh. He liked it. The smile was like a pat on the head.

'You're out, that's the thing. And lucky. I understand the RAF will have a seat for you from Hannover. I won't say it's been a pleasure having you with us. Here's something that might entertain you on the plane. Our papers are always out of date, but there's a little piece by the *Times'* Irish correspondent. It'll keep you up to speed with what to expect when you get home. I'd say we're meant to smile.'

Major Battersby folded a newspaper and pushed it across the desk.

'A letter to a newspaper from a chap somewhere, Kilkenny perhaps... he's seen some of the newsreels from Belsen... and spotted the flaw. All those bodies aren't even in Germany. Propaganda. We filmed it all in India apparently. And you'll see some of your politicians are very indignant about war crimes trials now. Victor's justice, that's it. We're being beastly to the Germans... know the words?'

'The words of what?'

'I won't sing for you, Inspector. "Don't let's be beastly to the Germans... When our victory is something, something won. Wasn't it all the nasty Nazis, something, something, something... So don't let's be beastly to the Hun." Anyway, now it's over some of your countrymen seem to think we're all behaving like bad sports. That's not on.'

'I don't think Ireland has a monopoly on idiots, Major.'

That was a weak return. I knew it as I said it. He didn't stretch himself for a reply. Raised eyebrows did the job, along with a bland, bored grin. I was as bored as he was, maybe more so. Besides I still had something more serious on my mind.

'What about the girl?'

'Oh, yes, the one that did get away.'

'What's happened to her?'

'I don't know. Displaced Persons are not my concern . . . but I think . . .'

'Is that what she is? She's only thirteen for God's sake.'

Battersby leafed through a pile of papers on his desk.

'That's what they all are, DPs . . . now there was something . . .'

He produced a sheet of teletype.

'Krista Friesack?'

'Yes.'

'She's in the DP camp here. The Rosalies Kaserne. The barracks.'

'And how long will she be there?'

'I've no idea, old man. Till someone claims her.' He looked down at the teleprinter page. 'The Russians haven't asked for her to be sent back. Not yet. You say the mother, your cousin, is in Soviet custody? That won't be much to write home about. What about the father? Reinhard Friesack, it says here. Is that right?'

'He's working with the Russians . . . I guess in Intelligence.'

'That should make for interesting family gatherings. Anyway, that's it.'

He was done. None of that mattered at all, just as now neither did I.

'I'll say goodbye then, Inspector.'

He stood and so did I.

'What would happen . . . if I claimed her?'

'Not with you, old man.'

'Krista Friesack. I get the impression her mother is going to stay where she is for a long time. You might know more about that than I do, but my instincts . . .'

Major Battersby shrugged. He didn't think my instincts were far off.

'And Reinhard . . . the father . . . he isn't going to try to get her back.'

'No?'

'No.'

Battersby shrugged again. This was the well-who-cares-anyway shrug.

'I'm her godfather . . . if I wanted to take her to Ireland . . . at least until . . .'

'That's charmingly old-fashioned, Gillespie.'

The familiar dismissal, but maybe not quite the familiar sneer.

'I don't know how these things work,' said the Intelligence man. 'I'll get you a lift to the Kaserne. See what they say . . . see what she says.. if you wait outside . . .'

Battersby picked up the phone as I left. I went out to the front of the building and sat on a low wall. I took out a cigarette. I didn't know whether I was doing the right thing. But I was doing it. For whatever reason, I had ended up doing it.

The major emerged a few minutes later. He handed me a piece of paper.

'There's a jeep on its way. At the DP camp there'll be an MP lieutenant. That's a note for him. The man you need to speak to is Ronald Knox, Red Cross.'

'Thank you, sir.'

'Good luck.'

'I hoped I might catch John Mackay before I went. Is he around?'

I wanted to say goodbye to John Mackay. But I had more to say. If it hadn't been for what I'd witnessed on my last night in Ilsenburg, I would have asked him about his investigation anyway. I had thrown my six-penn'orth in after all. Now I knew the case wasn't going anywhere, whatever the evidence. He needed to drop it. No explanation, just drop it. That's what I would have told him. I didn't need to.

'I'm afraid not.'

I didn't answer. The weight of his voice was heavier than his words.

'An accident . . . a very unfortunate one . . . a very unnecessary . . .'

I still said nothing. I was shocked. I'd only seen him days before.

'In Goslar. It was careless, one has to say . . . but that doesn't matter . . . you don't expect to see men dying when the war's over . . . just so horribly . . . pointless.'

'How?' Even that one word didn't come easily.

'Bloody curfew. I don't know why he did it, but he walked out by the camp perimeter and lit a fucking cigarette of all things. A sentry saw the light and fired. Facts aren't quite clear. He should have challenged him . . . but there'd been a spate of looting . . . the sentries were on edge. Why John did something so . . . he was a good man. I'll miss him.'

It was convincing, I have to say. I suppose he meant it. And that was that. He shook his head and walked away. I watched him go. I watched him walk to a parked motorcycle. I watched him as he pulled on a pair of goggles and strapped a helmet to his head. He got on the bike and started it. He took a red scarf from his pocket, wound it round his neck and tied it at the front. He drove away with a wave, as a jeep pulled up beside me and a cheerful MP sergeant beeped the horn.

'Mr Gillespie?'

I got in. As we drove away from Battersby's office, he was in front of us for several minutes before he turned off. Besides the man himself, only three people knew about the motorcyclist with the red scarf who led two British soldiers to their death. Possibly led, I might have said a few days earlier. Today, probably wasn't quite strong enough. Two of those men were dead. Unfortunate accidents. Now there never was a man on a motorbike. As I drew on my cigarette, I could feel my hand shaking. I was lucky. Lucky Major Battersby viewed the Irish with a mix of indifference and contempt. Maybe there was something in the Luck of the Irish after all. I was too Irish, too stupid and too unimportant even to need silencing.

As I stubbed out my cigarette, I immediately lit another. My hand wasn't shaking now. A nearer miss than I could have known. But a miss. There was something to be said for a country nobody cared about. The great game could be left to the ones everybody did care about. You'd have imagined the game wasn't worth playing in Germany's ruins, but there it was. The dice were still rolling. It shouldn't have come as any surprise that Russian Intelligence had people in British Intelligence. There would be British people in Russian Intelligence, along with any permutations other players on the board came up with. John Mackay was too bloody-minded to leave it alone. Maybe still too much of a policeman, maybe just too fucking Irish. If he'd been more English, he might have left it alone.

*

I sat in a small cold room with Krista. It wasn't a cell, but it wasn't far off. I think the Red Cross man only put us in there to give us some privacy, but as I sat on one side of a table and she sat on the other, privacy was all it did give us. I was used to the look of fear on Krista's face. It had been there in various guises since we met. I wasn't surprised that it was there now. The Rosalies Kaserne was a big stone building that had been a barracks and a prison, and probably, in its last incarnation as Nazi Germany collapsed, both at the same time. Now it was full of DPs. People from all over Germany and all over Europe, waiting to go somewhere, whether or not they had anywhere to go. There were people from the camps, some still in their striped clothes. There were Czech and Slovaks and Poles and Hungarians and French and Danes, who had worked as slave labourers, and pretty much anything else you could think of, waiting to find a way home. There were still Germans from bombed cities sheltering until they found their families or their families found them. There were soldiers too, according to the Red Cross director, who were masquerading as civilians. There were Germans who had come from the east, fleeing in front of the Red Army, and more, like Krista, who had only recently moved further west as the Soviet Zone had swallowed up more of Germany. It wasn't a big DP camp, but it was big enough. And it was a terrifying place to be for anyone, let alone the children who were there.

It didn't surprise me that Krista asked no questions. She said nothing. That was how she was. But she had questions. Her eyes asked one question above all.

'Your mother is safe. They took us to Ilsenburg . . .'

It wasn't a good start. Safe was true, but it wasn't the right word.

'I have to talk to you as an adult, Krista. I put it that way because it's the only way I can. I'll say what I have to say as well as I can. But it's not easy . . . and I don't know how to do it if I'm honest. I can only say the words . . . and you listen.'

'That's all right,' she said.

Starting was the most difficult part. I didn't know what the best place was. I remembered the certificate of baptism in my pocket. I took it out and laid it down.

'Your father gave me this. This morning.'

She peered at it, puzzled. It had nothing to do with anything.

'It probably doesn't mean much to you.'

'I know what it is.'

'It didn't mean much to me really,' I said. 'He wanted it to, I'd say.'

'I don't understand.'

'I'll tell you what's happened, as far as I can. Then, you're going to have to make a decision. A very difficult decision. Very quickly. We can't do it any other way. I think the decision you need to make is the one that your mother . . . and your father . . . would want you to make. I say, I think . . . that's the best I can do . . . For now, your mother is in the Soviet Zone. I don't know for how long, but she's in . . .'

'A prison, that's what you want to say, isn't it?'

'Yes.'

'I knew. And my father . . . will he take me back there?'

Another fear, an old fear. I knew now where it came from.

'No. He won't.'

Krista frowned, more surprised than relieved. It wasn't what she expected.

'You're on your own. I don't know what happens in these places . . . how long people stay. But you've nowhere to go and no one to go to. Is there anyone?'

'No, there is no one.'

'I think your mother and father . . . both want you to leave Germany . . . for a time. Things will change. When and how . . . is anybody's guess. I'll explain what I can, but in a way I'm asking you make a leap of faith. That sounds very grand!'

She laughed. There hadn't been many of those.

'Until things do change . . . you need a place . . . to call home. We have to decide, you and I, whether this piece of paper is worth anything. The day I signed it, I said something... in the Marienkirche in Ilsenburg. It was a long time ago. I've been called on that, you might say. Your father wrote the words on the back...'

I turned the baptism certificate over.

'The pastor said, "It is your privilege and responsibility, after Krista's baptism, to remember your godchild in your prayers, and whenever possible, to support her in mind and heart, especially if she should lose her parents... Do you gladly and willingly assume this responsibility?" I said, "Yes, with God's help."'

Krista looked at me with eyes that seemed older than her years.

'And do you think any of that meant anything?'

'Then, I don't know. Now, it's what you and I have to find out, Krista.'

NACHWORT
AFTERWORD

*R*eports *from the Red Cross present an alarming picture of the situation in Germany this winter. It is confirmed by personal observation. I had a useful conversation with Garda Inspector Gillespie, who was in Berlin with Cremin and travelled through the country at the war's end. He noted that even the military administration does not believe supplies of food can be maintained. The government has already provided 18,000 head of cattle, along with other agricultural produce, for transport to the British and US Zones. We also intend to offer temporary refuge in Ireland for groups of German children ... Our practice has been to discourage any substantial increase in the Jewish population. They do not assimilate but remain a colony of a world-wide Jewish community and a potential irritant to the body politic. The Minister, whose freedom from racial or religious prejudices will not be questioned, agrees that caution is necessary.*

Letter from Department of Justice to Department of Finance

NOTES AND ACKNOWLEDGEMENTS

Happenstance

The authenticity or lack of it in historical fiction is not determined by the degree to which it includes real facts and events. The truth, such as it is, rests with the story as is the case in all fiction. However, I know that many of Stefan Gillespie's readers like to know where bits and pieces of history are touched on. For those who do, these are a few things, small as often as large, that do mirror the times.

The execution of Anselm Ebbers echoes the death of Robert Limpert, in Ansbach, in similar circumstances, with American forces only hours away. In Ilsenburg the owner of the Landhaus Zu den Rothen Forellen at this time was a prominent Nazi politician who survived the use of his hotel by both American and British forces, only to die in custody when the Russians finally took over. After leaving Berlin in 1945, the Irish Minister, Con Cremin, did end up at the Schloss Babenhausen in Bavaria. The Irish tricolour was flown over the castle; signs (partly in Irish) were put up to placate the advancing US troops; and a group of retreating German soldiers did take enough umbrage at this to threaten to shoot everyone. The American colonel who arrived subsequently was indeed from Limerick. When Con Cremin left Germany for Switzerland, Joe Walshe at External Affairs sent a coded message asking for confirmation that 'no secret records' had been left behind. Since anyone and everyone could read the Irish diplomatic codes, this was probably more an invitation than a safeguard, though it's anybody's guess what secrets Ireland had at this stage. On several of Ilsenburg's streets there are Stolpersteine, 'stumbling stones', small bronze plaques set into the cobbles to record the Jews who lived in the town and were expelled or deported. Four of these, close to Mühlenstrasse and outside a house very like the one Clara Bloch lived in, commemorate a family called Eckstein. Tens of thousands of these stones appear now all over Europe, even Dublin has some.

The distinction between the Line of Contact, where British and American forces met the Red Army in Germany at the war's end, and the proposed borders between the different Allied Zones as agreed in 1944, was very significant. As a result, a large part of the territory occupied by the US and Britain in May 1945 was given over to Soviet control on 1 July 1945. Ilsenburg is close to what became the Soviet Zone border, later the border of the German Democratic Republic (DDR) until German reunification. The area around the Brocken remained a forbidden zone throughout the DDR's existence.

The concentration camp at Nordhausen, along with its satellites, became the main centre for manufacturing German flying bombs and rockets towards the end of the war. The Americans removed everything they could in the way of documents and equipment before abandoning the camp to the Russians. They took it all back to the US, along with many German scientists, some of them handily avoiding investigation for war crimes in the process. One load of documents the Nazis tried to get out of Nordhausen themselves was buried in a barn close to the Harz. Conflict within Germany's Protestant churches was an issue most believers avoided. At one extreme were the German Christians, who claimed Jesus was an Aryan, antisemitic hero, banned the Old Testament, and edited out references to it in the New. At the other end was the Confessing Church, led by people like Dietrich Bonhoeffer, who died for his opposition to Hitler. The majority of Protestants sat in the middle, either seeing nothing in the New Germany to challenge their beliefs or simply choosing not to look. Ilsenburg played a small part in this when a seminary for missionaries at the Kloster was closed due to its liberal teaching. The events surrounding the evacuation of Nordhausen and the death march that ended at Gardelegen are described as accurately as possible within the constraints of the story. It's not an easy decision to make such things part of a work of fiction, but it feels on balance that finding appropriate ways to remember matters in a time of forgetting.

Some concentration camps in the Soviet Zone were 'rebranded' and would eventually contain not only ex-Nazis and German soldiers, but Red Army troops who had made the mistake of letting themselves be captured by the Germans, and even anti-Nazis, like the Social Democrats, who were not pro-Communist. Sachsenhausen became Special Camp No. 7, and part of Russia's Gulag system. Although it would be years before the full extent of Soviet infiltration of British Intelligence was exposed, it is clear assumptions about this were around in the mid-40s, especially in US Intelligence. Accidental shootings during curfew, mostly of civilians but sometimes of soldiers, were not so uncommon that they demanded serious investigation, though we assume John Mackay's death was not an accident. One well-known example was the shooting of the composer Anton Webern who, having survived the Nazis, was killed by an over-zealous American soldier when he stepped outside for a smoke.

Most of this story takes place in and around the town of Ilsenburg and the Harz Mountains. Ilsenburg is a reminder not only that Germany has some extraordinarily beautiful landscapes but that its rural towns are, quietly and unassumingly, among Europe's greatest treasures. It is somewhere worth spending time and its lakeside hotel is no bad place to do that. Everywhere has a history that is dark as well as light. Germany in the 30s and 40s demonstrates that on a scale that makes it always important, but scale doesn't make it unique. I have only to travel a couple of miles from my home to a small town where randomly selected prisoners were slaughtered by their neighbours, even friends. An hour's drive away are the remains of a barn where hundreds of men, women and children were shut in and burnt alive. We visit Nazi Germany to encounter what remains all too human.

Acknowledgements

More than any other story in this series, over a lifetime too many books have contributed to what was in my head to be remembered, let alone listed. As ever, I can only put down what was on my desk while writing. On Germany at the end of the war, I found the most powerful history Ian Kershaw's *The End: Germany 1944–45*. Among other things it records the story of a young theology student, the above-mentioned Robert Limpert, tried and executed for a small act of resistance even as the Allies approached his town. For almost fifty years, a schoolroom scene in André Schwarz-Bart's novel *The Last of the Just* has haunted me. What happens to Reinhard Friesack in Ilsenburg isn't the same, but there is a profound debt to pay, and not only for what I have written here. On the Protestant Churches in Germany, the most thorough and disturbing account is Richard Steigmann-Gall's *The Holy Reich*. On Nordhausen and the Gardelegen massacre, Karel Margry's *Nordhausen Concentration Camp: Then and Now*. This book, in the *After the Battle* series, presents meticulous, relentless detail with a cold eye that I found gave me a way into how I wrote myself. No commentary, judgement, emotion, conclusions; only stark facts. Annie Jacobsen's *Operation Paperclip* is the definitive work on how Nazi scientists, especially rocket scientists, were brought to America in 1945; it opens up at least some of the murky activities of the Intelligence agencies involved. Niall Keogh's *Con Cremin: Ireland's Wartime Diplomat* is the best account of the last days of the Irish legation to the Third Reich. Dermot Keogh's 1989 paper on international reaction to de Valera's visit to the German Minister in May 1945, in *Irish Studies in International Affairs*, sheds well-researched light on a much-referred-to but often opaque event. The Royal Irish Academy's *Documents on Irish Foreign Policy* was an essential reference point. Obviously, the presence of Stefan Gillespie in a government document at the book's close is fiction. However, the view on the dangers of allowing too many Jews into Ireland isn't.